THE LEPER SHIP

Also by Peter Tonkin

The Fire Ship
The Coffin Ship
The Journal of Edwin Underhill
Killer

THE LEPER SHIP

Peter Tonkin

HEADLINE

First published in 1992
by HEADLINE BOOK PUBLISHING PLC

10 9 8 7 6 5 4 3 2 1

British Library Cataloguing in Publication Data

Tonkin, Peter, 1950–
The leper ship
I. Title
823.914 [F]

ISBN 0-7472-0520-5

Typeset by
Falcon Typographic Art Ltd, Fife, Scotland

Printed and bound in Great Britain by
Richard Clay Ltd, Bungay, Suffolk

HEADLINE BOOK PUBLISHING PLC
Headline House
79 Great Titchfield Street
London W1P 7FN

For Cham and Guy

LEPER SHIP   A ship forbidden to dock or unload in any
port or haven because of the hazardous
nature of its cargo.
Recent coinage, World Press.

All day I hear the noise of waters
Making moan,
Sad as the seabird is when going
Forth alone.
He hears the winds cry to the waters'
Monotone.

The grey winds, the cold winds are blowing
Where I go.
I hear the noise of many waters
Far below.
All day, all night I hear them flowing
To and fro.

James Joyce

CHAPTER ONE

The column of ancient Mercedes trucks thundered through the night south of Sidon like a division of Rommel's Afrika Corps come north fifty years out of time. The lights of the lead truck struck into the dead blackness ahead, chopping from side to side beyond the rough roadway out over the desert with each twist of track, each lurch over rolling boulders. The headlights of the others behind struck out also, but they were increasingly ghostly, shrouded by thickening clouds of sand. So it was only Salah Malik by the righthand window of the lead vehicle, Fatima beside him and the driver Ali ibn Sir who got a clear view of the figures lining the roadside.

In flashes, like snapshots cut out of the moonless darkness, the figures remained in their minds, each more horrific than the last. Men, women and children standing silently, watching the transports lurch past.

Silently.

Such was the noise of engines, gears and tyres in the night that they could all have been howling and not one sound would have reached the ears of the three in the lead truck. Such were the terrible tricks played by the light and the shade that it was impossible to guess which mouths were crying out and which simply did not exist. Local villagers, in helpless, horrific lines, withered, twisted, maimed and mutilated.

The mercilessly bright Bosch headlights glinted off blistered skin, open sores, red-pitted pocks. Puffed lips, slow black tongues. Hunched backs. Crooked legs. Stumped fingers adjusting keffiyehs and chadors beside white eyes too blind even to flinch in the sudden brightness; pulling tattered cotton cloth over the crusted craters of open nose-pits. Like lepers, but there was no leprosy here.

In the broad cab of that lead truck, the animated conversation which had raged between the two men and the woman all the way in from the almost laden freighter *Napoli*'s anchorage at the coast had fallen silent, the nightmare atmosphere emanating from those terrible, mutilated watchers too horrible to allow even the bitterest recriminations to continue.

Salah Malik looked out through the grit-grimed window beside him, forcing himself not to flinch away, feeling an urgent need to understand Ali ibn Sir's murderous rage. A girl with no hands seemed to leap into the spotlight holding a rag-wrapped bundle against her scrawny chest with rounded stumps of stick-thin arms. The bundle twisted, revealing pink paddle limbs. It was a baby but it looked more like a turtle. It turned its huge head. And Salah realised it had no face. Blind eye-pits stood astride an amorphous bulge of flesh above a lipless gash too shapeless to be called a mouth. Only the ears, perfectly formed but unnaturally large showed which way the featureless ball of its head was facing.

The Palestinian dragged his stricken gaze away from the silent horror just as the truck lurched round the final bend and descended screaming into the pit.

It was wide and shallow, the size of a small open-cast diamond mine, spiral terraces winding down its side under the halogen floodlights, like an architectural excavation, here at the heart of the Holy Land. At the lip of the pit sat three heavy earth movers and the mechanical digger responsible for fashioning the pit after the carefully positioned explosive charges had torn it open. But at the bottom lay no biblical city, no pagan temple anathematised in the Book of Kings, no Sodom or Gomorrah. Instead, there lay destruction of a much more modern kind than anything that had overwhelmed the Cities of the Plain. There were stacks of steel drums, battered, sand-bound, each drum perhaps five feet high and the same round. There were cubes of concrete – recognisable as concrete only to the experienced eye – also covered with sand, each cube six foot by six foot by six. Bizarre figures clad in white protective suits moved among the cubes, manhandling them on to wooden pallets which men in motley uniform were stacking ready to load into the backs of the trucks.

Salah's gaze quickly took in the number of cubes and barrels waiting to be loaded on to the trucks. This should be the last trip the convoy would have to make. His long dark eyes narrowed and clouded as they rested on Ali: the local man, the unknown quantity in Salah's calculations. Ali wrestled the big truck down to the collection area with fierce, ugly movements, as though the ancient vehicle bore some responsibility for all the horror surrounding them. Lying across his lap, secured round his lean torso by a loose shoulder strap, was an old but lovingly maintained Uzi. Salah knew the young man only slightly; well enough, however, to be certain that he could never take the weapon away from him. And yet disarming Ali ibn Sir and his men was the only way Salah could see of avoiding the threatened bloodshed. But, apart from Fatima, Salah was on his own here: the man from central office sent down to oversee the locals.

When he had come south from Beirut to see the job completed, he had brought with him only the sketchiest knowledge of what was really going on, and no real conception of the full horror or its lethal impact. He tried to imagine how he would have reacted had that faceless baby been his own. And he knew there was very little chance of getting any of the Italians back to their ship alive. He couldn't remember the last time he had felt so scared. No, that wasn't right. The last time he had been this scared was all too vivid in his memory. It had been a scant three months ago, on the ancient oil platform called *Fate* at the mouth of the Gulf. But at least he had had Richard Mariner and the others at his shoulder then. He would have given almost anything to have had Richard Mariner with him now.

As soon as the Mercedes ground to a halt he was out, striding towards the nearest Italians even before the first clouds of desert sand rolled forward into the stage-set lighting.

'Is that the last?' He spoke in English, both because the Italians understood it better than Arabic and because the local villagers did not understand it at all.

'Yes.' Cappaldi, the Roman company man, answered also in English, looking slightly surprised. He slid one finger round the collar of his silk Lauren shirt, betraying confusion more than nervousness. The two senior ship's officers behind him looked up sharply, very much more sensitive to danger. Niccolo, *Napoli*'s first officer, moved forward so that Cappaldi and the other officer, the captain, were behind the solid barrel of his muscular body, as though he was squaring up for a fight.

Salah hesitated, calculating how much he could risk revealing to them, but suddenly Fatima was at his side, speaking rapidly.

'When you have loaded the last of it, get your men together,' she spat. 'Do it quietly but do it fast. Salah and I will cover you as best we can. They mean to kill you if they get the chance and bury you here among this filth you have destroyed them with. It is in revenge for their children, and I, for one, don't blame them.'

The dapper Italian executive, the grey-haired captain and the solid first officer heard her out without moving a muscle, wisely masking their reactions from the busy eyes around them.

Ali ibn Sir watched the small group from the driver's seat of the Mercedes, stroking his Uzi unconsciously. He respected the reputation of Salah Malik, member of the Senior Executive of the PLO, and had been further impressed by the personal impact of the man, the sense of presence given by that core of absolute quiet which seemed to dwell at the heart of the tall, whipcord body. The light of intelligence and the fire of faith shone in those long dark eyes, tempered by occasional flashes of wry humour and a lively humanity unexpected in a man of Malik's reputation. Legends clung about the man like a magic cloak in some child's tale from The Thousand And One Nights. A man increasingly out of step, however they said. A man alone – except for the woman Fatima.

He was still trying to fathom the woman and to calculate her relationship with this Palestinian statesman who had come from Beirut to help them. There were tales enough about her as well, and now that he had met her, they weren't so difficult to believe. He was not sure that as a devout Muslim he could ever approve of her and the way she behaved but she, too, had begun to earn his hard-won respect. It was a pity, he thought.

Caught between the foreigners and the locals, they were powerless to control events. No amount of political wisdom could stand against the rage of the villagers. The Palestinian and the woman were warning the Italians of the judgement about to be meted out to them. Now they, too, would have to die.

For Ali ibn Sir, it had begun nearly a year ago. He had been born and raised here, but he was away in the north when the first rumours had started. Tales of strange sicknesses, tales of stricken children. The desert south of Sidon, they said, had become accursed.

Ibn Sir was a practical, well-educated man, no mere superstitious desert farmer, though sprung from generations of desert farmers. He was a scholar, educated locally at first, and then going on, with an inevitability ensured by his fierce intelligence, to the university in Beirut. He was still there when civil war broke out and his real education had begun, and he had remained there, learning political science the hard way, until they called him home. He had returned, not just as a local boy made good but as a junior officer – for lack of a more precise title – in the Palestine Liberation Organisation. He did not believe in curses, but he came home when Ibrahim his brother called, to find out the truth for himself. Ibrahim was a small farmer with herds of goats and camels. Ali had nephews and nieces here. He had parents here, who had lived with Ibrahim since he had gone north and joined the PLO.

He returned to find his family's herd gone. No one had told him that the animals too were suffering, but it turned out that they had been affected first, and Ibrahim's first of all, grazing out along the margin of the desert, furthest out of the village livestock. And his nephews, herdsmen to his brother's stock, had been among the first to fall ill. His youngest niece, newly weaned, taking little more than goat's milk, had been the first to die. He had left a contented family, prosperous, long-estabished and content. He returned to dull-eyed strangers, stricken by they knew not what, dying on their feet. Destroyed, apparently, by the land which had bred them for generations. 'Take me to the desert,' he had said. 'Show me your grazing lands.'

At first they had seemed to be the same grazing lands familiar to him from his childhood, with their hollows where enough moisture collected in the freezing nights to nurture thorn scrub and thin grass. But then the familiar terrain began to change.

Trackways he had grown up with vanished into encroaching sand. The desert itself seemed to have altered its character, to have become more forbidding. Out in the dead zone ten miles south, he felt his hair stir with an overwhelming certainty that something was terribly wrong. So strong was the sensation that he almost forgot that he had long been educated out of superstition. He turned to his brother who was driving the jeep with slack hands, almost letting the battered old machine guide itself, as though it were one of his dead camels. 'Ibrahim,' he said quietly. 'What has happened here? The desert has changed.'

'They say it is the curse,' Ibrahim told him wearily.

'They are stupid and old-fashioned and we know better. What has happened to make you like this, Ibrahim?'

'My children have started dying, Ali. Our parents have lost their hair and their teeth and their sight. My wife has a growth in her belly like a rock beneath her ribs. And I, I can no longer feel my fingers. It is as though the leprosy has returned.'

They drove on in silence across the stricken landscape until suddenly Ali called, 'Stop!'

There in front of them, imperfectly concealed, revealed more by the shadows cast by the setting sun than anything actually remaining on the sand, was a roadway. A roadway here where no one had ever wanted to come. Where no roadway had ever existed. It led to the coast, to signs of a makeshift docking facility.

Now, at the inland end of that road, nearly a year after he had found it, Ali sat cradling the Uzi he had been lucky enough to come across during his work, the whole sickening conspiracy lying open before him. It had been proved first by the scientists he had been able to call in; they had tested the soil and recorded levels of radio activity high above normal. It was proved next by the researchers who had combed land registries and company records until they had found two that matched, showing that the dead zone in his desert had been purchased by an Italian firm called Disposoco specialising in the disposal of toxic waste.

Had the stricken farmers been standing alone, they would have been all but helpless. They would no doubt have died quietly, and the desert, with its reputation, would have hidden its secret well enough. But the farmers were not standing alone. With them stood the PLO. Confused and lost for an effective alternative, Ibrahim ibn Sir had turned to his brother Ali. And Ali had turned to his friends. A message went to Rome, to Disposoco's board of directors: remove your waste from the desert or die. The message had been accompanied by a series of codes known only to the highest echelons of the terrorist organisation and the anti-terrorist police. The Italians were convinced; there had not even been the necessity of an example. Disposoco had sent *Napoli* with equipment and experts to blow open the desert dump and oversee the removal of the waste.

The bulldozers needed to exhume the waste would be left behind, as would the trucks needed to transport it. The villagers would need the former to fill in the excavation, Disposoco said; the latter would simply be a gift, though this should not be interpreted as any kind of admission of liability on their part. They had sent Enrico Cappaldi to ensure that everything went to plan. The PLO had sent Salah Malik to ensure the same. It was almost a civilised arrangement, as though the wrong being put right were some slight financial oversight. As though the horrors by the wayside, twisted by the thoughtlessness of the waste disposal company, had no families, required no restitution.

Did they believe that? Did they really expect that Ali and Ibrahim ibn Sir, last of their family now, and the rest of the villagers who had the strength to move and the burning will to fight would let this outrage go unavenged?

CHAPTER TWO

'When do you think they'll attack?' asked Fatima tensely.

'If it was me, I'd wait until we get this stuff back to the ship.' Salah's eyes were everywhere. Both of them knew that his estimation was a faint hope. They would be killed here at the scene of the crime. And that meant whatever was planned would begin as soon as the last truck was loaded.

'The only real chance I can see is to load the Italians into the trucks at the same time as the waste,' said Salah. 'Put the last of them in among the last of it. Use it for protection. They'll have to be careful, but it will protect them. Should protect them.'

'Not the sort of protection I'd want, I must admit!'

'It's all they've got.'

'Right. I'll have a word with First Officer Niccolo. He seems to be the most reliable,' decided Fatima. 'Captain Fittipaldi is old and slowing down.'

Salah watched the determined young woman walk off. From her demeanour it would be hard for even the most suspicious observer to guess her mission or its importance. She was truly extraordinary, the Palestinian thought. Born in Dhahran, raised in England, she was kidnapped back from a promising if fledgling journalistic career in London by a born-again Muslim father. She escaped, only to fall into the clutches of a half-sane terrorist with wild ambitions to capture the old oil platform called *Fate*, close the Gulf and hold the world to ransom. But she had come through it all to find a niche in the PLO as though specifically designed by Allah, blessings be upon Him, for the task. She had become his assistant – his right arm – with open generosity and absolute reliability, as though they had always been on the same side. As though they had always been friends and colleagues and he had never been forced to shoot her. He had shot her with a small-bore weapon high in the left side of her chest. She had been lucky to survive, but quick to heal. And swifter still to forgive, if not to forget.

His thoughts turned again to Richard Mariner and all the people he had fought alongside to regain *Fate*, all the people he could do with right now. Then he shrugged and made his way over to Enrico Cappaldi.

Disposoco's representative was the most at risk, although he did not seem to realise it. Cappaldi had not impressed Salah at all. Fashioned to be a male model rather than a businessman, the effete, arrogant young Roman got under foot at every opportunity and had such a capacity for irritating those around him that Salah had wondered more than once whether he had been sent out here on purpose to be killed. It did not require too much imagination to conceive of a senior executive, husband or father only too willing to use this as a means to save his company, marriage or family.

Cappaldi was standing by one of the halogen lamp standards. He had used a wing nut on the stem as a coat hanger for his suit jacket, after a pantomime of obvious concern that the combination of dust and perspiration might soil the garment. Now the temperature in the clear desert night was falling rapidly and he wanted to put it on again but before doing so he was checking it carefully to make sure that the lightweight cashmere fabric was unblemished. What he must have paid for it, Salah calculated grimly, would probably have kept one of these stricken families in food for a year. And they knew it. Even here, newspapers, magazines and television programmes kept the people well up to date with Western fashions, and what they cost. The certainty of this spurred the tall freedom fighter into speedier action.

'Stop fussing with that,' he said rudely as he approached, for all the world as though the young Italian executive was a child.

'Get yourself across to my truck as quickly as you can without making it too obvious. Get in the back and hide.'

The Italian's face registered shock and disbelief. The backs of the trucks were not just filthy, they were being loaded with containers of lethal waste that he had every reason to believe were leaking dangerously. 'What—'

'Do as I say!' Salah spat, walking straight past Cappaldi as though he were not talking to him at all. 'They'll kill you any moment unless you move!'

Without pausing to see what effect his words had, Salah walked on into the middle of the collection zone. Ali had parked the truck at the head of the column and it was fully loaded now. They all were, except the fourth and last. Six white-suited waste disposal experts were sitting in a group with their protective hoods thrown back, chatting and smoking as the sailors from *Napoli*'s crew loaded the pallets with fork-lift trucks. 'Any of you speak English?' asked Salah casually as he approached.

One of them nodded. He was the tallest of them, a dry-looking, almost elderly man. A professor of some kind. He was the leader of the scientists and, oddly enough, the one who had placed the explosives. Salah spoke directly to him. 'Tell the others to get on to the trucks now,' he said. 'Drivers and crew members into the cabs – as many as will fit. The rest in the backs. All the leaking drums have already been removed with the contaminated sand. This last lot is safe. You can hide behind them if you have to.'

The old man's eyes rested briefly on Salah as though he could not understand the rapid English words. Then they drifted away to the rim of the pit where there were suddenly a lot of shadowy figures in tattered Arab dress looking down on them. He nodded once and spoke to the other scientists. They were up even before Salah turned to the crew. Niccolo had anticipated him; he was already giving the crew orders. A few terse words and the men simply vanished. To cover them, the Italian officer and Salah stooped in concert and lifted the last pallet – providentially empty and light – up into the back of the last truck.

Then suddenly it was finished and there was silence. Salah

swung round slowly and walked out from behind the truck as
Niccolo slammed the tailgate up into place. The only other
outsider visible was Fatima, standing by the open door of the
first truck, waiting for him. Beyond and behind her, Ali ibn Sir
and the villagers stood in a wide, still fan, watching. The only
gun he could see was Ali's Uzi but that was more than gun
enough. He wondered how many of them would need to die
before the villagers would be satisfied. He wondered how they
expected to get the last of the stuff aboard the *Napoli* with half
of the crew here, dead. And the captain. And the first officer.
But they would have thought of that. Ali must have a plan, he
would have it all worked out, Salah was certain. Mouth dry,
heart thumping, he walked forward.

The engine of the lead truck coughed into life. Fatima swung
round, her face a mask of surprise and consternation, to look up
into the cab. Salah froze for an instant. They all did. It was the
last thing any of them expected. With a scream of tortured gears,
the truck was off, careering forward at Ali and the villagers. In
the thunder of its movement, the other lorries all fired up as
well and began to roll forward in convoy after it. Salah broke
into a sprint. The open door of the first truck swung wildly as
the Mercedes moved. It caught Fatima and hurled her away to
one side. The truck reached the villagers and they too flew this
way and that, most of them diving safely out of the way. Salah
pulled Fatima to her feet. The side of her face was darkening
into a bruise but her eyes were open and bright. 'Cappaldi,' she
called over the thunderous row, explaining everything with that
one word. They looked back down the convoy as the second,
then the third truck thundered past them, deserting them in the
panic rush to escape. But Niccolo was driving the fourth one
and he stood on his brake as he came abreast of them. Strong
hands pulled them up and into the cab then handed them back
like bundles of washing at a dhobi through the canvas partition
in the rear into the flat bed of the truck.

The barrels of chemical waste made an effective shield but
they were loosely loaded. It was easy enough to see between
them to the bright pandemonium rapidly receding behind them.

Ali and most of his men had picked themselves up now and were in animated conference, clearly debating the best way to give pursuit. As Salah watched them pick up the bodies of the two men who had not managed to dive out of the way of Cappaldi's truck, he knew there would be no quarter for them now. Then the sand thrown up by the convoy swirled in behind them and there was nothing left to see.

Two more dead, thought Ali savagely, and all because he had hesitated. He should have shot Cappaldi as soon as he sat up in the cab of the lead truck. Then he should have shot Fatima and Malik. That way all of them would still have been here, trucks and all. But there was no point in hanging about swapping recriminations. He looked around desperately for anything fast enough to follow the Mercedes trucks. The earth-moving equipment was still up on the rim of the pit. He could climb to the first heavy vehicle there almost as quickly as the convoy of trucks could grind up the corkscrew incline on the side of the pit.

No sooner had the thought come than he was in motion, scrambling up the sloping sand, with the quickest-thinking of his men close behind. The vehicle he was making for was a big Ford dumper. It was not fast, certainly not as fast as the trucks, but it was unladen and might well bring him up with the convoy if any of their drivers was less than expert. And Cappaldi in the lead truck gave every sign of being inexperienced in handling the huge vehicle; he might well slow the rest of them down.

At the Ford, Ali stopped. A tall, thin figure was standing just beside it, silent and unmoving. For a horrific moment he thought his father had returned from festering death to guard the vehicle for him. But then the figure stepped forward out of the shadows. 'You are going after them?' his brother asked.

'Of course, Ibrahim. At once.' At his word, half a dozen of the men who had followed him up the pit began to scramble into the rear of the Ford. Ibrahim turned and reached up with his right hand to open the Ford's door high above his head and Ali saw what was in his brother's left hand: a long, bolt-action

Lee Enfield rifle. As he looked at it, Ali heard again the voice of his father telling him about the weapon many years before: 'I took it from the British when I was fighting on the Gaza Strip. It works as well as ever.'

Ali gave a lean smile. 'Climb aboard quickly, Ibrahim.'

The Ford dumper-truck was surprisingly agile for such a large vehicle; the big tyres rode over the sand and boulders with an ease that the smaller Mercedes vehicles could not match. It had an automatic gearshift which gave Ali more time to concentrate on steering the most efficient course and working with the accelerator to coax the great diesel engine to efforts which must have been beyond its design specifications even when it was new. This was the road he had first followed with Ibrahim that long, terrible time ago when all this was just beginning, but it was not disguised any more. And Ali knew it well. Better than Cappaldi in the lead truck fighting it unhandily every inch of the way, trying to get his battered old vehicle to behave like a Lamborghini.

In the rear of the last truck, Salah, satisfied that Fatima was not badly hurt, looked back anxiously, waiting to see the light of the Ford come cutting through the dark sandstorm in their wake. But before that happened, something else caught them unawares. In their urgent desire to be gone, they had forgotten the maimed crowd that lined their way. Through it, like wind through a cornfield, ran an unspoken message, a suspicion of what was going on.

When the first stone bounced off the windscreen, Cappaldi thought it was just a freak, thrown forward and upward, somehow, by the motion of the truck. But the second shattered the sidelight and exploded into the cab beside him. Apart from himself, it was empty; there was no one to protect him from the onslaught of rocks and flying glass. A steady hail of rocks of all sizes hurtled in from out of the darkness. All of the side windows went. The windscreen starred and threatened to shatter. A particularly shrewd shot hit the cursing Roman on the side of the head and he lost consciousness. The Mercedes swung off the road, mercifully into a small gully where no one was standing, and came to rest, its motor still chugging gamely. The other trucks thundered past, but the last one slowed just enough to drop two dark figures over the tailgate to brave the hail of stones, sprint back and pile in to their crippled companion.

Salah and Fatima rolled the unconscious Cappaldi back through the canvas into the rear portion of the truck. Then they were off, driving wildly through the unforgiving night, trying to catch up with the others.

Cappaldi came to with a splitting headache and complete confusion as to where exactly he was. Indeed, at first he thought he must have taken a tainted line of coke at a party the night before and experienced an exceedingly bad trip. He half expected to turn over and find, as he habitually did at home, some vaguely remembered beauty snugly asleep beside him in the huge bed of his apartment on the Via Appia. Reality arrived with a deep rut in the trackway and a lurch which felt as though it had loosened his brain. And with a seemingly huge figure which erupted out of the darkness to hover over him like doom. He actually screamed as he sat up, but the sound was lost in the din of the truck's progress through the desert night. He found himself facing Captain Fittipaldi of the *Napoli* in a sort of redoubt behind a stockade of metal drums mounted on wooden pallets. He reached up and took the old man's arm, steadying himself as he looked around.

Such was the noise of the engine and the wheels and the flapping of the canvas sides in the wind of their flight that conversation was impossible. Looking over his shoulder through the soft perspex window of the cab's canvas back, he saw Malik and the girl who accompanied him everywhere. Young enough to be his daughter, thought Cappaldi, sidetracked; his mistress, no doubt. Fatima. She was thin and strong and vividly dark. Cappaldi preferred statuesque blondes; nevertheless, had they stayed any longer in this godforsaken place he would have taken Fatima for himself – out of sheer boredom if nothing else. But they were going back to the ship now. Once they had the last of this stuff loaded aboard her, he could see about taking the next flight out of the nearest available airport. He should be home within forty-eight hours.

The headlights which suddenly shone in on him took Cappaldi completely by surprise. From the look on the captain's puffy visage, it was clear he was equally taken aback by the utterly unexpected brightness. But their surprise was as nothing to their shock when the first bullet ricocheted off the canisters in front of them to punch its way out of the flapping canvas wall leaving a hole as wide as the captain's screaming mouth. It took very little imagination on Cappaldi's part to calculate that the damage done to the canvas could all too easily be repeated on the cashmere and silk currently pampering his own frame. His first thought was to hide; to cower behind the canisters and wait to arrive at the *Napoli*. But he, perhaps better than anyone else here, knew how dangerous the contents of those canisters really were. The thought of being showered with toxic waste should a bullet manage to pierce one of them was even more terrifying than the thought of being shot himself. It was this that spurred him into action. 'Come on!' he yelled at the terrified captain. 'We must put the Arabs off our track before they hit one of these canisters!'

'But how? They have a gun and we are unarmed! We cannot fight. We must hide.'

'I haven't time to explain, old man, but believe me, being shot is far better than being covered with the stuff in these containers!'

'But they are reinforced steel. They are safe.'

If you only knew the truth, thought Cappaldi. 'They aren't strong enough to withstand—'

Another bullet exploded through the side of the truck. Both men felt it pass immediately above their heads, and this time, instead of simply slapping through thick canvas, it chopped a metal strut in two. 'They aren't strong enough to withstand that!' yelled Cappaldi, and this time Captain Fittipaldi was convinced.

Ibrahim crouched in the Ford's cab beside Ali, the backs of his legs braced against the front seat, trying to sight through the raised flap-windscreen, along the length of the bucking bonnet. Dust billowed up in front of them and swept back into Ali's eyes. 'Wait for a moment,' he yelled to his brother. 'There's a straight section coming up, level and smooth. If you wait for that and then shoot quickly, you'll really be able to do some damage!'

Ibrahim frowned into the swirling dust ahead. 'They are doing something in the rear truck . . . Something I do not like the look of.'

Ali paid scant attention to his brother, concentrating fiercely on wrestling the unwieldy Ford along as fast as possible. The sand boiling up from the convoy in front of him was nearly blinding him. The twists in the familiar road seemed unexpectedly vicious. He was not used to the Ford's steering system. The figures at the roadside crowded almost on to the trackway itself in their eagerness to impede the speeding Mercedes trucks containing the Italians. It was a dangerous combination; Ali had visions of plunging into a crowd of villagers on a particularly sharp bend, doing yet more damage to them.

But then, as he had promised Ibrahim it would, the Ford suddenly steadied as the road became flat, smooth and straight. A wind from the north sprang up and abruptly the dust plumes were rolling away to his left and he could see the last vehicle in the column clearly. Ibrahim gave a howl of joy and worked the bolt feverishly, jacking another round up into the rifle's breech. Ali kept his eyes on the truck ahead; he could now see what his brother had been talking about earlier. Two figures, stark in the cave of the canvas, caught by the massive glare of his headlights, were wrestling with one of the canisters. It was clear that they meant to drop it overboard, hoping it would damage the Ford in some way. Little chance of that, thought Ali with grim satisfaction. The American dumper-truck was reassuringly massive around him. He allowed himself a wolfish smile. 'The young one,' he called to his brother. 'Spoil his suit for me.'

Ibrahim had in fact been aiming at the captain, wanting to kill the officer first, which seemed the logical thing to do. But at Ali's command, he swung his sight to the right, changing his target and aim. Just as the sight at the end of his rifle barrel converged with the apex of the V sight, pointing at the young Italian's chest, the two distant figures heaved the first canister up between them. He squeezed the rifle's trigger gently, trusting to the smoothness of the road. And as he did so, the Mercedes braked sharply, bringing his target leaping back towards him.

The third bullet thumped into the canister just beside Cappaldi's shoulder. It should have ricocheted off in a shower of sparks, soft lead shrugged aside by the curved steel, but it smashed through the rotting, sub-standard metal almost as easily as its predecessors had slapped through the canvas. At the far side of the canister, flattened but by no means spent, it thumped into Cappaldi's chest, straight through the centre of his breast pocket. The young man was hurled back, dead instantly, to lie on the bed of the truck. The canister, spewing its contents from the ragged wounds in its sides, rocked wildly in the captain's hands until by a power only terror could have lent him, he pushed it over the tailgate and down into the roadway. The instant he did so, the fourth bullet smacked through his temple and the sound it made splitting open his head was the last thing *Napoli*'s captain ever heard.

The flat section of roadway ran over a low plateau of rock which lay like an enormous step between the desert and a deep wadi which led down to the coast. At the end of that flat step, the roadway turned through the first of three hairpin bends leading down the valley side perhaps fifty feet sheer. Malik braked fiercely here, aware that this would bring the Ford up closer behind him but governed by the need to keep the screaming Mercedes under some kind of control; then he accelerated away into the bend. The canister, toppling backwards out of the truck under the captain's dead hands, was instantly thrown clear. Already ruptured, it hit solid rock and split further, sending a wave of its lethal contents out to either side across the road. On one side of it, the truck accelerated away down the valley side, turning into the first hairpin. On the other side of it, the Ford came thundering down, to collect the canister on its first bounce and complete its destruction with its radiator. Ali also braked fiercely, as Salah Malik's truck revealed the bend before them. The Ford's great tyres skidded through the mess on the roadway. A spray of toxic chemical came up through the open windshield, blinding Ibrahim at once. Ali fought with grim concentration to keep the bucking monster on the twisting road. Hand over hand he hauled the steering wheel round to his left while his feet, one on top of the other, both trod on the brake. Slowly the great vehicle answered his command and swung round into the hairpin, just barely under control.

The Mercedes seemed, if anything, even closer, for Malik was still driving with careful control. It was close enough for Ali to see who was driving. 'Try another shot,' he called to Ibrahim. 'You can hit Malik easily. Even in the PLO there are those I know who would be pleased to see him dead!' But Ibrahim made no response. 'Try another shot!' he repeated, glancing across at his brother. Ibrahim had dropped the rifle on to the floor of the cabin and was cradling his face in his hands. And there seemed to be smoke coming out between his fingers. Agony and the shock of realisation hit Ali simultaneously. He looked down. His skin was clinging to the molten curve of the steering wheel, like white gloves pulled off his hands. 'Jump!' he screamed to the men in the dumper's back, to his brother, perhaps even to himself. 'JUMP!' But it was already far too late.

Then the front tyres exploded as the contents of that one canister ate through their rubber walls, and a strange sort of silence enveloped the Ford as it took a straight, smooth, short road through the air beside the cliff. Ali had time to hear the men in the back screaming over his elder brother's quiet whimper and to mutter a prayer himself before they all crumpled against the valley floor and burst into red flames.

CHAPTER THREE

Salah swung the Mercedes round the second bend and the road sloped sharply down to the lowest hairpin which turned it back along the valley floor towards the coast. The picture the other trucks made, rolling forward through the night, froze in his memory as a dark shape dropped out of the sky and exploded like a bomb. The whole night seemed to light up and for an instant Salah thought the villagers must have got hold of some heavy artillery. But then he registered the shape of the projectile. It had been the Ford truck. It had landed just clear of the apex of the last bend, right in front of the lead truck.

By the time he had worked this out, he was all but upon it himself. The explosion did not seem to have done any damage; the convoy kept moving. Salah breathed a sigh of relief and braked. 'We must look for survivors,' he yelled at Fatima and she nodded curt agreement. They left the engine idling and jumped down. It took only seconds to establish that no one had survived. They leaped back into the Mercedes and left the great blazing funeral pyre behind them.

Salah carried the lurid vision of it in his mind's eye all the way down the dry wadi to the coast. Luckily, the driving here was much easier, for there were no villagers lining the road, and no pursuit, although the cracked windscreen had by now shattered and both the headlights were gone.

Down to the coast the convoy limped under a rising crescent moon, following the twists of the dry stream bed through the interlocking teeth of the steep valley sides until suddenly the hills rolled back and the land spread itself out. It stretched flat and featureless on either side, reaching down on the left towards the Israeli border, many miles to the south; ahead it sloped gently down to the mirror-smooth Mediterranean Sea.

At the coast the hill slopes did not fall back to leave a flat beach; instead they gathered themselves up into a plateau ending in a low cliff above a natural anchorage deep enough to admit a medium-sized vessel. The container ship *Napoli* had anchored alongside the cliff, her port side snugged up safely against sheer rock.

Salah swung the steering wheel viciously right and sent the Mercedes up to the anchorage at full speed. He joined the short rank of vehicles all facing inland towards the desert, their tailgates as close to the *Napoli*'s loading system as possible. The occupants of the first trucks were helping the crew and white-suited experts manhandle the steel drums and concrete boxes out into the floodlit night. The drums and boxes were then sorted and the drums were loaded into big wooden containers at the cliff edge by the black metal wall of *Napoli*'s port side. As each container was filled and sealed, it was marked and consigned. The concrete boxes went directly into the freighter's holds, the containers full of barrels to her deck storage. Her own cranes were more than enough to move both the boxes and the containers.

With Fatima at his side, Salah went to join First Officer Niccolo in the main work area. The square, reliable officer was in full command, overseeing the rapid disposition of the contents from his own truck. 'We have very little time,' yelled Salah over the dockside clamour.

'That much became obvious when they stopped throwing stones at us and started throwing Ford earth movers instead,' answered the Italian grimly. 'I have to get this lot sorted out, however. Perhaps you could find Captain Fittipaldi – he must be in the back of one of the trucks. He can get the departure procedure underway while I get the last of this filth aboard.'

He turned away, already filling his massive lungs to yell

another order, but Fatima impulsively caught at his arm and he swung back.

'I take back what I said earlier about the villagers having the right to kill you all,' she said to him. 'Not many people would hang around to pack up the last of this stuff, under the circumstances.'

'It is my job. It is what I think is right.'

'Nevertheless, it is brave.'

They might have said more, but at that moment, a white-suited form came panting up. Salah recognised the man he had spoken to earlier – the professor. 'You must come,' the scientist said. 'We've found Signor Cappaldi and Captain Fittipaldi.'

They had taken the barrels out of the back of Salah's truck and found the two corpses lying side by side. Niccolo and Salah first climbed up into the stinking cave at the back of the truck. 'Damn, this is bad!' was Niccolo's first reaction when he saw the bodies. And a fairly tame one too, thought Salah who had spent much of his life around sailors. The back of the truck was dark after the brightness of the lighting outside but there was quite enough light to see that both men were dead. The massive stain on the breast of Cappaldi's jacket told its own story and received hardly a second look from either man. Instead they gave their attention to the much more important casualty. But, again, what they saw allowed no room for hope. The right side of Captain Fittipaldi's silver-haired skull had been blasted open from temple to ear and it seemed that half of his brains were on the wooden floor. 'Look closely, please, before we move either of them,' rasped Niccolo at last. 'I may need your help when I make up the accident report later.'

Salah stared at the dead men on the bare boards before him, but he knew it was unnecessary; he would remember every detail of the back of that truck, from the broken strut and the bullet hole in the canvas, to the strange stench and oily taste of the air. He had seen much of death one way and another, and he had never forgotten one detail of any corpse that he had seen; these two would join the others, unchanging, in the nightmare picture gallery of his mind. 'I will give you my version of events later too,' he said. 'That will be important, though I don't think it will be particularly helpful.'

'You sound as though you have done this sort of thing before.'

'A little more than ten years ago I was on a tanker called *Prometheus*. Almost all her officers were killed in an accident in the pump room. I did my share of helping to fill in accident reports then. It is not something one easily forgets.'

'Any advice you feel you can give will be gratefully accepted,' said Niccolo as they climbed down. 'I've not had as much experience as you have, clearly . . .'

He let what he was saying drift off into silence. All the bustle of loading the *Napoli* had stopped. The ship herself still needed tidying up, her cranes needed to be secured, her hatches battened down, but the rocky plateau beside her was empty of all except the four battered Mercedes trucks and those few lights not standing on the laden decks. The ship was ready to up anchor and everyone was waiting. Salah could see Fatima on the deck. She had pause to lean against the deck rail. In the bright lighting, the bruised half of her face looked almost black.

Niccolo stood still, his eyes carefully travelling over the faces around him. He was silent for so long that Salah swung round, thrusting Fatima out of his mind, thinking he had frozen at the prospect of his sudden assumption of command. But as he moved, the Italian called out to the second officer, 'Cesar, the captain's been shot. Dead. I'm taking over command. Consider yourself first officer from now on. Get a party to carry two corpses aboard and send someone to break the news to Gina. Then get ready to cast off. Be ready to cut the shore lines if necessary. I'll be on the bridge or in the captain's quarters. Report to me there when we're ready.'

'Yes, Captain,' a voice called down from the deck.

'Captain . . .' Niccolo said the word over to himself, as if trying it on for size. Then he squared his shoulders and went to board the freighter.

Salah followed Niccolo's purposeful stride. He and Fatima had little option but to depart with the ship. If they stayed ashore and fell into the villagers' hands, they hadn't a prayer. They had driven down from Beirut. The car they had used was parked outside the Ibn Sir farmhouse, still packed with the clothes and papers they had brought down with them. He would have to find some way to report to headquarters. In the meantime, both he and Fatima, he suspected, would have to earn their keep until they could find some way of getting safely off this ship and back to Beirut. Under Niccolo's command – no matter how temporary that might be – everyone aboard the *Napoli* was likely to have to earn their keep. But where could an ex-bosun of supertankers and a woman fit into what should be the well-oiled machine of a fully-trained freighter's crew? Lost in these thoughts, he followed Niccolo down the length of *Napoli*'s main deck and, besides being slightly surprised at how quickly they reached the bridgehouse, he noticed very little about the ship.

He was struck at once, however, by the smallness of the bridge. He was used to the vastness of supertankers with deadweight tonnages in excess of 250,000. *Napoli* was little more than 20,000; she seemed cramped, confining. Struck by this, he stood quietly in the doorway while Niccolo crossed to a figure standing beside the helmsman, looking away into the distance. Salah's gaze was also drawn beyond the confines of the ship. A blaze of headlights was coming up the slope from the wadi mouth, and moving with them was a crowd in vivid chiaroscuro. Salah crossed to the front of the bridge where Niccolo was speaking in low Italian to the officer of the watch, who in turn was speaking into a hand-held radio. Salah had hardly started to try a rudimentary translation when Niccolo's hand went to the engine room telegraph. Figures down on the deck moved at the winches securing the anchors. 'Good,' said Niccolo after a moment. 'Let's get out of here.' As he spoke, over the sound of the generators, the engines, and of his quiet voice came the first familiar firework popping of automatic gunshots from the shore.

Half an hour later, they were well out to sea, riding easily through a dead calm. The moon had vanished behind thickening clouds and the shoreline was no longer visible from the bridge. Niccolo, who had been poring over the radar bowl, swung wearily erect and gave a series of orders in Italian. Immediately the engines reversed and, as the way came off the ship, went to idle. 'Come,' he said to Salah and Fatima. The two Palestinians were in a bright corner of the bridge behind the chart table; Salah was in the process of checking Fatima's bruised face – much to her obvious and increasing impatience. At Niccolo's word, she broke away and followed him off the bridge. Salah followed too, but more slowly.

The captain's cabin, bathroom and dayroom made up a small suite of rooms on C deck and to this Niccolo led his guests. The rooms were as anonymously neat as an hotel room, though someone seemed to have recently searched through the captain's clothes, for they alone were untidy behind half-open cupboard doors. 'Drink?' asked Niccolo. Both Muslims declined. Niccolo crossed to the captain's little bar fridge and took out a bottle of chilled white wine. As he opened it, he glanced at Fatima. He could see why Salah was worried – she was badly bruised – her left eye almost shut. But her right eye looked bright and alert. He poured himself a little and sat on the bunk, waving his guests into two seats. No sooner had he done so than an abrupt rattling came from outside, making both Salah and Fatima jump. It took Salah an instant to realise that it wasn't gunfire this time. It was chain. *Napoli*'s anchors had gone back down.

'Now, let's look at the situation we have here,' said Niccolo quietly. '*Napoli* is without a captain. There is no one aboard with the necessary papers to take this sort of cargo a hundred metres more, let alone to Italy. I hold command only because there is no one else to do so, not because I have the qualifications or the right. If I take her any further, we could be summarily arrested. If anything went wrong – if we collided, say, or even broke down – God alone knows what would happen. I would never sail again, that's for sure. Always assuming I wanted to, after I got out of jail. Of course, in these circumstances, I should refer to the charterers' agent, but he is currently lying dead beside the captain. I can phone Rome in the morning, but it seems unlikely that speaking to Signor Cappaldi's bosses will get us much further, especially as I understand this commission was to be completed under the strictest secrecy. So, here we are. We cannot go on and we cannot go back. And I rather fear our respite at anchor will be brief. There are a lot of deeply upset people ashore and they will be looking for us at first light, your organisation, Mr Malik, among them, I should think.'

'I can get through to the PLO in Beirut as soon as you allow me access to the radiophone. I will explain.'

'But even so, the people you contact will have to act fast if they are to stop the local people attacking us, even out here. We need someone who can take this ship to Italy, and we need them here at once.'

'I can get a captain to you within twenty-four hours,' said Salah slowly, with a glance at Fatima. 'Where could you be in twenty-four hours, if you risked setting sail again at once?'

'That's easy. The old girl can deliver about ten knots if we push her. We could be two hundred and fifty miles west of here.'

'North-west, perhaps . . .'

'But Salah,' Fatima burst out, *today of all days*!'

'You are right,' he answered. 'I had forgotten. They will all be at the wedding. Nevertheless—'

The cabin door burst open to admit a woman of about Fatima's age, as dark as the Arabian woman, but full-bodied where the freedom fighter was slim, and as turbulent as Fatima was calm and calculating. 'What have you done to him?' the woman screamed.

'Gina!' Niccolo was on his feet.

'Come with me! See what you have done to him!'

She was gone and Niccolo began to follow her out of the cabin. 'Perhaps you could come too,' he said to Fatima. 'You are the only other woman aboard. Why he had to bring her, I cannot imagine. She is his daughter. Captain Fittipaldi's daughter.'

The three of them followed at once, out into the corridor where Gina Fittipaldi awaited them. Silently, except for her sobbing, they went down to the infirmary together.

They had laid the captain out beside Cappaldi. It had been sensitively done. The pale forehead was bound with a bandage and the captain's cap disguised the odd shape of the right temple almost perfectly. Dressed in full uniform, the old man looked perfectly peaceful, as though he had dozed off at some official function and might awaken at any moment. But this reassuring illusion was utterly destroyed by the state of his hands. Folded respectfully on his breast, they were at terrible odds with the rest of him. From wrist to fingertip they looked as though they had been bathed in the most virulent acid. The skin was all gone and most of the flesh along with it, dissolved into semi-liquid matter that ran in dark stains down the serge-clad curves of his ribs. All that lay folded on the cooling corpse's uniformed chest were two skeletal claws of chalky calcium and yellow sinew, as though his hands had died and rotted to bone an age before the rest of him.

As the two men looked on in stunned disbelief, there came a gasp from behind them and the noise of a falling body. They swung round expecting to see Gina fainting to the floor – but it was Fatima. And it wasn't just a faint. Salah caught her up at once and placed her on the ship's operating table. Then, with gentle fingers, he traced the bruising down from her face to the collar of her shirt. He undid the buttons and opened the green material to reveal a mass of bruising on shoulder, breast and ribs. Niccolo was beside him at once – the First Officer was ship's medic. 'This is not good,' said the Italian, pushing the shirt wider to find the edges of the bruise. On the upper slope of her left breast – at the centre of the damage – was a recently healed bullet wound. Niccolo sucked his teeth and said nothing more, his fingers probing gently. At last he returned his attention to her head and separated the puffy lids of her black eye. Only the white could be seen between them – but it was not white any longer. It was bright blood red.

CHAPTER FOUR

Richard Mariner held up the glass of champagne and watched the bubbles fighting to reach the surface while he waited for the hubbub to die down. He was not a drinking man. He would do no more than wet his lips with the alcohol in honour of the toasts he was about to propose, then he would return to drinking Perrier. He had been a heavy drinker once; in fact he had come close to alcoholism after his supertanker *Rowena*, flagship of the Heritage tanker fleet, had exploded under him more than ten years ago, killing his wife and estranging him from Sir William Heritage, his boss, father-in-law and close friend. He had even left the sea, though exonerated by the court of inquiry, and set up his own company, Crewfinders. During the long, lonely nights and days he had begun to hit the bottle. His resumption of relations with Heritage, his return to the sea, and his marriage to Sir William's younger daughter, Robin, had saved him. He saw himself as a smaller, weaker man than others saw him. He knew he was not the creature of rock and steel he was reputed to be, and so now he avoided alcohol, the most dangerous of all his enemies.

Abruptly, he realised that silence had fallen and everyone in the great banqueting room at Heritage House was waiting for him to begin the toast. He cleared his throat. 'Ha *hum*!'

'Your attention, please,' joked John Higgins, the bridegroom. 'This is your captain speaking . . .'

A ripple of mirth went round the big room; as most of the wedding guests recognised the inevitable opening to Richard's invariable noon announcement aboard any ship he commanded.

'Thank you, John. Now, ladies and gentlemen, before I launch into my carefully researched best man's speech, John, and particularly his lovely wife Asha, have asked that I propose one special toast. I ask you to be upstanding for a moment, ladies and gentlemen, while we remember absent friends.'

Asha Higgins drew herself up to full height, topping John by half a head, careful to control the folds of her wedding dress. She raised her tall flute of lemon and Perrier and thought of absent friends and more: of Salah Malik whom she would have moved heaven and earth to have had here to share the happiest day of her life; of her sister Fatima, like Salah for ever barred England's shores because of her terrorist past and her current association with the PLO. Wherever they were, she was sure they were together, and she was sure they would be thinking of her and of John.

The room rustled as the guests sat down again. Richard put his glass on the table.

'Now, John,' he said, 'rather than giving a complete history of your childhood, education and training, or of our association, or of Asha's childhood and past experiences, I thought I would simply tell a little story.'

John groaned.

'No, no. Don't worry. It won't be the story of the nightclub performer in Singapore who removed all your clothes on stage . . .'

John covered his face.

'. . . with her teeth. Nor the story of how your underwear was run up the mast of a certain SS *Daphne*, only to catch the eye of the captain's wife who was heard to inquire, "Now what is John Higgins's underwear doing halfway up the mast?" And we are definitely not going to ask how it was that she could *recognise* your underwear, even at that distance . . .'

Most of the hoots of merriment came from those who

knew John's reputation as the shyest and most self-effacing of Lotharios.

'No, I would like to tell a more recent story. The background to your courtship of, and proposal to, Asha. That will, I think, give everyone here a flavour of your romance . . .'

'Nice speech, Richard,' said John an hour later as he and Asha prepared to leave for their honeymoon flight.

Richard smiled affectionately at this man who had started out as his most trusted lieutenant and was now his most trusted and respected senior captain. He put a brotherly arm across John's shoulders. 'Got everything? Tickets? Passports?'

'Yes. And we've plenty of time to get to Gatwick too. You've organised it like a dream, Richard. I really can't thank you enough.'

'No problem. Here comes Asha now. Let's try and get you out without too much noise and litter pollution.'

It was a nice idea but doomed to failure from the outset. John and Asha's car pulled up festooned with balloons and inscribed with the traditional 'JUST SPLICED'. They ran towards it through a blizzard of rice and confetti. They settled into it, shaking grain and paper out of their hair, and John started the engine. Immediately, another blizzard of confetti blasted out of the air-conditioning system. Pulling slowly away, he revealed a noisy tail of old boots and tin cans which they dragged gamely down Leadenhall Street towards the Bank of England and London Bridge. They stopped at the first convenient rubbish bin and got rid of the greatest excesses before proceeding towards Gatwick. They got as far as the Oval, on the A23 heading south, before their engine died on them.

'Good speech,' said Robin sleepily. Richard's wife sat back in a glow of cloth-of-gold, golden ringlets, golden tan. She was just coming up to her sixth month of pregnancy. That, too, made her glow when it was not making her sick.

'Thanks, darling. How's the baby?'

'Either practising ballet or getting ready for the rugger scrum.'

'Well, if she's going to play rugby, maybe we'd better get her name down for the school . . .'

They were driving through the early Friday-evening traffic towards Windsor, where they were booked into an hotel for the weekend. Richard's story of the courtship of John and Asha Higgins had been one of kidnap and piracy, of terrorists and terrible dangers, of high stakes and higher risks. It had also been the story of Richard and Robin's last, ill-fated, attempt at getting away from it all, and how it had met with such limited success that all of them were lucky to be alive. Now they were going to pamper themselves well away from work and all other responsibilities. Robin suddenly felt full of fun. She hadn't quite got used to the sudden mood swings caused by her advancing pregnancy but this was one she could handle. She sat up and looked across at Richard's profile illuminated by the lights from the dashboard. Full of love and longing for him she said, 'Do you mind driving Daddy's Mulsane?' He hadn't complained, but she knew he missed his old E-Type Jaguar, which was far too low-slung for her to sit in now. Her father Sir William Heritage had lent them his car for the weekend instead.

'How could anyone mind driving a Bentley? Idiot!'

She wriggled back into the hide seat, luxuriating in the feel of its contours against her back, bottom and thighs. She couldn't keep her eyes off him. He looked so distinguished. So handsome. Longing washed over her, and a sense of mischievous fun never far from the surface at the best of times. She lifted her left hand and studied the rings she wore; then, with a girlishly impulsive movement so typical of her, she slipped the hoops of gold and diamond off and popped them into her evening bag. Languidly, she considered her naked fingers, the ghost of a smile playing round the corners of her mouth. Then she picked up the handset of the Bentley's car phone and dialled.

Richard noticed none of this; he was concentrating on the road. It came as a complete surprise to him when he heard her throaty voice say, 'Hello, is that the Royal Court Country Hotel? Good evening. I am phoning for Mr and Mrs Mariner.

I'm afraid they wish to cancel their booking of the Prince's Suite for this weekend.'

'Robin! What on earth are you up to?'

'Sssh! Yes, I'm still here. Of course I understand the deposit is not returnable. I'm sorry if I have put you to any inconvenience.'

'Robin! We'll be there in five minutes! What has got into you?'

She hung up the phone and undid the top two buttons of her dress. Her ripening breasts gave her the sort of cleavage she had only been able to dream about before she became pregnant.

'I have a cunning plan,' she whispered, making the words sound like the most licentious proposition imaginable.

'What is it?' His voice was just trembling on the edge of laughter.

'Mr and Mrs Mariner don't want the Prince's Suite for the weekend. But Mr and Mrs Smith do. Mr and Mrs Smith whom no one will be able to contact or disturb. Mr Smith is so good-looking he turns heads wherever he goes, and the beautiful, mysterious Mrs Smith wears no wedding ring. Are they film stars out on some secret liaison? Will the truth of it all appear in the gossip columns on Monday? Is there any end to the wicked, wicked things they'll get up to in the meantime?'

Her eyes picked up the first of the brightness from the welcome lights of the hotel's driveway, and glowed like huge grey cats' eyes in the shadows of the car. She would have been utterly irresistible even had he felt like resisting.

As she had predicted, they turned heads in the reception area, she in her gossamer cloth-of-gold and he in his immaculate morning suit. Slowly, they walked through the stunned silence to the tall mahogany counter.

'Can I be of service, sir? Madam?' The receptionist fought to be urbane, then surrendered as Robin leaned forward conspiratorially and enveloped him in a cloud of Chanel. 'We want a room,' she whispered, her voice a gravelly alto. 'No. We want a *suite*. Immediately!'

'Well, I . . .'

'Any suite will do. It doesn't matter how large.'

'Madam, I . . .'

'Or how expensive.'

'Sir, I . . .'

'But we must have it *immediately*, do you understand?'

'Perhaps if you talk to the manager.'

'The Prince's Suite,' cooed Robin. 'I've always had the most burning desire to—'

'I'm afraid you're unlucky there, madam.'

'I beg your—'

'It was booked for the weekend, but our clients cancelled . . .'

'Perfect!'

'. . . so I gave it to that young couple over there not five minutes ago. They were actually standing here when the cancellation came through. They took it at once. I'm really most dreadfully sorry.'

'And that was the last available suite?' asked Richard quietly, his eyes just failing to meet Robin's.

'If you could just speak to the manager, sir. Perhaps madam would like to wait in the private lounge . . .'

Robin paced like a caged tigresss in the elegant little lounge, close to tears. Matters were made worse for her by the fact that it seemed to have been carefully and cunningly decorated to resemble the campaign headquarters of a French general on a desert expedition, all swathes of brocaded silk, overstuffed cushions and Louis Quatorze chairs. She found the rich sensuality of it tinglingly exciting. In a masochistic rage she picked up a pamphlet from a fine-legged walnut occasional table and began to read about the sport and leisure complex on offer to residents. The gymnasia. The heated swimming pools. The golf courses in the grounds which reached to the margin of Windsor Great Park (and please beware of the deer on the tenth fairway of the eighteen-hole course). The Jacuzzis in all the suites . . .

The door whispered open and the receptionist actually bowed.

'I'm sorry, Mrs, ah, Smith . . .'

Richard towered behind him with the most devilish look

behind the sapphire of his eyes. 'I'm so sorry, darling, but they have absolutely nothing left . . .'

Robin, a senior executive and full ship's captain with all the papers to prove it, actually stamped her foot.

'. . . except the Bridal Suite.'

The call came in at midnight and the same receptionist took it. 'Royal Court reception, can I help you? Captain and Mrs Mariner? No, I'm afraid we have no one of that name staying here . . . Yes, they were booked into the Prince's Suite but I'm afraid they cancelled. No, I'm certain. No one of that name here at all . . . Yes, of course I'll take a message but . . . Heritage House, yes . . . Extremely urgent . . . Could you repeat that? . . . Salah Malik, yes . . . Ship *Napoli*, I understand . . . Certainly. Of course I will tell them if I see them but I do assure you, madam, we have no one called Mariner staying here.'

CHAPTER FIVE

'Nah. Nuffin' I can do in that time, guv. It's knackered.'

'If I leave it here for you to work on, can you tell me where we could get transport to Gatwick at once?'

'Well, right here, guv. You're lucky in that at least. This isn't just a garage and repair shop, it's the headquarters for all the black cabs in south London. It says so over the entrance there. See? Black Cab Company.'

'Right. We can still make the flight, then. Is that all right with you, darling?'

'Whatever you say, John. You're my lord and master now.' Asha smiled serenely at the garage mechanic who was observing her, wide-eyed, and went outside into the providentially dry November dusk to sit on her cases and wait for the cab.

Five minutes later, John had sorted everything out as far as he could and came striding towards her across the forecourt as a black cab detached itself from the shadows behind him. She was much less serene than she seemed; in fact she was blazingly angry and unsure whether his calm acceptance of the outrage was making things better or worse. Worse, at the moment, on balance. 'Don't you ever lose your temper?' she hissed as he reached her.

He gave a short laugh. 'Sometimes. Too often, in fact. But it wouldn't do any good now. And who is there here to be angry with?'

'You don't have to be angry with anyone. You can just be angry!'

'Ah. That's just it, you see. I can't. I have to be angry with someone or it just comes out as though I'm being grumpy.'

The cab pulled up beside them and the cabby leaned out of the window. 'Give you a hand with them bags, Chief?'

'Yes please. We're in a hurry. Our flight from Gatwick closes in two hours.'

'Should be able to get you there in plenty of time, Chief,' said the cabby amiably, climbing out.

'It's captain,' snapped Asha.

'How's that, miss?'

'My husband isn't a chief, he's a captain. And I'm not a miss, I'm a doctor!'

The cabby paused, a case in each hand, and considered the flaming woman. Then he smiled dazzlingly. 'Right you are, Doc. Just leave those there, Cap'n. I'll get them in the back.'

They were beyond Croydon before the atmosphere in the back began to cool. John sat quietly, waiting for Asha to calm down, knowing her well enough to know that her display of temper would not last long. He wondered what her marriage to Giles Quartermaine had been like, for the journalist was famous for his artistic temperament and impatience. Sparks must often have flown in the Quartermaine household, he thought. Well, things would be quieter *chez* Higgins. Wherever *chez* Higgins was going to be. He had a yacht in the harbour at Peel in the Isle of Man where he had been born and raised. That was the closest thing he had to a home apart from his tanker commands. Asha had no roots in England either. For the foreseeable future, the master and the ship's doctor of *Prometheus II*, flagship of the Heritage Mariner fleet, would simply share the Captain's cabin and call it home. It would be everything he had ever dreamed of.

John had never wanted anything other than to be a sailor. Of Irish/Manx descent – by no means an uncommon combination on the island – he had grown up on and around the sea. James Higgins had been captain of a trawler going after the herring which became Manx kippers after smoking at Peel and his mother had been one of the Quiggin family of shipwrights, related to the Quirk family of chandlers. John had spent his childhood on that mountainous little island halfway between Barrow and Dundrum, growing up in the hurly-burly of a big family half of whom were Quiggins, Quirks and Qualtroughs and half of whom were Higgins, Hursts and Hacketts. He had cousins spread west from Bride to Ballyconneely, from Maughold to Mallin Beg. No sooner had he come to terms with the dour grey waters of the Irish Sea than he found himself in Donegal wrestling the epic rollers of the great green Atlantic. And it was love. There never was a time, it seemed to him, when the sea had not filled him with almost uncontrollable emotion. Awe, at the sheer size of it. Fascination with the mysteries it contained. Respect for the unfeeling, dangerous power of it. Hatred for the grasping, unforgiving greediness which took his father's trawler and all her crew a week before his thirteenth birthday.

'If we miss the plane, that will be that, will it?'

It took him a moment or two to come back to the present. This was Asha, calming down.

''Fraid so. It's one of those package deals. Fabulous price, ruinous small print. But we shouldn't miss the plane. Excuse me, driver, but how long will it be?'

'Just coming down on to the M23 now, Cap'n. Twenty minutes should do us, as long as there's no trouble with the M25 interchange.'

'Thank you. There, darling, you see? There's nothing to worry about. We have more than an hour before the flight closes. That's plenty of time to check in the luggage and decide about the duty-free.'

Asha breathed a sigh of relief, stretched luxuriously and began to look around her. It was late evening but not yet full night. The sky was clear and still had a little colour to it. The cab came under the bright yellow lighting of the M23 motorway and began to pick up speed. The traffic flow around them thinned at once. 'This is better,' said John cheerily. 'We should make good time in this.'

'It'll thicken up again,' the driver warned. 'There's still the interchange to come.' And even as he spoke, the tail-lights ahead began to glow more vividly red.

Now that the atmosphere was easier in the back, the cabby began to chat to his passengers. 'Just married, I see. What a way to start, eh? All uphill from here, I expect. Just bad luck about your car. Mind, my marriage got off to a bad start too. Wedding joke! You know the sort of thing that can happen. They found out where me and the missus was going and took the screws out of our bed. Whole thing collapsed. Hell of a noise in the middle of the night. Manager thought it was burglars and nearly threw us out of the hotel. Very amusing! And it's not as if it's easy to find a bed in the middle of the night in Southend . . .'

John's mind began to drift again. It had been a hard few months and, although he mentioned it to nobody, when he got tired his side began to hurt where a terrorist bullet had ploughed through it, back to front, following the curve of his ribs, only thirteen weeks ago. Asha snuggled up against him, clearly tired too. It had been a long day for both of them.

Suddenly the driver stood on the brake, hurling both John and Asha to the floor; they were lucky not to be hurt. John pulled himself up at once, only to be thrown down again as the car behind careered into the back of the cab, shunting it left on to the hard shoulder. The noise was appalling, compounded of shrieking metal and blaring horns. As the taxi juddered to a halt, John pulled himself up again and clutched Asha to him until he was certain she was all right. Then he turned to the driver.

'Are you all right?'

'Yes, guv.'

'What happened?'

'Damned if I know.'

'Are we safe here?'

'Should be. We can sit on the hard shoulder here while I check the damage and . . . JESUS!'

John jerked forward, scarcely able to believe his eyes. As they had been talking, the three lanes of traffic on their right had come to a complete halt. But now, as though driven by a blind person, a Porsche came down the road, far too fast to have any hope of stopping. Seeing the jammed traffic, the driver swung fiercely on to the hard shoulder immediately in front of the cab then tried to swing straight again. The manoeuvre was a total failure and as the three of them watched, horror-struck, the sleek sportscar tore through the protective rail at the outer edge of the hard shoulder and vanished. The last thing they saw was its wheels leave the ground and its body begin to roll. Then the sound it was making was lost in the other sounds around them.

John tore open the door and ran to the broken rail at once. The road was at the crest of a low bank here, with the curving viaduct sloping down from the M25 to join it just behind where they had stopped. Ahead and to the left, where the Porsche had gone, the slope fell away on to scrub and a little coppice of trees. In the blaze of light from the motorway, John could see the track the crashing car had made before it vanished into shadows. In a sudden silence when the brakes and the horns were all suspended for a moment, he listened carefully for a sound from below, but there was nothing. He ran back to the cab. 'I'm going down there,' he snapped. 'I'll need a torch, if you have one, and your jack. I doubt whether the Porsche will be upright or able to supply any light itself. Darling, is your medical bag handy? I think we may need some stuff out of it.'

'I'll come down too,' she decided at once.

'Hadn't we better wait for the emergency services?' asked the driver.

'Normally, I'd say yes,' John answered. 'But the traffic is closing in fast behind us and it'll take them a hell of a time to get through. I'm a ship's captain, trained in practical engineering and in emergency work. My wife is a fully qualified doctor. We should be able to help. And the people in that Porsche need help now!'

'Right, Captain,' said the driver at once. 'I'll get you what you need. I'd better stay with the cab, though. I'd like a word with the pillock who ran into the back of us, then I'll just have to wait till this starts getting sorted out.'

'Good idea,' said Asha. 'If we need more help, one of us will come up again. Do you have a pair of boots, by any chance? High-heeled going-away shoes will be no good at all down there.'

'I do, as it happens. Me and my boy like to do a bit of fishing of a weekend and our boots is in the back. I'll lend you the lad's if that'd be all right, Doctor. Your feet are nearer his size than mine.'

John felt a fleeting urge to laugh at the figure she presented in her Aquascutum travelling coat and dirty black Wellington boots.

Together they followed the bright beam of the cabby's torch over the edge of the embankment. The grass was winter dead and the ground frost hard. The scrub of fume-stunted bushes was black and leafless, designed like something in a circle of the Inferno to catch and trip and hurt without offering any compensatory beauty. Even the mist which drifted low among it was dirty and smelly. The light and noise of the motorway soared overhead and almost immediately became irrelevant down here, as though of another world. There was enough quietness to throw up scurryings and snufflings – the all but silent swoop of a hawk, hunting, the regular wheezing breath of a cow in a nearby field, the tinkling of a running brook.

But no. It was too cold for little brooks to tinkle. It was some other liquid, running. And that quiet sighing was just too regular to be an animal. It was the sound a tyre might make, spinning on a broken axle.

And there it was, at the end of a short crash path, like a little aeroplane which had landed incorrectly. Its doors open, like broken wings. Its bonnet crumpled pathetically against a mess of shattered tree stumps. Its torn body resting upside down. It had been painted bright blood-red, and the fluids running across its flanks from cooling, brake and fuel systems made it appear to be bleeding as they approached.

The stench of petrol was powerful and five feet back along the car's track, the ground felt muddy underfoot. 'Wait here,' said John. 'I'll go in first for a look. You may well be wasting your time.'

'If I'm wasting my time, you're wasting yours,' she countered. But she did as he asked.

He went right up beside the Porsche, moving stiffly, favouring his wounded side. He lay down on his stomach and shone his torch into the passenger compartment. At first it was difficult to see what was in there. The roof was almost level with the bonnet and the door linings had folded in as the doors themselves folded out. The windscreen had burst inwards and some of the contents of the luggage compartment – in front of the passengers, under the bonnet – had been shoved back to get tangled up in the mess of the dashboard. But gradually he worked out the inverted puzzle until he could see that the moulded seatbacks had taken some of the weight and the headrests seemed actually to be supporting the car so that the young man in the passenger seat and the girl behind the wheel seemed almost to be sitting normally, secured by their seat belts, upside down. There was no movement. He had no way of telling whether they were alive or not; both bodies seemed intact from what he could see, and there was not an excessive amount of blood.

The car would have to be moved. But first he had better do a little clearing out and shoring up so that Asha could get in here. He pulled the door lining free and gently eased out a mess of clothing from around the passenger. Then he wedged the jack under the top of the inverted door sill and wound it up gently until it was taking weight but had not yet started to lift this side of the car. He could not lift the side until he was sure that the action would not flip the whole thing over and crush the girl on the other side. When the Porsche was as firm as he could make it and the path to the passenger reasonably clear, he backed away slowly, like a retreating tortoise, and motioned Asha over.

Asha was as thoughtless of her finery as he had been. Without hesitation, she went belly down in the muddy mess of petrol and oil beside the car, slithering in much deeper than he had gone, following the beam of his torch to her first patient. He kept close behind her, lighting her way until she was in place, then rested the torch on a pile of ragged clothing and pulled himself out again. Now he had to get round to the other side of the car and start clearing a path to the driver.

Perhaps it was the darkness on this side of the car, or perhaps things actually were worse here; whatever the reason, John had real trouble getting to the girl. Slowly and carefully, calling a desultory conversation to Asha who seemed to be a great distance away in spite of the fact that she was closer than the width of the Porsche, he worked his way inwards. This door had not opened out so widely. He had to twist himself into agonising contortions to get his arms in through it. Then, when he started to ease it wider, the whole car shook and he stopped, worried that it might crash down on Asha's head. Very carefully he managed to get his head and shoulders into the chassis and started feeling around in the utter dark.

The first time he touched the girl he did not realise he had made contact with flesh, but then the contour of her leg registered and he slid his hand along an inch or two until he felt her knee. Immediately beyond that it met a twisted tangle of metal – the steering column, he guessed, and some cables from the dashboard. No sooner did he feel the obstruction than he felt something else as well: a shock of electricity which numbed him from wrist to shoulder and sent him jerking back to smash his head on something hard and start the whole car shaking. Damn! You fool, Higgins! It was the first thing he ought to have checked. The ignition was still on and the slightest spark could set the whole car alight like a Roman candle.

'Asha, darling,' he called, trying to make his voice sound casual. 'Do something for me, would you? Come out of there a moment and stand back a little way.'

'Hang on. I have a very faint pulse here. I want to give him something to knock him out. If he comes to like this the shock would probably kill him,' she said, too preoccupied to read the underlying message of concern in his voice. 'Almost no other vital signs at all, though, so we can't take any liberties. We'll have to move the car more than this before we move him at all. How's the driver?' He could hear her moving as she spoke.

'Cold,' he said. 'But that could be shock. And I haven't felt anything more than her knee. It's pretty tangled up in here. I haven't tried for a pulse. Are you clear?'

'Yes,' she answered, her voice more distant. 'I'm just setting up the injection. Why?'

He plunged his hand back among the wires, searching blindly

for the girl's leg again, knowing that it was the surest and quickest guide to the relevant section of the dashboard. Time and again electricity jolted him but he worked quickly and carefully, forcing his arm to the shoulder into the car. And there, below the relative warmth of her lap, he felt the keyring hanging. 'Still clear?' he called.

This time Asha did pick up something from his voice. 'John, what are you . . .'

The torch beam shone faintly on his side of the wreck. She was coming round. He closed his eyes and turned the key. It was fifty fifty. He would never have been able to work out for certain whether the key, in its present position, was going to turn the engine off or on. He took a chance and was lucky. The tiny shaft of metal turned two clicks and came away in his hand. And just in time.

The torch light smote hard against his face, dazzling him. 'John,' Asha repeated urgently. 'What's the matter?'

'Nothing.' He began to wriggle out again. 'I don't think we can even get an injection to her until we've moved the car a bit.' He stood up and slipped the key into his pocket. Then he checked all round the car again, looking for a way to move it safely. Asha shrugged, moved back to the passenger and injected him.

A motorcycle policeman was talking to the taxi driver as they scrambled up the bank. The two men turned towards them at once. 'How does it look, Captain? Any sign of life, Doctor?' asked the cabby.

'I think they're both alive,' said Asha, 'but I can't really tell what sort of condition they're in.'

'We'll have to move the car,' said John. 'Got a tow rope?'

The cabby had and went to get it. John looked at the policeman. 'Perhaps we shouldn't be doing this,' he said.

'From what the cabby tells me, you're both pretty competent to do the job, sir. I wish I could advise you to wait for the emergency services, but we have a ten-mile tailback in both directions now and nothing will be through for hours. If you think you can help the people in that Porsche, you're probably their best bet. Sorry I can't wait around to give you much of a hand. We have a report of a larger pile-up futher down. I'm the only one who can get there at the moment.'

'That's all right. But you'll want to take a look, I expect. There'll be reports to fill in and such.'

The policeman nodded. 'You'll be here yourselves most of the night one way and another, I'm afraid, sir.'

John's eyes met Asha's; so much for their honeymoon.

The policeman started to move away, then he turned back. 'Of course you made sure at once that the ignition was turned off?' he asked. 'To cut down the risk of fire?'

'First thing I did,' lied John grimly. Then the policeman went down the embarkment and they were alone.

'So that's why you wanted me to stand back,' said Asha at once. 'You darling fool, John. Don't you know I wouldn't want to live if anything happened to you?' John caught his breath – it had never occurred to him that she loved him this much. And suddenly the missed honeymoon seemed utterly unimportant. He swept her into his arms and kissed her as hard as he could, until the cabby's tactful cough interrupted them.

'What I'd thought was this,' explained John a moment or two later. 'We loop the tow rope round the front axle there and run it up through the fork in this big tree immediately above. Then we should be able to raise the front of the car. It shouldn't be too heavy. The engine's in the back so all we have to contend with is the frame, the spare tyre, and the front wheel steering. I think the chassis is resting on a sort of roll bar above the headrests. If we're lucky, that will act like the fulcrum on a seesaw so the weight at the back should counterbalance the front and make it easier to lift.'

'It'll still be difficult to hold it up for any length of time, though,' mused the cabby. 'Not what you'd call insubstantial, your average Porsche.' He crouched down beside the policeman to look at the still figures inside the crushed car, his face twisting with concern. He glanced up at Asha, his eyebrows raised in the mute question, 'Any hope?'

She shrugged.

'I've thought of that,' John continued. 'Two things. First, as we raise the front, it will be possible to move your jack in to hold it firm. I've looked for the Porche's kit but I can't see it anywhere, so it's probably in that mess under the bonnet. Beyond that, what I thought we'd try is this. You see how that tree fork is shaped? On this side it's smooth but on the other its sharp like two fingers up in a V sign?'

The cabby and the policeman stood beside him and looked, seeing at once what he meant and nodding.

'Well, if we knot the tow rope at intervals and feed it in from this side, the knots will slide through the fork, but they won't slide back.'

There was a short silence, then the policeman said, 'That's very ingenious, sir.'

'Bloody clever, Captain,' agreed the cabby.

When the policeman had helped them set it up, he left. The cabby eased the front of the car upwards towards the fork in the tree with John helping until the first knot snugged safely home. Then they rested for a moment, easing the rope back to find John's makeshift ratchet worked perfectly.

'Right, driver . . .'

'Alf. Alf Patterson. I'd shake your hand, Captain, but I'm not sure I trust this tree to carry the load.'

'How d'you do, Alf. We're going under now. When I call, I want you to raise it up until the next knot goes through. Easy enough.'

'Right, Captain.'

'It's John,' said John, crossing swiftly towards Asha, who was on the driver's side this time. 'John and Asha Higgins.'

John went in beside the icy passenger. The jack had fallen over and he could find nowhere to set it up again, so he decided to put his faith in his makeshift block and tackle and in Alf Patterson. He pushed himself right into the tiny, gloomy car and slid his hand beneath the young man's shoulders. Immediately he felt something hot and vivid moving against the back of it and he almost called out with surprise before he realised it was Asha, similarly supporting the girl.

'How did you get in through the door and all that tangle?'
he asked.

'Came free as the car went up. I've got most of it out of the
way. Not all of it, though. Can we go up a little more? Then I'll
have room to inject her, too.'

'Up to the next knot, Alf,' he called, and the car slowly began
to ease up. When it stopped, the young man's head was hanging
free of the ground altogether. John's right arm was across the
broad shoulders, his elbow supporting the neck.

'Any sign of life?' he asked Asha.

'I have a pulse here.' Her voice was surprisingly close at hand,
intimate in the dark. 'I'm injecting her now, then you can try to
get her free.'

'Right. I think I can get this chap out if we go up one more
knot. But don't you try to move the driver yet. Look, I tell you
what. You leave her a moment and check on this chap when I
get him out. Okay?'

'Okay.'

He half heard, half felt, her move. Then he held his breath
and pulled the release on the young man's seatbelt. The body
slumped down on top of him, far heavier than he had imagined it
would be. Surprised, he almost lost his grip on it but he managed
to stop the head hitting the ground. Slowly and carefully he
rested the shoulders in the mud, then checked again to make
sure no part of the body was caught. Satisfied that it was free, he
began to squeeze himself backwards out of the narrow opening
between the door sill and the freezing ground. It took him five
more careful minutes to pull the inert passenger out entirely and
by the end of it he was shaking with a lethal combination of cold
and tension and fatigue. But at last it was done and Asha came
across to check again for life signs.

'Can you take her up one knot more, Alf?' he called, crossing
back at once.

He went in after the girl flat on his back with his eyes closed.
Asha had the torch so there was nothing much to see in any
case. But it was spooky. She had long hair and as he moved
it brushed across his face in a most disturbing manner. He felt

up past her shoulders and across her body in a way that would
have got his face slapped in any other circumstances. He traced
her torso. It was free. Her hips and lap. Good! They had not
been completely trapped by the steering wheel or dashboard.
Only her legs to check. He traced them down carefully, his
calloused palms snagging in her stockings, wishing she had been
wearing jeans. Just above her ankles, he discovered apparently
immovable shackles of twisted rod and wire.

He was half sitting up now, his head against her hip, facing
down towards the accelerator, clutch and brake, his arms at full
stretch as his hands tried to separate the invisible mare's-nest
into single strands with which he could deal. His mouth was wide,
gasping great choking breaths, fighting against the petrol fumes.
The strain on his scarred flesh made his side feel hot enough to
set the whole lot alight. But he could get no grip on any individual
strand, nor would his increasingly numb and shaking fingers give
him any sense of shape or form; he simply could not visualise the
tangle and so could see no way of undoing it.

At last, more out of frustration than through any real hope
of doing any good, he simply took what hold he could of the
whole mess and shook it. There was a tearing sound and a
muffled thump. The bunch of wires came free and the girl's
legs flexed. He gave a choked shout of victory and wriggled
feverishly back down until he could slide his left arm under her
shoulders, gathering her hair gently as he did so as though he
were her nurse, or her father.

It was at this point he smelt burning. His own hair stirred.
He opened his eyes but could see nothing. He reached up to
the release of her seatbelt, calling, 'Asha, I'm bringing her out
but I think I can smell burning. Can you see anything?'

He heard her move at once and the sound made him immediately aware of another, sinister sound, something between
crackling and a rustling. It was a sound he recognised: an
electric current shorting out.

When he pulled the release, she fell into his arms just at
the exact moment he heard Asha calling, 'John! The car's
on fire!'

Then her words were drowned in Alf's bellow of, 'Captain! It's burning! Get out of there!'

'I've almost got her!' he called back, steeling himself against panic so that he would move her carefully and gently. His head slid out from under the door now, his arms still reaching in, positioning the girl so that she would follow the path his body had already cleared. As he did so, there came a quiet explosion and there was flickering light close by on the right.

'Captain! Get out! For God's sake, it's going to blow up! *Doctor!*'

And Asha was there beside him, between him and the terrifying brightness, kneeling at his right hand to help guide the girl's inert body out into safety. Full of fear for Asha more than for himself, he twisted over on to his knees and caught at the girl's right arm. Together, side by side, they shuffled back at feverish pace as the brightness grew rapidly and spread like a sinister dawn. 'Alf, let go of the rope. Move the man back,' called John the instant that black tangle of wires round the girl's ankles was dragged into the light. Then the three of them were pulling the two bodies back with all the speed that care for their condition would allow. Flames flowed around the inverted car in little rivers, following the streams of leaked petrol. They joined into a lake below the dangling wreckage and suddenly the whole lot went up. But by the time it did so, the five of them were just clear.

It was after midnight when the first ambulance got through. John and Asha had used their now useless honeymoon clothes to make makeshift beds for the man and woman from the Porsche and Alf had told and retold the story of the rescue to onlookers attracted by the column of flames which had once been a sports car. But then, after the sightseers drifted away back to their own jammed cars, the three of them sat quietly and Alf lit a cigarette. They chatted inconsequentially and Asha nursed her patients. Oddly enough, it was not until after the two from the Porsche had gone in the ambulance, the necessary formalities had been completed and the snarl-up was clearing that Alf thought to ask, 'Where were you going, then? On your honeymoon, I mean?'

'Hawaii.'

'Oh, John, how clever! I've always wanted . . .' But then she remembered.

'Wish I could drive the pair of you there,' supplied Alf. 'But I can't, so that's that. Where do you want to go now? Anywhere in London and this is on me. I've never seen anything like you two in my life.'

John had been thinking about this. 'Back to Heritage House,' he said. 'The executive flat there will be empty. We can use that for the rest of tonight and sort ourselves out in the morning.'

The moment they walked through the doors into Heritage Mariner's great London headquarters, the security guard came up to them. 'Could you go upstairs to the Crewfinders offices at once, please?' he said.

And the strain in his voice was echoed as soon as they got there by Audrey calling from the twenty-four-hour emergency desk, 'Captain Higgins. Doctor. Thank God you're here. We've been getting urgent signals all night from the freighter *Napoli*. Salah Malik and Fatima are aboard and something's badly wrong. They need a master and a ship's doctor most urgently. They'll be off Cyprus in eighteen hours and they must have someone then. We can't find Sir William or Captain Mariner and someone has to get out there at once . . .'

CHAPTER SIX

'Your attention, your attention please, this is the captain speaking . . .'

The familiar words dragged John back up out of an exhausted doze. Disorientated for a moment as he came to full wakefulness, he supposed he had nodded off in a comfortable chair on one of Richard Mariner's ships. But a wave of vertigo soon told him otherwise.

He loved flying, always had; but this trip hadn't been much fun so far. Asha was not too good a traveller even at her best. Now she was exhausted and refractory. He glanced at her and could not tell whether she was sleeping or sulking. They still had not been alone together since they took their wedding vows. During the hours of delay at Gatwick, he had tried to sell her the idea that what they were embarking upon was a romantic cruise across the wine-dark Mediterranean. He found he was a bad liar. All his enthusiasm could not mask his half of the disappointment they both felt at losing out on their real honeymoon.

And things were going from bad to worse.

'We will be landing at Larnaca in five to ten minutes. Arrangements have been made to take you all to Nicosia as soon as possible.' A ragged cheer went up. It served to relieve most of the tension that had crept into the passenger cabin with the worsening weather conditions outside.

John looked out of the rain-streaked porthole at his left shoulder more to hide his frustration than to study the view, which was one of dirty-laundry cloud in any case. As a captain he was used to making decisions, taking control, getting things done. He just didn't want to have to sort out another problem today. But he would have to sort out this one. The cloud cover was snatched away with breathtaking suddenness. The waters of the Mediterranean swept by beneath, sluggish and slate-grey, ruffled by a sudden downpour. They were probably still heading east, or north of east, he thought, into the teeth of quite a breeze by the feel of things. The plane jumped and dropped, then seemed to stand still in the air. They would turn soon and come in low across Akrotiri Bay, over the docks at Limassol. That was where they would get a boat out to *Napoli*. She might even be somewhere under the airliner's current flight path, somewhere on Akrotiri Bay, Larnaca Bay, or the choppy seas beyond. He and Asha would have to find a way of getting out of the airline's clutches, with their baggage, or they would be dragged all the way up to Nicosia with the rest of the passengers only to have to turn and come all the way back down here again.

'I don't even know whether I need to speak Greek or Turkish down here!'

'English will do,' said Asha quietly. 'You're almost in the colonies here, remember. Empire hath its privileges.'

He hadn't realised he had spoken aloud. He must be even more tired than he had supposed. 'Did I wake you?' he asked solicitously.

'No, darling. I was just dozing.'

The cabin tilted as they started to turn. Asha strained across him to look through the thick perspex of the porthole. He was suddenly aware of her musky perfume and the soft sensation of her breasts against his chest. He could feel the heat of her almost as though her fine silk and his thin cotton were not there at all.

Get a grip, Higgins, he thought.

'So much for Homer,' she observed, mournfully. He had actually used the poet's phrase, 'the wine-dark sea', when describing it to her.

'That was the Aegean anyway,' he said. 'And three thousand years ago.'

Certainly, Homer's romantic description could hardly have been further from the prosaic sight beneath them. A grey bay swept past, the dull water increasingly close to the plane's belly – apparently dangerously close.

Then a dazzle of lights on a promontory gave a sense of perspective. They were still quite high after all. And as he realised this, he recognised the land. The promontory had been Cape Gata; the lights the NATO base at Akrotiri where the old RAF camp had been. Now they were sweeping across Akrotiri Bay itself and a bustle of thoroughly twentieth-century shipping was revealed clustered around the Limassol docks and coming and going across the bay – ferries, smaller pleasure craft seeking a safe haven from the north-easterly, one or two larger freighters further out. He looked at them closely. Was one of them *Napoli*? He hoped not; they looked tired, beaten. One of them was even ugly, though he always sought beauty in women and in ships. But this aged hull had nothing about it but functional ugliness, weariness, defeat. There were four skeletal gantries before the bridge, stretching in line down the deck, ropes hanging as though they were gibbets on an execution dock; and a heavy gallows behind the bridgehouse finished the effect. He saw her for an instant only as she flashed by below him; nowhere near long enough for him to make out her name or anything else about her. But the sight of her stayed in his mind as they came on down. Let it not be her, he thought to himself. Please God, let it not be her. But no, he decided an instant later; this ship was riding too high. *Napoli* was supposed to be fully laden, she would never be riding that high.

The sea came nearer and nearer as the plane settled down on its final approach over Cape Kiti towards Larnaca's runway. The water folded like soiled grey silk, and heaved. There was no lack of perspective now; they really were this close. He could see branches of dark weed on the backs of the waves. He could see the individual bubbles in the spume. He could no longer distinguish what on the window was rain and what was spray. Of all the airports in the world, Gibraltar was his least favorite with its runway actually running out into the sea, invisible to the passengers until after they had apparently landed on the waves. Larnaca he disliked almost as much from this angle. He had no desire at all to land on the sea, as they seemed to be doing now.

'I hear Kai Tak is worse,' said Asha conversationally. 'You approach it down a steep valley, brushing the mountainsides with your wings.'

'No. I like this less than Kai Tak. And Gibraltar less than—'

The plane seemed to give a bound and the sea was chopped away by a scimitar of land, bladed with beach, made bright as day by a sudden dazzling flash.

The rumble of rubber on runway was echoed instantly by reverse thrust powerful enough to drown – almost – the last ragged cheer and the first snarl of thunder.

'Well,' Asha said philosophically, 'at least we're down safe and sound. That's a good start. Let's set our watches forward and pretend we're on holiday from now.'

The holiday started at 20.00 local time on a raw, stormy November night. By 21.00 all the baggage was off the plane and by 21.30 it was clear that their luggage was simply not there. The tour guide stayed and tried to help, in spite of the fact that they were not with her party, and the rest of the passengers, waiting on the Nicosia coach out in the thundry rain, became increasingly restless. But there was really nothing anyone could do, and, as Asha pointed out, looking on the bright side, most of their best holiday gear was lying bloodstained beside the M25 anyway. They had even seen it on their way back to Gatwick for the ten o'clock flight this morning.

'And what with the French flight controllers' industrial action and the delays and everything,' she concluded, 'it's a wonder they got *us* through to the right place.'

'Yes,' John agreed. 'No use worrying any more. If we hang around here much longer we won't be able to get a taxi down to Limassol docks.' His voice was deep, calm and reassuring, but he was just about ready to scream. The tour guide smiled understandingly and went, leaving them stranded and alone.

That same reasonable calm, no matter how thin, soothed the feathers of a defensive airline rep who gave them the forms to fill in to try for a trace on the cases. Then John made a phone call to his personal insurance panic number to assure them that the cash and the plastic were safe, but that the luggage was gone. 'They'll sort it out,' he said, putting an arm round Asha's drooping shoulders. 'They'll find it and have it waiting for us wherever we come to port. They might even get it out to *Napoli* herself. They've done that sort of thing in the past.'

In the back of the taxi, hurtling along the dual carriageway under the frowning walls of Larnaca Fort, they made a list of what they would need to buy in the shops and chandleries of the port.

Even at half past ten on a wet Saturday night this late in the season, Limassol was lively. They took energy from the dogged cheerfulness of the holidaymakers in their T-shirts, shorts and see-through rainwear, and went after the necessities on their list. Within the hour they had, if not everything they needed, at least as much as they were going to get. John hailed another taxi and asked to be taken to the Port Office. Limassol was a busy port, the only legal way in and out of southern Cyprus. The Port Office was open. Yes, *Napoli* was out in the roadstead. Naturally they would be pleased to contact her at once. Of course they had a cup of tea for two people who looked as if they had had a *long* day.

'You couldn't imagine the half of it,' said Asha feelingly.

'Well, what with one thing and another, we shouldn't keep the Immigration or the Customs officers too busy,' said John brightly.

In the event it was well after midnight before they got down to the quayside where *Napoli*'s cutter was waiting for them, chafing restlessly against a heavy rope at the foot of a steep, slippery set of steps. None of the crewmen aboard seemed to speak or understand much English, but they knew the name of their ship so that one word served well enough. The rain had stopped by now and the cloud cover was being torn apart by the wind to reveal a few pale stars and, occasionally, a low, mean moon. Akrotiri Bay looked huge as they pulled away from the docks, for it was shallow, and opened wide to the sea; there was nothing beyond it until Tripoli one hundred and fifty miles east or Port Said two hundred and fifty miles south.

Soon the cutter started to pitch uncomfortably through waves made steepsided by the contrary wind. There was no way to keep out of the stinging, icy spray. Asha's stomach started to rebel at once. She was nauseous already from strain and fatigue, and had eaten nothing except an airline lunch since her one slice of wedding cake thirty-six hours ago. John held her fiercely. He was in the grip of that formless rage again. What a start to a marriage! Maybe they were just being handed all the bad luck for the first few years in the first few hours. He fervently hoped so. He couldn't bear to think of it going on like this for very much longer.

Asha started to heave. That was all they needed. 'Don't worry,' he bellowed. 'Nelson always—'

'*Napoli*,' shouted the coxswain.

John looked ahead, vainly trying to make out the shape of his new command. All he could see were her riding lights. Asha tore herself away and leaned out over the gunwale, retching helplessly.

There were three men apart from the coxswain at the helm of the cutter and they were all looking steadfastly forward. John followed their gaze again as the coxswain repeated, '*Napoli*.'

As he did so, the moon emerged from behind a cloud. A murky, bronze light flashed across the bay, casting into sickly relief the execution dock of cranes and that high, sinister gallows behind the bridge. It couldn't be true! He actually closed his eyes and looked again like a child confronted with a ghost. But there was no mistake.

She was broadside on to the low moon, seeming to tower out of the water above the little pitching cutter. The darkness claimed her again almost at once, but her image remained in

John's stunned mind with all the aching clarity of an old sepia photograph, this time with more than enough detail for him to see the name *Napoli* clearly written on her forepeak.

CHAPTER SEVEN

There was a simple Jacob's ladder down *Napoli*'s dark flank with rope sides and flat wooden rungs. The ship was by no means sitting still in the water and the rungs were wet with rain and spray, but the crewmen held the ladder firmly enough and supported them both on to it while keeping the cutter as still as possible. Asha managed it without too much trouble. Nevertheless it was a longish scramble with plenty of scope for more disaster so John followed her up as closely as he could. He was not best pleased when he arrived on deck to see a long and much safer hydraulic accommodation ladder lying snugly retracted in its retaining clips. He was gruff with the square-bodied first mate waiting to greet him. With hardly a word to the man, he turned and strode across the deck towards the bridgehouse, his arm solicitously around Asha's bowed shoulders. His first impression was of an elderly, battered, badly maintained rust bucket with too much cargo piled on her deck and not enough ballast or cargo below to hold her as steady as he would have liked. And of a first officer untidily dressed with uncombed hair. Was he also unshaven or just shadowed in the wan moonlight?

Stepping through the great iron-framed bulkhead doorway into the main corridor of the main bridgehouse deck, they were overcome with shrieks of welcome and surprise. Suddenly, there were the 'absent friends' mentioned in their wedding toast a mere thirty-six hours earlier. While John and Asha knew who would be waiting, it was immediately clear that Fatima and Salah had not known who was coming.

'Asha! Darling!' The sisters swept each other into a tear-
ful embrace, which was broken again at once while Asha
looked more closely in Fatima's face. Then the two of them
bustled away, leaving John feeling excluded and suddenly a
little lonely.

'John!' Salah sounded surprised. 'I thought Richard would
come himself.'

'Couldn't find him in time. He must be gone for the weekend.
The wedding was yesterday afternoon – Friday. He might not
show up again until Monday, day after tomorrow. I thought this
was urgent. I can see why you needed a doctor. Is the need for
a captain equally pressing?'

'It is. But not so urgent that you should cancel your honeymoon!'

'Don't give it a thought. Our honeymoon was cancelled for us
long before we started out for this place.' Belatedly, perhaps,
John stuck his hand out and Salah shook it.

The first mate came in at that moment. 'Cutter stowed away,
Captain,' he said in laboured English. 'The men say you had no
suitcases.'

'Thank you, Mr . . .'

'Niccolo.' He did not offer to shake hands. His fists were full
of Asha's plastic bags.

'Thank you, Mr Niccolo. I will see you in the captain's cabin
in ten minutes. We will not be leaving until the morning.
Just a harbour watch for tonight. If you've sea watches, you
may dismiss them.' Niccolo nodded and was off. For such a
solid-looking man, John observed, he moved extremely quietly.
He drew his hand down his stubbled chin, looking around. Salah
stood silently.

'Right. Where's the captain's cabin? Or, more to the point,
after what I've been through during the last day and a half,
where's the captain's drinks cabinet?'

Considering the obvious age of the ship, the captain's quarters
on C deck, just below the bridge, were surprisingly sumptuous,
though they had clearly seen better days. A teak doorway opened

into a small vestibule with an office on the left, a shower and toilet straight ahead, a day room on the right with sofas and easy chairs like a lounge. Here John found the bar, complete with an elderly little bar fridge. He poured himself a hefty Scotch, added chilled soda and a handful of ice, then sipped it, looking round. The door into the captain's sleeping quarters stood far enough open to reveal the foot of a good-sized bed. John sipped his Scotch again and continued to look about in silence. The pictures on the pale walls were all of Italy, by the look of things. He recognised enough famous views and buildings, bays and harbours, to suspect that they were all pictures of the same place: Naples. Salah moved into view deliberately, blocking a vivid Vesuvius.

'How much do you know?' asked the Palestinian quietly.

'Not much, but I can work out quite a bit.'

John was used to arriving aboard ships in mid-voyage. For many years he had specialised in picking up the threads of crews caught partway to their destinations, their progress halted by accident or tragedy. He had worked for Crewfinders before it became part of Heritage Mariner, and had been routinely sent all over the world at a moment's notice. He had stepped into the shoes of maimed officers, crippled mates and dead captains in every sea there was. He was adept at summing up a vessel, crew and situation at a glance. He had a routine which he would be starting with the first mate in a few minutes and continuing with a full inspection in the morning and an unexpected lifeboat drill the instant they set sail.

'An old, battered, half-laden freighter, caught between the Lebanon and God knows where. A rust bucket with a polyglot crew probably picked up at a moment's notice in the whorehouses of Piraeus. I know I'm in trouble. This ship has trouble written all over it. That I can work out. But what sort of trouble? What's in those crates on deck? What filth is she carrying below?'

Salah's eyes widened with admiration. He had forgotten how easy it was to underestimate John Higgins. He drew breath to answer. There was a knock at the door. John glanced at his watch. Ten minutes to the second. That was better.

'Come in, Niccolo,' he called.

In the light of the cabin Niccolo looked better than he had on deck. He was neat and tidy, hair slick, no longer ruffled by the wind. He was carefully shaved though grey-jawed. He looked almost as tired as John himself felt, but perhaps he was competent after all. To be fair, he had brought the ship here and had put her hook down in just the right place, even though he didn't have the papers for full command. One small test lay to hand. 'What's the matter with the accommodation ladder?' he asked.

Niccolo nodded as though John himself had passed some test.

'Is fucked,' he said. 'But I get the engineers to fix it tomorrow, now I am first mate again.'

'Good enough,' said John.

The three of them were still in the captain's office going through *Napoli*'s papers and sailing orders when John heard the main door open and close and the sisters moved through into the day room. Their quiet conversation proved a distraction to the tired men and John soon called a halt to their deliberations. There was nothing much else they could do tonight anyway and it would be an early start in the morning. He wanted to complete a full inspection before they got underway. 'That's all for tonight, then,' he said. 'I may take a look up on the bridge before I turn in, but that's all I want you chaps for tonight. Please tell the chief steward I will take tea at six in the morning. We will up anchor at eight.'

Niccolo glanced at his watch. 'Tea in four hours. Anchor up in six hours . . .'

John laughed. 'We'll have plenty of time to catch up on our sleep while we cruise across the Med.'

Niccolo didn't look convinced.

Five minutes later Asha and John were alone. He freshened his whisky and gave her a Perrier. 'We'd better get our heads down,' he said. 'I've ordered tea at six.' Then he remembered the bruises on his sister-in-law's face. 'What on earth happened to poor Fatima? She looks as though she got hit by a speeding truck.'

'She did.' Asha began to explain what Fatima had told her about the Lebanese incident during her physical examination. Or, more to the point, what Fatima could remember about the incident, which was not all that much. There was enough memory loss to worry Asha and make her fear concussion. 'In other circumstances, I'd be tempted to put out a Pan Medic call,' she said, frowning with concern. 'But that wouldn't help now. Fatima would be put in prison first and hospital later if she entered any country near here. I'll just have to treat her the best I can for the moment and let Gina Fittipaldi carry on nursing her whenever she feels giddy or sick. Rest will probably be the best thing for her in any case . . .'

Talking about how the two invalids Fatima and *Napoli* should best be nursed along, they went through into the bedroom. The bed was as big as he had hoped: easily big enough for both of them. He pulled his shirt out of his trousers thoughtlessly and began to unbutton it. It was still a little damp. Asha moved around the little room opening and closing drawers and cupboards into which she and Fatima had packed the shopping from Limassol while the men wound up their meeting. Wearily, he chucked his damp shirt on to the nearest chair as though he was still a bachelor, and began to undo his belt. He turned his back on her and sat on the bed to untie his shoelaces. His mind was full of what he had learned of the ship and her situation. He was busily planning the morning, completely withdrawn from the present. Withdrawn from his fingers also, working at his laces. They too were wet and the double knots were slippery and difficult for his short nails to get a grip on. And the position was making his bad side cramp up again. He sighed. Then she said, 'Here, let me.' And before he could protest she was on her knees in front of him untying them herself. And he hadn't even been aware that she was watching him. Her presence came as a kind of a shock though it shouldn't have, this was their wedding night, after all. But that shock was as nothing compared with the impact of her undress. She wore the last piece of her going-away outfit, the only piece which had not been soaked, ruined, used for bandages or lost. It was a Teddy by Janct Reger, made of sheer black lycra trimmed at breast and gusset with lace. It had been purchased at a very exclusive lingerie shop and had cost a small fortune, but the effect it had upon him made it worth every single penny.

He found himself looking down upon her statuesque red and gold body from above. His gaze moved from Titian hair to tanned shoulders. Here shoestring straps quivered with the gentle movement of her breasts as she untied his laces. From cleavage to hip it was as if she had been stencilled in a lacy pattern with black body-paint. The garment stretched over her athletic frame like another skin. It seemed to glow as it became transparent and the paleness of her flesh shone through. Below the waist, it was cut high above her square hips and plunged dizzyingly, to emphasise the depth of her pelvis and the length of her thighs.

The instant his shoes were off she rose, as yet unconscious of the effect she was having on him, and stood immediately in front of him. The black silk dimple over her navel was level with his forehead and the taut thrust of her stomach immediately before his face. He found himself reaching round to gather her in his arms. He pressed his face into the warm, fragrant softness between her hip bones. She leaned forward tenderly to cradle his head. Somewhere deep within her an artery pulsed audibly, its steady beat matching the throb of *Napoli*'s generators.

After a moment, John stood up, sliding his face and hands up her body as he rose. She stood half a head taller and leaned down slightly to kiss him. Without a pause in that long, hot kiss, he took the straps and pulled them off her shoulders. Their bodies hardly moved as the warm black film slid down between them. Then it was his turn to kneel for a moment and slip the wispy bundle down her legs until she could step out of it. They had not slept together before the wedding. It was actually the first time he had seen her like this.

'I love you,' he said, looking up.

Then, smiling, she looked down at him. Her eyes were russet brown and seemed to hold the light like amber. There were flecks of gold in them. And something more; something irresistible.

He did not visit the bridge after all.

'So,' she asked him later, just before they went to sleep, her voice a deep, contented purr. 'Where are we taking the *Napoli* and her cargoes of mutilation and death?'

He thought of the sailing orders in the office next door signed by Nero of Disposoco. He thought of the ship's name and of the pictures in the dayroom. Vesuvius, the Castel dell'Ovo thrusting out into Naples Bay.

'We have orders to take her home,' he said.

In his dreams John reread the papers on the captain's office desk, desperate to know his command as quickly as possible. She had been built at Gdansk in 1960 and heaven alone knew how she had arrived in Akrotiri Bay. The first few pages of her records were in Polish or Russian and it was impossible even to make out her original name. Her measurements had been written in English in the margin of the first page, however, beside the figures and the Cyrillic jumble of the original record. Her displacement was 20,000 deadweight tons. She was 543 feet long and 82 feet wide at the broadest point of her hull, though her bridge wings overhung her sides, he had noticed. She was 40 feet deep from deck to keel and her bridgehouse stood 40 feet high. Her single screw should push her forward at a service speed in the region of 15 knots. Somewhere along the way she had fallen out of Soviet hands and into Italian ones. During the great container boom she had had some money spent on her – a complete refit and the replacement of her coal-fired steam turbines with an oil-fired diesel motor. With her new engine had come the new name *Napoli*. Everything was repainted. Everything was replaced. That was almost a pity; now they would never know whether the legends were true that Gdansk ships arrived ready for sea even down to the complete canteens of silverware, the last cup and glass.

The four practical cargo handling cranes had been left on her foredeck; and the brutal gantry behind the bridge. She wasn't pretty, but she was self-sufficient, the original naval architects knowing too well that it would be a long time before the ports she was destined to visit around the Soviet coast were themselves mechanised to any great degree. The men who refitted her had clearly followed their logic and decided that the independence the cranes gave her would also serve their ends. And they had been right, for she had been destined to spend much of the next few years carrying cargoes to ports and harbours in the Third World, which were even less mechanised than those in sixties Russia.

But the container boom had come and gone and no more money had been spent. She had passed from owner to owner until she became the property of CZP, a Cayman-registered transport company with branches in Zurich and Palermo. Never beautiful, she was now also old and unloved. The perfect vessel in which to transport chemical and nuclear waste. Perfect from the point of view of her current charterers, Disposoco, not from the point of view of the conservationists. What on earth would Greenpeace make of such a cargo in such a vessel?

John began his inspection of her at half past six next morning. Showered and shaved, he felt quite restored by the three hours' sleep he had had. Niccolo looked refreshed too and the view from the bridge, where the inspection started, was enough to energise a corpse. The storm had cleared during the night to be replaced by a bright dawn, washed and scoured clean by rain and wind. *Napoli*'s head was facing into Akrotiri Bay and the broad, rectangular windows looked over the piles of deck cargo, past the strong arms of the four cranes away across a vista of burning blue sea backed by bright beaches, low promontories and vivid hills. John strode across the bridge and threw open the door to the bridge wings. The air was sweet and surprisingly warm. He breathed it deeply and appreciatively. This is more like it, he thought. Wait till Asha sees this! But even as his mind was occupied with her, his eyes were busy. 'What's this?'

'It belongs to El Jefe. Is for star-gazing.'

The item in question was standing in the shelter of the bridgehouse, leaning up against the blistered, peeling paint on the salt-grimed metal wall. It was a celestial telescope, its long tripod legs folded shut.

'Who is El Jefe?'

'The chief engineer. He is from Spain. Torremolinos. La Carihuela; the son of a fisherman. He will tell you all about himself. Unless you mention stars to him first. Or engines.'

Everything on the bridge seemed fine. Old, but functional. And the same seemed to be true of the rest of the bridgehouse. John went through into the radio shack behind the port side of the bridge. No one was there at present, but the sets were on open emergency frequencies and all correctly disposed. Niccolo had clearly put the word about and the inspection caught no one unawares. Going on down, John looked in some of the cabins – just enough to establish the layout of the accommodation in his mind. He checked in the library, the mess rooms, bars. There was no cinema but a television stood in one comfortable lounge with a video player under it and a pile of videos beside it. Like the books in the library, the videos were in various languages, but they were films he recognised, for the most part, and the rest mostly seemed to be football matches played by the likes of Real Madrid and AC Milan. He found some officers and crew taking breakfast; they were still on harbour watch until they got underway in an hour's time, and they watched him silently as he toured the dining rooms and galleys. The rest were still in bed, as were the engineers and the supernumeraries: the scientists who had brought the cargo aboard, the late Captain Fittipaldi's daughter.

The engineering areas were all in the same state as the bridge, though John's expertise here was more limited. This was what was called a UMS system – unattended machinery space. No one was here yet, though he knew the engineers would be down soon to start warming up the diesel prior to getting underway at eight. He glanced around the control room, looked out over the three-deck-deep hole which contained the engine, patted the boiler and nodded knowingly at the alternator. He would be back when El Jefe was about. Certainly there were no obvious failures of maintenance, though the place could have been cleaner and tidier.

Out on deck it was the same story. The lifeboats were properly stowed, but not quite what John would have called 'shipshape'. The decks and exterior paintwork were dirty and the metalwork dull. The deck auxiliaries all looked ancient, but he had no intention of starting up winches and cranes just to check them now. The whole ship needed a refit she would never get and a paint job she would never have. Niccolo and El Jefe seemed to be doing the basic minimum, snowed under by the more immediate demands of keeping her afloat and moving forward. WHAT'S SO DEMANDING ABOUT THAT?

It was time to look at the cargo. He started with the deck cargo as it was the more accessible. There were fourteen piles of it, seven pairs, each pair astride one of the three main hatch covers, each pile consisting of nine containers three wide and three high. Each container was separated from the others by battens of wood so that it was possible to see between them. They looked well-secured and absolutely safe. Steel hawsers reached across at every level and at each end, securing them to the deck.

'You have made a good job of this,' said John appreciatively, taking the last hawser in his hand and shaking it. It remained as firm as an iron bar.

'I was careful. I saw what that stuff can do.'

That had been a part of the meeting last night. Salah's story and Niccolo's report. The logs and accident books were in Italian, so oral reports were all John had to go on. 'The captain's hands,' he said.

Niccolo grunted in reply.

'I hope you were as careful below.'

'I was *more* careful below. Down there it's atomic.'

John glanced at his watch: 7.30. 'Just time for a quick look.'

Napoli had three holds. They were each thirty-five feet deep, seventy feet wide and one hundred feet long. Above each of them stood the raised rectangle of a McGregor single-pull weather deck hatch cover and above the three covers stood the four cranes. John and Niccolo walked back between the containers on the deck to the nearest hatch. This was the furthest forward, closest to the raised forepeak with its stubby communications mast. John reached down and opened the control panel, then pressed the release button and waited for the first segment of hatch cover to slide back. The resulting hole at their feet was absolutely black and seemed infinitely deep. John swung his foot in, sure of the position of the hold ladder, but stopped with his foot on the first rung as a thought struck him. 'Is it safe? Is it radioactive down here?'

'The scientists, they say it's safe. There is a Geiger meter beside the torch there at the first rung. Take that to be sure. But Captain, with a torch and a Geiger meter, I think you're more likely to die of falling off the ladder than of radioactivity.'

John was inclined to agree with him. The torch and the Geiger counter were bulky and the ladder was narrow and difficult to climb. But he was glad of them both. The hold he was in was cavernous and cold. The bright morning light following him down from the deck didn't make much impression on the darkness and he felt as though he were potholing until he got to the bottom and stepped off on to solid decking. He had been concentrating so hard that it wasn't until he did this that it occurred to him to ask the obvious question. 'Where's the switch for the hold lights?' he bellowed up to Niccolo.

'Fucked,' came the distant reply.

John had kept the torch and the Geiger counter switched on all the way down, each hanging by a wrist loop from a forearm, each giving off light, neither of them giving off any sound. John echoed his first mate's last word and turned, allowing both the torch and the Geiger counter to fall into his fists. The torch was powerful and he followed its broad beam into the middle of the hold. As he approached the pile of great grey concrete blocks, he kept checking the counter, but the needle stayed in the green and the occasional quiet click set his mind at rest. This was just as well, for what he could see was not designed to do the same. Whatever the chemicals on deck were in – drums or barrels, he assumed – they were all neatly stowed in the containers. That was not the case down here. The nuclear waste was exactly as it had been when it was lifted out of the desert. The great pile of grey blocks in this hold – identical to the contents of the other holds, according to Niccolo – looked like part of some antique ruin. Part of an Egyptian temple, perhaps. A pile of giant building blocks square enough to fit together in mock walls dusted with sand and standing on a miniature desert. John almost expected to see a fallen statue beside them, the Sphinx, or a gargantuan mask of Rameses. He was forcefully put in mind of Shelley's *Ozymandias* and he found himself shivering and muttering, 'Look on my works, ye Mighty, and despair . . .'

He walked round the ruin looking up at it from every angle and checking on the Geiger counter. Satisfied at last, he began to look round the hold more generally. There was nothing else inside it. That explained why the ship was riding so high, he thought. While he was down here – not somewhere he proposed to come back to too often – he decided he would check the hold walls in more detail. He didn't trust *Napoli*. She was too old and battered.

There was nothing to see until he reached the end of the hold. Between this hold and the next nearer the bridge, the middle hold, there was a double wall. In the centre of it at floor level was a massive door designed to allow passage between the holds. It towered before John now, almost on the same scale as the blocks behind him. But it was not the scale of it that held his attention; it was what had been done to it. At some time, and very recently by the look of it, the door had been closed, bolted, secured and then welded shut. John reached out and touched it, thoughtlessly letting the Geiger counter drop to swing on its wrist loop. 'No way of opening this!' he said to himself.

He stood there for some moments deep in thought, with the short hairs at the back of his neck prickling uncomfortably. At last he shook his head and started back. All the way across the hold and back up the ladder to the deck, he wondered who it was aboard who was so frightened of the cargo in the holds that they had gone to such lengths to prevent those sinister grey blocks moving directly from one hold to the next.

CHAPTER EIGHT

Because they were near her head anyway, John sent Niccolo down to the fo'c'sle to get the anchors up. Then he walked smartly back along the deck and ran up the companionways mounting the outside of the bridgehouse until he came on to the bridge itself from the outside. The brisk walk and the exercise of running up four flights of steps in the clear, bracing morning air had put him in a much more positive frame of mind. But his mood began to darken again when he stepped in off the port bridge wing. The bridge itself was empty. John checked his watch, looked at the digital chronometer above the wheel. They both agreed: ten past eight. The deck watches should have started ten minutes ago. The third officer and the bridge crew should have been standing by since then. His mouth set in a thin, disapproving line, John crossed to the engine room telegraph. Beside it was a microphone. He snapped it to the setting he assumed would contact the engineers direct. He was right. When he said, 'Engine control room?' the machine answered at once.

'*Si*, Capitan.'

'Are the diesels warmed up and ready?'

'*Si*, Capitan.'

'I will be giving the order to make way as soon as the anchors are up. Ten minutes at most.'

'*Si*, Capitan.'

'I'm relieved someone down there understands English.'

'*Si*, Capitan.'

'What is your name?'

'*Si*, Capitan.'

John broke the connection. His nostrils flared. His lips, already set thin, disappeared altogether. The muscles of his jaw tightened.

And that was the face young Marco Farnese, third officer, saw as he entered the bridge at a leisurely pace, finishing a croissant as he came. He was a big, blond boy from Bari, easygoing and a bit dim. He knew trouble when he saw it, however, and reacted like lightning. The last morsel of his breakfast went out through the door with enough force to carry it clear of the bridge wing. The bridge crew behind him were inundated with a flood of orders couched in stinging terms. John recognised the tone and the results if not the Italian invectives. Within thirty seconds the wheel was in the hands of the helmsman, the sailing radar was on and under close scrutiny, and Marco himself was making up the log as though he had been here since eight on the dot.

John decided to let it go this once.

On the port side of the bridge, sitting on a slightly raised section just abaft of the bridge wing door, was a comfortable chair. It was covered in black imitation leather and had a deep bucket seat, a broad, padded back and overstuffed arms. It was the watchkeeper's chair. John crossed to it and picked up the handset lying on its seat. He switched to SEND.

'Niccolo?'

'Here, Captain.'

'You may proceed.'

'Yes, Captain.'

John put the handset back in the rack where it clearly belonged and crossed to the microphone by the helm.

'Engine room?'

'*Si*, Capitan.'

'Make ready. Anchors coming up now.'

'*Si*, Capitan.'

Well, he thought, whether they understood his English or not, there would be no mistaking the directions relayed on the engine room telegraph in five minutes' time.

He crossed to the comfortable chair again, then turned and walked straight back from it towards the rear of the bridge. There was a door here, the exact balance to the chart room door on the starboard side. He pushed it and stood in the threshold of a small room, half within and half on the bridge. A small, wiry Spaniard with thinning black hair and narrow brown eyes sat there. He was in full uniform, neat and dapper. John remembered his name because it had seemed appropriate in a vaguely sacrilegious way. This was Jesus the radio officer.

'Get me the Port Office first, please, Sparks. Then I will need to talk to the owners.'

Jesus nodded silently and made connection through the short wave, handing a telephone handset to John.

'Limassol?' The voice emerged through a hiss of static.

'This is *Napoli*, call sign Delta, Delta, Delta. We will be under-way in five minutes, outbound for Naples. We are far out in the Roads and do not need a pilot.'

'Thank you, Delta, Delta, Delta. There are no standing orders in force at the moment. I have just been speaking to your radio officer. He has all the current frequencies and call signs. Good luck, *Napoli*; safe journey home.'

John broke the connection and turned to Jesus to ask about the owners, when the radio handset in its rack above the chair squawked. John crossed to it at once, but he knew from the feel of the deck beneath his feet what Niccolo was going to say.

'Anchors up, Captain.'

'Good. Report to me here, please.'

He crossed to the engine room telegraph and pushed the handle over and back until the display read SLOW ASTERN. He paused there for an instant until he felt the metal beneath his feet begin to throb to a new, purposeful vibration. The distant land began to move, swinging away to their right.

'You know where we're going,' he said to Third Officer Farnese. 'Lay in a course.' Muddy eyes regarded him earnestly with not one ounce of understanding. John crossed to the chart and pointed. 'Naples,' he said. '*A Napoli!*'

Comprehension dawned.

The door to the starboard bridge wing opened and Niccolo entered in time to hear the end of this exchange. John was suddenly extremely glad to see his square, competent bulk. 'Please check that Mr Farnese has actually understood my order, Niccolo. I want a word with the owners. Then I would like a list of everyone aboard who speaks any English.'

The name of *Napoli*'s owners, CZP, was not familiar to John. He suspected that their Cayman and Zurich offices were there for tax purposes and the actual work was done in Palermo, but as long as CZP had the money to pay the crew's wages and supply and maintain their ships, they could have offices on the moon for all he cared.

CZP was responsible for the upkeep of the hull and the hire of the crew. Disposoco owned the cargo and paid the owners to transport it, and from that money came the funds to run the ship. CZP was also responsible for paying Crewfinders in London for the new captain, until such time as they could find another captain of their own. Crewfinders guaranteed John's pay. It was Sunday today. First thing tomorrow, Crewfinders would be on to CZP to complete their contract. They might replace John, but this seemed unlikely. It was less than a week's cruise past Crete, round Sicily and up to Naples, all things being equal.

Having reported in at some length to a slow, deliberate, Italian-speaking clerk in the owners' office in Palermo, John handed the handset back to Jesus and returned to the bridge proper wearing a frown. True, it was Sunday, but he was surprised that no one senior at CZP had been available to speak to him. That boded badly for the way they were likely to conduct their business. But then again, there was still no sign of anyone senior at Crewfinders either, and that was unheard of!

Cape Gata was sweeping past on their starboard now, the NATO base at Akrotiri coming into view. John checked the line of their course on the chart and then crossed to where he could see the heading on the display in front of the helmsman. A little south of west. Perfect. 'You may enter that heading into the automatic steering system, Mr Farnese, and the helmsman may stand down to other duties.'

As soon as he began talking, an irritating, mumbling echo started and he swung round, frowning, like a schoolteacher interrupted in class. Of course, it was Niccolo, translating.

John crossed to the watchkeeper's chair and sat, deep in thought, while Marco Farnese carried out his instructions. Niccolo looked across at his new captain as soon as the third officer was clear what to do. 'I could get some engineers and fix the ladder now, Captain,' he said quietly. 'Or do you want the list of men who speak English?'

'Later, thank you, Niccolo.' John looked down at his watch. Eight thirty-five. They would just be serving breakfast for the off-watch crew and the passengers. This was going to make him extremely unpopular – with Asha, quite apart from anybody else: 'Sound "Abandon Ship", please.'

John called a halt to the shambolic lifeboat drill half an hour later, just after Gina Fittipaldi had escaped death by inches when the forward fall on Number One lifeboat snapped and all but dropped five tons of wood and metal on her head.

Napoli had four big lifeboats as well as the cutter and some smaller survival equipment. Everyone aboard had a place assigned in one of them. It was Niccolo's responsibility to see that each person aboard knew their place, and it had been Captain Fittipaldi's responsibility to hold drill regularly, to ensure that everything went smoothly in an emergency. Within minutes of the first alarm signal it became obvious that this was the first lifeboat drill most of the crew had ever experienced. Instead of making their way quickly and calmly to their assigned posts, most of *Napoli*'s complement ran around in panic, blocking up important passageways by standing in groups to ask what was happening or pausing by noticeboards to try and discover what they should be doing. John's estimate that breakfast would be underway was correct, but many of the off-watch officers and crew had not even got themselves out of bed yet, or were still in the head or the shower. Gina Fittipaldi was among the latter and John first made the acquaintance of his late predecessor's daughter as she ran in a blind panic and a very small bathtowel along the C deck corridor towards the stairs. At the moment they collided, Asha came out of the captain's cabin. 'Take her,' snapped John at once. 'She's in our lifeboat.'

'I know,' answered his wife calmly. 'So are Fatima and Salah. Is this a drill, John?'

'No. It's a sodding disaster,' he snapped.

This estimate was perhaps a little unkind. Most of the crew went to their assigned stations and thence to the lifeboats. Eventually. But what should have taken seconds took minutes instead. And the minutes began to stretch out. John and Niccolo, both increasingly angry, chivvied the men along and timed their reactions on stopwatches. They doublechecked who was where on Niccolo's lists; the only men missing were the watch on the bridge. John stood between boats One and Two on the starboard while Noccolo stood by Three and Four on the port.

'Well,' bellowed the mate in Italian to the milling crowd of sailors and engineers, stewards and scientists, 'What have you got to do next, deadheads? The sea is licking at your bloody feet!'

His voice carried easily across the deck to the crews of the lifeboats on the starboard. Jesus the radio officer, who was in the captain's lifeboat, and Cesar, second mate, leaped forward as one man to pull the solid craft out of its retaining clips and swing the davits round. The lifeboat swayed out over the blue water like a huge swing, the blocks creaking and falls protesting. Before the two officers could steady her with the inboard lines, a huge crewman, with a battered boxer's face and copper crewcut hair, reached forward to free the forward fall. '*Belay* . . .' began John automatically, but his stentorian bellow meant nothing to the man. The rope came free of the cleat and the crewman took the sudden strain badly. Hemp stripped through the palms of his leg-of-mutton fists as the lifeboat swung in towards the people waiting to board her. Cesar saw what was happening and threw himself on the rope at the same time as John did. The movement of the lifeboat's head was brought up sharp. Then, incredibly, the three men were tumbling backwards again as the rope simply snapped. John was hurled back against the bridgehouse wall and he watched in helpless horror as the sharp, metal-sheathed prow of the lifeboat fell towards Gina Fittipaldi like the blade of a guillotine.

It stopped at the last second, perhaps an inch above her skull, and there was Salah holding the last foot of the broken rope safely belayed round the ship's rail.

Silence. Even Niccolo's men on the other side were still, aware that something terrible was going on.

John took a deep, shuddering breath, fighting to control the rage in his chest. Gina looked up at the boat swinging in, then out, brushing her wet hair, whispering past with the sound of a headsman's axe. She screamed. A massive, terrifying sound, echoing and re-echoing off the steel. Asha swung her round and gathered her into a strong embrace, drowning the sound with the shoulder of her bathrobe. Fatima joined the huddle until Gina's tears ceased.

Suddenly Niccolo was there, his face white and his fists huge and John had had enough. 'That's it!' he snapped. His eyes met Niccolo's and held them until he knew the mate was paying attention again. 'Dismiss!' He swung round to Salah, 'Thanks . . .'

'It's OK – I didn't want to lose Fatima's nurse . . .'

Everyone began to troop dejectedly away except for Cesar and the huge seaman who made the rope safe and started pulling the lifeboat back inboard.

John and his first mate stood face to face. Niccolo was a head taller, half again as broad of shoulder, at least three stone heavier and none of it fat, but he seemed almost insignificant under the weight of John Higgins's fury. 'That was the biggest, stupidest, f—'

'*FUEGO! FUEGO! AYUDA RAPIDO! FUEGO!*'

The cry was accompanied by a smell of burning so that even if neither of them had understood Spanish, the panic call would still have made immediate sense. Niccolo set off at a dead run with John close behind. There were only two sets of Spaniards aboard: the engineers working for El Jefe and the stewards working for the chef. The engineers hadn't had time to get back to their stations yet, so this call had to be coming from a steward.

The galley was at main deck level behind the dining saloons. There were doors into it from the outside deck as well as from the bridgehouse. One of the outer doors stood wide, belching smoke, and a small group of stewards stood outside calling for help.

'Where's the chef?' asked John, but the blank looks prompted him to use his rusty Spanish at once. '*Donde esta . . .*'

'*Alli!*' They pointed in behind the belching smoke.

Once again his eyes met those of the first mate. Niccolo gave one of those minuscule, almost invisible shrugs which can mean so much and which brand a man as a Neapolitan. The slightest stirring of his shoulders disposed of the pathetic group of men on the deck; perhaps of the whole Spanish nation.

Side by side, they rolled through the door, trying to keep as low as possible. Immediately inside the door was the first galley storeroom. Floor to ceiling it had shelves crammed with sacks, bags, boxes and tins, none of which was alight. On the floor was a crate of bottles and John lifted one out as they crawled past. It was a bottle of Perrier. Pulling his handkerchief from his pocket, he smashed the top off the bottle on the next doorframe and wet the bundle of cotton before jamming it over his nose and mouth. He glanced across at Niccolo in time to see him pull his shirtfront out. John drenched his stomach for him and the mate used the wet cloth to filter out the fumes.

The next room was the dry goods store. Smoked meat – well smoked, thought John wryly – hung from hooks above. Sacks of flour, rice and potatoes stood on the floor. Nothing here was burning either. And that could only mean one thing. The galley itself was on fire.

The first thing John saw in the galley was the chef. The plump little Frenchman was face-down on the floor, apparently unconscious. Above him stood his cooking range and it was instantly clear that he had realised the range was on fire and had come in here to turn it off. John crawled across to him and rolled him over. The cherubic face was grey-streaked with soot, the cheeks livid with incipient asphyxiation. Both his hands seemed to be burned also. John glanced up to see that the power switches to the hotplates, blackened and melting, were in the OFF position. John took hold of one arm and began to drag the man back the way he had just come. At the door he met Salah and Cesar and handed the body over to them. As he did so, Niccolo loomed out of the smoke with a fire extinguisher in each hand. His shirt was comically bunched over his shoulders and lower face, displaying a hirsute but muscular torso. John reached back to knot his handkerchief in place over his lower face and then took one of the fire extinguishers.

The whole range seemed to be on fire, every hotplate giving off its own column of dense black smoke. In perfect unison the two men went through the routine of readying the red cylinders and pointing the black nozzles, then the blazing remains of the crew's breakfast was inundated under two roaring clouds of white foam.

CHAPTER NINE

The clock on the captain's desk said it was eleven thirty and John had no reason to doubt it. His own watch, covered in foam, had stopped altogether, its digital display blank and silvery, like the back of a long-dead codfish. In half an hour Cesar would relieve Marco on the bridge. Were he Richard Mariner, in half an hour he would begin his noon broadcast. But he was not Richard Mariner; there would be no broadcast. It was not that he had nothing to say to those under his command – quite the reverse – but the chances of them actually understanding most of what he had to say seemed remote.

He leaned back in his chair, put his hands behind his head and gave a deep sigh. At once he started to cough, a combination of the fumes coming off his ruined clothing and those already in his lungs. The coughing tore at the wound in his side and the acute pain filled his eyes with tears.

Savagely, he drove his fist down on to the desk top, making the captain's clock dance. He had been aboard less than twelve hours and it had all gone from bad to worse. He didn't like the cargo, especially that stuff below decks. Niccolo had explained that Captain Fittipaldi had undertaken the work on the hold doors at the suggestion of Enrico Cappaldi. The first officer had no idea why the late, unlamented Disposoco man had made the suggestion. The only thing the captain had understood about the cargo was the fact that it had scared him. And the more John thought about that, the less he liked it. The ship was a mess. The officers were slack, the crew a shambles and the safety routines a disgrace. All he had done so far was to discover one failing after another. And he hadn't even said a proper good morning to his wife. *And* he hadn't bloody well eaten, and quite possibly never would, now.

Still coughing, he heaved himself to his feet. The newspaper with which he had been protecting the seat fell gracefully on to the floor. He kicked it across the room.

There was a knock at the door. Niccolo entered.

John cleared his throat. 'Report, please.'

Niccolo's voice was as rough as his own. 'Number One lifeboat secure. Fall replaced and block freed. Cook is in the infirmary under the care of Dr Higgins and she says he will make a swift recovery. Even his hands are not too bad. The fire is out, as you know. I have not yet sent the men back into the kitchen, neither engineers to assess damage nor stewards to clear up. I have brought you the list.' He put a list on the table in front of John, who snatched it up eagerly. This was what he had been waiting for. Here was the beginning of control over the polyglot mess of *Napoli*'s complement.

The list was handwritten and it included the name of every person aboard *Napoli*. The names were not arranged according to responsibility, though against each one was a bracketed designation showing whether they were deck officers, engineering, crew, stewards, passengers, scientists. They were arranged in three columns as speakers of Italian, Spanish or French. John was relieved to note the absence of Greeks, Portuguese, Pakistanis. At the top of each list were names bearing asterisks, – at least one per group. These were the men and women who also spoke English. It wasn't much, but it was a start.

'I want to speak to them all together. Everyone except the watch. Where is the best place?'

Had he been on his beloved *Prometheus* or any other of the Heritage Mariner tankers, he would have used the gym, or the ship's cinema. On *Napoli* the only place large enough to hold the forty-five or so people was the crew's dining room. They all packed in there, standing, with the tables pushed back hard against the walls and the stench of smoke coming through the black-rimmed kitchen door behind them, even though it was still closed tight.

John waited a moment outside the door before entering to allow Niccolo time to sort them out and when he entered it was to an apparent confusion of uniforms, overalls, shirts and jeans. El Jefe, the chief engineer, a bull of a man with a long back and short powerful legs, glared at the Spaniards from bright blue eyes deep-set between shaggy brows and a great spade of a beard which put John forcefully in mind of Professor Challenger contemplating the Lost World. Beside him stood Professor Étienne Faure, leader of the scientists, a tall, dapper, dust-grey man with gold-rimmed half-glasses over which he was peering at the French speakers. As John entered and paused, fighting to prevent the fumes starting up that tearing cough again, Niccolo stood forward, moving silently but with graceful assurance and swung round to face the Italians.

John just knew he was going to hate this. 'Good morning,' he began.

'*Buenas dias.*'

'*Bonjour.*'

'*Buon giorno.*'

The tripartite running translation cramped his style. He had a burning desire to explain to them, one and all, that they were a pathetic excuse for a crew, who were a worrying danger to themselves, sailing around in a disgusting old rust bucket that they had maintained so badly that he himself would not have transported guano in it, let alone the lethal combination they had above and below decks. If what he had seen so far was anything to go by, they presented a terrifying danger to all the other shipping in the Mediterranean Sea and by God he was going to spend the next week pulling them into some kind of shape.

Stewards were going to scrub out the kitchen until it glowed like an advert on the television. The engineers were going to fix the hot plates and from here to Naples the cooks were going to salvage enough from the smoke-damaged stores to cook food that would impress Robert Carrier. The engineers were then going to fix the accommodation ladder and everything else aboard that didn't work. The first officer was personally going to review the current state of all the lifeboats, davits, blocks and falls and the captain would take his afternoon watch in order to let him do so. Under the second and third officers, the deck hands were going to wash, strip, polish and chip every bit of deck, paint, brightwork and rust aboard. And the supernumeraries had until the end of this watch to decide which work gang they belonged to. And if that didn't keep everybody out of mischief until they picked up the Naples pilot, then he would be very pleased to come up with one or two other little jobs which obviously needed doing aboard. And, just to keep them on their toes, there would be another lifeboat drill at 18.00 hours this evening and a third at 08.00 tomorrow, and there would be lifeboat drill twice a day until everybody got it bloody well right!

On *Prometheus*, had he ever had to give a speech like that, that's what he would have said. That's what he meant to say now, but somehow it didn't come out like that. It lost something in translation, he supposed. Much of the venom seemed to go astray between his thoughts and his lips. And the rest of it vanished between English, Italian, French and Spanish.

But the message seemed to have got across: the minute the four of them finished speaking, everyone trooped out of the room with an impressive show of unity and purpose.

Feeling a little deflated, John went up on to the bridge just in time to see Marco being punctiliouly relieved by Cesar and to linger for a self-indulgent moment watching Paphos fall away on the starboard with the Troodos mountains lost in thunderheads behind. Alexander the Great had built the little port, he remembered inconsequentially; and Antony had brought Cleopatra here, Richard the Lionheart had brought Berengaria, Othello had brought Desdemona . . .

She was in the ship's infirmary. She had not been at the meeting, but she had featured on Niccolo's list: Mrs Higgins (ship's doctor).

'Look at this, darling!' She was bubbling with enthusiasm, almost dancing round the facility. The infirmaries on supertankers tended to be small. There were ship's doctors on the largest of Heritage Mariner's supertankers, but the usual run of crewing the massive ships was that the first officer was in charge of medical matters using the books of advice and guidance supplied for treating minor ailments at sea. Anything major resulted in a Pan Medic call on the radio and the almost immediate removal of the afflicted crewman by helicopter. Infirmaries were therefore unnecessary, and they tended to be poky, almost afterthoughts. Not so aboard *Napoli*. The infirmary here consisted of a surgery lined with lockable pharmacy shelves, fully stocked. Behind that lay a proper hospital ward of half a dozen beds, presently occupied by the chef, deep in a drug-induced sleep with his hands in white boxing gloves of bandage peeping over the green counterpane. Behind that again there was a fully equipped surgery complete with an operating table, bottles of anaesthetic gas, chilling arrays of instruments. Here Salah and Gina were seated on either side of Fatima whose face was looking worse than ever under the bright surgery lights, smeared with ointment. But she raised a smile for her brother-in-law.

'And look!' Asha's voice still had that edge of excitement, but was hushed now almost with awe. Behind the operating table, built out from the wall was a great silver cabinet, almost like a giant's filing cabinet. John understood what it was, the shock of the realisation driving the last thoughts of romance from his head. She pulled open the drawer. He looked down, riveted. He had expected to see a body lying there open to his gaze, as they were in films and on television. Instead, there was a white clouded plastic bag, like a suit protector. He had the vague impression of a shape beyond the plastic skin, of a head and shoulders and . . .

The main door from the corridor opened and Marco's voice called through the surgery and the ward, 'Capitano! *Loro combattono!*'

John's gaze swung away from the corpse and his eyes met Asha's. 'I think someone's having a fight,' she said.

John nodded once. He caught Salah's eye and gestured to his friend to sit still. 'I'll handle this,' he said, and turned. 'I may be bringing you more business,' he flung over his shoulder on the way out.

'If it's big Bernadotte I don't want to know,' she called back. 'Gina here says he's bad trouble.'

Following Marco along the corridor and down the companionway, John felt irritation building in him again. Where was the first officer? Why wasn't Niccolo sorting this out? This kind of thing was the mate's job – and not just because he spoke the same language as the crew. The man was an enigma. He gave the impression of massive competence, and yet the ship was a shambles. He looked as though you could trust him with your life and yet he couldn't organise a simple lifeboat practice.

The fight was outside the door into the storeroom that led to the ruined galley. There was a shouting mob of crewmen and stewards looking like some ill-disciplined rugby scrum surging to and fro on the deck, but it soon became clear that these were simply the spectators. With Marco at his side yelling his orders, John pushed through towards the heart of the mêlée. As soon as they realised the captain had arrived, the crowd split apart and began to slink away. At its heart stood the huge seaman who had nearly dropped the lifeboat on Gina Fittipaldi's head.

His fists were clenched and his knuckles swollen and bloodied. They were the biggest fists John had ever seen. Lying in front of the enraged seaman were three stewards, out cold. From the state of their faces it was obvious that not all the blood on those massive knuckles was the seaman's own.

Marco pushed a little further forward and shouted a string of orders. John understood nothing of what the third mate said, except one word: Bernadotte. The big man laughed and spat on the deck, staining the green paint with red spittle. His battered face, squashed between simian eye-ridge and lantern jaw wore a coldly threatening expression. He moved towards Marco and the boy simply melted away. John stepped forward, suddenly wishing he hadn't told Salah to stay in the surgery. 'Bernadotte, you will report to your quarters. Now!'

Bernadotte shook his bullet head and continued to move forward. John had never seen anything like the expression on that battered, pugilist's face. Bernadotte was out for more than blood. He was going to kill someone.

'*Tua cabina! Subito!*' John bellowed. He had not been knocking all round the world for the last twenty years or more without picking up the basics. A different air entered the gathering on the deck. Disobeying boys was one thing. Failing to understand a captain's orders spoken in a foreign language was little different. But failing to obey a direct, understandable command was something else. Bernadotte either didn't care or was simply too far gone in his bloodlust. With a wild yell, he charged. Marco ran. Even the hard core of onlookers fell back. Only John stood his ground.

'*Ferma!*' he yelled, pleased to have remembered the Italian for Stop.

But it might as well have been Greek as far as Bernadotte was concerned. He swung a round-house punch at John that would have killed him if it had connected. John dipped under it and moved sideways just enough to let his opponent past. As the massive flank, like a side of beef in a string vest, passed, John hooked a left in under the short ribs which should have given the Italian pause for thought. The shock of the blow numbed John's arm and for a moment he thought he had broken his wrist. But the pain was dulled by two other things. Firstly, horror at what he had done: his instinctive punch had opened him up to actions at law from everyone from the seaman's union to the owners' lawyers. Secondly, dismay that he had not done enough: Bernadotte swung round with no sign of discomfort and every sign of wanting to tear his captain's head off.

John dropped his fists and stood, calculating rapidly. He had no doubt that he could move faster than the big man, but he couldn't keep dodging for ever. And what was the long-term plan? There was no chance of out-boxing Bernadotte in a fair fight. Should he try to win at any price, using all the foul tricks at his command and hope that they would not be matched by more from Bernadotte? Should he run away like Marco Farnese? Die?

Bernadotte charged again. At the last minute, John dropped to the deck, jarring his knees, tearing his side and gathering himself into a ball. Moving too fast to dodge and too slow-witted to jump, Bernadotte tripped over him and fell head first on to the deck. His brows, nose and chin took full force: they all split open. Dazed, the massive seaman rolled on to his back and sat up. John pulled himself to his feet quickly, but the moment his weight came properly on to his legs, his joints warned him that he had sacrificed a great deal of speed in pulling that little trick. He hissed quietly and tried to dance.

Bernadotte was up; what little could be seen of his expression behind the mask of blood was murderous. He gathered himself to charge again, and again John waited. He had not risen empty-handed. Clutched in his fist was a wet rag which someone had dropped on the deck. This time when the sailor charged, John hurled the sodden material straight for the bleeding eyes. The cloth wrapped itself round Bernadotte's head and John charged him, shoulder first, driving all the weight of his wiry body straight into the giant's solar plexus as though it were a door he was trying to break down. And down it went, enfolding him as it did so. Twisting wildly, he managed a half-turn before they hit the deck, but even so he fell badly and had the wind knocked out of him. His scarred side felt as though the wound had been torn wide open by the fall.

Only the ominous stirring of his huge opponent gave him the strength to move. In a wrestling match he stood no chance at all. He twisted and broke the Italian's grip not an instant too soon, for Bernadotte's head had reared back to butt him in the face. As John slid out of the way, the solid forehead grazed past his ear and rang against the deck again. John pulled himself up, feeling old, unsupported, at risk, in danger. Not one man of the crew had offered any help at all. He got as far as his knees and gave up. But Bernadotte was beginning to pull himself up again, too.

This had gone far enough! Suddenly imbued with a rage nearly as murderous as his foe's, John shuffled forward, so that as Bernadotte's head came up and turned to look for him, there he was beside the Italian while the massive crewman was still on all fours. And swinging both his fists high, clenched together like a Wimbledon player's double-handed backhand, he drove down a blow at Bernadotte's jaw just beneath his left ear. So powerful was the blow that his knees lifted off the deck. When it connected, it had all the force of his body behind it and a good deal of his weight as well. The impact folded Bernadotte's arms and sent his head down to butt the deck for the third time. The observers must have felt the impact through the soles of their feet. John felt it reverberating through his bruised and battered knees. Bernadotte, apparently, didn't feel it at all, for he rolled on to his side and lay quite still. John pulled himself up again and began to scramble awkwardly to his feet. Guiltily, the crew who had been witness to the struggle began to drift away.

'*Resta!*' bellowed John with the last of his breath. He didn't really care whether it meant Stop! or Stay! He just wanted to get the name of every man here because he was going to log the sodding lot of them and dock them one day's pay. He came erect, his knees protesting and his legs none too steady. They met his gaze and for a moment he thought they were all going to line up behind Bernadotte to come at him as well. 'You two.' He pointed at the nearest pair. 'Pick up this man and take him to the infirmary.' He pointed not at Bernadotte, but at the nearest of his victims. 'You two.' He turned, ready to direct the next couple in a similar fashion. But there was no need. There at last was Niccolo, his face a blank mask, directing the others silently, by curt gesture. John began to walk towards him.

Then, abruptly, Niccolo was coming towards him, his right hand swinging up and his left hand reaching out. John didn't have time even to react. In the right hand as it swung up he noticed a short club. Then the left hand caught his shoulder and swung him aside and the charging bulk of Bernadotte exploded into his view. The club fell on the crewman's head, just behind the left ear, with a percussion that sounded to John like a Magnum pistol going off. Bernadotte went down again.

The two men stood and looked down at him. With each choking breath he took, blood sprayed over the deck from the ruins of his nose and lips. 'Dr Higgins said she doesn't want Bernadotte in the infirmary,' said John after a while. 'Miss Fittipaldi has warned her that he is trouble.'

Niccolo laughed, a hard bark of sound. 'Then I have a rest cure for him.' He tossed the club up in the air and caught it reversed. John saw it was actually a rust-chipping hammer. 'A rest cure in the chain locker.'

John turned to go, then turned back again. 'In among all that holidaying,' he said, 'get him to tell you what started this.'

If John had gone to her for sympathy as well as tending, then he was disapointed. The men who had carried the beaten stewards to her had managed to describe the fight in a surprising amount of detail. He found her enraged. He stood like a schoolboy while she cleaned up the last groggy steward in icy silence and shooed him out of the surgery. Then she swung on John. 'Was there no other way?'

'Well, I . . .' The same feeling swept over him now as he had felt when he realised the crew were not going to back him against the giant. Except that this was more difficult to deal with. He could hardly attack his own wife. Or dock her one day's pay.

'Bloody men! Good God, what's the point? I mean what's the point of us women nursing you and tending you when all you do is go straight out and get yourselves hurt again?'

'Really, I . . .'

'Don't you try to defend yourself, John Higgins! How long have I known you? Hardly more than six months and in that time you've got yourself hit over the head, beaten up, kidnapped and shot. And damn near suffocated. Now here you are, starting the same cycle all over again! Take your shirt off.'

'Actually, it's my knees . . .'

'Take your trousers off as well then.'

'Asha, darling, can we do this in the cabin, please? It's just scrapes and scratches. The odd bruise. Bring some iodine and tincture of Arnica.'

'This isn't the Dark Ages! Tincture of Arnica! Shall I bring some leeches as well?'

Her voice was increasingly high. John thrust past her and closed the outer door. There was a lock on it so he locked it; he didn't want this to get too public. There was no way of knowing what the effect of his fight with Bernadotte might be, but he could see only damage being done if he fought with his wife in public too. Then he remembered that the chef was in the ward and went through there. But no. The chef had gone. So had Salah, Fatima and Gina. They were alone.

'All right!' he snapped. 'Forget the leeches.' He ripped the shirt tails out of his trousers and tore the garment off. If he heard her gasp of shock at the state of his torso, he didn't show it. He unbuckled his belt and undid the zipper with almost insane force. The last shreds of his self-control had gone now. He had completely lost his temper with her. He couldn't even begin to work out why it had happened. The rage just swept bitterly over him. The trousers fell and he kicked them off tangled round his shoes.

His knees were black, as though he had been playing in the dirt like a naughty boy. Her practised eyes saw the swelling and understood the pain he must be feeling from the puffy discoloration. From head to foot he was a mess. His torso was scratched and bruised. The pit of his gunshot wound was so florid she thought for a terrible moment it was bleeding. His thighs too were bruised and welted and his shins looked as though they had been kicked.

'Where do you want me?' he snarled.

'On the examining couch,' she snapped.

He walked over and lay down in icy silence. She had never seen him so angry. Had, herself, never been so angry with him. She opened her pharmacy cabinet and started getting out the ointments and salves she needed. 'I might need some support on the knees,' he said. 'Have you any tubular bandage?'

'You don't need support. You need to lie down.'

'I can't.' He glanced at his watch. Swore. 'What's the time? I'm taking Niccolo's watch at sixteen hundred so that he can start getting this piece of floating scrap iron into some kind of shape.'

'Very noble. So you're not only Neanderthal, you're worka-
holic. Why didn't I notice this earlier?' She began to tend him,
none too gently.

'I've got no bloody choice. Ow! This ship is a danger to
navigation. The standard insurance certificate up on my desk
isn't worth the paper it's written on. If anything, *anything*, goes
wrong, we're all in deep trouble. And from the look of things, all
too much is waiting to go wrong! Think about it, for God's sake!
Think about what's on the deck. In the holds. That fiasco this
morning proved that if we went down now, no one would stand
a chance of getting in a lifeboat. Would *you* want to swim around
waiting for help while a couple of thousand tons of chemical and
nuclear waste washed up out of the sea underneath you?'

She was half sitting beside him now, one buttock on the edge
of the couch, rubbing ointment on to his chest. She shuddered.
'No,' she said. She had looked in Captain Fittipaldi's plastic
body bag. She had seen what the stuff could do.

'Right. I've got to lick this crew into some kind of shape!
I mean, there's more than a week to go before we pick up
the Naples pilot. We've a lot of busy waters to get through.
If you think this calm weather's going to last, you're wrong.
The only man aboard I really feel I can trust is Niccolo and
he keeps getting even the simplest things wrong. And on top of
that I've got that great ox Bernadotte all but declaring mutiny.
Jesus!' The exclamation came as a combination of frustration
and Asha's application of a salve to the tender scar tissue over
his old wound.

'About Niccolo,' she said.

'What?'

'I don't think it was all his fault. I've been talking to Gina.
She's a nice kid but not too bright. And she's still in shock.
She's been talking to Fatima and me a lot and I've been reading
between the lines a bit, I suppose.'

'What has she said?'

'I get the impression that her father was a bit of a failure.
Niccolo may not have been up with all the things that a first
officer ought to have done, but that's because he's been doing

the captain's job since the *Napoli* set sail. And, from the sound of it, Cesar does a fair amount of Marco Farnese's job too.'

There was a short silence, then John nodded wearily. 'Yes,' he said. 'I thought it had to be something like that.' He sighed. 'That's better.' She was working on his knees now, and his knees had been really sore.

'What *is* the time?' he asked again.

She glanced at her watch. 'Two.' She finished one knee and started on the other. He leaned back and closed his eyes. After the fight, a combination of reaction and exhaustion rolled over him.

'I'm wiped out,' he said. 'Have you got anything that would pep me up a bit?'

She flexed his right leg gently and rolled a tube of elastic bandage up his calf. She unrolled it and smoothed it into place. She reached across his lap and took his left leg. The strain on her blouse caused several buttons to pop open.

'Pep you up?'

'Keep me going.'

She pulled up the second tube. As she settled it into place, she pressed herself gently against his upper thighs. To tend the stewards, she had donned a starched white coat. The coolness of it against his flesh made him gasp. She leaned down as though she hadn't heard the sound and kissed him just above the edge of the bandage. The flesh of his leg was hot and the hair tickled her lips and nose.

'All better,' she said, sitting up again.

He was watching her now, and he didn't look quite so fatigued. 'I'm not pepped up yet, though,' he observed.

'Well, let's just see what we can do about that,' she answered.

She moved out of his sight and his attention wandered for an instant. Then she was back beside him, tantalisingly close, her fingers busy with the top button of her starched coat.

Dreamily, he slid an arm round her hips, hugging her to his chest, running his hand lovingly down her flank. He repeated the caress twice before he realised what she had done. The starched cotton was too warm. Too smooth. Surely even that gossamer Teddy would have seams or ridges to be felt through the crisp cloth.

'What . . .' He began to sit up but she pushed him gently back. As she did so, she leaned forward and a glimpse down the front of the coat confirmed what his fingers led him to suspect.

'Asha! What are you doing?'

'I'm pepping you up, darling.'

'Wearing me out, more like!'

'Oh no. This is just what your doctor ordered.' She undid the lowest button and pulled the flaps of the coat wide. 'See?' she purred, 'it's working. This little bit's pepped up already.'

She undid the next button and climbed nimbly up on to the table to kneel astride him. 'Now don't tell me,' she said gently, leaning forward on to all fours, letting her hair fall in a fragrant veil around his face, 'don't tell me you've never played doctors and nurses.'

CHAPTER TEN

Doing Niccolo's watch for him that afternoon proved to be three well-invested hours for John. He did little enough at first other than sit in the watchkeeper's chair in a daze, kept awake only by the combination of aching knees and sharp hunger. He viewed the dazzling afternoon sun on the flat calm of the Mediterranean with every evidence of distaste and spent so little time looking at it that he would have been lucky to spot a craft on a converging course, let alone have stirred himself to do anything about it before disaster struck. But he felt at peace with the world. With himself. With his wife.

At about five thirty, Professor Faure appeared. John shrewdly suspected the elegant old man was only up here to escape the activity he could hear going on at boat deck level and below, but he was pleased enough to see him. He had some things to get sorted out.

'Tell me about the deck cargo, Professor.'

'That is difficult, Captain. I am afraid I don't know exactly what it is.'

'Tell me what you can about it.'

'Firstly, I do not know where it originally came from, what it is a product of or what it was used for. I assume it is all some kind of chemical waste but it might conceivably have biological elements as well. I have not worked for Disposoco for very long, I'm afraid. I don't even know whose idea it was to take it and dispose of it in the desert. Whoever had that bright idea is no longer on the same payroll as I. That I *am* sure of!'

'I can tell you a little more about what it is contained in and what it can do, however. It is contained in specially strengthened drums within those containers piled upon the deck. The drums are packed into the containers themselves particularly carefully. Niccolo oversaw that, along with just about everything else. I made it clear to him that the drums should not be allowed to roll about or strike each other. We do not want them ruptured!'

'Could they be explosive?'

'*Merde!* I hadn't even thought of that. But no. It is highly unlikely that there is anything explosive in there. Explosive, no. *Corrosive*, yes.'

'How corrosive?' John was thinking in terms of the deck paint being damaged.

Faure paused. 'You have, perhaps, heard of the film *Alien*?' He wrinkled his nose as though referring to the cinema was beneath his professorial dignity.

John couldn't see where this was leading at all. 'Yes,' he admitted. He had seen both the film and the video; they were popular on tankers.

The professor nodded. 'Perhaps you remember the scene where they try to cut the first creature from the face of the man who discovered the eggs.'

John remembered. A creature like a silver lobster had wrapped its legs round the head of one of the characters and his friends had tried to cut it off.

He sat up straight, catching his breath.

When they cut it, it had bled a kind of acid which had burned its way with incredible rapidity straight through the spaceship's metal deck. And it had done so with enough power to leave a considerable hole.

He looked across at Faure and met his gaze. The Frenchman was deadly serious about this.

The acid in the film had gone on to burn its way through the next deck as well, its force hardly abated. And, dripping down from the molten deckhead, it had burned through the next deck too.

He had to be exaggerating. 'You're not serious? I remember that stuff in the film burning through three steel decks!'

'Really? I remember it burning through four steel decks. And yes, I am serious. That is what I meant by specially treated containers. That is what I mean by corrosive. Have you seen Captain Fittipaldi?'

Asha had mentioned something about the late captain. Perhaps he should take a look. He shook his head. Faure nodded. 'When you see what it did to his hands, you will have a clearer idea.'

'Very well. What about the stuff in the holds?'

'I cannot be any more precise about its origin or its nature. I'm not sure whether it is plutonium, for instance, or another of the heavy metals. It is highly radioactive, however. It is the equivalent of what they call a "dirty" bomb, I believe. We discovered a slight crack in one of the casings. That is all we found. We found no flaws in any of the casings you have aboard here. But that one flaw was enough to irradiate a whole section of the desert. And we are carrying several hundred casings.'

'Did you tell any of this to Captain Fittipaldi?'

'Yes. He had not seen *Alien*, however.'

'But he understood about the nuclear waste?'

'Fully. More so than you, perhaps. He may not have seen the movie, but he saw what the radiation did in the desert.'

John sat silent for a moment. 'Niccolo said Mr Cappaldi advised Captain Fittipaldi to have the doors between the holds welded shut.'

'That's right. It scared them, you see. What the radiation had done to the local villagers. It scared me too. I advised them both to ensure that the nuclear waste be loaded in such a way that the casings could not be damaged. You have heard, perhaps, of the China syndrome?'

'Another film.'

'Really? I was referring to the idea. That if nuclear material is insufficiently protected from the influence of other nuclear material, it will heat itself up to such a temperature that it will burn its way right through the earth's crust. So that, if such a thing happened in the United States, the nuclear waste would burn its way through to China.'

'Except that it would in fact settle at the earth's core.' John knew his elementary physics as well as the next man.

'It would, yes, if not for the Chernobyl effect.'

John shook his head, not really understanding this.

'Water,' said the professor quietly. 'The molten core would hit water long before it hit the centre of the earth. And a hot nuclear core hitting cold water results in a huge explosion, a kind of atomic bomb. Yes. That is what Captain Fittipaldi was frightened of creating in *Napoli*'s holds: an atomic bomb.'

Just then Niccolo came in through the door from the starboard bridge wing. 'Captain, I have brought the third officer to relieve you for the next few minutes. We are now more ready, I think, for this evening's lifeboat drill.'

'Right,' said John and stood. Faure's visit had had its effect: he was now wide awake; his appetite was gone, and the pain in his knees seemed less important somehow. 'Professor, if you would just go to your lifeboat station. Marco, you have the con; sign on to the log, please. Niccolo, sound "abandon ship".'

Niccolo had drawn up a manifestly sensible set of lifeboat lists and this time there was much less confusion. The passengers designated for each lifeboat assembled in straight lines according to the order that their names appeared and it was easy to see who belonged where. The lifeboats were swung out on their davits without incident and the whole exercise was completed within twenty minutes.

The crew returned to their late-running day work, the officers returned to their hard-working gangs. The stewards returned to their dining rooms and the chef took his team back into the galley to finish preparing dinner. The scientists had been reluctant to join any of the work gangs and John popped his head round the door of the video room on his way back up to the bridge to catch them there, settling down to watch some football. Professor Faure crossed the room to him. 'It seems your men think deck work is beneath them,' observed John.

Faure had the grace to look a little sheepish.

'Right,' snapped John. 'You can organise them into watches. At eight in the morning and four in the afternoon I want all of the deck and hold cargo checked for damage and leakage. All of it. Carefully.'

When he walked out into the corridor he was overcome by the aroma of dinner cooking and suddenly his appetite returned. Forty-eight hours ago, he had enjoyed a light wedding breakfast of smoked trout and noisettes of lamb at his wedding reception. Twenty-four hours ago he had thoughtlessly consumed a thin gammon slice with a round of pineapple, two fingers of potato croquette, a small brown roll and a glass of red wine. He was not a great trencherman, but so much had happened during those two days that his intake of food seemed totally inadequate. Whatever he could smell now was going to be served in half an hour, at seven; for a moment, he poignantly regretted taking the four to eight watch.

Back on the bridge, he relieved Marco, crossing to the log to sign on. Glancing up the page over Marco's untidy, boyish record of wind, weather and kilometres sailed, he was surprised to see something he had not noticed before. It was a list of names. Marco was on his way out, but John called him back. He pointed to the list.

'*Il combatto*, is the battle . . .'

At the top of the list was the name Bernadotte. At the bottom, the words, 'cause of incident: Burned breatfast.'

'Niccolo write it.'

As though summoned by the mention of his name, the first mate entered. 'I have dismissed the deck gangs to dinner,' he said.

Marco stumbled out at this point, made clumsy by his hurry, his priorities clear. John crossed to sit in the watchkeeper's chair. The digital chronometer above the helm clicked up to 19.00. Deep from the bowels of the bridgehouse below them, the percussion of a dinner gong was greeted by a ragged cheer. John's stomach growled.

'Captain, perhaps you had better go to dinner.'

'I don't think so, Niccolo. I relieved you for the whole watch.'

'Yes, sir. But at twenty hundred hours I am due to be in the officers' salon eating my dinner and Cesar is due to be up here. Everybody else is due to be listening to the captain reading Mass. Is *domenica*. Sunday.' His eyes met John's across the width of the bridge. Their corners crinkled; the points of his lips stirred into a speaking smile, the brother of his minute Neapolitan shrug. 'And they will need something to take their minds off the fact that I have locked away all the alcohol aboard.'

At a quarter to nine, John closed the book. He looked down at it feeling very strange indeed. He was a devout Anglican and counted himself fortunate that Asha, educated at an English school though the daughter of an Arabian Muslim, shared his simple faith. Reading Mass seemed to him disturbingly close to heresy and his Irish blood stirred at the thought of it. He stroked the black leather of the service book and, for the first time in his life, he blessed those hours at King William's College he had spent in the study of Latin. With the last 'Amen' still seeming to echo from the speakers, he reached over and switched off the intercom mike on the captain's desk in front of him.

No sooner had he done so than the phone beside it buzzed. He picked it up at once. 'Captain speaking.'

'Jesus, Capitan. I have a call incoming for you.'

'Can you transfer it down here?'

'*Si.*'

The handset went dead and for a moment he thought the Spanish radio officer had cut him off, but then with a crisp crackle it came to life again and he was talking to the person he had most wanted to contact since Friday night.

'*Richard!* It's good to hear you.'

'You too. You'd better fill me in on what's been happening to you. Even Audrey at the Crewfinders office has been confused by it all.'

John took a deep breath and began to explain.

'Right,' said Richard, some time later. 'Let's try and get this into some kind of order. We've confirmed your command with both CZP the owners and Disposoco the charterers. Under the circumstances, they seem happy to have you and so they should be. Now, I can replace you myself if you want and see about getting you off on that honeymoon you're missing.'

'No. It's Fatima, you see. Asha wouldn't leave her now.'

'Yes, I see that. What is their position?'

'Salah's been in contact with his people but there doesn't seem to have been much progress on that front. The circumstances have thrown everyone into quite a bit of confusion, I'm afraid.'

'So they're both trapped aboard until someone sorts it all out?'

'They've no papers or anything. I can't put them ashore legally anywhere.'

'And you can't go back to where you picked them up, of course.'

'From the sound of things, that would be the worst thing of all to do.'

'You'd better leave the whole mess with me. I'll see what I can do. You're heading for Naples?'

'Slowly.'

'I see. And you're happy to stay in command until you get there?'

'I don't see any alternative, not unless we can get Salah and Fatima off safely. And anyway, Asha and I aren't due anywhere else for a week or two.'

'You're sure?'

'If we change our minds, you'll be the first to know.'

'Right. Well, it's just coming up to midnight here. There's nothing I can do until tomorrow morning. I'll get on to the Foreign Office then, unofficially, and see whether we can get Salah and Fatima sorted out in any way. In the meantime, is there anything I can do for you?'

'It sounds a bit petty, but . . .'

'Don't worry. What?'

'Well, our luggage all went missing on the way out to Cyprus . . .'

*   *   *

While John was talking to Richard, Salah was sitting silently by Fatima's bed. He was pleased with the privacy her move out of the sick bay to the cabin next to his had brought her, for he knew she hated being fussed over. Now he watched over her as she tossed in restless sleep dressed incongruously in one of Gina Fittipaldi's see-through nighties. And, in the quiet little room, he had time to think.

The fact that they had had to borrow so much simply emphasised their isolation. They had come aboard almost destitute, possessing only the clothes they stood up in. And those had been dirty, stained with sweat and blood. Quite apart from their lack of identity papers and money, they lacked the most basic necessities. Toothbrushes, toothpaste, soap, flannels, towels; underwear, night attire. Niccolo took Salah to the ship's slop chest at the earliest opportunity but Fatima had had to rely on Gina, who fortunately was a generous friend as well as an attentive nurse. Salah had been fortunate to find a prayer mat in the slop chest under all the old clothes, but even the most careful search of the ship's library had failed to reveal a Koran. Still, he prayed at the appointed times each day, using the freedom of his position aboard to check with the ship's compass before each prayer so that he knew precisely the bearing to Mecca.

At least Ramadan was finished now, so that there were no special dietary requirements or fasting times – at least they could eat the same food at the same time as everyone else aboard. On the one hand he had no desire to mingle with *Napoli*'s crew but on the other hand they seemed to be trapped aboard here and he didn't want to see them more isolated than they already were. Repeated discussions over the radio with men he did not know in Beirut and Tunis had got him nowhere. Trying to reach Yasser Arafat had been out of the question, even for Salah. The only other man he could trust, Tewfik al Ashrawi, could not be reached. The PLO had other concerns at the moment. There was no one there to help them, no one to take responsibility, no one to care. He felt isolated aboard *Napoli*, but his sense of isolation from the PLO was even more absolute.

Abruptly, he came back down to earth to find Fatima looking

quizzically at him with her good right eye. He leant forward and gently swept a tangle of hair out of the black swelling of her left. The black locks were heavy with the greasy ointment that Asha had smeared liberally over her bruises. 'What time is it?' she asked, her voice slightly slurred by the thickening of her lips.

'Nine o'clock. You just missed Mass. Do you want anything to eat or drink?'

'No.' She moved restlessly.

'What?'

'I feel filthy. This stuff on my face, in my hair.'

He was not surprised. During the months of their association he had been impressed by her cat-like ability to keep clean. In the dustiest, filthiest bombed-out ruin in Beirut she was inevitably dapper, neat and faintly redolent of soap. She would never rest as she was now. 'You need a shower,' he said. 'Shall I call Asha or Gina to help you?'

'No, it's all right.'

He leaned forward and pushed back her bedclothes, then he slid his hand beneath her shoulders and sat her up. Gina's nightie fell transparently to her waist and there it stopped altogether. As though she were a child she lifted her arms – though it was hard to move the left one. As though he were her father he lifted the garment gently up over her head. When it was clear of her hair she fell back against her pillows as though exhausted.

The whole of her left side, from the point of her hip-bone to the curve of her hairline, was black. The flesh was all swollen, though nowhere was quite as bad as her eye. The pock of the bullet-scar on the upper slope of her left breast, where she had been shot all-but through the heart, was as bright as fresh blood. He could certainly see why Asha feared concussion, sprains and hairline fractures. There was nothing at all erotic about the battered battle zone of her nudity.

He helped her rise and walked her to the shower stall, then he stood ready to help her should she need it while she pampered herself at length with the overpoweringly scented soaps and unguents that Gina had been happy to give her. While he waited, his thoughts returned to their earlier mode and his sense of isolation closed in again.

But Fatima had one more surprise in store for him. As she stepped fragrantly out of the cubicle into the towel he was holding for her, she looked deeply into his eyes and gave voice to his darkest, nagging worry: 'Do you think someone sent you down to that village because they hoped you'd be murdered there?'

Weariness threatened to overcome John at last. Talking to Richard had relieved him of the nagging sense of isolation he had felt. It had assured him that Salah and Fatima were going to get some help. This and the simple fullness of his stomach seemed to have unleashed a bone-deep fatigue in him. It was not just the lack of sleep he had suffered during the last few nights – for if the truth be told, he had not slept well before his wedding day either – it was also a reaction to the frenetic activity and taxing danger he had faced. Asha must be shattered too, he supposed. He would tell her of the conversation as soon as she came up to bed.

And the thought of her put something else into his mind. The one last chore he had to perform before he tried for a good night's sleep. As she was nowhere to be seen, he went down to the infirmary himself and unlocked the door with his pass key. He switched on the lights and walked through to the surgery at the back. The cold cabinet was just as he remembered it: like a giant's filing cabinet. He slid open Captain Fittipaldi's drawer to the fullest extent. The corpse lay there, shrouded in white plastic. With his mouth dry and the back of his neck prickling, half expecting the corpse to move, John reached down and undid the zipper. The sides of the bag parted and fell back to reveal the dead captain's livid face. John did no more than glance at that bleached countenance and yet it burned itself into his mind, brown-stained cap and bandage and all. But he had to look more carefully at the hands. Faure had said something about the hands; that they bore mute testimony to the potency of the contents of the drums in the containers on deck.

But Faure had to be joking.

Frowning with concentration, his fatigue slowing everything down as though he were a drunk, John looked again, peering closely at the dark-uniformed chest where the captain's sleeves crossed.

Of course Faure had been joking. Nothing else made sense.

The sleeve cuffs were flat and empty; Captain Fittipaldi had no hands at all.

CHAPTER ELEVEN

At eighteen hundred hours on Tuesday evening, on the third day of the voyage, John was on the starboard bridge wing looking moodily north towards towards Cape Krio – the Ram's Forehead – where the south coast of Crete turned its mountainous cliff faces northwards. If Tim Severin was correct, they were crossing Ulysses' sea-lanes now, ploughing all too slowly through the waters where he – and Menelaus and the rest – had been driven south by the prevailing winds to the land of the lotus eaters before beating north again to the coast John was watching through the binoculars, whose wild cliffs had been home to the Cyclops. It was a clear, calm evening with a slight south wind bringing north to his keen nostrils the faintest odour of the Sahara which swept down to the sea a hundred miles behind him. Evening was gathering, and the sea was gaining an indigo hue as shadows moved across the depths of water still reflecting on its surface the colour of the cerulean sky.

Then among the jumbled scents of distant sand and immediate sea, he smelled something of Paris and Asha slid her arm across his shoulder. 'Penny for them,' she whispered, her voice almost lost beneath the calling of the officers on the deck, dismissing the afternoon day-work men to wash up for dinner.

She snuggled up beside him. She was wearing a loose T-shirt and a baggy pair of shorts purchased in Limassol, and Gina Fittipaldi's spare trainers. He hugged her in return, his thoughts still elsewhere. Should he tell her that they were at last crossing Ulysses' wine-dark sea? The great Greek voyager's galley probably moved more swiftly than this old tub currently averaging only ten knots. Should he tell her that the wily old captain's ill-disciplined, short-tempered crew could hardly have been more darkly mutinous than the discontented Italians and Spaniards trapped aboard a ship they were growing to hate, with a cargo they absolutely feared? And with a dead captain moldering away at an unnatural rate in the infirmary below.

Even Niccolo, with his Neapolitan strengths of world-weary cynicism and wry humour, was getting restless; he had also the Neapolitan weakness of superstition. And the Frenchmen, the urbane, intelligent Faure's scientific team, were growing apprehensive because the more intimately they checked their cargo to keep the crew's minds at rest, the more nervous they themselves became. John knew that if he moved across to the front of the bridge wing now, he would see two teams of them walking down the deck to check the containers and the holds. To begin with they had carried out their twice-daily inspection in their normal clothes. Now, however, they went down kitted out in the full gear of white environmental protection suits and air tanks. The two groups of disturbing, unearthly creatures would be shouldering their way through the worried crewmen coming in from their work, he knew. He could almost hear the nervous muttering. He could certainly feel the tension cranking up.

'Look,' he said, by way of answer to Asha's greeting. He handed her the binoculars and gestured north towards the horizon. She focused the glasses and caught her breath. He started to explain to her what he could remember of Severin's *The Ulysses Voyage*, an explanation of Homer's epic story based not on historical research but upon a voyage along the route in the bronze-age galley *Argo*; and which, in common with most mariners, John found absolutely convincing.

They were interrupted a few minutes later by Niccolo. 'That is the main deck finished for the time being. I think we had better start on the upper works soon.'

'Particularly the cranes and cargo handling equipment. I want all that in tip-top order when we get to Naples. That'll be in five more days at this speed.'

'We will start on those first thing in the morning.' The first officer paused. He was clearly unhappy about something but was hesitant about speaking. John wondered whether he should ask Asha to leave the bridge, but it was not her presence that was the trouble.

'Captain, is there nothing you can do to stop the scientists wearing their protective gear when they check the holds? The morale of the crew is not high. They have many worries and grievences and they have no natural outlet for them. None of them are union men – not even communist sympathisers were allowed aboard when the owners were recruiting, so it is a miracle that we have any Italians at all.'

'Except, of course, that they will have lied about that.'

'True. But the union matter is more difficult. Under normal circumstances they would at least have someone to complain to, someone who would promise to sort out their difficulties at the end of the voyage if not before. And there is no one. And even if there was, even if someone had lied about being a union man to get a berth aboard, the minute he reveals himself and tries to meet their grievances, he will automatically face dismissal. So there is no . . .' Niccolo searched for the word. 'No safety valve.'

'Lazar, the bosun?'

'They see him as an officers' man. A captain's spy.'

'And that divide exists so deeply? Between officers and crew?' John felt more isolated than ever. This was not at all what he was used to.

'Yes. Perhaps because there is no trusted system for grievances to be aired. Perhaps because Marco is seen as being useless and something of a coward. Because Cesar is so unapproachable. Because I . . .'

'Yes?'

'Because of what I did to Bernadotte.'

'I thought it would come back to Bernadotte.' There was a pause which began to lengthen into a silence. 'But we couldn't just let the great ox slaughter every assistant cook he thought had left his breakfast to burn.'

'Nevertheless, he is stirring trouble.'

'Maybe more than you know,' interjected Asha. 'You should see the way he looks at Gina.'

'He is not alone in that,' said Niccolo quickly.

John nodded. The unseasonal weather pushing up out of Africa, a boon in many ways, nevertheless had its negative side. With nothing else to do except mourn her father and worry about her future, Gina fought back against grief in the only way available to her. She spent every waking hour in some activity. Morning and evening she nursed Fatima. During the day she was everywhere about the deck, sometimes sunbathing, sometimes just sitting reading, often jogging or exercising, pausing always like a princess on 'walkabout' to talk to the men, apparently utterly unaware of the effect on them of her bathing costumes, tiny shorts or skin-tight, sweat-stained exercise outfits.

Like Asha – like Fatima in many ways – she was a twentieth-century woman, well educated and liberated. It never seemed to occur to her that she might be viewed, not as a complete person but as a collection of secondary sexual characteristics: a centrefold come to life. In her present situation, John suspected she would find the idea not only surprising but shocking. Sick. Nevertheless, it was a situation they might well have to deal with in one way or another. And soon.

It was not the only bone of contention currently beyond his control either, he thought glumly; none of the crew liked having Salah and Fatima around. They were almost as nervous about the possibility that some terrorist – or anti-terrorist – organisation would come aboard, guns blazing, as they were about the possibility that their cargo would destroy the ship in some terrible way. Thank God, thought John grimly, that Fatima's injuries at least kept her away from the men for the most part. If only Gina was less visible.

Abruptly, there she was, skipping through the bridge wing door behind Niccolo. She was wearing a dayglow pink sweatshirt which fell loosely to her hips and beneath it a pair of black pedal-pushers as tight as a layer of paint, which ended just above her knees.

'Come on, Asha,' she said, bouncing on her Nike'd toes. 'You promised to run round the deck with me twice before dinner.'

John glanced at his wife then across at the first mate, just in time to see the tail end of an expression leaving Niccolo's face. My God, he thought as the Neapolitan's eyes flicked up to meet his own, their black pupils huge and irises so dark it was difficult to tell the difference between them. He fancies her himself. John schooled his face into bland innocence at once, and hoped he had done so quickly enough. The least invasion of the Italian's privacy on that point could well have the most disastrous consequences. If he alienated Niccolo as well, running the ship would become well-nigh impossible.

'Of course he fancies her,' said Asha half an hour later as she sat naked before the mirror in their bedroom, towelling the russet profusion of her hair. 'In other circumstances he'd have made his move by now.'

'That makes things even more difficult!'

'Yes.' She put the towel down and picked up the hairbrush they were sharing.

That was one of the things he loved most about her: she understood so completely. She was the perfect wife for a man such as he was. She knew all about shipboard life; she was intelligent and sensitive enough to see how social – and sexual – tensions could destroy command structures in an instant, and wise enough to watch out for things she knew he would miss or notice too late, never labouring them, just there ready to discuss them when they came up. He remembered how well they had worked together when they had been trapped on board *Prometheus*, held captive by terrorists a scant three months ago.

'How do you think he'll react if things go any further?' he asked quietly.

'He's kept quiet so far out of respect for her father's memory, I think. But he's under increasing pressure. The crew are getting really randy, I'm afraid. Some of their language is getting very pointed. If Bernadotte actually takes action along the lines he's been discussing, then Niccolo will kill him.' She put down the hairbrush with more care than was necessary, as though her hand were involved in her thinking processes.

'Do any of them realise you speak Italian?' he asked quietly, as though there might be eavesdroppers listening at the door.

'Not yet. But they will soon, I'm afraid.'

'Why's that?'

'Well, if I'm going to be here for another week, then I think I ought to be ship's doctor in fact as well as on paper. As soon as she's well enough, Fatima and I will be working properly in the infirmary and that means sick call twice a day as well as treating longer-term sick or injured. If they give me their symptoms in Italian, it will become obvious I understand them when I start to treat them.'

'Well, there's no real point in your eavesdropping anyway. It's not the way I like to run a ship. I'll rely on the officers and Lazar the bosun. But mostly I'll rely on Niccolo.'

'There must be a lot of personal pressure there, too, between Niccolo and Gina and the rest of them,' she continued, rising and starting to climb into her underwear. 'It's not obvious, I know, but he is definitely Italian in that respect. Macho. The real thing. Machismo. The attitude of mind, not the sexist posturing.'

'There's a difference?'

'I don't know. If we stick around, we're going to find out, though.'

'Maybe the hard way?'

'Maybe.' She stepped into a summer frock and they were ready to go down to dinner.

John sat at the head of the long table in the officers' dining salon with Gina on his right and El Jefe on his left. Asha sat at the opposite end, as though this were a dinner party, with off-watch officers, engineering officers and scientists ranged along the sides. Many captains, John knew, preferred to have the dining room arranged with small tables, allowing groups of three or four to eat in relative privacy. That, indeed, had been Captain Fittipaldi's way. But John let only Salah and Fatima sit apart, for there was no way they would easily become part of this group. And the idea of the group was important; he was working hard to make a unit out of *Napoli*'s officers, in spite of the natural division between deck and engine room, the inevitable gulf between sailors and landsmen, and the language barrier. At least the food was superb. The chef could not hold a saucepan yet, but the best of his assistants had avoided Bernadotte's revenge.

John leaned across his *Fegata alla carbonara* and fixed El Jefe with a stare he hoped was not too anxious. 'Jefe, can't we go *any* faster than this?'

The chief engineer looked up thoughtfully and stroked his beard. 'What j'ou know abut RND-M Sultzer engine?'

'It's a single-acting, slow-speed, two-stroke, reversible diesel engine.'

'*Bueno!* That is what we have. She is good engine. Simple. Powerful. Light. Direct drive to the shaft. Turns single, single-pitch screw at one hundred revolutions per minute.'

'Right. Good. So?'

'Is *old*.'

'But it can't be that old. This ship was only built thirty years ago and the original steam turbines were replaced with your diesel, what, ten years ago?'

'J'es. But the diesel was old. Secondhand.'

'*What?*'

'J'es. Secondhand. Is now too old. Is . . . What does Niccolo say?'

John closed his eyes. He had a shrewd suspicion exactly what Niccolo said: 'Fucked.'

'J'es. Auxiliary blower is fucked. Loop scavenging system especially is fucked. J'ou understand what this means?'

'If the engine gets too hot, you're looking at a scavenger fire.'

'J'es. Engine catch fire. We stop. Engine cools. We inject fire fighting foam. We wait for fire to die. We clean out foam. We heat up engine. We start. J'ou want this?'

'No, but—'

'Also, Starting Air System. Flame traps not trap much flame no more. Valves sticky. Fusible plugs fucked. J'ou know what this means?'

'It could all blow up.'

'*Muy bien!* Is good to talk with captain who really understan's engines.'

'My pleasure, Jefe.'

If the Spaniard understood irony, he gave no sign of it.

He was still sharing Asha with Gina and trying not to be petty about it, so when the two of them vanished into the Italian girl's cabin for 'girl talk' after dinner, he decided to have a bit of a prowl around. He had a lot to think through. Marco, on the bridge, was in a talkative mood, practising his pidgin English and too insensitive to be quietened by anything other than outright rudeness. Jesus, in the radio room, was lost in a novel, his feet on the console and the FM radio tuned to a Spanish radio station which was playing haunting guitar music. It was quite dark now and there was little enough to see around them on the quiet sea except for the distant lights of passing ships and boats. Nothing was particularly likely to cut their path – unless they came across someone following an unlikely smuggling route from Benghazi to Kalamai.

It was a clear night, with a dazzling array of stars hanging low in the blue-black sky, seemingly magnified by the clarity of the air. John knew he would bump into El Jefe as soon as he stepped out on to the bridge wing, but this time he reckoned he was safe from discussion of the engine. Sure enough, the bear-like engineer was crouching at an odd angle over the end of his telescope, but he was looking down across the end of it instead of up towards the sky. John paused, fascinated. After a moment, El Jefe straightened. 'Capitan,' he said, 'j'ou know as much about stars as about engines?'

''Fraid not, Chief. Well, I know about celestial navigation, not astronomy.'

'AhHA! There is much difference. I explain! Look here . . .'

Half an hour later, with his hands deep in his pocket – most uncharacteristically – and fists bagging the thighs of his trousers, John wandered on down the exterior companionways outside the dark-curtained bridgehouse. He was lucky to have got away so soon, he decided, wandering on, deep in thought until he was on the main deck. The last warmth of the day still lingered. The faint spice of the desert was long gone beneath the salt smell of the sea and the sharpness of metal. He crossed to the deck rail and stood for a moment, his flat stomach resting against it, then turned sideways and stared past the black castellations of the containers down towards the forepeak.

Napoli was by no means a small ship; he was looking down nearly three hundred feet of deck. Yet she felt small, he realised, almost with a shock. He was used to tankers many times her deadweight, if not her actual size. She was confining. Almost claustrophobic. And, of course, his big tankers carried small crews. *Prometheus* could get by easily with thirty aboard and here, on this much smaller vessel, were forty-five. The thirty on *Prometheus*, moreover, would be a team, all pulling together. This lot were all in small armed camps, suspicious of each other, pulling in different directions, dangerously close to tearing apart completely.

He thought best when in motion, and felt like taking a stroll in any case, but the forepeak was too forbidding; those gallows cranes still made his blood run cold. He turned until his back was to the deck rail, and used it as a fulcrum to swing himself into motion. Slowly, thoughtfully, placing his feet with all the care of a child avoiding the cracks in a pavement, he began to walk across the deck. Halfway across, he drew level with the windows of the crew's video room and walked into a beam of brightness – the curtains had not been properly pulled. Automatically, he approached the bridgehouse front, his hand raised to rap on the window and summon someone to close the curtain and douse the extra light, which could so easily confuse his own navigators – or those of any passing vessel. A raucous shout brought him up short, however. His first thought was that they were watching one of their videotaped football matches, for the shout was like that of a cheering crowd. But no. On the television screen, a plump brunette was taking off her clothes to the loud ecstacy of her audience on *Napoli*.

When he knocked briskly on the door a moment later, Lazar answered. 'What are you watching in there, Lazar? Is it a video?' More than ten years ago, on board the first *Prometheus*, John had seen the damage done by hard-core pornographic videotapes. There the foul material had heightened tensions, brought out hidden antagonisms, and all-but split a well-trained, coherent crew apart. His voice, therefore, was much more abrupt than the picture on the set actually warranted.

Lazar was surprised and his shaggy eyebrows rose. 'No, Capitano. Is Italian TV programme. Is on live now. Live show.'

Behind him, the roaring got louder.

John walked in. Lazar stood back until his captain was past, then he followed as John crossed to the curtain and twitched it shut. The crew, silent now, watched him while behind them on the screen the amateur stripper, still safely in her underwear, was further covered by the title of the show and was then replaced by a far more graphic advert for lingerie.

That night John had a nightmare and, waking in a sweat at four when the watch was changing, he remembered that he had had a nightmare the night before as well.

The next day was hot and surprisingly like summer. *Napoli* pushed slowly across a dead sea through a dead calm while the mercury in the ship's thermometers climbed through the 20s Celsius. At noon the air conditioning broke and the atmosphere in certain areas of the bridgehouse became positively unpleasant. After a late, hot, lunch, the crew in their work gangs went out with Marco and Niccolo to work on the cranes down the middle of the deck.

Gina, in spite of Asha's gentle hints, went out to sunbathe on the forward hatch. She wore the briefest bikini, high-cut and clinging, seemingly transparent – especially after she had covered herself with oil. Work on the lower gantries of the forward cranes suddenly gained in popularity and the officers stood and fumed as the men worked lingeringly out over Gina's unconsciously erotic body, slowly applying paint to metal and discussing the possibility of applying their basic attentions to the girl below.

John watched the situation building up but knew that if he moved to confront it, he would do more damage than good by undermining his officers and offending his lovely passenger. He would be far better occupied in cooling things down in the bridgehouse. He went down to the engine room. 'I know, I know,' bellowed El Jefe from down by the alternator beside the main engine at floorplate level, three decks down. 'The air conditioning. J'ou want it back. I cannot leave this work. It is the purifier extraction fan, she breaks all the time. J'ou know where this is, this fan?'

'Yes.'

'Is good. J'ou take two boys and bring it to workshop. Is all right you do this, Capitan?'

Not really, thought John, and nodded wearily. Off he went, trying to think of one other captain he knew who would even think of taking orders from a chief engineer. Still, needs must, he thought. He reached the offending piece of machinery, accompanied by two engineering assistants. 'Get the extractor fan down and take it to the workshop, please.'

They looked at each other, faces blank.

'We must take the fan to the workshop.' He enunciated each word very carefully.

They looked at him.

He pointed. 'The fan.'

Ah. They understood: the fan. They nodded. They smiled.

'It's not working. You must get it down and take it to the workshop to be fixed.'

They understood: the fan. They nodded and smiled. They did not understand what to do, however.

He took a deep breath. Tried to remember the Spanish for 'broken'. Or the Italian. He failed.

'The fan . . .'

They understood, smiled.

'. . . is broken.'

They nodded at the fan.

'It's *broken*!'

They smiled.

'*BROKEN!*' He had promised himself he wouldn't shout.

They did nothing.

'It's *FUCKED*!'

It was down and in the workshop within fifteen minutes.

'I think there is *some* improvement in communication.' John had just taken over Niccolo's watch from Cesar and was taking the opportunity for a quiet word with Salah Malik. The two men had known each other for ten years and more but had seen little of each other for much of that time. They knew all about each other, as did most of the Heritage Mariner team, but they remained little more than strangers, though they had always got on well when their paths crossed. But that did not make the subject of Salah's current position and immediate plans any easier to broach, especially as John really wanted the two ex-terrorists off his ship at the earliest possible moment. He was as aware as anyone how nervous they were making his already frightened crew. 'I have some hopes of welding them into some kind of unit before we get to Naples. And, talking of Naples, what do you and Fatima reckon on doing when we get there? We'll have to be careful, I think. Your presence aboard could be as explosive as that nuclear waste out there.'

Salah nodded, his long, sculpted face dark and sad. 'It is difficult,' he said quietly. 'My people in Beirut have had no chance to take any action to help us. They are not quite as magically powerful as many people think, you know.' His voice was heavy with exhaustion. A kind of spiritual weariness John had never realised Salah could feel. The tall Palestinian was always so vibrant, so dominatingly active. 'We left without papers. Even had we passports with us, we could hardly just show up at the Italian immigration counter.'

John pursed his lips. 'If I swung her well to the south while we were rounding Sicily at Cap Boeo,' he said slowly, 'we could just brush the exclusion zone and drop you off in a dinghy

within twenty miles of Cap Bon. Would you be all right in
Tunisia?'

Salah was surprised. That could well be the answer. And here
he had been thinking that John was wrapped up in his own
problems.

'Come across to the chart,' John continued. 'I can show you
what I mean.'

They were halfway across the bridge when the scream came
up the deck to them. John swung round, just in time to see the
figure falling from the second furthest crane. He tensed himself
automatically for the thump of it hitting the deck but it vanished
through the green steel and he just had time to wonder whether
this was some weird kind of mirage when the dead sound came
after all – though the scream continued to linger after it.

The pair of them hit the door out to the companionway
side by side and it was not until they were halfway down
the second flight that John remembered about his knees. But
they seemed to be holding up. Once on the deck, they ran
along the outside track beside the piles of containers. John
suddenly realised how much they looked like giant coffins.
Frantically he tried to remember whose team was working on
the cranes. Was it Marco's or Niccolo's? Please God, let it not
be Niccolo.

Marco was standing at the top of the open hatch looking down
into the night-black hold. He was white as a sheet and shaking.
Beside him, Eduardo, one of the work crew, was supporting a
near-fainting Gina.

'Where is the first mate?' gasped John, winded by his run.
Marco looked at him uncomprehendingly. 'Niccolo?' snarled
John.

The third officer shook his head and pointed downwards
past the hatch. John felt his stomach twist. The whole afternoon swam before his eyes. He walked forward and looked
down.

In a square of brightness on the floor of the hold, Niccolo
was kneeling by a crewman. The body was spread out on the
solid steel and a great splatter of blood reached out from it

away into the shadows as though the body had exploded on impact.

Niccolo looked up.

'Who is it?' asked John, his voice surprisingly firm in his own ears.

'It is Lazar,' called Niccolo.

CHAPTER TWELVE

They sailed out of the summery spell that night, as though they were leaving the good weather behind with the bosun's soul. Lazar's death cast a deepening gloom across the ship in spite of, or perhaps because of, the fact that nobody much had liked him. To the extent that the accident had any good side, it was in the way it brought John and Niccolo even closer together. John knew what to do well enough. He remembered all too vividly the procedures Richard Mariner had followed in situations identical to this on his ships, beginning with the first *Prometheus*. Not the great flagship of the Heritage Mariner fleet, currently being refitted after the depredations of terrorists, but the older, original *Prometheus*, a battered old tanker destined to sink with all her crew aboard, including Richard, Robin and John himself. Salah Malik had been aboard that *Prometheus* as well, John remembered with a shock. He might make a useful witness, and he would pick up on any errors of commission and omission during the inquiry. The inquiry had to be thorough and correct, and above all quick.

As soon as Asha had established officially that the wreck of the man, strangely flattened by the impact with the steel, was indeed dead, the body was taken to the infirmary and John called an inquiry with a speed and decision that impressed even the crew. He set up a three-man tribunal consisting of himself, the first mate and Salah, with El Jefe on hand to translate as necessary, for there had been Spanish engineers working with Niccolo in the hold. In his day room, John interviewed everyone who was anywhere near the

site of the accident. Marco had been in charge of the team up the
crane. He gave their names and explained that something had made
him feel faint. He had been sitting on the deck chatting to Gina
when it happened, he said, and neither of them had seen anything.
Bernadotte had been up on the gantry, effectively under Lazar's
direction in Marco's temporary absence. As fate would have it,
Lazar had just sent Eduardo down to the deck for more paint.
Bernadotte, therefore, had been the only one to see anything, and
even he, he admitted, had not been paying much attention until
the scream – which was Gina's – began. Lazar had been standing
by the crane operator's cab, giving orders, when he had slipped.
No one had been standing anywhere near him. Perhaps the sun
had blinded him. Bernadotte shrugged his massive shoulders. Cesar
had checked the spot and found a large area of grease with a long
footmark in it at the point where Lazar had fallen. There had been
nothing else to see.

Niccolo had nothing to add about the beginning of the
incident. He had been working with a team of electricians
on the light system in the hold. At the sound of the scream
he had turned, looking up. The angle of the sun had dazzled
him and he had seen only the vaguest outline of the crane, so
he could not bear out Bernadotte's story that Lazar had been
alone. Then, falling out of the glare had come Lazar, waving
his arms as though trying to grasp the insubstantial air around
him. He had landed face down. He had seemed to bounce. He
had made no other movement. A light drizzle had persisted for
a moment, warmer than the air.

That was that, really. It was written up punctiliously, signed
where necessary, entered into the logs and accident report books.
And all the while *Napoli* pushed westwards after the sunset into
the night.

After the others left, John called Eduardo back. The crewman
had impressed him. Eduardo was unusual, almost remarkable
among the men aboard. He was the crew's equivalent of Niccolo
in that he did not fit into the third-class mould of his fellows.
He had Cesar's whippet-like strength, his face all sharp angles
and dazzling blue eyes. He was quietly intelligent and he spoke

English. He had been a cadet with an ill-fated shipping company, working up to his first set of lieutenant's papers when the company had gone out of business, effectively throwing him on the beach. He had no savings, no professional insurance and no standing. His family were poor and could not support him. He had taken work as a crewman until he could find another trainee officer berth. It was not such an unusual situation for young men to find themselves in, under the current depressing circumstances in the shipping world. John was tempted to make him acting fourth officer, or at least use him to replace Lazar. In the future, maybe; in the meantime, he sent him off. But he decided to keep a close eye on the young sailor.

During the next two days they proceeded under lowering skies, through a cooler wind freshening from the north-west. As they turned towards that heading, their progress began to slow even more and the steepening chop brought out the worst in the lightly laden ship so that she pitched and corkscrewed with increasing restlessness and every now and then one of the crew would be found pausing by the containers on the deck, listening for the percussion of clashing drums. It was a tribute to Niccolo's care in loading them that no one heard a thing.

This made little difference, however, to the darkening mood of the crew. The air-conditioning had been fixed, but now they needed some heat and the heating began to falter. It was an ancient twin-duct system which may even have been part of the original Polish fittings, and not even El Jefe could track down the reason why the cooled air was not reheated on demand. The quality of the food began to falter too.

After all, the chef explained, there had been *some* damage from the fire, not only to the fittings but also to the stores. Smoked bacon and smoked ham were all very well but did the men want smoked pasta? Smoked potatoes? Bread made with interestingly grey smoked flour?

At least the rain held off, though as far as the crew were concerned this just meant that Niccolo could keep them at deck work. The new motion of the ship combined with too

vivid memories of Lazar's accident made work on the cranes
particularly unpopular, so much so that Niccolo and Marco
swapped duties. Niccolo, grimly, forced the unwilling men aloft.
Marco hung on the ladders just below the rim of the hatches,
secured there by ropes, watching the engineers trying to discover
the fault in the holds' lighting system. It was an uncomfortable
place to be, and particularly nauseating when the ship began to
ride the chop, but at least he felt safely removed from the sinister
grey containers squatting so massively on the double bottom.

As they proceeded towards the Strait of Sicily, the shipping
around them became thicker and the watchkeepers actually
began to earn their pay; but then the traffic began to thin
again because the bulk of it ran north, through the Strait of
Malta, while *Napoli* took the southward passage, nearer the
African coast. They ran almost due west again after they had
passed Malta. They came south of Linosa and did not turn off
the westerly heading until they hit the old 100-fathom line, now
marked as the 200-metre contour on their nautical chart. They
followed this almost due north as the evening closed to night
on the second day after Lazar's death. There was tension on
the bridge now as well as in the crew's quarters, for *Napoli* was
going deeper into Tunisian waters with every revolution of her
propeller, and she had no business there at all.

Marco came on to the bridge at 20.00 hours as usual and was
surprised to find John there with Niccolo. As he signed on, he
was further surprised to see the chief steward arrive with a plate
of sandwiches and four cups of soup. He gave one each to the
senior navigating officers, another to the helmsman, and carried
the last through into the radio room where Jesus was monitoring
the airwaves as closely as the helmsman was watching the sea.
Marco went across and checked the heading; made a bit of a
show of doing all the things an officer taking over the watch was
supposed to do. He wanted to be punctilious in all things when
the captain was present. And, although he knew well enough that
he and Niccolo were not here to test him in any way, he suspected
that their eyes would be on him while there was nothing else of
importance for them to look at.

Because they were running north, the sun was setting on their port quarter and, although the cloud cover was thick overhead, it thinned a little in that direction. A glow lit up the western sky; not a red glow, such as might give sailors delight and hope for the morning, but a silvery glow as though the sky had become molten pewter. Against this, the mountains behind the coast loomed up, more than twenty miles away but standing black against the lower sky like a mirage. Here the two lines of the Atlas Mountains joined, thrusting into Cap Bon as though reaching out to Sicily. Here was a landfall known not to cunning Ulysses, but to Aeneas, bound for Rome via Carthage, which had stood on the north shore of the bay whose southern arm was Cap Bon.

'We'll lose the light in a minute,' observed John quietly. Already the shadows of those mountains seemed to be reaching out to them across the dull steel of the water. The chop was still a rough confusion, made more vicious by the way the wind was being twisted by the coasts and by the action of the cooling desert stretching for more than two thousand miles due south of them. The confusion of waves attained a pattern for a moment, however, as every surface facing the port bow of the ship, and the eyes of the watching men, became coal black.

Then it was dark. 'Watch your radar,' said John at once, and Marco, without a second thought, crouched across the green bowl. There was nothing to see but the dark loom of the cape.

The outside door opened and Salah brought a jumble of sound in with him. A confusion of sea thunder and the roar of a rising wind. 'Watch your helm, Eduardo,' ordered John quietly. 'I don't want to be blown ashore. There are dangerous shallows and flats for miles all along this coast.'

'What's the plan?' asked Salah.

John led him over to the chart table and the two of them pored over the chart itself. Salah's eyes narrowed as he took in the pattern of dangerous shallows between *Napoli* and the land.

'I'm going to get as close to civilisation as I can and drop the pair of you off. You'd better use the dinghy. I'll report it lost in the bad weather and hope the crew stay quiet.'

'When?'

'Near midnight, I expect. You have plenty of time to get ready. I'm certainly not going to drop you this far out. You wouldn't stand a chance of getting twenty miles to shore.'

'But if we get in much closer, God knows what you will hit or trigger off.'

'I know. What I want to do is get up nearer the point of the cape. That should find us a bit of wind shadow and give you a better chance of getting ashore. Nabeul is out of the question, but you should be able to reach Kelibia, and get a lift to Tunis from there, even without identity papers. Your face should be well enough known in Tunisia, after all.'

Tunis was the headquarters of the PLO. Salah had once been famous there. John was right: he would be familiar to most Tunisians. 'I'll go and tell Fatima,' he said. When he went out, the noise spoke of a wind freshening quickly from the north. An on-shore wind, born of the fact that the desert had not yet lost all its heat. It would moderate later; might even turn before dawn as the sand became icy and the water remained relatively warm.

At midnight, when Cesar came on watch, they had still not found the wind shadow behind the point of Cap Bon, though on the radar under Marco's dazzled eyes, the dark outline of the outland was swinging west into greenness at last. Cesar looked round the dimly lit bridge with no expression of surprise on his lean, sallow face. He had known they would be there: the crew was agog with speculation as to what was going on, and why Eduardo had been called up to take the helm. The dapper little man checked their position and heading before signing the log. Frowning, he looked up. 'You'll have to make a decision soon, Captain,' he observed.

'I know, Cesar,' said John.

Salah, Fatima and Asha crowded on to the bridge then as well. John looked across at his battered sister-in-law and the tall Palestinian beside her. 'We can't wait any longer,' he told them. 'I'll turn *Napoli* side on to the wind and drop you in her lee. Even then, we'd better put a lifeboat down and help you launch the dinghy out of that. It'll take longer and tie us down a bit, but it'll be safer.' Fatima's bruises were mending quickly now – but she still moved stiffly and he didn't want to run the risk that she might fall into the water. He turned to his officers, giving the necessary orders. The helmsman swung *Napoli*'s head due west and John rang down for dead slow on the engine. 'Keep watching the radar,' he ordered Marco. 'Cesar, you have her. I'll take a portable radio down with me. I want to know the instant anything stirs.'

Outside, the wind began to buffet them at once; they had to grasp the rails of the companionways quite firmly. They climbed down the port side so that as *Napoli*'s head came round, the wind was slowly blocked out by the superstructure, but this benefit was somewhat undermined by the fact that the ship began to roll in an increasingly vicious manner.

On the main deck, Niccolo and John took hold of the falls of Number Three lifeboat and held tight as the others freed it from its retaining clips and swung it out on its davits. At once the heavy little vessel picked up the motion of the ship. Out and in it swung with such force that the two on the falls could only hold it because the blocks had been rigged as pulleys, allowing them to lower the pitching weight of it as though they were four times as strong as they were.

As they did this, Salah held a line trying to keep the boat by the rails long enough for the two women to get the cover off. But his line was not rigged through a pulley and he got the full effect of its weight every time the *Napoli* leaned away from him. Nevertheless, it was done in short order, and within ten minutes the lifeboat was sitting on the water, banging against the container ship's black side. Niccolo tied off his fall and ran to get the inflatable life raft. As soon as he had brought it back, he pitched it over the side, keeping tight hold on the line tied to it, and let it inflate itself in the water.

John, meanwhile, had put the Jacob's ladder in place and guided Salah down it. Then Fatima was over the side, and the process paused for a moment as John passed their kit to her and she passed it down to Salah. Niccolo ran back down the last few feet of deck, pulling the inflated life raft into position behind the lifeboat. Salah put down the last piece of luggage and leaned back to secure the two small craft together. Then he stepped across into the rubber dinghy and Fatima began to pass the kit to him.

John clambered down the ladder into the lifeboat as quickly as he could. The dinghy's outboard was in the after locker of the lifeboat. He pulled it out and carried it carefully across into the pitching little shell of black rubber. Lowering it into the water, he caught his breath – how cold it was! His fingers went numb almost at once, making it more difficult for him to secure the outboard properly. And even that was not the end of the process. In the near dark, with numb hands, beginning to shake with the chill of the wind which was blasting round the end of the ship with vicious force, he had to pour the fuel into the outboard.

He had just positioned the funnel to his satisfaction, when the portable radio rasped. He hesitated. Should he stop what he was doing and check what the touble was? Yes. That would be the safest thing. In any case, Salah was finished with the baggage now, and could take over. He yelled an order and handed over the petrol can. Then the handset was pressed to his numb ear. He thumbed SEND. 'Yes?'

'Marco says there's something fast coming round the Cap.'

'Boat? Plane? Helicopter?'

'Boat. *Fast* boat.'

'ETA?'

'What?'

'When will it get here?'

'Marco, *quando arriva*?'

A mumble of reply.

'Capitano? He thinks maybe *un quatro d'ora*.' The strain was beginning to affect Cesar's careful, considered English. Even as John thought this, there came a sudden rush of sound over the radio and Cesar was back. 'Capitano, Jesus is in contact with the vessel. He does not understand Tunisian and they speak little French but he thinks they are threatening to sink us. They are heavily armed. He thinks they will try and sink us.'

John swung round, eyes narrow, looking down the length of
the ship as though he would be able to see the Tunisian patrol
boat in the distance. There was only darkness with a sharp, ugly
sea coming out of it. If they moved at once they had a chance.
They were only just in Tunisian waters. If they moved now, they
would be safely out in Sicilian jurisdiction by the time the vessel
reached them. But he had to make the decision immediately.
Salah span the starter on the motor and it caught at once. The
little craft began tugging at its rope as though eager to be gone.
John swung round. Salah looked at him, his long face etched by
shadow and varnished with spray. 'There's a patrol boat on its
way. I have to get *Napoli* away.'

Salah nodded once and leaned down to adjust the outboard
motor. John swung back and looked into the lifeboat where
Asha and Fatima were standing, saying goodbye. 'There's a
patrol boat coming!' he yelled. 'They're threatening to blow us
out of the water. They think we're smugglers, I suppose. But
they could well shoot first and ask questions later. I can't wait
any longer. Think what a round through the deck cargo would
do. *I can't risk it.*'

The sisters gave each other the briefest of hugs and then
Fatima was pushing past her brother-in-law. John shoved his
hand out and Fatima paused, her own hand half out as though
expecting to shake hands in a formal English farewell. But no:
John was offering his walkie-talkie. 'Just in case,' he yelled.
'Good luck.' She took it and was gone.

John leaped aboard the lifeboat and shoved Asha up the
Jacob's ladder. He glanced back as she began to climb, just in
time to see the dinghy powering away into the dark. Then he
was following her upwards. As soon as he stepped out of the
lifeboat he heard the falls creak and as he scrambled upwards,
so the little vessel rose up *Napoli*'s side just beneath him. At the
top, Cesar stood, still clutching his walkie-talkie. 'Niccolo has
the con,' he yelled over the buffeting wind. 'He said I should
come down here.'

'Tell him to come to five knots,' yelled back John. 'Best course
for Italian waters.'

Leaving Cesar's men to secure the lifeboat, the two officers and Asha ran up the deck and took the lift up to the bridge. Coming out of the lift, they rushed across the bridge-deck corridor, John's eyes already busy, looking through the glass panels which formed the wall behind the wheelhouse itself. But even when he reached Eduardo's shoulder at the ship's wheel, he found himself looking not dead ahead but away to the side – towards Tunisia and the invisible dinghy.

Suddenly, in the distance there, a fireworks display began. Lights flashed, rockets soared, Roman candles blazed. And even before Cesar's walkie-talkie began to rasp with Fatima's incoming message, John was yelling to Eduardo, 'Back, turn her back!' and ringing down on the engine room telegraph for full speed ahead.

The little dinghy was running flat out through the dark, bumping from wave top to wave top in an increasingly dangerous way. Fatima was kneeling in the front. She took the brunt of the icy spray, hurled back by the relentless wind. Salah, crouching in the stern fought to keep her on a northerly heading, exactly into the wind, back along the track they had just taken. The track which should lead them to *Napoli* if they lived long enough.

The fire was coming in low over their heads now and they could actually hear the whispering hiss of the tracer rounds scything the air above them. The wind brought the sulphurous smell of the burning rounds as they fell into the sea just ahead. The only reason they were still alive was because the rubber sides of their little vessel gave no echo on the Tunisian gunboat's radar-guided targeting system and the gunners were firing blind.

The dinghy was not absolutely invisible, however, for a great searchlight had caught them in its blinding beam just before the guns opened fire and no matter what Salah did, it held them still, pinned like a moth to the black velvet background of the night. Fatima had known there was a risk they would be shot at from the moment John had relayed Jesus's message, but she was still shocked by the ferocity of what was going on. Like Salah, she had supposed the coastguards would probably arrest them. And arrest by the Tunisian authorities could well be the answer to all their problems. But there had been no question of it – just that blaze of light which had framed Salah the moment he had stood and waved, then the withering fire. Her mind leaped back to the accusation she had made earlier. Was there someone in the PLO who wanted Salah dead?

She jammed the walkie-talkie to her lips and yelled again, '*Napoli*! We are running due north back along our track.' She jammed the freezing instrument to her all-but-numb ear. She hardly understood what she heard, but she turned and yelled it to Salah word for word. 'They say *bear right and look for the surf*!' A great wash of icy foam heaved out of the darkness in front of them and almost carried her away.

Salah did not try to work out what the message meant. He simply obeyed it, turning starboard into the shoulder of a wave which threatened to swamp them. He was not thinking about his enemies in the PLO or about why the gunboat was firing on them. He wasn't thinking about anything except survival. He could see past Fatima into the stormy darkness and his seafarer's eyes saw more than hers did. The searchlight, coming from behind, showed the mass of steep-sided waves running in towards them. Even the tracer rounds seemed to give off a little more light to help him see, but beyond them, the dark night clamped down again. Salah grimly searched the shadows there, looking for that one steady pattern of starlike brightness which would spell their only chance of salvation: *Napoli*'s running lights.

But abruptly he saw something else entirely – a change in the wave pattern dead ahead. He remembered the chart John had showed him of this area of the coast, and the last cryptic radio message began to make more sense. He remembered the light patches denoting shallows and the red notes warning of shoals. John must have been careful to drop him just at the edge of one of these and now, running back to starboard of their original course was taking them across the middle of it. The shoal revealed by that breaking surf offered their only real chance of escape. The gunboat was far faster than they and would run them down if the chase went on much longer. But the dinghy had almost no draught while the Tunisian boat probably drew two metres or more. Where Fatima and he could skip over the oncoming obstruction with only the outboard's propeller at risk, the gunboat would be forced to turn aside.

But it was going to be a rough passage. The surf on the shoal's back, whipped up by the northerly gale, looked vicious and extremely dangerous. 'Hang on!' yelled Salah. Fatima looked round at him, her face etched brightly in the blaze of the searchlight. It was tense but calm and fearless. The skin was white except where shadowed by departing bruises and both her eyes were open. Something stirred deep within Salah then, something he thought had died twenty years ago with his wife.

And they were amidst the surf. What had been a pattern of waves became a wilderness of heaving foam. It was like riding the rapids of a wild river. The dinghy leaped erratically, tossed up by the head one minute and by the stern the next. Fatima seemed to leap into the air. The only parts of her which retained any contact with the dinghy were her hands, closed to fists around the bow rope. Salah crouched, his left hand wedged in a tangle of cordage like a rock in a mare's nest of branches – so numb was it and so hard were they. His right hand held the outboard's control lever twisted hard over, throttle as wide as it would go. He had stopped even registering the tracer fire falling around them.

Fatima felt as though she was on the rack. Her body was healing but it was by no means healed. As the boat tossed her up in the air again and again, her wounded muscles tore and it became a matter of some debate as to whether the firey pain or the numbing cold would claim her first. The front of the dinghy slammed up into her face like a canvas-covered inner tube and teeth already loosened by the Mercedes rattled in her head. She realised that the walkie-talkie had gone but could not recall having dropped it.

Darkness closed down on them. Salah risked a swift glance back. The gunboat had swung away at the outer edge of the shoal and the searchlight had lost them. Now the long beam was probing away to their left as the boat sped west in search of the shoal's end. The guns, too, found themselves firing wild and the brightness of the tracer faltered and died. Elated, he swung round and almost screamed. Immediately in front of him was a cliff edge falling away into some immeasurable abyss and just beyond it stood another cliff face reaching upwards to the sky. To his staring eyes, wildly trying to make sense of the shadowy picture he could see, it was as though he had come to the edge of the world and just beyond it was a black wall built between heaven and hell.

The propeller, two scant feet beneath them, struck against rock and sent a shock of agony tearing through him. The front of the dinghy reared up for the last time and the brave little craft leaped out into the dark. For a moment they actually seemed to be flying, with the wind coming from beneath them and nothing but dark air all around them, and the bent propeller screaming out of the water as though they could sail up to the clouds. Then the head slammed down again and they were on a helter-skelter ride down the wave wall at the northern edge of the shoal, hurling forward, wildly out of control, towards the second, iron cliff, dead ahead.

Immediately beyond the northern edge of the shoal, where the wave wall defined the resumption of deep water, *Napoli* was waiting to pick them up. It had been easy for the officers on the old freighter's bridge to bring her to the light-show the gunboat was making and in fact, the dinghy had been under the scrutiny of several pairs of binoculars since she turned on to the new heading dictated by John's radio message. And the moment the gunboat stopped firing, all *Napoli*'s lights came on so that the black cliff immediately in front of Salah and Fatima abruptly became a staircase to safety.

There was no mucking about with lifeboats this time. John had put the accommodation ladder down. Salah ran the dinghy up against its foot and he and Fatima leaped out. The dinghy sped away before they could even think of securing it, and vanished into the darkness to the west. They stumbled up the metal steps as *Napoli* turned and began to run north once more. As soon as their heads were at deck level, Cesar hit the retract lever and Asha ran forward with towels. Five minutes later they were on the bridge, wrapped in warm towelling clutching mugs of steaming cocoa. Away to the west on the port quarter, a brief blaze of brightness stained the dark.

John's hands fell on the shoulders of both Salah and Fatima on either side of him. 'That was your dinghy,' he said, loudly against the wind.

Salah went to dry himself off in his cabin and John watched Asha going off with her sister. He followed them, crossing the corridor behind the wheel-house, and ushered them safely into the lift. Then he went back on to the bridge. Niccolo was there already, but Cesar was still in charge. Marco was gone and the first mate was watching the radar. 'Back in Italian waters and nothing in sight,' he said quietly.

'Good. Thank you. Thank you both,' said John with feeling. Then he remembered Eduardo at the helm. 'Thank you all.'

'Capitan!' Jesus stuck his head out of the radio room and into the bridge. 'I think you should hear this.'

The radio room was small and cramped but there was space enough for both of them. Jesus had tuned the big FM receiver to the BBC World Service. 'I picked it up retuning from the Tunisians. I thought you should hear.'

The way Jesus said it made John's hair stir.

'. . . BBC world news at midnight. Today . . .'

'Is this it, Jesus?'

'*Si*, Capitan.'

'Stories have been coming in since late last week of renewed disturbances in southern Lebanon. Our reporters have now confirmed that there was in fact an outbreak of violence at a village near the coast which involved an Italian cargo ship. Simon Wheeler reports from the spot . . .'

'God! Is that us?'

'*Si*, Capitan.'

'. . . can confirm that last Friday night the Panamanian- registered container ship *Napoli* was attacked, here, in southern Lebanon. The *Napoli*, chartered by the firm Disposoco, was loading a combination of chemical and nuclear waste which seems to have been buried in the desert nearby. According to local villagers, the waste has been here for some time. Now, they say, it is in a highly unstable condition. They blame contamination from this waste for the destruction of their farms and for the mutilation of their children, and they claim that the crew of the *Napoli* also killed several villagers in a gunfight before the ship sailed. There has been no report of the *Napoli* since she sailed from Limassol harbour in Cyprus on Sunday morning, but she is understood to be heading for Naples, where she is due to discharge her load of toxic waste for disposal in Italy. Now, back to the studio . . .'

Jesus switched the radio off and there was silence.

CHAPTER THIRTEEN

Niccolo ran on to the bridge, his face as white as spindrift and John knew at once that it had started. Almost in slow motion he turned to Marco and made a gesture. The third mate nodded. His hair was wild, standing up as though the boy had seen a ghost. Niccolo leaped back out through the door and John followed him, hurling down the companionways through the storm.

The deck was awash with spray which slopped from port to starboard and back again as the ship heaved. Together they ran forward, the spray exploding up off each of them as though the men were cliffs, rocks, natural things rising from the sea, anchored safely in beds below.

The crates were shifting wildly, the wrist-thick hawsers seeming to stretch and contract like elastic. The two of them skidded to a halt. Crouching on the pitching steel, they looked beneath the restless containers. The stuff was drizzling out, slow as syrup among the quick water. It was oozing out of black-rimmed, steaming holes. It was settling, to squat smoking on the deck. Then, quicker than the eye could see, it was gone and the water whirled in new patterns on the green metal of the deck, as though running down plugholes.

And when he went down into the dark hold, John looked up and could see through the deck, the holes like stars, letting in the rain and spray. *No, that wasn't right. It couldn't be like that.* But then his eyes, having looked up, looked down. Glowing faintly in the pitching dark, the mocking piles of effluent lay on the bottom. Then, they were gone again. And every star-hole in the deck above was echoed by a fountain of seawater bursting out of the double bottom here below. It was as though the steel was skin which had been stabbed and stabbed and stabbed again. The hold began to roll. The water foamed up round his knees as he ran for the ladder as though through treacle. But the hold was tilting. Toppling. It would be over and under long before he made it to the ladder. Choking, he looked round in desperation. The wall of nuclear containers broke like a wave to come thundering down on his head. He felt each block of concrete with its heart of lead crunch down upon him. He felt them squeeze his feet and ankles as flat as a fishtail. He felt them pinch his legs against the deck until his shin bones shattered. He felt them squash his kneecaps through his knees. He felt his hip bones spread and level to the deck and tasted his blood come fountaining up his throat as the black, hot water closed above his head.

And, crushed and drowned and screaming, he jerked awake.

'Again?'

'Yes.'

'That's five nights in a row.'

'I know.'

'You're soaking. I'll get a towel.'

'You think Richard Mariner has this trouble?' He spoke in a croak, his throat was raw.

'Richard? Why?' Her voice was distant in the dark as she answered from the shower room.

'Well, he's been in enough tight situations. Makes you wonder.'

'Lean on me.' She climbed back on the bed behind him, receiving him like a warm pillow.

'That's better.'

'John, you're as tense as a bow string. Your shoulders are like rock.'

'It's the dream.'

'Is it the same one every night?'

'God knows. I can't remember what I was dreaming about just now. I never can. Aaaah!'

'What is it?'

'Cramp in my legs. *Ah!* No. It's no good, I'll have to walk about a bit.'

There was a moment or two of silence in the cabin. The wind thudded suddenly against the porthole. A second later, a big sea echoed the squall by smashing into *Napoli*'s side. She shuddered, swooped. John staggered a little. Something of the dream returned.

'Lie down here, I'll massage you,' Asha gently invited.

John wearily eased himself face down on to the damp wreckage of the bed. Her strong fingers gripped the great triangle of muscle which joined the back of his neck to the point of his right shoulder, her nails grazing the collarbone at the front. He hissed. The muscle was as tender as the backs of his legs. It was stress. Ever since his youth he had reacted to protracted stress by dreaming and by running in his sleep.

'Still,' she soothed quietly, 'it's almost over. We're due at Naples soon.'

'Lunchtime tomorrow.' He looked across at the luminous dial of his bedside clock and corrected himself: 'Today.'

It was six a.m. on Sunday. They were due to enter the port in six hours' time. But the promise of it didn't seem to have eased his nightly nightmares.

It was thirty hours since they had run from the Tunisian gunboat. A short, restless night's sleep after the excitement. A long, tense day's sailing north as the crew's resentment continued to simmer. Union men or no, they would be on to the dock authorities in Naples as soon as they were off the ship. Strange cargo, snatched from Lebanese villagers at gun-point. Two men dead then. Crossing the eastern Med under the command of a man with no papers, giving succour to terrorists. Picking up a new captain who only took them further into danger: it was like being commanded by Jonah. The fire. The fights. The assault by officers upon crew members. GBH with a chipping hammer. The injuries. The extra work. The extra death. Sailing an untrustworthy vessel with an engine that didn't work properly

into foreign waters. Brushes with gunboats. The terrorists still
aboard. The cargo increasingly dangerous. So much so that the
Napoli was now the subject of speculation in news broadcasts on
the radio – and, for all they knew, the television would be next.
No wonder the recruiting agent in Piraeus had been so specific:
you hold a union card, then you look for another berth.

But it wasn't right. It wasn't legal. Something would have to
be done. And, by all accounts, Leonardo Bernadotte was the
man who was going to do it. As soon as he got ashore.

Dawn came late, the sun seeming to drag itself up out of the
Tyrrhenian Sea and immediately into thick cloud so that it never
really emerged from dull grey water at all. The wind remained
fresh and northerly, whipping up enough spray from the choppy
waves to conceal the land though it was little more than twenty
miles away. But then, even Capri would have looked like just
another slate-bellied cumulus on a day like today. Niccolo's
deck work was done – or as nearly done as made no difference.
Marco and his team of engineers had given up trying to find the
fault in the holds' lighting circuitry. Just in case there would be
work, though, Asha and Fatima found a long, doleful line of
men waiting to describe a terrifying array of symptoms at sick
call. Gina, roped in to help the sisters, was suddenly extremely
depressed, brought face to face with the loss of her father by the
fact that she would be taking him ashore soon. Ashore into a city
where she had no family left, into a country where she would
be absolutely alone. Her deep sadness disturbed Asha and the
men. Even Niccolo had become edgy and short-tempered. The
air of defeat which John had seen come into the faces of Salah
and Fatima as the plan to land them in Tunisia fell apart had
only deepened as they followed the route of the Tunis to Naples
ferry northward towards the unwelcoming coast of Europe. And
their depression had further affected Asha, already strained by
nightmare nights with him. Marco Farnese remained childishly
self-absorbed, but he knew that he would not emerge unscathed
from John's report and feared he would be lucky to keep his
berth in the officers' mess. Only Cesar remained aloof, standing

behind Marco as he brought the freighter towards Naples Bay during the last couple of hours of his watch.

As the news came through that there would be no day work, Asha's sick queue melted away. The crew began to pack up their kit and, having established what action Bernadotte would take the moment his feet touched the concrete of the Stazione Marittima, they began to discuss what they would do when they got ashore themselves. An air of grudging excitement began to enter the atmosphere of the crew's quarters. Not so much like a school looking forward to the holidays as a group of prisoners wrongfully convicted but finishing their sentence soon.

In the suddenly deserted surgery, the two sisters sat side by side. Gina had departed with the last of the men but Fatima had shown no real desire to move. Asha tidied up a bit then sat beside her twin, knowing Fatima wanted to confide.

Theirs was a strange relationship, put under added strain during the last few days. Almost psychically close since infancy, they had been pulled apart and clashed together wildy during the last few years, and fate had put secrets between them without any emotional distance to make the secrets easier to bear. It was agony to both of them that there were things Fatima could not tell – but her secrets were Salah's secrets and she could not easily divulge them to anyone.

'He's up there on the radio again,' Fatima began quietly, in a matter-of-fact voice. 'But there's no one for him to talk to. Not in Beirut. Not in Tunis. Not even Tewfik al Ashrawi will talk to him. He's been thrown out of the club, made a pariah, and I don't know what we will do.'

Asha sat silently, waiting for more. She wondered how much of this she should tell John – though John had known Salah for ten years and should be able to see the situation clearly enough. He might not know about Tewfik al Ashrawi, though. Perhaps she had better mention him, for the name was familiar: it belonged to a senior PLO spokesman.

'When he came out of Beirut in August to help Richard Mariner and the others rescue *Prometheus*, he moved without permission and he upset many people, though I think he was already isolated, even then. And his absence allowed his enemies to undermine his position.'

Fatima paused. Part of the reason that this was so difficult for her lay in the fact that Asha and John had been aboard *Prometheus* and Fatima herself had been involved with the terrorists who had kidnapped them. It was against Fatima and her friends that Salah had been forced to move. That was why he had shot her – to prevent her from shooting him.

She took a great breath. 'He is a religious man in a secular organisation. He has come to think that the Palestinians should negotiate with the Jews. He works for the PLO in Beirut and yet he mistrusts the Hizbollah, advises against strengthening links with them and says they should give back the western hostages. He has flown in the face of Arafat himself and spoken out against Saddām Husain. As far as I know, Arafat is in Baghdad at this very moment linking the PLO cause to the Iranian position and Salah is the one man who advised him not to go. And the result of all this is that Salah gets sent to some Lebanese backwater to oversee something that anyone could have taken care of. He is attacked by local villagers and PLO representatives. He is trapped aboard this filthy tub, cut off and helpless. And Tunisian coastguards open fire the moment they see him. And, Asha, he was wearing the very keffiyeh that Arafat gave him. Wearing it in the style that Arafat taught him – folded to represent the map of Palestine. They must have seen that. They must have known who he was. And yet they still opened fire.'

'You say you don't know what to do; but what would you like to do?'

'I'd like to make him give up. Now, while we have a chance of survival. I'd like us to go ashore in Naples with the rest of you and give ourselves up to the police.'

John, too, was thinking about what he would do when he got ashore. He was sitting in the watchkeeper's chair on the bridge. He had a lot of making up to Asha to do. They ought to be lazing on a Hawaiian beach, just beginning their second week of honeymoon. Her marriage to him so far could hardly have been less idyllic. Exhausted, tight in the grip of that depression which comes from stress and results in sleeplessness, more exhaustion, greater stress still, he felt almost self-pitying. But then a wave of love for her swept over him. She had been so strong. So understanding. He had never relied upon anyone before, except, perhaps, Richard Mariner. To tell the truth, he had been worried about relying on her. But in every test she rang true. He could not believe how lucky he had been to meet her. How lucky he had been to engage her interest. Certainly, looking coldly at himself, there was precious little about him to catch any woman's eye, let alone Asha's.

Lord, he had wanted it to be so perfect for her. And just look at the mess they were involved in instead. Still, with any luck, Disposoco or the owners CZP would have a new captain waiting to relieve him this afternoon. Someone trained in overseeing the unloading of dangerous waste. Perhaps they would let Niccolo do it: he had got the stuff aboard ably enough.

The electric 'bells' sounded on the bridge chronometer: time to change watch. John stirred. His first thought was, good, now Cesar can bring her in. Even though this was Sunday, Naples was bound to be busy and he didn't want his third officer blundering about the port with or without a pilot. But where was the port? Were was *Italy*? The outlook was the same view of tossing waves and flying spume that had been there since day had broken.

'Niccolo, what can you see on the radar?'

'We're just coming up into the bay now, Captain. Capri is perhaps a mile off the starboard. Jesus should be talking to the port authority any minute.'

John got up out of the bridge chair and walked back towards the radio shack. 'Any traffic?' he asked Niccolo as he passed him.

'Nothing close to us. It's very quiet.'

'Good.'

'*Very* quiet. You think there could be anything wrong, Captain?'

It was not an unusual concern for sailors: long out of contact, as they had been for a while, homecoming mariners often thought things might have gone badly wrong in their absence. Wars, plagues, Martians; anything seemed possible.

'No, Niccolo. I'm sure there's nothing—'

'Capitan!' Jesus stuck his neat, dark head out of the shack. 'The port authority wants to speak to you.'

'There, you see, Niccolo? Everything's fine. The anchor will be down in half an hour. An hour at most.'

In the shack, John took a VHF handset and gestured for Jesus to take another: the radio officer could make notes while he talked. 'Captain, *Napoli*. Hello, Naples port authority. Hello, Naples.'

'Capitano, you must turn to a heading due east of your present heading. You must proceed on that heading for ten miles and then you must anchor at map reference 40.38N; 14.22E.'

John was hardly paying attention. So sure had he been that the port authority were just going to go through the formalities of pilot pick-up, port-official rendezvous, discharge point, unloading bay, that he was completely taken aback by the urgent instruction.

'Say again, Naples.'

As the orders were repeated, John automatically plotted the manoeuvre on the chart of Naples Bay he carried in his head. They wanted him to anchor on the edge of a shallow submarine shelf below Sorrento. They didn't want him in the port at all.

'Acknowleged, Naples. May I ask why you are queuing us up outside the port? Are there no unloading bays available? How long will we have to wait before we can come ashore?'

'There is a lighter waiting for you at the point where you must anchor.'

'A *lighter*! Our cargo is far too dangerous to unload into a lighter in this weather, Naples.'

'It is an oiling lighter, *Napoli*, carrying supplies and representatives from your owners and charterers. You will not be allowed to enter the port of Naples, *Napoli*.'

'Say again?' John simply could not believe what he was hearing. It simply could not be true. He looked at Jesus and the expression on the radio operator's face confirmed it before the distant voice on the VHF spoke again: 'I am sorry, *Napoli*. The port of Naples is closed to you. Every port in Italy is closed to you.'

Sorrento was out of the worst of the wind, but the swell was still coming south across the bay. There was a line of foam defining the outer edge of the ledge and John put *Napoli* in the first calm inside this and had the anchors dropped. As they were moving into position, a large lighting vessel detatched itself from the grey crags of the coast and began to steam purposefully out towards them. There had been nothing to do on the way over here so John had called the chef up to the bridge almost the instant he had come out of the radio shack. 'We will be anchoring off Sorrento in an hour. There will be a lighter coming out to us, but nothing much for the men to do. I will dismiss them down to lunch at one. And make it a good lunch.'

The chef was an independent-minded Gascon. He took direct orders from no one, and, in his day, he had left a good few captains choking on his barbed ripostes. On this occasion, he took a close look at his captain's expression. '*D'accord*,' he said and was gone. He might almost have saluted, had he known how.

Marco looked across at Cesar, his eyes round with wonder. Cesar's face was like stone, so the amiable third officer glanced at Niccolo, his humorous expression saying, 'What's got into the chef?' But then he met Niccolo's eyes and looked back at the captain again, his open countenance folding into a worried frown. He had never seen an expression like this upon the quiet Englishman's face.

'What is it, Captain?' asked Niccolo.

'They've closed the port. They've shut us out.'

'Shut us out of Naples?' Niccolo was aghast.

'Shut us out of *Italy*!'

The oiling lighter *Parthenope* nudged up alongside *Napoli* at one thirty local time. The accommodation ladder was down but there was no one on the deck to take a rope. Only the first officer waited to welcome aboard the three people who climbed up out of her. They walked down the gusty deck and clambered unbidden up the outside companionways to the bridge. They entered the silent bridge in a little flurry of wind and noise that emphasised the silence in the long, bright room. A silence made all the more striking by the presence of so many people. The captain was here, with his other navigating officers. The chief engineer was here. The radio officer. The leader of the scientists. A tall man in the battle fatigues of a Palestinian freedom fighter. Three women: the other freedom fighter, the doctor who was also the present captain's wife, the late captain's daughter. Ten pairs of eyes whose expressions were uniformly hostile.

One of the new arrivals was a small ball of a man, red of face and thin of hair with a narrow black moustache exactly bisecting the distance between his button nose and his cupid's-bow lips. The other man was taller, but stooping, self-effacing, ground down. There were dark bags below his lugubrious eyes, making them look like black stones at the hearts of pale prunes. The third visitor was a woman.

The small man bounced forward, brushing the pudgy fingers of his right hand to and fro across his moustache. 'Captain . . . ah . . . Higgins. I am Michaelangelo Verdi of CZP, the owners of *Napoli*.' He thrust his hand out vaguely towards the heart of the phalanx of officers before him. No one moved to take it, perhaps because the gleam of gold rings was outshone by the glistening moisture on the digits. The little man danced back, gesturing vaguely behind him. 'This is Signor Nero from Disposoco.' The tall man moved forward. His prune-puffed eyes looked at Salah for a second. He fell back. His hands were shaking.

'I had expected to talk to the captain in his day room.' Silence. Stillness. Verdi's rubicund face gathered into a frown. Clearly he was not used to being treated like this. 'I had expected to find a team of men ready to oil up the ship. You do not have very much time. You must turn round and get underway as soon as possible.'

'Where to?'

Verdi's eyes zeroed in on the speaker. It was the captain: he had known it would be. 'To England, Captain. To your home.

They dispose of such things as your cargo there. You sail with the tide for Liverpool.'

John's lips twitched. The tide in this area ran to a foot on a bad day.

But it was no laughing matter. Liverpool was the better part of three thousand sea miles away: twelve days' sailing at the speeds El Jefe's diesel was capable of. In this kind of weather – and there was no improvement promised – across the Bay of Biscay, the prospect was grim indeed. There was a brief murmur as the news was translated. The atmosphere of hostility intensified. Verdi wiped his moustache again. 'We have no choice,' he persisted. 'The ports of Italy are closed. Only England will accept the cargo.'

'Only England has the capability of disposing of it safely,' intervened Nero. His voice was deep and slow where Verdi's was light. His prune eyes studied the floor as he spoke, avoiding contact with everybody else's gaze.

'Oh,' said Fatima, her voice deceptively quiet, 'I thought it could be disposed of almost anywhere. Lebanon. Nigeria. South America. Anywhere a little more death might go unnoticed!'

The tall Italian jumped, twitched, fell back. The woman said nothing though her keen gaze seemed to take in everything.

Verdi leapt into the breach. 'Only in England can it be disposed of safely,' he reiterated. 'They have facilities—'

'This is getting us nowhere.' John was in motion, coming towards the visitors as he spoke, the others falling in behind. 'You'll have to discuss your ideas with the crew. They only signed on for Naples. They'll probably be getting off here anyway no matter what you say.'

'No.' Verdi's sharp monosyllable brought them all to a standstill.

'That's not what they think.' John's voice held a distinct warning.

'Then they are mistaken. They signed on for the port of delivery. The contracts do not specify what port.'

'They were told it would be Naples.'

'*Told*. Ah. But nowhere does it *say*. Even were they union men . . .' Verdi gave a Neapolitan shrug. They were not, of course, union men. They were not getting out of these contracts. They were not getting off *Napoli*. They were hardly close enough to shore to risk jumping ship. And if they did, they would have no papers, no pay, no berth, no comeback, no hope of finding another job. John glanced round the bridge. The expressions on the faces of his officers told their own story. Only Gina would be going ashore here. Gina and the dead men. Perhaps Lazar had been the lucky one after all.

They all crowded into the crew's dining saloon, and if the hostility on the bridge had been intense, it was nothing to the atmosphere that greeted them here. Forewarned of his reception by the officers, Verdi launched into voluble Italian at once. Down here, Nero seemed to have more confidence and he stood beside his colleague, adding silent stature to his arguments. Only the third figure, the woman, remained aloof. The fact that he did not understand a word unsettled John; he edged out of the room as Verdi's speech was greeted with a stunned silence followed by a howl of outrage from Bernadotte.

In the corridor, Asha joined him and they stood together for a moment as though eavesdropping on the furore beyond the door. 'What are you going to do?' she asked.

The weight of it ground down on him like whatever it was weighing Nero's bowed shoulders. He longed to say, 'I'm going to phone Richard at once and get us off this rust bucket.' He could, of course. They had signed no contract with CZP's shark-agent in Piraeus. They were nothing to do with Disposoco. But in fact they were as completely trapped as anyone else aboard. John spoke to Richard Mariner every night, but neither Heritage Mariner nor the PLO seemed capable of solving the Palestinian problem. Asha would never leave Fatima and Salah in the lurch. And John could no more desert his command or his men, quite apart from his wife. 'I'm going to take her to Liverpool, of course,' he said gruffly. 'You want to come?'

She swept him into her arms and for reasons he could not perfectly fathom, she tried to crush the life out of him.

The pandemonium in the crew's dining saloon rose and fell

as the door opened and closed. The honeymooners sprang apart. John swung round to see who had come out. It was the third of the visitors. The woman. She stood a robust five foot eight. She had brown hair and intelligent blue eyes. There was a power about her, an authority. She gave the impression of being a person used to getting things done. She thrust out her hand to John. 'Captain Higgins?' she said. Her voice came as a shock to him. It was deep, forceful. American.

He took her hand automatically and was again surprised: she had an extremely firm grip.

'Captain Higgins, Mr Verdi just got through telling your crew that he wants me aboard this ship for the good of his company's reputation and that he's not taking no for an answer from anyone. And I guess that includes you. So, if you're taking this mess to Liverpool, then I'm coming with you,' she said. 'My name is Ann Cable. I work for Greenpeace.'

CHAPTER FOURTEEN

The formalities of unloading Gina and the dead men were complicated only by the late Captain's filing system, which refused to disgorge Lazar's papers. At last Verdi shrugged, 'He doesn't need them. We go. You go.'

It took them two days to cross the Tyrrhenian Sea but at least the wind moderated and the air cleared so that they came past Cagliari on a bright, calm evening.

John asked Niccolo, who was on watch, to take her off the automatic helm and drift her to the north of her progammed course. They were heading south of west and the sun was setting swiftly on their starboard quarter. The western edge of the sky was clear and the orb of the great star swam down slowly into view, blood-red and seemingly flattened by some quirk of the crystalline air. Great beams struck across the bellies of the high cirrus overcast, turning a mackerel sky to bright smoked salmon. Asha, who was standing beside John's chair, caught her breath. Her hand stole out to rest on his shoulder. He pulled himself erect as though her touch had electrified him. 'Come on,' he said. 'I've something to show you.'

He led her past the radio room and out of the port side of the bridge. The air was cool with just the faintest intimation of the winter currently reaching down Europe towards the Mediterranean basin. It was late arriving here, as if it had become dammed up behind the north-facing slopes of the Alps.

Asha gathered her light cardigan about her shoulders and John slid his arm across them too, for they were on the shadowed side of the ship. 'Where are we going?'

'You'll see.'

They went down the companionways with John taking the lead on the steps but waiting to embrace her at the foot of each flight, gently solicitous, and guide her to the next with his arm warm and tight round her shoulders.

As they moved, they talked quietly. 'What did Richard say last night?' She had made a habit of trying to be with him when he contacted Richard, but last night she had been involved in the far more important task of trying to get to know their new passenger.

'Same as before. If we want to go home, he'll have us 'coptered off at the drop of a hat. I think he'd actually come out and take over himself if we asked.'

'But I couldn't leave Fatima.'

The two sisters, twins born only minutes apart, had received an unusual upbringing. Daughters of a minor playboy Arab prince, they had been given a liberal education in England during the late seventies and early eighties until their father had discovered the True Faith and had called them home to Dhahran to take up their place in Muslim society. They had refused and so he had resorted to trickery and managed to kidnap Fatima, with disastrous results. As a result of this the two of them, always close, had become closer still, and it was only Fatima's terrorist involvement that now kept them apart. Asha would never abandon Fatima, even if Richard Mariner promised to take over *Napoli* himself.

'I know you couldn't leave her. I'd never ask you to,' he said. 'And in any case, it's not so bad. This sort of thing is what I did before I settled down into the Heritage Mariner fleet anyway. I think Richard is only so worried because he thinks we should be on honeymoon somewhere.'

She said nothing, for she felt as Richard did on that point. If only they had been able to drop Salah and Fatima off safely in Tunis!

'Still, mustn't grumble,' he said after a moment. 'We're

certainly on our way home now. And Richard hopes to have some plan dreamed up of helping Salah and Fatima at Liverpool. As for honeymoons, well, after we get free of this lot, the rest of our life will probably feel like a honeymoon.'

They were on the main deck and he led her slowly sternwards. She had never been behind the bridgehouse and was surprised how secluded it was. The great gallows stood above them, black against the thrilling sky. It had two great steel legs standing nearly forty feet high, seated on massive rollers fitted in turn on to rails in the deck. The tops of these legs were joined by a huge gantry reaching right across the ship. The whole structure gave an impression of forbidding strength and its shadow lay heavily upon her as she hurried past.

Beyond it, the deck was flat and largely uncluttered. Winches and cleats stood to port and starboard. The rails to guide the gallows lay along the steel, but there beyond, beneath the little flagpole with its drooping CZP house flag, bound in by the afterdeck rails, was a little area where the green metal and modern machinery gave way to something very different. The green deck ended a yard beyond the gallows rails. And set square against it, reaching out to the rounded stern, was an added section of dark teak boards. To walk on them was a different sensation to walking on metal. For a dizzy moment she felt as though she had stepped off concrete on to turf. Her feet tingled. Absurdly, she wanted to dance. She turned towards him, thinking this was what he had wanted to show her. But his eyes were narrowed against the sunset and looking away behind her to the north. She turned and he guided her the last few steps to the little pulpit of the after rail.

Sardinia crouched below the horizon then reached up high above it. Asha found herself looking into the bay of Cagliari from the south-west, looking past Capo Spartivento across to Capo Carbonara. The impression was of great wooded shoulders of land, clad in forests of beech trees, but turreted and fortified at their crests. One stood close on her left and the other further away behind her. Between them, the land swooped down into a great placid bay, still and mirror-calm, as though it was filled not with water but with mercury.

Nothing moved. No boat disturbed its perfect reflection. No car wound along those pale, reflecting ribbon roads. No dark land-bird rose flapping from its nest among those black-green forests, and no white gull swooped calling to break the spell. Nothing in the town which climbed up the hillsides and down to its image inverted in the bay stirred or sounded in that perfect moment. Until, over the mountain, came the evening breeze. It seemed to make the air dance at the distant, knife-edge crest. It brought a sea swell to the forest branches. It set the washing in the town to flapping and doors and shutters to slamming, and when it drew its fingers across the water of the bay it seemed to set the whole evening a-ripple. The flags on the distant turrets waved and *Napoli*'s flag waved in return.

The smell of the land, of the forests and the city settled on them; the odours of beech nuts and olive oil, of rich earth and hot stoves, of salt drying and dinners cooking.

The breeze took her hair and spread it out so that the sunset picked up its auburn highlights. The glory of the sight still lingered in her eyes as she turned back to him, the wizard who had made this magic happen. A quiet, modest, almost self-effacing man, he had no idea at all of the effect he could have on women. And was having on her, at this moment. She threw her arms round him and crushed him to her in an excess of emotion which went far beyond any thought or words. And he, who had brought her to this romantic place just in the hope of pleasing her a little, was overwhelmed by the reaction and surrendered to the emotion as swiftly as she did. His final rational thought moments later in their cabin was that they would be late for dinner.

The contentment of the captain and his wife went a certain way towards lightening the atmosphere aboard. And that atmosphere did need lightening. At Sorrento, Verdi and Nero had left a stunned crew to oil their ship and bring aboard their supplies like sleepwalkers, deep in shock. They had carried up the bodies

of the three dead men like zombies and put them aboard the
lighter with Gina Fittipaldi and her kit. They had brought Ann
Cable's luggage aboard and put it straight into the guest cabin,
effectively swapping one woman passenger for another. But so
deep was their shock and disbelief at Italy's rejection of them
that they did not even try to size up their new sex object. Even
Bernadotte failed to assess the cubic capacity of her bust and
the lissomness of her waist. His eyes passed blindly over the
length of her thighs and the breadth of her hips. There were
no quiet whistles at the way in which her jeans clung to her
buttocks. Niccolo watched, amazed. Not one salacious comment
or hopeful leer. Generations of sexist breeding seemed to have
been wiped out at a stroke. It came as little surprise, therefore,
when they went about their work uncomplainingly and even
seemed to be doing their duty and their best. He and Cesar
put their heads together at once and drew up a list of things they
needed to get done and put the men to work on them before the
stunned mood changed.

The work was important. The two senior officers were grimly
amused but by no means laughing. When the effect of Verdi's
words wore off there would be a backlash. It would manifest
itself in slow and sloppy work, refusal to do dirty, difficult or
dangerous jobs. And if the mood changed when they were in
the Bay of Biscay, there could be real problems. They looked
at the long-range weather forecast with narrow eyes and grim
lips. Still, it was early days to worry yet.

In the meantime, while the crew seemed to have left her out of
their daily intercourse, Niccolo and Cesar entered into a rivalry
to engage Ann Cable's attention. Niccolo had spent some time
in distant homage to the captain's daughter Gina Fittipaldi, but
she left the ship with no word to him and he knew in his bones
that she had no real regard for him at all. Perhaps he was on the
rebound. He didn't really think about it; he was acutely aware,
however, of the woman from Greenpeace.

She made no demands; seemed content to get to know the
ship in her own time. Obviously she was here to monitor the
cargo, but she had a couple of weeks to do that. During those

first two days, therefore, she simply wandered around with a notepad, a camera and a small personal tape recorder. She talked to the scientists and went down the deck with them to look at the containers. But she did not get into a white suit. She did not go into the hold. Niccolo and Cesar both watched her and watched each other watching her.

Niccolo thought he would have the edge over the second mate, not through any misplaced over-confidence, but because he spoke better English and because he had been in charge of the disposition of the load which was of such interest to her. But, then again, the obvious time for social chat was at the dinner table. And dinner was served at seven, during the last hour of Niccolo's watch. This he found very frustrating. And his confidence was further damaged by Cesar's quiet revelation that his limping English had proved no handicap after all; the American woman spoke perfect Italian.

Early in the third afternoon out of Sorrento, however, it seemed that the tables would be turned. Cesar had taken over the watch at midday and was prowling the bridge restlessly, his eyes everywhere, as the automatic helm guided them along the pre-programmed course across the western Mediterranean towards the first narrowing of the sea lanes south of the Balearic Islands. They were about 350 miles south of Marseilles and 50 miles north of Cap Carbon, though neither could be seen. Niccolo was on the deck with a day-work gang chipping rust away from the safety rails and strengthening them where necessary so that they would be reliable across Biscay. The first he knew of her presence was a kind of stirring among his men and a whisper or two, the least offensive of which was '*Che bella regazza!*' What a stunner!

'She speaks Italian, *pene*. Watch your mouth,' he spat in a rapid Calabrian undertone. Then he was on his feet, wiping his hands.

She was almost as tall as he was, and her blue eyes looked quizzically directly into his own. It was not their size or their colour which engaged him at once: it was their cool intelligence. The whole of her delicately chiseled face, from the slight raising of one finely curved, dark brown eyebrow to the merest upward curve of her lip, bespoke powerful intelligence. He met her gaze, all too aware of the untidy picture he must present with his hair plastered low across his perspiring forehead and his hands and overalls – his face, too, likely as not – liberally sprinkled with flakes of rust and paint.

'Signora?' He gave her the title out of respect. He had looked at her hand and seen no wedding ring.

'It's time I had a closer look at your handiwork, if that wouldn't be too much trouble, Mr Niccolo.' Her voice in its own way matched her eyes. It was cool, reserved. The sort of voice he could more easily imagine delivering a dissertation than swearing undying love. She was speaking English and he answered in English.

'Of course, Ms Cable.' He paused. He had never actually said 'Ms' before. But the title suited her. 'When?'

'As soon as would be convenient.'

'Now?'

'Perfect.'

'Right.' He looked around for Eduardo automatically, but he was helping Marco on the far side of the deck. 'Bernadotte, you're in charge,' he said at last. 'Carry on with that chipping and for heaven's sake, check any weaknesses carefully. We don't want that lot giving way if we hit bad weather in Biscay.'

He turned away at once, confident the big seaman would see the importance of what they were doing and make the others take care. The fact was that Bernadotte was twice the seaman of any of them; only his truly foul temper and utterly unacceptable attitude to authority kept him off first-class ships.

'Don't you want to borrow one of the scientists' protective suits?' he asked.

'Haven't seen the need for one.'

'What exactly do you want to see first?'

'It's a tough decision. Most of the people I've spoken to since I came aboard seem more scared of what's in the barrels than what's in the hold.'

He gave a bark of mirthless laughter. 'So?'

'So, how easy is it to get into the containers?'

'The only one worth opening is the top one nearest the fo'c'sle head.'

'Why?'

'I packed the others full of sand round the barrels. I had time to do them all properly except for that last one. Except for sand, there's nothing to see in any of the others.'

'That was very sensible.' She sounded impressed. He liked that.

'It was the obvious thing to do. I had to pack them in with something. We dug them out of a desert and brought them to a beach: there was a lot of sand available.'

They came down to the last set of containers before the fo'c'sle. Ann paused here, looking up, and Niccolo went on down to the foot of the forward cargo-handling crane. He collected a ladder and a box of tools, then he returned to her side.

The containers were secured one on top of the other. They were each ten feet square at the end and twenty feet long. 'We'll go right up on top and open up from there,' said Niccolo and put the ladder in place. 'You first.'

Without a further word, she climbed upwards. He caught up the box of tools and followed her. The top of the container was more than twenty feet above the deck and it did not feel like two hundred square feet of moulded and riveted metal affording sure and solid footing. Even though *Napoli* was riding smoothly and surely, the height above the deck and even greater height above the water was disconcerting. Niccolo found Ann sitting down to wait for him, even though he was only a second or two behind her. It seemed absolutely natural for him to sit beside her for a moment.

'Some view,' she said, looking around. It had not occurred to him that this would make such a satisfactory lookout post. It was only half as high as the bridge, but the openness of the place gave a feeling of being able to see much more than the watchkeepers there. Europe and Africa were both invisible. Mallorca and Menorca were below the horizon to the north-west and there wasn't even any cloud clustered above their mountain tops to betray them. But they were by no means alone on the apparently boundless sea. A tanker was approaching them, obviously inbound from the Strait. It sat low in the water and looked every bit as large as *Napoli*. Beyond the tanker was an old-fashioned freighter, following roughly the same course. Bound for Italy or Yugoslavia, no doubt, with a cargo of trade goods and a few passengers. Crossing north to south in front of them, but far enough ahead to be clear in plenty of time, was a ferry. Probably the ferry on the regular run from Marseilles to Algiers. Beyond it, to the south of them, heading lazily south-west, was a cruise liner, her upper works a dazzling white, so bright that she was easier to see than the battered old ferry which was so much closer. Closer still, closer than any of the other ships, was a small fleet of fishing boats, all of them chugging purposefully southwards, low in the water, with their nets piled on their long, low sterns like bright orange seaweed. A cloud of seagulls followed them, screaming and swooping. It was an idyllic scene.

Close to where they were sitting on the container was an inspection hatch a little like a manhole, secured with four clips, one of a number of hatches which enabled the container to be accessed section by section. The hatch was set into a larger hatch which could also be opened with relative ease. And this in turn was part of a yet larger hatch fully half the top of the container. The whole top could be removed in one section as well.

Niccolo snapped the small hatch open and lifted it back. A wave of hot air, fetid with the stench of rust, filled his nostrils and he turned away. He reached into the tool box for a torch. 'You want to go first again?' he asked.

Ann crossed over to look down the hole. A shaft of brightness revealed a simple stairway of carefully packed drums. 'Yeah,' she said, lengthening the word while she continued to move, swinging her leg in and down on to the first step. Carefully, she reversed in as though climbing down a ladder. Niccolo followed her at once.

At first it was quite easy to climb down the drums for there was plenty of light from the open hatch by which to guide fingers and feet. But the arrangement of drums was as much like a staircase as a ladder and soon it moved away from the beam of brightness. In the dark, it was less easy to place fingers and feet correctly on the rims of the drums and he heard her slip and swear more than once before they were safely on the floor. Niccolo flashed his torch round the echoing tomb-like place they found themselves in. It was as big as a small room, its ceiling more than four feet above their heads. The drums rose in safe, solid series immediately in front of them, bound firmly in place by strong ropes, just as the container itself was secured in its present position by steel hawsers hooked through the loops on its sides. They were further held in place by battens of wood wedged against their metal sides and stepped against the floor. 'What's next?' he asked, his voice echoing eerily in the steel sarcophagus.

'You were serious about keeping these things still, weren't you?'

'Have they told you what this stuff can do?'

'The captain's hands.'

He nodded, his mouth a thin line. 'The captain's hands,' he said.

Cesar had no idea that they had gone down into the container because all his attention was on the little fishing fleet. The boats were forty-footers designed in exactly the opposite way to the *Napoli* for they had tiny fo'c'sles with their bridges immediately behind them. All the rest of their long, low length was open and uncluttered. Only the piles of nets sat on the empty decks. There were no crew visible, but there must have been someone there, for as the *Napoli* began to close with them, they seemed to speed up, apparently to clear the way. But then the incredible happened. No, not the incredible, the impossible. The last of the boats, all but under *Napoli*'s bows but chugging purposefully clear, heaved abruptly over a cross wave. The movement threw its carelessly secured nets overboard into its creamy wake. The bright, nearly indestructible web spread out on the back of a wave and slipped swiftly across *Napoli*'s course. A line of floats bobbed up as the drift net sank like a curtain beneath it. A hundred yards of it unfurled in a moment, spread right across their path.

Cesar watched for an instant, horror-struck. They would ride over the net easily enough. The frail floats and bright plastic posed no threat to the hull. But unless they swerved round the end of it, the net would slide under their keel until it met their propeller. The little fishing boat would in all probability be pulled under the water and torn apart. The propeller would be wrapped in a mare's-nest of net. The main shaft, trying to turn it, would warp and spring out of its bed. The engine, caught in direct drive, with not even a gear box to fail and relieve the pressure, would overheat. The fires El Jefe was always warning them about would explode into flame. They would be crippled, at the very least.

Cesar crossed the bridge at incredible speed and hit the button beside the automatic helm, which was the HARD A-STARBOARD button. Then he pressed the switch that sounded the foghorn, as *Napoli* seemed to leap aside. Vaguely, because his attention was elsewhere, he noticed that the deck cargo was having a hard time in the forces released by the emergency action. One of the containers seemed to have torn loose and was swinging from side to side. No time to worry about that now. He grabbed the engine room telegraph and wrenched the lever across to HARD ASTERN. *Napoli* had enough way on her, even at ten knots, for the steering command to be effective. The engine command hopefully would give them just that little more time. He hit the siren again. A figure appeared on the afterdeck of the fishing boat and began to wave its arms in a pantomime of surprise. An ants' nest of fishermen boiled out of the squat bridgehouse to join him. They ran back and started to pull the bright net out of *Napoli*'s path.

The four of them sat in Asha and John's cabin, the sisters side by side under the paintings of Naples, the old friends opposite them. Typically, it had been Fatima who dominated the conversation that was just coming to an end. She had embellished her description of Salah's isolation and made it the foundation of a plea – John and Asha should do all in their power not only to get the ex-terrorists off *Napoli* at Liverpool, but to find some way of helping them make a new life away from all association with the Middle East. Further thought had convinced her that political events in the Gulf States and North Africa were simply making it inevitable that a man of Salah's views, with Salah's reputation and standing, would die as soon as he went back.

Salah himself remained silent. He was not surprised by Fatima's proposition. He was not offended to have himself spoken of in such terms in front of outsiders. He was simply surprised that anyone should care so much about him. If the truth were to be told, he thought little enough about himself. A man of fierce personal pride, enormous courage, and infinite loyalty, he had lost everything dear to him years ago when his wife had been killed in the earliest days of the Palestinian conflict and when, soon after, his son had been tricked, robbed and murdered by the captain of a tramp steamer called *Sanna Maru*. Salah had met Richard Mariner, John and the rest while he roamed the world on tramps and tankers looking for his son's killer. It had been aboard the old *Prometheus* that he had caught up with his prey. He had been trapped aboard for the rest of the voyage after his revenge had been accomplished and he had come to respect and to like the men and women he got to know during that voyage.

But after *Prometheus* came to port, he had returned to his roots – an incredibly intelligent, experienced man with nothing left to live for except his first fierce loyalty, and no one left to care for except a friend of his youth now known as Yasser Arafat. And now, where was he? Estranged from Arafat, adrift from his organisation and falling back into the strange old ways of caring and being cared for.

Fatima was probably right. He was nearing sixty and slowing down. She was half his age and loved him. They could have ten, maybe twenty good years if they were lucky, but if he was going to make the break it must be now – while he still had the time and the energy for a new start.

A new start: suddenly the idea was very tempting.

'We will see,' he acquiesced. 'In the meantime, you have to get this tub across Biscay, and I am sick of being a passenger. Let me do what I am good at. Let me replace Lazar. You will never get *Napoli* running smoothly without an experienced bosun.'

John looked around the room. The atmosphere at last seemed to be lightening. Asha was contented and Fatima was positively glowing. For the first time on this cruise it was possible to see the woman beneath the bruising. His calm gaze settled on Salah. 'You know who the troublemakers are and who will stand by you. You know where to look for help among the officers if you need it. If Richard was here you would probably already be doing the job.' He slapped the arm of his chair like an auctioneer accepting a bid. 'That's it. Let's go.'

And the moment he spoke, the emergency siren screamed.

Cesar found he was yelling orders and advice liberally mixed with obscenities at the fishermen. He was still doing so an instant later when the captain burst on to the bridge with the Palestinian one pace behind.

One glance told John everything he needed to know: it revealed the situation and the fact that Cesar was taking the correct action. There was no one at the wheel. 'Take the helm,' he ordered Salah, then he went to the front of the bridge. He noted that one of the containers seemed to have come loose and was mildly surprised, for the emergency manoeuvre, though urgent, was still sedate. At ten knots, it was hardly like being in a swerving Ferrari. The cable must have been weak. The spectral memory of his recurring nightmare rose just below his consciousness. It had enough force to make his hair stir. Sidetracked, he tried to pin down his sudden horror. Then Bernadotte burst on to the bridge yelling an impenetrable jumble of Italian. Cesar swung round to face his captain as though he too was remembering the nightmare. 'Capitano, Niccolo, the American woman – they are in the loose container!'

CHAPTER FIFTEEN

John and Bernadotte ran side by side down the deck, their eyes riveted to the swaying container which each moment threatened to come crashing to the deck. But there was more than one hawser involved here and Niccolo's care in loading had ensured that, though one had snapped, there were at least three more capable of restraining the restless metal box. Even so, the thought of what must be going on inside the great steel cave made John extremely fearful for the safety of his first officer and their American guest.

At last they were beside it, looking straight up as though at the underside of a giant swing. The first thing that needed doing was to get up there and try to quieten the movement. 'Bernadotte,' John called. *Christ!* What was the Italian for 'ladder'? He'd better try 'steps' and that one was easy: that opera house was named for its staircase. 'Bernadotte, *la scala.*'

Miraculously, his words made perfect sense to the big man, who caught up the ladder, which had fallen at the first wild swing, and held it against the end of the container, where the movement was least violent. John ran up at once and threw himself flat on the metal top. It was immediately clear to him what the problem was. Niccolo had separated the crates with great battens of wood, and the movement of the huge metal box had loosened one of them so that the container was swinging on the second, like a mad, sideways seesaw on a fulcrum. His weight on the far end should be enough to engage the swinging section with the top of the box beneath and bring the movement to an end.

He squirmed forward and was gratified to feel the container cant slightly. The next vertiginous swing ended jarringly and abruptly. The containers crashed together and the top one ground to a stop, wedged against the bottom one. John moved back experimentally. The container's far end lifted, but the wild sideways motion did not begin again. He stood up and walked forward. After the container had settled once more, he moved with more confidence and a great deal more urgency down to the open hatch. Here he knelt, looking down.

The sunlight revealed less destruction than he had feared. The first step or two remained intact. He would be able to climb in, at any rate. But what good would that do? When he got in there he needed to be able to move things about, quickly and surely. And there was only one way he could do that. He looked up. Hanging above him, swaying slightly, were the falls of the first great crane, the one Lazar had fallen off. At the end of the falls were great slings of webbing. He knew well enough how to work their standard adjusting buckles. They could be set wide enough to lift a container or small enough to lift an individual barrel.

'Bernadotte!' he yelled at the top of his voice, moving over to the edge and looking down. The massive man broke away from the little group of his day workers he had been a part of and looked up. John had no idea at all what the Italian for 'crane' was, so he just pointed forcefully and hoped for the best. The big man lifted a hand and began to make his way forward.

'Niccolo!' This time his yell was not as loud, as though he was afraid of disturbing a church – or a cemetery. 'Ms Cable!' No reply.

He was busily unfastening the clamps which kept the bigger trap door closed. The small inspection hatch was all very well for popping in and out, but he needed light and a hole big enough for the crane to operate through. The last one sprang open and with a bellow of 'Look out below' he heaved, sending almost a quarter of the top clanging on to the deck.

Once the section was gone, it was relatively easy for him to scramble down on to the first step made out of firmly lashed drums.

'Hello!' His voice echoed eerily and was answered only with silence and the queerly distorted sounds from outside. He began to climb downwards into the deeper recesses of the container. With the quarter section off above, the whole interior was flooded with light so that he had no difficulty in seeing what had happened further down. Here the regimented rows of the barrels very quickly became a treacherous jumble, as though there had been a sort of avalanche. He went as far down as he dared, and even then he was stopped not by fear of personal injury but by the lively awareness that the two missing people he was here to help could well be underneath the very barrels he was walking on.

He looked up towards the brightness. Across the great square of haze-silvered sky swung the black arm of the crane, the falls uncoiling as it moved and the slings of webbing coming down towards him at surprising speed. Just before the buckles bashed him on the head, they stopped, jerking in the air and making clapping noises as though applauding their own performance. John looked back along the skeletal arm above his head. At its shoulder with the upright hung the controller's cab and here, just visible through the glass, Bernadotte was standing, leaning forward over the controls so that he could see what was going on in the container.

As John looked another black outline was chopped out of the sky. Asha had thrust her head over the edge of the container. 'John?'

'I'm OK. Just getting these barrels moved.'

'Need help?'

'One-man job. No room for more. Can't have people tramping around down here. God knows what they'd step on.'

'I'll stay up here then. Marco is down with the gang on the deck now.'

'Leave him there.'

John had reached up and taken one of the slings in practised hands, checking it as he talked. It was set wide, for lifting containers. A swift adjustment not only made the sling more suitable for slipping round a barrel but also gave him an extra length of webbing. It was the work of only a moment more to adjust the second sling. Then he was pulling them impatiently down towards the first barrel he wanted to move. The barrels were like massive beer kegs, with ridges running round them a quarter of their length in from each end. The ridges, designed to strengthen the barrels, also had the effect of making them easy to handle. Even when they were lying on their side, as this first one was, it was easy to slip a sling round each end because the ridge raised them clear of the floor.

John tightened the webbing in place and stood back. Bernadotte saw his movement and the barrel swung upwards. It was only when the thing was hanging, whirling slowly, just above his head, that John realised how stupid he had been. He had not checked to see whether the drum had been damaged by the fall; he had no idea whether or not it was leaking. And he had trusted Bernadotte, the man who, controlling the barrel just above his head, was the one most likely to drop it on him. But then his second thoughts were overridden by the sound of a groan somewhere near his feet and he crouched down to look among the jumble surrounding the barrel he was standing on. The urgent sound of his 'Hello?' drowned the swish of the barrel above him being lifted up and out on to the deck.

'Who's there?' It was Ann Cable's voice; she sounded woozy, shocked.

'John Higgins. Where's Niccolo?'

'Here, I think. I can't seem to be able to see or to move. The last thing I remember is Niccolo pushing me under a batten by the wall and diving on top of me.'

'Well, he *is* Italian.'

'Pardon me?'

'A joke. Passionate.'

She gave a dry chuckle which surprised him; his jest wasn't

exactly well timed. 'Yeah. But not even Neapolitans work that fast.'

Looking up, he saw Asha's outline. 'Ann Cable's here,' he called, but more than that he did not want to say. Her voice was coming from beneath a pile of barrels which was a wild reflection of the steps coming down from the hatch. Heaven knew what things were like under there.

He stepped off his safe barrel on to its lower slopes, rocking uneasily on a curved, unsteady surface. 'Tell me if there's any movement which looks dangerous,' he said, and could have kicked himself for choosing the wrong word: she had said she couldn't see. She might be blind. 'Did you get hit on the head?' he asked innocently.

'Not hard enough to affect my sight.'

Lord! She was quick. Sharp as a tack. He remembered that it was her obvious intelligence which had impressed him when they first met.

'Good. You should begin to see some light soon, then.' He stepped back on to the steady barrel and the second one swung up and out.

'Anything?' called Asha's voice from above.

He repeated the question more quietly. 'Anything?'

'No. But I think I'm facing the wall. I think Niccolo's sort of on my back.'

'OK. I think you must be wedged right in there under the batten. Can you feel anything wet?'

'No. If there's blood I wouldn't be able to smell it either. Everything down here stinks of metal. But if there's any stuff leaking out of the barrels, I'd surely know about that, I guess. Though judging from what they say about Captain Fittipaldi, I might not be able to *feel* it.'

His grunt of laughter at her grim humour coincided with the arrival of the sling.

'So,' he said as he worked on securing the next barrel, 'Asha tells me you work as a journalist as well.'

'Yeah. It's not unusual. Greenpeace is as much a state of mind as a profession.'

'Is that what you're doing here, looking for a story?'

'What do you think, Captain?'

'I think CZP and Disposoco were mad to let you aboard.'

'Yeah. But we had them over a barrel.' That dry chuckle again. John felt his lips twist in an answering smile. The next barrel swung up and away. Bernadotte was doing a good job. He had great hands. Gigantic but great. John went further on to the pile of barrels so that he could secure the one immediately above the place her voice seemed to be coming from.

'So,' he said conversationally, 'why *did* you join Greenpeace?'

'I have to know you a bit better before I tell you that story, I'm afraid.'

'Fair enough. You freelance out of Rome?'

'As a journalist? Yeah. Usual thing. A little magazine work, research. A little newspaper work. Stringer for Reuters. Trying to break into television.'

When the webbing cradle came back, he attached it with more care than ever to the barrel he had been checking out as he talked: the one immediately above her. He raised his hand, heard Asha's call, watched the way Bernadotte eased it up.

And this time he was rewarded: '*Hey!* I see the light, Captain. I see the light.'

He smiled to himself and said nothing, but he flashed a 'thumbs-up' to Asha.

The next barrel uncovered the batten they were under and the fourth revealed a piece of white overall. Progress slowed for a minute then, for he had to move some of the lower barrels. One or two of them, leaning across others, were neither upright nor horizontal. These he simply wrestled round until they stood back in their places, giving him room to step down on to the floor. He was assessing his next move carefully – the barrel he had been standing on seemed to be supporting a slope of horizontal barrels like a stake holding back a pile of logs – when he heard a masculine groan.

'*Hey!*' cried an outraged Ann instantly.

'What?'

'He moved.'

'Good.'

'Good for you, maybe. You don't know *what* he moved.'

'He's stirring,' John called up to Asha.

'Is he all right?' Her voice echoed down strangely, as though he were hearing her through a faulty radio.

'Too soon to say. I think I'll need some help down here now. Marco and two men.'

While he waited, he sent up another barrel but getting to it made the batten under which Ann and Niccolo lay creak worryingly. Niccolo groaned again. This time Ann said nothing. 'Is he still moving?' asked John anxiously.

'Yes,' she snapped.

'Capitano,' called a voice from above, and Marco came scrambling down the barrels with all the youthful energy he expended on most of the things he did. The container began to shake again, a worrying movement which was exacerbated as his men climbed down behind him. John was heartily thankful he had asked for only three helpers. Any more would have toppled them on to the deck. 'Put these barrels back in place.' He gestured at the barrels which were lying about. *'Not that one! No!'* This last to Marco who was thoughtlessly reaching for the one that held all the others safe.

By a combination of pushing, pulling and pointing, he got them to place the barrels so that he could climb up safely to the top of the dangerous slope without putting any weight on the two trapped under it. Then it was just a matter of time before he had placed the slings round the last few barrels and had them lifted away. Finally, he let Marco move the upright barrel so that he could roll the last one away. There they lay, wedged under the batten in a space which should not have contained one of them, let alone two.

Asha climbed down and knelt beside the groaning man while Ann, patiently, lay still between him and the wall until they had checked that it would be safe to move him. Marco and his men stood ready to carry him up and out. As Asha gently rolled

Niccolo out on to the floor and began to check him more carefully for broken bones and internal injuries, John gave Ann
a hand to roll out into the light and climb to her unsteady feet.
Then he began to wave at Bernadotte.

Once again the webbing straps came down. 'This'll be the
safest way to get Niccolo out, as long as it's not going to damage
him to strap him in,' he said. 'The alternative is to let Marco's
men carry him.'

Asha looked at Marco's men. They looked like extras from
a pirate film. She looked at Marco. He smiled. He was exactly
like a great big, cheerful, willing, over-friendly, clumsy puppy.
'Use the straps,' she said.

John treated him like a barrel and tightened the straps round
his chest and thighs. While he did so, Asha turned to Ann
and they had a muttered conversation which apparently put
the doctor's mind at rest. Bernadotte could see what John
had done and he used a great deal of technique to raise the
unconscious man gently into the air. Asha immediately took off
after her patient, and Ann, a little more stiffly, followed after
her. John went up after the women, but paused and turned to
find Marco and his team following him. 'No,' he said, slowly,
trying to think of a word which would encapsulate the complex
of orders he wanted to give. '*Ordinato!*' It meant 'tidy' as far
as he understood. And that was how he wanted the interior of
the container. With long faces, the three men went back down.
John went on up. At the top of the container he paused, his
head and shoulders in the sunlight, his hips and legs still in the
container. He looked down to see the men working slowly and
fractiously below.

Then the shouting started and he was up and out in a flash.
'What is it?' he yelled down to Asha who was on the deck, beside
Niccolo already.

'Bernadotte!' she yelled back. 'The stupid bastard's dropped
Niccolo!'

In the container, Marco's men paused to listen to the
exchange. It was in English so they did not understand it.
Their eyes, however, followed the angry footsteps of the

captain as though they could see him through the steel of the container top. But their hands remained busy, and blind. They swung the next barrel back into position without noticing the slow drops of dull yellowish-green liquid leaking out of its side.

CHAPTER SIXTEEN

John hurled across the deck to where Niccolo's body lay sprawled on the green. Asha was crouching anxiously over him and the men of the day work gang stood in a solicitous circle. 'I think his leg is broken,' she flung over her shoulder. 'I can't say any more until I've checked him over thoroughly.'

John shot up the ladder to the crane control cockpit, but as he stepped on to the small steel balcony outside its door, he realised he had been beaten to it. Ann Cable was standing there, her slim figure tense with outrage, bellowing in fluent Italian at the stunned deckhand. John had no idea what she was saying to him, but the big man was clearly not enjoying it. She paused for breath. 'He says the control lever slipped,' Ann informed John. 'How could the control lever slip?' And she was off again, hurling a tirade of Italian at him. The big sailor had clearly just about had enough. He surged to his feet, huge paw raised.

'*Resta!*' snarled John, as though Bernadotte were a dog. But he need not have bothered. Ann was more than capable of holding her own against inarticulate, macho threats of violence. Indeed, having disarmed the huge man with her flow of invective, it was she herself, carried beyond control by his sullen, mute insolence, who struck the first blow, hurling herself into the little cabin to rain a series of slaps upon his simian face and bullet head.

John reached in and grabbed her round the waist. She paid no attention to his firm grasp and so it was easy enough for him to swing her out of the cab and set her feet on the top rung. 'That's enough,' he gasped, winded by her fury. 'Leave this to me now.'

She froze, as though waking unexpectedly from a dream. 'Go down,' he prompted, and, thoughtlessly obedient, she moved.

He swung back and met Bernadotte's eye. The giant's expression was murderous. I'm going to have to keep him under lock and key, thought John. '*Fuori!*' he snapped, emphasising the order with a jerk of his thumb.

'Zis bitch she hit me bad,' grumbled Bernadotte unexpectedly as he moved obediently.

'I'll sort it out later.' John was still so angry that the crewman's linguistic ability hardly made any impression. 'Go to your cabin now.'

John followed the bear-like back down to the cabin Bernadotte shared in the lower deck of the bridgehouse. His cabin mate was off watch and lying reading on his bunk, which was lucky. 'Which kit is yours?' John asked the man and such was his obvious rage that he was answered, not by the usual universal shrug but by instant action. The man pointed to a pile of clothing and books. 'Out,' snapped John. '*Fuori.*' The crewman picked up his stuff and shuffled out into the corridor. 'In!' he snarled at Bernadotte and, apparently in the grip of shock, Bernadotte obeyed.

John slammed the door and jammed his pass key in the lock. Let Bernadotte cool his heels there until he had this sorted out, he thought. And, he reckoned, it would give Salah a little more leeway as he settled into the bosun's job. 'You. Find yourself new quarters,' he ordered Bernadotte's erstwhile cabin mate. Then he spun on his heel and was gone. He would see the chief steward and make sure the man he had moved was comfortably housed. He would have to see the chief steward in any case to arrange Bernadotte's food. He was tempted to make it bread and water. When he was calmer, he would talk to Bernadotte and try to discover what exactly had happened. He would need to make a report in the log and accident report book. In the meantime, he had better see how his first officer was faring and arrange to take over his watches himself. Thank God Asha was here.

Niccolo was just coming round when John arrived in the infirmary. Both Asha and Ann were there at his bedside, and the only person who seemed to be doing any work was Fatima. The Neapolitan was shockingly pale and when at last his eyes did open, he was so unwell that he hardly registered the presence of the women at all. He strove to move when he saw John, and seemed to be trying to sit up. John crossed to him at once. 'Don't disturb yourself,' he said gently.

'The container . . .'

'It's fine. Marco's team are repacking it.'

'The drums . . .'

'They all seem fine. You just rest. You've had a rough time. We'll talk later.'

Niccolo lay back with a sigh. John was surprised that he did not ask about Bernadotte, but then he realised Niccolo knew nothing about his fall to the deck. He obviously assumed his injuries had originated inside the container. Well, they would sort this all out later. Niccolo was sinking back under the influence of the sedative Asha had given to him. He had regained consciousness only to fall asleep almost at once.

'Well?' asked John.

'I'm still not sure about his leg,' she said. 'I think he's all right otherwise.'

'Good. Ms Cable?'

'Call me Ann. I ache all over and losing my temper like that always pisses me off. Other than that, I'm okay.'

'If we can call it a day for the time being, I'll take you down into the hold myself, but later. I have some sorting out to do now.'

'That's fine, Captain,' she said.

His eyes met Asha's. She smiled at him with loving pride. And he realised the tone in Ann's voice betrayed the fact that when she called him Captain she really meant it.

During the next forty-eight hours the land closed in on either side and the traffic around them became denser as the shipping in the western Mediterranean was forced into the funnel of the Gibraltar approaches. John took Niccolo's watches between four and eight in every twelve hours. On the one hand, the

16.00–20.00 watch allowed him to get the feel of the ship and the way she worked more satisfactorily than he could as the captain. On the other hand, the watch between 04.00 and 08.00 took Asha and himself back to feeling that this was not a very satisfactory honeymoon. But she was as often at Niccolo's bedside as he was on duty; he was also concerned with checking the disposition of the containers and with holding an inquiry into the accident.

He had no time to keep his promise to show Ann the hold. Instead she took the opportunity afforded by his work on deck to watch him and his men replace the broken hawser and check all the others. They had to leave the loose container resting directly on top of the one beneath it because the timbers that had separated them were broken. She watched with fascination as every line was checked and tightened. She also attended Bernadotte's hearing which John held the morning after the accident in the infirmary so that Niccolo could listen. He was much improved but would have to stay in bed for a little longer, especially as the infirmary was not stocked with crutches.

Bernadotte was brought in by Cesar at nine o'clock while Marco held the watch. He looked mutinous, and presented himself as being perfectly innocent. He explained that the controls of the forward crane were faulty and had slipped in spite of his best efforts to lower the first mate gently. Cesar had already checked it at John's order. He found that it worked perfectly with heavy weights. Marco, too, had found no difficulty in lifting the barrels from the deck and lowering them back into the container yesterday. But when, at Salah's suggestion, Cesar tested the crane with several lengths of chain weighing about the same as a man, the gears slipped once in every five attempts. Bernadotte's claim might be true; the crane could be faulty. John kept him in custody while he continued to think things through.

They came under the Rock at the end of the first officer's morning watch on the third day after the accident. John was on the bridge. It was an overcast morning, with a low sky and a mist of thin rain almost obscuring the great white rockface. The wind and tide were running against them but *Napoli* chugged doggedly forward into the Strait. John went to stand beside the helmsman, one of a team Salah was training.

He stared narrow-eyed through the clearview, but there was little to see. The Atlantic proper did not begin until after Tangiers and Cap Spartel. The biggest waves they had met so far came in in series, however, causing *Napoli* to pitch a little. A fitting preparation for the Bay of Biscay.

The rear door to the bridge opened and closed. John turned and was surprised to see Niccolo limping in. His left leg was bound in a firm bandage. He had a length of metal piping in one hand which had been bent into a makeshift walking stick. He saw John looking at it and grinned. It was the first time John had seen him smile. 'Ann thought of it. She got one of El Jefe's men to do it. I'll take over my watch now if you like, sir.'

'All right, Number One. Take the watchkeeper's chair. Do you want a footstool?'

Before Niccolo could answer, the door was pushed open again and Ann Cable came in carrying one. The senior officers' eyes met. Both men smiled. Ann put the footstool down without seeing the shared look and straightened. 'Okay, Nico?'

Niccolo nodded and sat, swinging his leg up on to it. Ann turned to John, thoughtlessly wiping her palms down the thighs of her jeans. 'I think you've got time to show me stuff in the hold now.'

'Yes. It's a good time. I want to doublecheck it before we get into the Atlantic anyway. Even if Biscay fails to live up to its usual reputation, we need to be certain it's safe and sound.'

John had only been in the first hold but the other two were identically stowed. Once again, Ann disdained to wear the protective clothing the scientists had brought, but they both put on rainwear as the drizzle was beginning to thicken. John took a flashlamp since the hold lights were still not functioning and Ann armed herslf with a small Geiger counter. Together, they scurried down to the relative shelter between the first two piles of containers which stood astride the hatch cover to number

one hold. They went down the ladder with extra care; for the
first time in a while the decks were wet with rain and the metal
rungs were slippery beneath their feet.

'Is it just me?' asked John, sweeping the broad, bright beam
across the pile of grey concrete blocks. 'I find this lot very sinister
indeed.'

'No,' she said, watching the display on the Geiger counter.
'This stuff is sinister. Worse than the barrels. I didn't much relish
being trapped under the barrels but I would sure as hell hate to
be under a pile of these. I'm getting a reading here. Did any of
Faure's men get a reading?'

'No.' John turned, his first instinct to get well out of the place.
She saw his reaction and laughed.

'Don't worry. It's not enough to do you any damage. You're
sure they didn't mention it?'

'No, I'm certain. I would have remembered.'

'Yeah,' she said quietly, 'I guess.'

In the second hold, there was no reading. John was relieved
but Ann was not so sure. As they moved up, across and down
into the forward hold, her face was folded into a frown.

In the third hold, the Geiger counter again buzzed quietly
and Ann hissed almost angrily. 'I want to see Faure about this,'
she said.

'I'd better come down with them on a regular basis,' said John,
worried by her readings, even though she had said they were low,
nothing to worry about.

'Yes. Me too,' she answered. 'And I take back what I said.
In future, we'd better wear the protective outfits.'

'But it's nothing to worry about, right?' he persisted.

'No. As it stands, you have nothing to worry about at all.'

'Good.'

She went to find Faure the minute they got back to the
bridgehouse. He went up on to the bridge again. They were
off Tarifa now. The coast of Africa was running almost parallel
to their course off the port beam and would continue to do so for
a while; but after Tarifa, Spain pulled away sharply northwards
up towards Cadiz. John stood silently, looking forward, his

eyes blind to the movements of the traffic coming and going before and beside them, though he would have reacted quickly enough if anything threatened to cut their course. Dead ahead, the Atlantic was concealed behind curtains of rain. The sea was turning green below its silvery surface. There was a feeling of change in the air.

Two figures walked down the deck towards the first hold. They were wearing bulky protective clothing. He didn't need to see their faces to know they would be Ann and Faure.

His mind turned uneasily to the radioactivity Ann had detected in the holds. If Faure's equipment had registered anything he would have mentioned it. He had not. Therefore his equipment registered nothing. Ann's Geiger counter did register something in the first and third holds, however. Not much, but something. This might mean that the Greenpeace equipment was more sensitive than Disposoco's. That would not surprise him. But there had been no register in the second hold.

So, then again, perhaps the discrepancy was not in the equipment. And if that was the case, then even a low reading was worrying today, for it had not been there yesterday. And if a progression – a deterioration – was starting, then God alone knew what the reading would be tomorrow.

Napoli seemed to stand still. Spray exploded up and away on either side of her flared bow. John rocked forward on to the balls of his feet and smiled at the familiar motion as she swooped forward down the back of her first real Atlantic roller. It would soon be time to turn her head north for Liverpool and home.

And not an instant too soon.

CHAPTER SEVENTEEN

Although they turned onto a heading north of west almost as soon as they exited the Strait of Gibraltar, they did not turn due north until they had cleared Spain and Portugal at 35.30N;12.30W. Soon after that, Salah himself swung them back eastwards, onto the heading they actually needed to follow in order to get round Biscay, across the Western Approaches and up through St George's Channel to Liverpool. All through that time – and it took them another week to reach the English port – the prevailing wind was from the west and as soon as they came north of Coruna a north-westerly gale whirled in hard. This meant that waves and weather were always pushing them towards the distant coast – prevailing conditions which were at the root of Biscay's reputation.

If the Mediterranean had taken them from unseasonal summer to dull autumn, there was no doubting that these were winter waters. Tall and grey, the Atlantic swells thumped relentlessly on *Napoli*'s port quarter, rhythmically, unvaryingly, except that, as the storm wound up, the power of their impact intensified. The wind, which also intensified as time went on, brought squall after squall of rain, so that the decks were never dry and even the containers standing twenty feet above them were awash with rain or spray.

Now it was easy enough to see the difference between the sailors and the landlubbers aboard. Of the latter, only Ann Cable remained unaffected. Even Asha went off her food and Faure's scientists all seemed to vanish without trace. With or without them, twice a day, John and Ann clambered into the white protective clothing and checked the contents of the holds. This was a difficult procedure in the bulky suits with their thick gloves, cushioned boots and unwieldy compressed-air packs, but as the weather deteriorated, it became positively hazardous.

Even going on deck became dangerous, so much so that John, Cesar and Niccolo arranged for lifelines to be strung. Bernadotte cheerfully stayed snug and dry locked in his cabin, mysteriously supplied with an almost infinite selection of varyingly pornographic magazines, until John and Salah made a great show of relenting with the big seaman and released him. Then they put him to work with the gang rigging the lifelines. Cesar and John himself were in charge of this and for almost a whole watch, first one then the other worked out in the blast, faces numbed by the vicious rain and eyes slitted as though against sleet, heaving the lines tight against their anchor points with the deckhands grumbling and swearing around them. But everyone felt safer when it was finished.

Helping the crew to feel safe was increasingly important, for there was no doubt that Ann's readings in the hold were accurate: the nuclear waste in its lead coffins jacketed in cement was stirring, like some legendary, long-dead vampire hungry for blood. The readings were slight, but the fact that they existed at all gave cause for concern. And that concern had an impact far greater than it actually warranted. It seemed to open unimagined doors, like positive proof of a haunting or a UFO. Ann kept her records meticulously and showed them to John, carefully explaining the precise meaning of the slight variations from the flat horizontal on her graphs. To John, the little peaks, the coming and going of reaction on her Geiger counter, looked like readings on a heart monitor. They looked like life. And even though she persisted that they were nothing to worry about, that they might even be residual readings from previous cargoes, he chanced to overhear her talking to someone on the ship-to-shore, making one of her routine reports to Greenpeace in London, and she sounded worried to him.

He did everything he could to spoil his nervous crew without making them actually suspicious of his motives. The chef was prompted to outdo himself with culinary delights, and the indisposition of the scientists meant there was more food to go round. As the weather worsened, day work was scaled down and John released more and more of the videos *Parnethope* had supplied along with the oil and food in Naples. He tried to have the television permanently retuned to some worthy, challenging, educational channel; his objective was to give the men something other than the cargo to think about, but whenever he left the set unguarded, it mysteriously returned to French or Italian game shows – especially those involving loss of clothing as a forfeit. Still, he would rather they thought about sex than fission. And, in truth, there was little or no day work to be done in these conditions. Above decks and outside the bridgehouse became increasingly no-go areas. Enthusiasm for making do and mending inside their own quarters was strictly limited. Niccolo nursed a burning ambition to get the engine up to scratch but El Jefe was jealous of his terrain and allowed only his engineers down onto the engineering decks and, with his leg only mending slowly, the first officer was no match for the chief engineer.

At the end of five dour days plodding up across the unforgiving ocean, they passed some fifty miles off Land's End, a little less than twenty miles west of Bishop Rock, with the distinctive, fifteen-second flash of the light briefly visible between gale squalls which kept trying to attain storm force.

It was 18.00, the time when John and Ann now regularly inspected the holds while Salah stood at the wheel and Niccolo held the con. John had released a carefully calculated amount of liquor from the stores and, as on Heritage Mariner ships, the crew would now retire to the bar for a drink or two before dinner at 19.00. On the bridge, Niccolo stood uneasily on one firm leg and watched them walking along the deck. The wind was whipping so hard across the open expanse of green-painted steel that the paint itself seemed to be rippling, in danger of being peeled away by the blast. Even when the rain died down, spray still slid like sheet ice across the deck and the two white-clothed figures leaned at strange angles, moving awkwardly and keeping hold of the lifelines as though scaling a cliff face.

Out on the deck itself, communication was impossible. The wind buffeted out of the gathering murk of the early evening as though silent explosions were occurring regularly beside them. The water plucked at their feet and, whenever a wave broke over the hull to windward, tried to rugby-tackle their knees. The thickness of the gloves made the lifelines hard to hold but at least they protected hands which would otherwise have been numbed and torn. John followed Ann down the deck, pausing once in a while to wipe the spray off his face mask, taking a brief opportunity to look around. There was no real sense of sky or sea, merely a writhing greyness darkening and gathering in. Once, away to eastwards, he saw the flash of Bishop Rock Lighthouse like a star and it gave a kind of depth to the day, enough to make him feel insignificant in the face of the granite-coloured vastness. But then another squall closed down and it was gone. This ought to be the last visit under these conditions, he thought gratefully. They would have swung into St George's Channel by the end of Niccolo's watch and with any luck, the bulk of Ireland would give them some protection.

He opened the hatch only a little, just enough to let the pair of them scramble down. They had a simple routine which they had worked out nearly a week ago: he held the torch and she explored with the Geiger counter. As he stood at the foot of the ladder, keeping the broad white beam steady on her, he felt almost glad to be down here. Things were so foul on deck that the sepulchral stillness below decks was a positive relief. Stillness of air only. The double bottom was pitching and heaving beneath them. The seas were throwing themselves against the hull with thunderous force. It was not even dry; spray and rain from the deck above came drizzling in through the open hatch and fell through the torch beam like diamonds in the air. The metal beneath their feet was shallowly awash with a dull, dirty little sea of water, made as agitated as its great wild cousin outside by the motion of the ship beneath it. After a few minutes, Ann was back at his side, shaking her head: no change in the reading.

It was the same in the other holds. The news should have cheered him, especially as they were little more than thirty-six hours from their destination, but something else was nagging at his mind. In the last hold before they went up and returned to the relative calm of the bridge and warmth and dinner, he paused. She stood at his side and waited as he flashed the beam of the flashlight up the dark grey metal walls. They were running with water, slick as sea rocks. Yes. That was what they reminded him of. As a boy he had been taken to the Wexford coast near Cahore Point. Of all the things he had seen there, what had impressed him most had been the look of the sea sliding over the black peat-stained clay where the rivers ran across the beaches. This looked the same: glassy water sliding over a black-grey surface. And, as it had at that seaside of his childhood, grains of vivid sand collected in the nooks and crannies; not much, just enough to emphasise their outlines. He knelt and pushed his gloved fingers through the restless surface of the water. His padded boots had disguised the fact that he had been standing on a thin sprinkling of sand which was washing over the steel. Frowning, he flashed the torch around and around again. There was nothing else to see but something of it stayed in his mind. Had the water in the holds simply washed the sand down off the concrete blocks, or was there more sand coming into them from somewhere else outside?

It was the lights that guided them up the Irish sea, though they could not be seen through the storm and in any case they fell back below the horizon as soon as the land did, into the Bristol Channel north of Land's End. But their call signs were there for Jesus to contact as *Napoli* butted northwards. His radio remained tuned either to them or to his favourite fading station with its lilting Flamenco music. Round Island and Longships, then Pendeen, Godrevy and Trevose all came and went. Hartland Point and Lundy gave over to Skokholm, Smalls-Rock and South Bishop.

But the stately progress was constantly interrupted. First John bustled in for his evening call to CZP's office in Palermo. Then he ordered Jesus to contact Heritage Mariner and route the call through to the captain's office. Here he talked at length to Richard. The two men discussed the progress Richard was making on their plan to get Salah and Fatima into a new life together. They had little time to pull things off – Liverpool was less than thirty-six hours away.

When John was finished, Ann turned up. She contacted Greenpeace's offices in London most evenings and, although she made no great show of secrecy, Jesus never quite managed to find out what she was saying. She was relaying her readings on the cargo – that he understood; but her reports sometimes lasted for twenty minutes or more.

Now that Salah had stopped trying to contact his erstwhile colleagues, that was all the outgoing business Jesus had come to expect. After seven he went down to dinner, and left the receiver on automatic for the rest of the night unless he wanted to listen to his Flamenco station before he went to bed. He could do this safely in the knowledge that the watchkeeper would inform him of any unexpected incoming messages. And all through the passage so far, there had been no incoming messages after seven.

Until tonight.

The first that John knew about it was the sound of some-one banging on his outer door, calling his name. He sat up and groped for the light switch. 'What time is it?' mumbled Asha.

'Not quite midnight.'

'That's Fatima,' she said, waking up properly. 'I'll come out too.'

Fatima tumbled in through the door in a state of high excitement, halfway between elation and frustration. 'Salah's on the radio now,' she gasped. 'They want us to go at once.'

'Who?'

'It's the PLO. Tewfik al Ashwari at last. He came through ten minutes ago. He wants us to go ashore now. He has a route to get us back.'

'Ashore? Where?'

'The Irish Republic. There's a way to get us back along an IRA gunrunning route.'

Asha sat down suddenly, her face dead white. John too felt a little faint. The brush with the Tunisian gunboat was one thing – an episode with an almost dreamlike quality – but this was something else. This was uncomfortably close to home. The thought of these two being smuggled east by IRA gunrunners as though they were semtex being returned to Libya was deeply shocking and quite terrifying.

John opened his mouth to say something but then the phone in his office buzzed. It was Salah, speaking from the radio shack. 'Has Fatima explained?' His voice was abrupt, yet vibrantly alive.

'Yes.'

'Can you do it?'

'Where exactly do you want to go?'

'There's an estuary south of Cahore Point, the River Black-water.'

John was stunned. He knew it. It was the very place he had been thinking of in the hold so recently, where the ribs of black clay ran out across the white sand beach.

'Where are we now?' he asked, his mind still reeling.

There was a rumble of sound as Salah called through into the bridge. Then, 'Just coming up to 52.30 north, about twenty miles out.'

John closed his eyes. He could see the Irish coastline in his mind, cut across with the eastings. It was not only possible, it was easy. The rendezvous was well chosen. 'Take the helm yourself,' he ordered. 'Bring her round to due west. I'll give you a more precise heading later. Get Jesus to ring the chief. We need maximum revolutions. Is Cesar up there?'

'Yes.'

'Tell him we need a good man on the Collision Alarm Radar. I'll be up in five minutes.'

In fact it was nearer ten. He dressed quickly and then, while Asha and Fatima continued their conversation next door, he squatted in front of the ship's safe in his office. At the very back,

in a small wooden case, there was an old but well-maintained
pistol with a couple of boxes of cartridges to fit it. John knew
little about guns, but he recognised this as a Beretta. It was, in
fact a Model 34, chambered for the 9mm cartridge and marked
with the letters RM denoting Naval issue. It had been issued to
Captain Fittipaldi when he had been posted Lieutenant in the
Italian Navy so many years ago.

As John pulled the box out into the light, something else came
with it. A small book. John glanced at this, sidetracked. It was
Gina Fittipaldi's passport. That was a surprise – he remembered
giving Gina her passport before she left the ship. It was Lazar's
passport which had been missing. He put the document back
where he had found it. He would think this through later. He
had more important business now.

On the bridge, he called Eduardo up to take the wheel while
Salah went below to make his minuscule preparations. He had
lost two sets of kit in little more than a week and had almost
nothing left. Cesar remained bent over the Collision Alarm
Radar. Niccolo appeared. Ann turned up.

John and Salah pored over the chart of the Wexford coast
as the Palestinian explained what his mysterious contact had
required of him. Once again, John was struck anew by the
coincidence, but his surprise was immediately subsumed in his
feeling of how lucky it was that he should know the area. The
instructions were simple but even so, it would be a good thing to
have a man with some local knowledge along. It never occurred
to him that he should let Salah and Fatima go alone, though
the thought that he might find himself confronted with active
members of the IRA made his flesh crawl.

Napoli anchored off the mouth of the Blackwater at two and
by the time the anchor had settled on the shallow silty bottom,
the cutter was in the water and its motor was pushing them
shoreward towards the little river's mouth.

'Asha may never forgive you,' warned Fatima, raising her
voice over the slap of the waves, the grumble of the engine and
the moaning of the wind. 'I don't know whether she was angrier
about you coming or about you forbidding her to come herself.'

John shrugged, though the movement was all but invisible in the near dark. Above them, the last rags of storm cloud ran away from the waxing moon. In the bow, the hunched shape of Salah moved. There was a double click as he worked the action of the Beretta. John put all thoughts of Asha and their brief disagreement out of his mind and concentrated on the black rise of the shoreline and the river valley cutting between the dunes. The dunes were only twenty feet high and the river not much more than ten feet wide. The cutter drew eighteen inches but, even so, they wouldn't be able to get all that far up – to the first great reed bed, that was all. He gunned the engine as they entered the river's outwash; the force of the water had been intensified by the storm rain of the last few days. The west wind gusted past them, heavy with rich land smells. The little cutter pitched, then settled into the Blackwater's dark stream, pushing them forward across the pale expanse of beach between the low black clay banks and into Ireland itself.

They got further up the river than he had thought they would, for he remembered it in summer drought whereas now it was winter flood. 'A mile upstream,' Salah had said. 'Well behind the dunes. There is an old landing stage. If we leave the boat there, we can follow a path across the fields.' This too John remembered, though what lay beyond it was vague. Even as a child, he thought grimly, he had remembered water, not land.

It took them thirty minutes to cover that mile, through the deserted, wind-whispering pastures. It was a short enough time, but for each of them it had a strange intensity. For John there was a dreamlike double focus given by his half-remembered memories of the place. For Fatima the quiet countryside falling away on either hand behind the dunes into rich broad water meadows was a mockery. So much gentle peacefulness was just a pathway for herself and the man she loved back into the violence she had thought they had escaped. For Salah, the whole short river voyage was the beginning of a test. A test of himself as he was now, of the past he had lived through, of almost the last friend he had in the Arab world. Though he was a peaceful man in spite of his warlike expertise, the Beretta still felt comforting in his hand.

He wanted so much to believe what Tewfik's familiar voice had promised over the radio link a couple of hours ago. He wanted to believe that they needed him back in spite of his unpopular beliefs, his unique points of view and his unwelcome advice. But he really believed that this was a trap. That there was someone out there across those silent, silver, moonbathed fields who was waiting to kill him. He would have to be extremely careful to make sure they did not kill Fatima and John as well.

The landing stage was ancient and rotten; a worm-eaten pier lost in tall rushes, three crumbling brick steps up to an overgrown path. They climbed like poachers over a crazy five-barred gate and followed the scar of the ancient pathway across a field full of sleeping cows. John looked ahead. Beyond the hedges defining another couple of fields was a clump of trees. The rendezvous was in whatever lay at the heart of those trees. He had promised Asha that he would just drop them off and come straight back to *Napoli*. 'I'm only going because I know the way and so that I can bring the cutter back,' he had told her. It had been the first conscious lie of their marriage.

The second hedge was actually a dilapidated estate wall overgrown with blackthorn and briars. They had to climb over it for the pathway led them to a great arched gateway with padlocked iron gates. 'This is Blackwater Hall,' breathed John as they clustered by the wall. 'I came here as a child. I remember it now. It was closed during the troubles in the nineteen-twenties. I never dared go in – they say it's haunted.'

Had the other two felt any inclination to laugh at his childish superstition, they lost it when they climbed down into the grounds. They found themselves in the feral remains of a formal garden. Rhododendrons run to seed loomed massively, concealing rotting moss-grown statuary. More than one marble nymph eternally contemplating her pale nudity in a long dry carp pond almost had her head blown off by Salah's Beretta. Rose bushes, deformed by years of growing madly out of control, caught at them like caged monsters from the ruins of decorative arbours. The stench of rotting honeysuckle escaped from fragrant walks untrodden for seventy years and threatened to choke them whenever the wind fell. And when it was high, they were surrounded by the sounds of dead things moving and the skittering of live things running amok.

At the foot of a great stone staircase twenty feet wide they stopped. Some way above it, still cloaked in shadows, stood the house. Salah looked at the luminous dial of his watch. 'We're to be there at three or they go without us,' he breathed.

'Do we go on in together?' whispered John in reply.

'We go on together but I go in alone,' ordered Salah and was off before Fatima could begin a debate.

They went up the staircase three abreast and across a rutted expanse of treacherous tufts which must once have been the croquet lawn. Then there was another, smaller, staircase which led up to an ornamental balustrade and, beyond it, the house.

Originally, Blackwater Hall must have stood five stories high. The bottom three remained in the centre, though the wings stood only two stories high. Above fat, ivy-cankered walls, skeletal chimney stacks clawed up through disintegrated attics and seemed to tremble in the wind. The glassless gape of the windows seemed to soak up the pale moonlight while the crazy pile of rotting masonry gave the wind a hundred new voices – and none of them sounded sane. In the centre of that frowning Gothic folly stood a pointed Norman arch where doors massive enough to grace a cathderal leaned crazily half open, mutely inviting them to enter.

John understood very clearly how superstition had been so quick to flourish around the place. When he was ten nothing on earth would have got him in through those doors. He had no intention of letting Salah go in now. 'You're not going in there,' he said.

'It's where the rendezvous is, in five minutes' time.'

'Let's just wait a bit and think this through.'

'John's right, Salah. Let's wait a moment.'

They sank back down so that their heads were just level with the balustrade. From here they had a clear view of the whole front of the hall.

Salah asked, 'What was the point of coming if we don't go in?'

'We can go in,' answered Fatima. 'We just don't want to go rushing into a trap.'

'That's right,' said John. 'You don't want a repeat of the Tunisian gunboat. If anyone shoots at you here they won't be shooting blind.'

'Our first objective is to stay alive,' insisted Fatima.

'And this is the IRA you're dealing with'.

'After twenty years of dealing with the PLO. If we are not there by three, Tewfik says they will go without us.'

'If they really mean to help us they will wait.'

'If there's actually anyone there at all,' said John. 'The place is as quiet as the grave.'

And so they sat and watched the apparently deserted house, but all that happened was that time ticked by – five past the hour. Ten past. Then a flash of movement jerked them all to full alertness. But it was only a fox running in through the open door. 'That's it,' hissed Salah, 'I'm going in.'

And from deep within Blackwater Hall came a great flash of light followed immediately by a clap of earthbound thunder. The three watchers were hurled down the steps to lie in a bundle at the bottom while a great force swept by above them and bits of plant debris, rubble and smouldering wood rained down on them.

Then they ran in silence through the fire-bright garden and out across the scarred field milling with terrified cattle to the rushy landing place where *Napoli*'s cutter tugged at her line as keen to be gone down the river as they were. They checked it from stem to stern for bombs before they went aboard.

They got back to *Napoli* before four and John ordered a course full ahead for Liverpool, then Salah, Fatima and he accompanied Asha to their cabin. They sat in silence for a while, the three of them trying to come to terms with what had happened and what it meant and the fourth trying to come to terms with their silence. At last she could bear it no longer. 'What happened?' Asha asked.

Salah got up and walked to the door. Fatima rose and followed him. At the door itself, the tall Palestinian turned. 'An old friend sent me a message; that's what happened,' he said. And he left John to explain what he meant.

No one saw anything much of any of them during the next day or night; even the usual radio traffic was suspended while they caught up on some much-needed sleep as *Napoli* crossed the Irish sea and Niccolo pushed her firmly back onto her schedule. Then John came up onto the bridge just before the first morning watch twenty-seven hours later as they ran along the north coast of Wales towards the mouth of the River Mersey.

Niccolo remained on the bridge at eight, with Ann content to stay sleepless too. Marco arrived right on time but even before he could sign on Asha had arrived as well. Within moments, Salah and Fatima, Cesar and Jesus had all arrived. They watched the late daybreak pull back the grey horizons until the land was revealed, a brown bulge ahead and to the starboard, which seemed to be leaking down into the brownish, dirty sea they were ploughing through. It was the outwash of the Mersey and it turned even the foam of her wake to the colour of old ivory.

When the helicopter dropped out of the overcast, it came as complete surprise. John swung round to see through the open door of the radio room that Jesus was fiddling with the tuning on the VHF.

'*Napoli* . . . I say again, please respond . . .'

'This is *Napoli*, helicopter, please repeat.'

'I have orders to bring Captain Higgins ashore at once. Please contact Liverpool harbour master on . . .'

The radio relayed orders and frequencies. Nobody except Jesus paid any attention. All the others were looking at John. John himself seemed deep in thought. This was worryingly reminiscent of Naples, quite apart from possible repercussions of more recent adventures. His flesh crawled. Suddenly he regretted having stayed so much out of contact. But no. He gave himself a mental shake. If there had been anything important, Richard would have contacted him.

'Right, Niccolo, you have her. We're still a longish way out and I have no doubt I will be back before we actually get into the river. I expect you'll be picking up the pilot soon, though, so you'll be able to refer to him in any uncertainty. I expect we will be taken to the Seaforth container terminal, though we may have to wait for the tide. If any port authorities, Customs men and so forth come aboard before I get back, tell them they will have to wait for me before they can proceed.'

He swung round to look at Salah and Fatima. 'I will make a phone call as soon as I get ashore and find out what Richard has in mind for you. He'll have thought of something to get you off safely, I'm sure.'

He put his arm round Asha and pressed his first husbandly kiss against her cheek as though he was just off to the office. She hugged him and whispered, 'Darling . . .'

There was nowhere for the helicopter to land; but it hovered and John climbed a Jacob's ladder up to its silver side. As he climbed, he was forcefully reminded of his arrival, by the same means, on *Napoli* for the first time. It was typical, he thought wryly, the accommodation ladders were fixed and working perfectly now he had no need of them.

In the body of the helicopter was a crew of two. One to welcome him aboard and one to fly the machine. Neither of them had anything to tell him. He looked back for *Napoli* but she was already out of sight as they raced across West Kirby and the narrow Wirral penisula to Birkenhead, then over the river to the port buildings on the north shore and the heliport behind them.

There was a car waiting but, again, the driver was unforthcoming. In silence he drove John back into the port itself, eventually dropping him outside one of Liverpool's great container terminals.

A light flurry of rain dashed across the grey cobblestones and thundered into the thin walls of the huge, hangar-sized building. John was inside at a run. When he stopped and looked around, he noticed how quiet it was; he was utterly alone. The huge building was as darkly cavernous as *Napoli*'s holds, but seemingly infinitely larger. John's footsteps echoed eerily and he was suddenly overcome by a crushing loneliness. Since the wedding he had been surrounded by people. He remembered how crowded the old freighter had seemed. He missed that feeling now. He thought how slow the *Napoli* had been, making her dogged way here. Well, now he was here and nothing was happening. There was a wrenching, painful feeling of anticlimax. He turned his head automatically, and realised with a shiver that he was looking for Asha. How much he had come to rely on her – and so quickly. And here he was, stuck in an empty container terminal like the last kid left in a boarding school on the final day of term.

Never one to stand and mope, he pushed the feeling down and went off to explore. He knew these gigantic port buildings well and he was certain that if he crossed to the far side, opposite the door he had entered by, he would find an exit to the quayside. And so it proved. Great hangar doors reached up to the roof far above him, far too massive to be opened by a mere mortal, but in one of them was a smaller, man-sized door. He opened this and stepped out. On either side, the tarmac stretched away, marked with the steel tracks of huge cargo-handling gantries, giant cousins of the gallows aft of *Napoli*'s bridgehouse. Beyond these structures rearing stark and silent against the sky stood cranes; more distant still were the great oyster-grabs which bit into cargoes of coal and the like. All of these iron monsters stood along the margin of the Mersey like dinosaurs frozen in time. They were absolutely silent. Utterly still.

John crossed to the railing and looked down into the wide, dark and dirty river. Its surface was marked with the rainbow-coloured slicks of oil and petrol, rippled by lines of wind, pocked and blistered by the increasingly heavy rain. Flotsam swirled idly in the brown grip of the current and swept past the vertical plunge of the quayside he was standing on, looking for a bank which would let it rest as jetsam. A gull screamed, loud enough to make him jump. He tried to count the number of times he had been here or nearby, offloading ships or catching the Isle of Man ferry. It seemed an alien place, lonely, vaguely threatening; nothing like home at all.

On the far side of the building, a car drew up. A door

slammed. John turned and went back in. Distantly, a figure entered the terminal and hurried up the echoing football-pitch length of it towards him. John gasped with recognition. It was Richard Mariner. Already suspecting something was very wrong, John hurried forward towards his old friend. Richard's face was drawn. He disregarded John's outthrust hand.

'Let's move,' he rasped without preamble. 'The press'll be here in a minute. We've got to get you away.'

John had no idea what his old friend was talking about. My God! he thought. Could it be what happened in Ireland? Was that it?

Richard wrestled a newspaper out of the pocket of his Burberry. 'Didn't you see the news last night?'

'Not the English news, no.' John's took the paper and began to unfold it.

'You mean you don't even *know*?'

LIVERPOOL DOCKS CLOSE, said the headline on the top of the front page.

John felt a kind of relief wash over him. He looked up at Richard. 'Damn! That means—'

'Read on,' Richard said.

John's eyes followed the page down and widened with shock at what he saw: DOCK WORKERS VOTE TO STRIKE: 'WE WILL NEVER HANDLE LEPER SHIP *NAPOLI*'S CARGO'.

CHAPTER EIGHTEEN

There weren't many places they could go in order to think; John had not passed through any of the official channels coming ashore and might technically be seen as an illegal immigrant. Further, the whole of the British press would be down on him like a ton of bricks once they knew he was here. And where the press went, the authorities might well follow. If anyone official went aboard *Napoli* before they had thought of some way of dealing with Salah and Fatima, there was a very real danger that the two PLO members would be arrested. That was in many ways Richard's most agonising frustration. All his hard work and planning had borne fruit. He had made arrangements to smuggle Salah and Fatima ashore and then away into safety, plans which relied on *Napoli* docking quietly and unloading with no attention being paid to her. There was nothing he could do about getting them ashore now. Once again, they were doomed to remain aboard *Napoli*. John listened to his old friend, wondering when it would be best to mention Blackwater Hall – and the message the bomb there had sent to Salah.

The heliport had a small coffee bar; it was unnaturally quiet while the docks were closed, and it had a public telephone available. It would do well enough to work out their next move.

John bought a couple of coffees and some biscuits, glad to have something positive to do. Then he sat silently at a small, mock mahogany table. Richard went off with his company phone card to get in touch with Heritage Mariner's main office.

'So,' said John when Richard returned. 'Where do we stand?'

'I've been on to Italy all morning, ever since the news first broke. I'm surprised no one's been on to you. But I expect that's because the man's flying in himself. He should be here in twenty minutes. We've got time to make some plans.'

'Ok,' said John, 'but first I've something I have to tell you . . .'

In fact it was nearly half an hour before Verdi arrived, fizzing with energy and wanting to get straight down to business.

'CZP are happy that Disposoco's chartering of *Napoli* should continue,' he said.

'At current rates?' asked Richard. He wasn't directly involved, of course, certainly not with that side of it. But the shipowner in him couldn't resist the question.

Verdi flashed the big Englishman a venomous look. 'The rates will of course be open to negotiation when we know more.'

'They will have to be,' said John abruptly. 'You got away with your performance in Naples by the skin of your teeth. If you wish to avoid an open mutiny when you break this news to your crew, you'll have to offer them a great deal more money.'

Verdi was affronted. 'Captain, it is hardly your place—'

'He's right, though,' interrupted Richard. 'And you'll have to keep it in mind. What does Disposoco propose? Responsibility for *Napoli*'s cargo is theirs.'

'Of course they are looking for somewhere to place this industrial waste. Mr Nero will be contacting me via Heritage Mariner at any moment. Thank you for facilitating this, Mr Mariner.'

'Nigeria,' murmured John wearily. It was not a suggestion; it was an accusation.

'No!' Verdi was stung. But not, perhaps, outraged. 'There is no suggestion of dumping it in the Third World. We all wish to have it properly disposed of.'

'Then your options are limited,' said Richard.

'Severely so,' agreed Verdi. 'I understand Disposoco were relying on the English, after the trouble in Italy.'

Richard nodded. Silence fell.

John looked at his friend over the rim of his coffee cup. They had discussed a wide breadth of plans and possibilities while waiting for the Italian. They were both men of action, used to thinking on their feet, but even so they had chosen to talk through a range of scenarios, variously contingent on what Nero in Italy arranged and what Verdi in Liverpool demanded. But they could hardly discuss these in front of the man from CZP.

'How is *Prometheus* coming along?' asked John, as much for something to say as from any immediate desire to know. He had spent a lot of time thinking about his command of the Heritage Mariner tanker. But not recently, he realised with a start. Recently he had become absolutely involved with his current command. He had stopped being a caretaker, a stand-in. He had become the captain of the *Napoli*. And he wanted to bring her safely to port.

'Getting restless?' asked Richard. 'I don't blame you.'

'As a matter of fact, no. I just want to know how she's getting through her refit.'

'Slowly and carefully.'

'So she's not ready yet in any case.'

'Not yet.'

'Right.'

'Oh, by the way,' said Richard suddenly. 'I forgot to tell you, we found your cases. All safe and sound. I have them in the back of my car outside.'

'Hey, that's wonderful,' began John, feeling quite bucked up by the unexpectedly good news.

The phone started ringing. It was the Heritage Mariner office transferring a call for Verdi. Five minutes later, he came bustling back into the room. 'Is solved,' he said, rubbing his hands in glee. 'Is all solved, *semplice*!'

All three of them went back on board. The helicopter flight began as a tripartite discussion but soon John and Richard were locked in a deep, quiet discussion which excluded the suspicious Italian.

Napoli's speed had been cut the moment John left and so they found her, only just holding steerage way against the current and tide, almost stationary in relation to the shore. All had not been quiet, however, for the crew began to get restless the moment the headway fell off, and Jesus was inundated with calls from news reporters which would have taxed his English even had he known what his interrogators were talking about. The minute they climbed out of the helicopter, tension on the battered old ship rose further. They felt eyes following them as they ran up the wet deck through the desultory rain, a feeling which intensified as soon as they entered the bridgehouse, in spite of the fact that there was no one to be seen. No one, even, to be heard.

On the bridge itself, the same reception committee was waiting as had been in attendance the first time Verdi and Nero had come aboard, under Sorrento. John automatically crossed to the watchkeeper's chair, pointedly vacated by Niccolo the moment his captain entered. He dumped down the cases he was carrying and stood for a moment, thinking. Richard crossed to that side of the bridge too, standing just in front of Ann Cable, with Asha, Salah and Fatima, to face the Italian. Verdi glared at them, clearly not happy with what was going on here. John waited, testing the silence, his mind racing. What happened during the next few minutes could do irreparable damage to his command and the only way they were going to come through this now was if they all stood together.

All of them.

'Mr Verdi,' he said, before the company man could speak, 'the entire ship's company can fit into the crew's dining salon and I suggest that we assemble the whole complement there except for the watchkeepers and allow you to break your news to everybody at once. I do not want any rumours starting that the officers and other senior interested parties got special treatment here.' He looked round, and everyone nodded.

'I hold the papers,' said Richard. 'I'll take the watch if I may. Salah, will you stand it with me? You've been bosun on enough ships of mine. I know I can trust you with the helm. Fatima, could you keep an eye on the radar, perhaps? I think the three of us have something to discuss in any case.'

And so it was done. The outsiders stayed on the bridge, giving the crew a chance to stand together. After all that had happened, all the tensions and suspicions that had been grown up, it was a necessary move. Richard felt it with a sensitivity almost as strong as John's knowledge.

The crew's dining salon was split as it had been for that earlier speech of John's – could it be only three weeks ago? – along lines of language understood rather than responsibilities undertaken. As on that other occasion, the crew stood and faced speaker and translators with a sullen resentfulness. They expected trouble because that was all they ever got; that was the kind of seamen they were or they would not have been in Piraeus, willing to sign CZP's shady contracts. The deck officers and the engineering officers looked guarded. They were no prize crewmen either. Only the scientists looked unconcerned: they were company men. They expected company protection. The company men were also the only ones in the room not to register the increasing revolutions of the engines and the slow swing to port, the only ones who did not check round furtively to look for El Jefe, who was missing.

Verdi spoke. 'Well, gentlemen, and . . . ah, ladies, I am sure you have some idea of our current situation. The *Napoli* and you who crew her, having been leased to Disposoco, are still legally under their control until such time as we have delivered their cargo. That is in the contract we hold with them, and in the contract we hold with you. No matter where that cargo is delivered, or when.'

The silence was glacial. He licked his lips and looked around. 'As you know,' he continued, raising his voice over the running translations, 'we have aboard a cargo of industrial waste taken from the desert in Lebanon and intended for delivery in Naples. The situation in Italy made it necessary for us to send it, and you, to England. But the English have gone on strike rather than handle it.' The expression on his face showed clearly what he personally thought of the English. A hiss of shock went round the room.

'Yes. It is true. The English will not touch it. Only one company will touch it. They will meet the *Napoli*, they will unload her, they will oversee the transport of the waste to the disposal site and they will guarantee its safe disposal. Needless to say, Disposoco are well aware that this situation must be reflected in a new contract with CZP and in turn in an enhanced rate of pay for yourselves. I have personally made it my business to ensure a considerable rise in your pay for—'

'*Dove?*' It was Bernadotte. Of course it was, thought John wryly. Bernadotte seeing through the bullshit at once. Not 'How much?' but '*Where?*'

'Under the circumstances,' persisted Verdi angrily, 'I have arranged a *considerable* rise . . .'

But Bernadotte was not alone in smelling a rat. The cry of '*Dove?*' was taken up by the rest of the crew until it drowned Verdi's voice. He looked to John for help, but John was far too astute a boardroom politican to offer any now. He did not want his crew to become confused as to whose side he was on.

So Verdi was forced to turn back and bellow for silence. Eventually, he got it.

'As I was just about to tell you, had I not been interrupted in this manner, the company that has agreed to take the cargo work out of Sept Isles. They wish the cargo to be delivered to them there as soon as possible and Signor Nero has therefore arranged for you to be refuelled at Cork in Southern Ireland.'

A whisper ran round the room like the first rumour of a plague. Those who had not yet been at sea long enough to learn where the minor seaports were soon found themselves enlightened by the old hands. The whisper went round the room and died. The stillness became absolute. John expected Bernadotte to speak next, but he was wrong. It was Marco Farnese. The third officer, childlike in his geographical knowledge as in most things, was riven by the news. 'Canada!' he yelled. He spoke in Italian, but even John had no trouble following his general gist. And, in any case, Asha leaned close enough to whisper a translation in his ear. 'You seriously expect us to take this old tub all the way to Canada. You must be mad!'

'We at CZP place our absolute trust in Captain Higgins, in the *Napoli* and in—'

'But not enough to come along yourself!'

Verdi began to bluster.

John judged this to be the moment to intervene. He stood up and started speaking. 'This is more than an old tub, Mr Farnese. It is a first-rate ship. It has to be. We have to make it so. We must get our cargo safely to Sept Isles to be disposed of properly. There must be no more mutant children like the ones in Lebanon my sister-in-law has described to me. No more ruined farms. No more damage to the environment. Both Disposoco and CZP are keen to ensure that. They trust us to make it absolutely certain. That is all. Dismiss the men to their watches and duties please, Mr Niccolo.'

He turned and exited, followed by Asha and Ann Cable. He had taken only one step when his wife threw her arms about him and hugged him. And Ann was there too, shaking his hand. 'That was quite a speech.' She was smiling, but her eyes were guarded. She might have said more, but the reason for her expression came puffing self-importantly out of the crowd of silent crewmen.

'Ah, there you are, Signorina,' he said ingratiatingly. 'If you will pack your bags now I have made arrangements for you to come with me back to Italy.'

'Thank you, Mr Verdi,' she answered carefully, 'but if the others are staying aboard, I guess I am too.'

'No, no. That is not what we agreed. And Signor Nero is most specific also. To Liverpool only.'

'Same as you said to the crew? *Specifically?* To Naples only. To Liverpool only. To Sept Isles only.'

'It is not the same! You are here as a guest of CZP and Disposoco and—'

'And of the officers and crew of the *Napoli*,' John interjected. 'If Ms Cable wishes to remain aboard, we'll be only too pleased to have her.'

Verdi eyed John wrathfully. His moustache actually seemed to bristle with irritation. But he was caught in a cleft stick: he could not threaten the Crewfinders captain and he could hardly manhandle the woman off the ship.

Eduardo suddenly appeared. 'Signor Verdi's helicopter will be ready to lift him off in five minutes, Captain.'

The deck was blustery and wet, and the overcast low and drizzling. Even so, two helicopters kept station with *Napoli*, a couple of hundred feet off, dull light catching on the lenses of video cameras.

'Aren't you going to wave, Mr Verdi?' asked Ann quietly. 'You'll be on the news at home tonight.'

'Very well, you can stay. But only as far as Ireland. When they refuel . . .' But then he paused, realising that getting her off in the Irish Republic was even less of a possibility than getting her off here.

'Mr Mariner,' he said suddenly, as though he had just made an important discovery.

'What about him?' John asked.

'He is still aboard. Miss Cable can get off when Mr Mariner gets off.'

'Ah, but he isn't getting off.'

'*Che?*'

'No, indeed Mr Verdi, I thought you realised. Captain Mariner is coming with us too.'

CHAPTER NINETEEN

As they came back down St George's Channel between Wales and the east coast of Ireland, the wind behind them began to moderate, so that when they turned south-west off Carnsore Point at midnight it was into quiet water. Atlantic swells, born a thousand miles further still south-west, came in regular series under her bow but the seesaw motion of her pitching was gentle enough. The coast of Ireland swept past, visible only as occasional points of light at first, but then emerging with the dawn, so green after the long rains that it seemed to glow even in the overcast. The Saltee Islands. Hook Head, guarding Waterford harbour. Cork.

'The harbour there used to be called Queenstown, but they changed it,' said John to Richard as they watched from the starboard bridge wing. They had not gone into the harbour itself, but were waiting off Crosshaven for the oiling lighter to come out to them as arranged. The Swansea ferry came out first, all white upper works and passengers waving, in holiday mood, even on a dull December morning. The oiler was just behind it and it was soon snugged up beside them as they filled their bunkers for the long journey to Sept Isles, the better part of two and a half thousand miles distant.

The bustle of the brief contact was enough to bring everyone topsides as the oiling team got to work under Cesar's watchful eye. Niccolo remained in the watchkeeper's chair, leg raised. Marco had just relieved him, agonisingly aware that there were now two captains aboard and both of them were just outside the bridge wing door. Right now they were keeping an eye on the crew lining the foredeck rails around the pipe which was pumping the oil aboard beneath the crane swinging up the supplies. Salah joined his old friends on the bridge wing and Fatima soon followed him. Asha and Ann were not long in coming up either and so the end rail got quite crowded.

'It's your last chance too,' said John to Ann. 'As Verdi said, you were supposed to get off at Liverpool. Haven't you got a life to get back to?'

Ann gave a negative flick of her head in reply. 'I'm supposed to keep an eye on that stuff down there.' She gestured down the length of the ship. 'If you'd unloaded at Liverpool, I'd have written a report. Now it'll be a fully fledged article; maybe more. I'll see what I can scare up on the far side of the pond. We need a combination of accurate fact and wide publicity on this one. It's the sort of thing that happens too often and it shouldn't be happening at all.' She looked at them all and smiled wryly. 'And of course I'm really here to make sure you don't just dump it over the side one dark night, or scuttle her altogether.'

Richard laughed humourlessly. 'I know it's been done,' he said quietly.

'And all too often,' said John. 'Mind you, if we are going to pull the plug on her, we'd better do it soon or we'll have a bloody long swim home.'

'Hello, *Napoli*!' came a call from below. The lighter had finished her business and her captain let her drift back a little until his bridge was just below the freighter's. 'That's you filled and vittled.' The soft brogue made almost no distinction between the 'f' and the 'v', poignantly reminding John of his childhood holidays. 'Where are you bound?'

'Sept Isles, Quebec,' called back John.

'And aren't you the brave boys to be running that a'way.'

'Why?' asked Richard.

'Sure and isn't there a terrible storm coming down out of Hudson's Bay.'

'That'll either pass far north of us or blow itself out long before we get anywhere near it,' countered John.

'Indeed it will, indeed it will. But they say there's another one behind it that makes it look like a dead calm.'

The lighter captain seemed content to leave the conversation there but John was not. He looked across at Salah and Fatima standing beside Richard. The western clothes he had brought aboard for them yesterday made them look different. For once Salah was wearing a sports jacket and slacks, though he would be changing back into his bosun's overall soon. Fatima also was wearing slacks – it would be a while before she wore a skirt again, he reckoned. Even so, the clothes emphasised the new start they were trying to make. It was hard to believe that less than two days ago, less than a hundred miles from here, the three of them had nearly been blown to kingdom come. And no one had said a thing about it. Oh, they had talked to Richard and he had discussed it with Asha, but there had been no news reports on the radio or the television; nothing in the papers. Nobody beyond *Napoli* seemed to know or care. 'I hear there was a big fire up in Wexford a couple of nights ago,' he called down to the Irish captain.

'Is that a fact?'

'Up beyond Enniscorthy. Near the coast. A bomb, I think. In an old house.'

'Ah. Blackwater Hall. No, that was no bomb. Sure, who'd want to blow up an old place the likes of that? T'was just the gas, they say, and t'was a fox or something set it off.'

By the end of lunchtime the Old Head of Kinsale was visible from the bridge. John and Richard were back up there again. It was a strange, do-nothing time; they had made another departure and yet had not quite started on the last leg of their voyage.

John and Richard had worked together on and off for years, but had shared the bridge only once with John as captain and Richard as senior captain. On *Napoli*, Richard deferred to John. He was not in command here and was anxious not to interfere with the way John wanted to run his ship. Richard's reasons for coming were complex, but nowhere among them was there any distrust of his most experienced captain and friend. He had always believed in leading from the front and if any man or woman from Crewfinders found themselves in trouble, then they knew they would find Richard there beside them. Had he been available when Salah's original cry for help arrived, instead of indulging Robin in the bridal suite of that Windsor hotel, then he would probably have come himself in any case.

He hated to be away from Robin, especially at the moment, and he didn't like being away from his desk at Heritage Mariner, but following *Napoli*'s course from disaster to disaster during the weeks of her voyage so far, he had felt a nagging worry, not least about how to get Salah and Fatima safely off the ship. Now returning them to the Middle East seemed impossible. If they were going to be handed to any authorities, then the Canadian or American would be the best. Neither of them had been directly implicated in any act of murder or sabotage, as far as he knew, and there were no warrants outstanding against them which would cause automatic extradition. America might be a good place for them. And he had lawyers in New York who would make cases which would last for years if necessary. He had well over a week to try and think of anything else that might be done. In the meantime, Salah and Fatima were trapped aboard. And while her sister was there, Asha would not leave. And while Asha was there, John would stay, at the mercy of CZP and Disposoco.

Richard trusted neither organisation. Of CZP he knew little, and his myriad contacts in shipping had been unable to enlighten him. They seemed to be a faceless company quietly building a fleet of old, self-reliant freighters. Go anywhere, do anything ships. He found the way they recruited, contracted and looked after their men particularly disturbing. They obviously started out with the assumption that everything would go wrong and they made sure they had a shady edge over everyone involved. Working for them must be like working for the Mafia, he supposed. And if CZP were bad, Disposoco were worse. Here was a company that secretly purchased great tracts of desert land specifically so that they could bury waste products no one else would handle. It was 'out of sight and out of mind' as far as they were concerned. And, when babies began to be born deformed, it still needed the direct intervention of the PLO to make them take any responsibility or action. And that action had not been impressive either.

As for the ship's company, Niccolo and Cesar both appeared to be good officers, but he knew nothing of their qualities as men. He was not overly impressed with El Jefe in the engine room, and by and large the rest of the crew left a lot to be desired. He had no knowledge of the late Captain Fittipaldi, but he suspected that if his command had run the same course as John's had, *Napoli* would never have got out of the Mediterranean. Or, if she had, she would have been en route for Nigeria, as John had cynically suggested, simply to dump the waste on a beach somewhere and slip away into the night. Richard also wondered about the bona fides of the nameless company in Sept Isles and he hoped John had thought to put the explosives Faure and his scientists had brought aboard safely under lock and key.

As the dull afternoon began to darken towards evening, they seesawed on over the groundswell past the increasingly craggy coast familiar to John from his forays in the Fastnet, that great yacht race which is the climax of Cowes Week. Beyond the great thrust of the Old Head came Courtmacsherry Bay and, beyond that, Galley Head. Cliff followed cliff as the rugged jaw of Ireland squared itself against the great Atlantic blows. The Stags, Toe Head, Kedge Island. Dark mountains gathering themselves grimly into the overcast behind Skibbereen, and Baltimore. Then the view deepened, stretching away behind Clear Island to the first lights of Schull on the thrust of Mizen Head to the north and, almost indistinguishable, the Caha Mountains beyond, reaching out towards Dursey Head. Then the black shoulder of Cape Clear cut it all off and the darkness came with it as they made for the hopeful gleam of the Fastnet Light.

John and Richard were on the bridge again as they butted past Fastnet and carried on away, out to sea. John felt a brief sense of worry, as though he were doing something badly wrong by failing to order the helm hard over. Just for a moment, he felt a shiver of unease as they went on out into the gathering darkness instead of safely back to the Isle of Wight. He walked forward to check the course from Fastnet to their destination. They would be following the logical, usual route of any ship going so far across the open ocean: Great Circle to the Corner at 42N;47W, then choosing their best course in past Cape Race, between Cape Ray on Newfoundland and Cape North on Nova Scotia.

He was, perhaps, a little psychic tonight – fey, his mother would have called it – for there was something about their new course that he found disturbing as well.

Richard noticed the tiny shudder he gave. 'What is it, John?'

'I haven't done this often, but once in a while when I lay in the Great Circle from Fastnet to the Corner, I can't help thinking of poor old Captain E. J. Smith doing the same.'

Richard was miles away – he only half heard: 'Captain Smith? Don't think I've met him.'

'Well, you've left it too late to meet him now. He went down with his ship.'

Richard looked closely at his friend. John's attention was back on their course, making sure it was correctly entered in the automatic steering gear. 'What ship was that?' Richard asked.

'The *Titanic*.'

CHAPTER TWENTY

Next morning found them far out in the east Atlantic with the Fastnet a fading memory. Much more real, and increasingly so as long hours became days, was the first of the storms that the lighter captain had warned them about in Cork. It affected them only indirectly, for it whirled along a track far to the north of them, coming east out of Hudson Bay to close over Labrador. It sent north winds screaming down from Cape Farewell to the Grand Banks, made navigation of the North Atlantic between Greenland and Iceland almost impossible and all but swamped the Faroes and the Shetlands alike before roaring over the Baltic and blowing itself out against the Ural Mountains.

To *Napoli* over the days of its tyranny, it was a series of weather warnings to the north, moderating as they came south towards *Napoli*. It was a series of radio messages from ships in trouble too far away for the old freighter to help. It was a series of lines on weather charts gathering darkly in the high latitudes, but separating as they came down towards the waters she was crossing now. And it was slate-grey weather with low skies roiling slowly over choppy seas where the south-westerly groundswell bickered with storm waves running across them, pushed by the last breath of north wind. But most of all, it was a warning of what the men and women aboard *Napoli* had to look forward to when the gale's big brother followed in its footsteps in a few days' time, just as they would be nearing the Grand Banks, exactly in its path.

'We could always alter course to avoid it,' said John at one planning meeting when he, Richard and Niccolo were together on the bridge. 'But we'll be hard put to meet the schedule as it is. And I'm a bit like Captain MacWhirr, I suppose.'

Niccolo looked to Richard, as he had learned to do when confronted with his captain's arcane shiplore or history.

'MacWhirr is a character in a story by Joseph Conrad,' Richard explained. 'He was warned to avoid a powerful typhoon but he didn't do so because he couldn't believe that the people who predicted it actually knew anything about it because they were all so busily avoiding it themselves. He brought his ship home,' he added, turning back to John. 'That's a more cheerful reference than usual from you, John.'

'Yes. I don't know what's got into me. I have a bad feeling about this. Nothing I can put my finger on, or I'd have done something about it by now. Perhaps it's just that I've been aboard here too long now. I suppose I am beginning to feel trapped. I wish I hadn't brought Asha along, I tell you that. We've a day or two in hand before the outskirts of this weather start to make things difficult,' he continued. 'Forty-eight hours, maybe a little more, to get this tub really shipshape. It's all very well expecting her to get through a blow in the Med in her current condition, but this will be a little more testing, I think. We really do need to be able to rely on her hull, especially her bows. We need to know that nothing is going to break loose below or above. We need to be able to rely absolutely on all the electrical and communication equipment.'

'Hard work for Jesus,' commented Niccolo.

'Hard work for all of us,' John told him. 'Even for the chef and the stewards. We'll need to have food ready-prepared to keep us going no matter what – hot and cold, ready to go no matter when. The galley's going to be working overtime for the next few days. And the stewards will need to check out the bridgehouse thoroughly making sure everything is tied down tight. We'd better hold another lifeboat drill too; we'll wait for the weather to deteriorate before we do it, though; make it feel authentic. What else?'

'The engine?' asked Richard.

John closed his eyes, remembering that conversation he had had with El Jefe. 'We'll keep the chief engineer posted, of course,' he said at last, 'but I really think all we can hope is that he can continue to nurse us along at some kind of speed.'

'We're making only eleven knots now.'

'I know, Richard. But all I want is steerage way if the storm does turn out to be a bad one. I'll be happy enough if I can *rely* on steerage way.' He put the engine out of his mind, too, for the moment. He could do nothing beyond chivvying his chief engineer and trusting him to do his best. But the thought of an engine fire breaking out in the middle of a North Atlantic storm did nothing to lighten his feeling of depression.

He completed the list of things to be done and left Niccolo on the bridge to keep the watch and to co-ordinate as was necessary while the more mobile officers and Salah, the bosun, took work gangs and began to make them live up to their names. He and Richard went down to the fo'c'sle head to begin their inspection.

Marco's gang were on the foredeck, making sure the lines round the deck cargo were absolutely secure, a task that was made difficult and unpopular by the chill drizzle gusting fitfully out of the overcast. Numb fingers slipped and got cut, caught or crushed as steel ropes were tested and tensioned. The ladders stood in place but their rungs were slippery and no one was keen to try and get up them to check the tops of the containers. Halfway down the deck, John was forced to step into a confrontation between Marco and Bernadotte. The two men were standing face to face, the officer holding a pair of heavy work gloves and gesturing upwards. It was clear that the seaman was refusing to obey Marco's order to climb the ladder, either on his own behalf or as a representative of the whole gang. John caught the word '*Su!*' from Marco. He remembered it meant 'up' and added his own weight of authority to it: '*Su. Subito!*'

Bernadotte glared down at him for a moment, but then obeyed. Thrusting aside the work gloves, he stamped across the deck and made quite a performance out of mounting the ladder. John waited until he was up on top of the containers and had obviously settled to his task there before he turned and rejoined Richard.

'That's a nasty piece of work,' Richard observed as they went down the rest of the deck.

'It's like putting a maneater with an amateur lion tamer,' said John. 'Marco Farnese seems to bring out all the worst in Bernadotte.' He began to tell the tale of the seaman's transgressions and the junior officer's place in them. 'It's a difficult one. With Niccolo off the deck, Bernadotte has to go to Marco. He's got precious little standing left with the men, but if I take Bernadotte and add him to Cesar's work teams, nobody will take any notice of the third officer at all.'

Their inspection began with a look at Bernadotte's work. Down in the cramped confines of the chain locker, they examined the state of the bows. Bernadotte had been sent down here by Niccolo with orders to chip rust and make good with paint. But time and again they found areas of white-painted blisters on the walls which burst at a touch to cascade dull red flakes over their work clothes.

Nor was that all. Set into the floor of the starboard chain locker was an inspection hatch which opened on to a pair of ladders designed to take them right down the inside of the hull, on either side of the cutwater itself. In the constant thunder of the surf against her stem, talking was difficult, but as they went down the inspection ladders to a level near the surface of the restless water outside, Richard raised his voice in an inarticulate shout which attracted John's attention. Richard pointed at the metal wall and shone his torch down it. John watched as a wave hit and the whole wall flexed in response. The movement was not great. Only the shadows from Richard's carefully positioned torch revealed it at all. The movement indicated that the metal in *Napoli*'s hull was not wearing well. It would have given little cause for concern under normal circumstances. But with a storm coming, John was not in a mood to take risks. The ladders down the inside of the hull were effectively on the forward walls of a deep but narrow gully whose rear walls were the front ends of storage areas and the forward hold itself. It would be possible to wedge timbers down here and hold the bow still in the same way that Niccolo had used battens of wood to wedge the barrels in the half-filled container. That was work which had better start right away. Silently and a little grimly they climbed back up.

That flexing of the bow raised some unwelcome questions. How sound were *Napoli*'s sides? How much real metal was left under the paint-bound rust of her decks? How would those decks react to a container falling down on them? Or a couple of thousand tons of water, if a big wave broke over her? How much pressure from shifting cargo would her holds stand before they burst open? Quite simply, could the old ship handle the massive forces unleashed by a severe storm without falling apart around them?

They found Cesar busy with his team in checking the lifeboats, their contents, fittings and fixings. With a few terse words, John explained the situation in the bow and what he wanted the second officer to do about it.

Four of them then went down into the dark holds: John and Richard to check the disposition of the cargo and to discuss whether it was necessary, and possible, to make it safer than it was; Professor Faure to advise on what was possible, within safe limits; Ann Cable to run her daily check on the level of radioactivity. The cargo presented a problem for the seamen. Niccolo, in a hurry and expecting that the great grey blocks were bound only for Naples, had been content to pile them like massive children's building blocks without securing them in any particular way. But the movement of *Napoli* in a severe storm was likely to send the topmost blocks crashing to – perhaps *through* – the bottom of the ship. In each of the three holds, John, Richard and Faure stayed together, discussing how best to overcome the problem.

'You'll have to open the hatches and use the cranes,' Richard commented.

'Yes, it's the only way. We'll do the maths back up on the bridge, but I think they'll all fit. One level right across the deck, not piled up at all.'

'If they'll all go in like that, then there will be much less risk of them shifting in a storm,' agreed Faure. 'The danger to them, if any, will come from up there.' He gestured to the deck above.

'We'd better triple-check Marco's work,' rasped John. 'We definitely do not want one of those containers breaking through the deck and bursting open down here!'

'Talking of things bursting through deck heads,' Richard said, 'who is your best crane man?'

John gave a dry bark of laughter. 'Even Niccolo still agrees our best crane man is Bernadotte. But I'll ask Salah to keep an eye on him just in case.'

They began work at once because the task of spreading out the concrete blocks would take time. They had six protection suits, and so no more than six men could work in the hold at any one time. Further, although the compressed-air packs were designed to hold two hours' worth of the precious gas, hard work meant the user ran out more quickly. John organised the gang as a group of four working in the hold, one – himself – overseeing and one getting his tank recharged at the compressor. Bernadotte would be in the crane above.

Although the grey concrete blocks seemed absolutely feature-less at first, closer examination revealed that, like the barrels of chemical waste, they had two slight ridges running round them, which separated them from each other and raised them from the deck sufficiently to allow a strap to be passed round them. Borrowing the ladder from the deck, John and his men climbed up on to the top of the pile of blocks in the most forward of the holds. Then, as Bernadotte carefully lowered the tackle from the first crane, they grabbed the webbing straps and made them fast round the outermost of that top level of blocks. Then Bernadotte lifted them one by one with the most delicate touch imaginable, and lowered them to the deck like thistledown.

That first square of blocks was simply lowered straight down to lie in a larger square round the outside of the bottom layer. Then those in the middle were lifted up and swung further out still until the last pile, from the very middle of the top layer in the forward hold, went furthest out of all, along the walls of the hold, filling it completely to one level, side to side and fore to aft. It all seemed quite easy, although the fit was very tight indeed. The last few, in fact, had to be jockeyed quite carefully to allow the last one of all to swing easily from the very middle to the last corner, furthest forward on the port side. Here, the last space stood waiting, to John's anxious eye only just big enough to take the last block.

Of the team working in the hold, only Eduardo spoke any English, and so John had used the ex-cadet as his assistant in the hold. By the time the last block was ready for positioning, the two of them were the only ones who had not been away to have their tanks replenished. They were all dog-tired, and John was as exhausted as any of them, but this last block had to be put in place. 'Eduardo,' he called, his voice hoarse and his throat sore from using the dry air. 'Let's put this one down and go topsides.'

The crewman came willingly enough, though he looked tired and John suddenly realised how unfair he had been, almost penalising the man for being able to communicate with him. The pair of them, he reckoned grimly, must have done as much hefting and heaving as the other four put together. But it was almost finished now.

He caught the straps as Bernadotte lowered them, and pushed one towards his helper. Eduardo caught it and they knelt together, fastening the webbing in place and clinching it tight. The light was going fast now, filling the hold with shadow like a flood, but John reckoned he was still easily visible in the last island of brightness right beneath the hatch. He waved to Bernadotte up above his head. The block rose fractionally and he and Eduardo swung it across the hold towards its allotted place. Behind them, one of the others stepped into the place John had just vacated, ready to signal to Bernadotte on Eduardo's translation of the order.

It was hard work positioning the block just right, but the two of them had had enough practice to get it done quite quickly. Just as it was swinging into position, John yelled, 'Ready!'

'*Pronto!*' called Eduardo.

Timing was all important here, for the block was unwieldy and the space was small. It had to start coming down just as it swung into position so that it would catch on the blocks round it and settle into place before it had a chance to swing back again.

'Now!'

'*Subito!*'

The block hesitated, exactly in place. If it was eased down by as little as six inches it would fit perfectly. If it was eased down immediately. 'Now!' snarled John again, but even as he spoke he began to feel it swinging back against him, its mass and momentum overcoming his strength. His feet began to slide back, only to be stopped short by a ridge on the top of the block he was standing on. He tried to hop over the long, low protuberance but it caught at his clumsy boots as though it had a malicious will of its own. The block still swung back towards him and, as he couldn't move his feet quickly enough, it pushed him over. There was nothing violent about it; the force of the thing was simply overpowering. The block continued to swing back, moving inexorably over him. Desperately, he threw himself to one side, jerking in his legs and arms to form himself into a tight ball. A ball which could roll clear before the thing came down on him. How many tons must it weigh? He wouldn't stand a chance.

A force gathered him and pushed him forward; a force centred at the curve of his back. He could not visualise what was happening to himself at all, but later he realised Eduardo had thrown himself forward, also under the block, to gather his captain like a big beach ball and half roll, half hurl him forward.

The block came down then, brushing the seaman aside with the same gentle force, then exploding down on one corner to pivot and fall against the wall. The flat steel gathered the concrete edge to itself and John sat up just in time to see it settle into its place. He ran to Eduardo; he was out cold. 'Get him to the infirmary!' snarled John to the stunned team. Whether his words made sense to them or not, it was abundantly clear what required and they all leaped forward together.

John didn't pause to check on what they were doing. He went

up the ladder like a madman, swearing under his breath with language he had not used in years. He stumbled across the deck and on up the rungs of the crane. This time there was no one on the platform to prevent him tearing the door of the control cab wide, and, with a voiceless cry of rage, he hurled himself forward.

Bernadotte was sitting there with a slightly puzzled look on his face.

John grabbed him by the shoulders and pulled him out on to the metal balcony. Bernadotte came easily, giving no resistance at all. He simply toppled sideways off his seat. John went down on one knee beside him, his fist closed as tightly as the bulky glove would allow, raised high above his head to deliver the most powerful punch he was capable of. But then Salah was there, pulling the enraged man back, holding him until he calmed.

Bernadotte seemed to have noticed nothing of what was happening beside him. The big man rolled over, put his hands on the wet metal and tensed to push himself up. But he fell down instead. He tried again. Again. Until John, calming down now, began to see the pattern. As soon as Bernadotte put any weight on his hands, he simply fell.

John pulled his headgear back. The windy cold of the late afternoon hit him round the head like a bucket of water. But that was not what made him catch his breath. What made him gasp with shock was the fact that Bernadotte was crying. Actually crying aloud. Sobbing like a child.

'There's something wrong with his hands,' Salah was yelling.

Gently now, John took hold of those massive shoulders again and heaved the giant back until he was sitting half propped against the cockpit door. Then, glad of the gloves, he took the great ham hands in his own and looked at them. They were pale; no, white. They looked as though they had been boiled for hours and then left to cool. And there was the slightest chemical smell to them. He looked up at Salah, mouth open with shock – then he leaned forward and sniffed again. It was the same smell he had noticed on the empty sleeves where Captain Fittipaldi's hands had once been.

CHAPTER TWENTY-ONE

John leaped upright, his flesh creeping with horror. He must get Bernadotte to the infirmary at once, but even with Salah there just to get him down the ladder to the main deck would be impossible without further aid. Clearly, the big seaman could not use his hands any more. And, John guessed, he was in such pain that getting him to understand anything would be out of the question at the moment. John looked around for rope to lower the huge crewman. There was none. He glanced up at the crane. Its falls were still attached to the concrete block in the hold. But the crane did offer a solution, for in the cab was a phone which could contact the bridge. It was there so that bridge officers could give orders to crane operators, but it worked both ways. He picked it up and recieved an immediate reply.

Fifteen minutes later, both Eduardo and Bernadotte were lying side by side in the infirmary and Asha was moving anxiously from one to the other, while Fatima tidied their bandages. The small crewman was deeply unconscious. The big crewman was the opposite. All too wide awake, the pain of his hands was clearly going to overcome even the powerful painkiller Asha had given him. John stood anxiously by. 'Any idea about his hands? he asked.'

'It's obviously the stuff from the barrels. But it's diluted. There are none of the effects I noted on Captain Fittipaldi. Not that I looked too closely at him. I wish I had, now.'

'He was working on the containers and he wasn't wearing gloves. Stupid!'

'Check back in half an hour. After you've gone over the containers with Ann and Faure.' She was reading his mind again. 'Fatima,' she continued as he bustled out of the door, 'don't bandage his hands yet – just a light gauze.'

A minute examination revealed nothing specific at all. There was no obvious leakage from within any of the containers, though the weather made absolute certainty difficult. The drizzle had been replaced by steady rain and the exteriors of the containers were awash with rain water and dripping on to each other and on to the deck in any case.

They retreated back to the shelter of the bridgehouse little the wiser. Faure had taken samples from the puddles on top of the containers, and from the water-washed deck below. Ann was content to watch his tests before deciding whether to take any samples herself.

In the meantime, John needed advice on what to do with the containers now.

'If I were you,' said Faure, as the three of them stood dripping in the bridgehouse's main deck corridor, 'I would hose the whole lot down with salt water, just to clean the surfaces. Then I would try to cover them with something waterproof.'

'Yes,' Ann agreed. 'It looks as though anything coming out of the barrels is being washed out by water seeping through the containers. If you can stop that, the leakage should stop.' The more she said, the less convinced she sounded.

'Well, I suppose I can try,' answered John doubtfully. 'But it's a tall order. Keeping the deck cargo dry is difficult enough under ideal circumstances. Doing so through a December gale in the North Atlantic may not be possible at all. But you're right, we must do what we can. The crew has to at least think we have things under some kind of control.' The more he said, the more decisive he sounded. 'Ann, check with Asha whether there's anything about Eduardo or Bernadotte I should know, will you? I'd better get this under way as soon as possible.'

He put together three teams. Using Niccolo's expertise, he first put together a team of experienced deck-swabbers under

Cesar's command. Niccolo knew the crew well enough to be able to advise on the men who would have the good sense to take the apparently menial task seriously. These men were dressed in the protective suits and given old mops to use. Secondly, there was a team on the hoses, under Marco's charge. These again were chosen carefully because John wanted to be certain that the powerful jets of sea water were carefully and precisely directed. The third team, under Salah's watchful eye, would need to dress in the first team's protective clothing at the end of the exercise, but to begin with all they had to do was get out the great tarpaulins from the ship's store and lay them out on the deck immediately in front of the bridge and check them for holes and tears.

Half an hour later the first white jet of sea water hit the side of the first container. The water exploded into foam against the corrugated side, making a sound like distant thunder. Carefully, Marco's men played the cleansing jet over the vertical steel side, then switched it off. The swabbing team, in place on top of the container, swiftly cleaned the top – which had not been hosed – and got it as dry as the conditions would allow. Then the hose moved down and when its work on the side of the next container was done, the swabbers got to work again on the horizontal surfaces. John had calculated that any water going on top of the containers, even salt water designed to clean them off, would only add to the seepage problem. The only horizontal surface given the benefit of a direct hosing was the deck beneath the containers. And so the washing process continued. Sides and ends were hosed down. Tops were swabbed. Decks were washed and swabbed alike. And when the swabbing was finished, the swabs were thrown overboard, just in case. Then the third team took the first team's protective clothing and, under John's supervision, made huge tarpaulin parcels out of the deck cargo.

By 18.00 it was all finished to the best of their ability. The officers retired to the bridgehouse exhausted but also satisfied that they had at last achieved some sort of control over their terrifying cargo. Salah took the men down to clean up for drinks and dinner. 'Tomorrow,' said John to Richard, 'I'll ask Salah to find the second best crane driver aboard and sort out the other two holds. Then we'll be as ready as possible.'

Dinner that night was among the social highlights of the voyage. The chef outdid himself and produced the sort of meal that would form the foundation of much pleasurable reminiscence in the future. The feeling that they were at last exerting some control over their sinister cargo and that they had a guaranteed welcome at their destination far outweighed the threat of the gathering storm or their lingering concern about the way the voyage had gone so far.

The mood was further lightened by the fact that, in the infirmary, things were improving. Eduardo was awake and Bernadotte was asleep. Faure's tests had established that the rainwater from the top of the container did in fact contain a substance of a strongly corrosive nature. Asha had at once bathed Bernadotte's hands in the most plentiful chemically inert medium they had to hand: salt water. This had apparently soothed the pain sufficiently to allow him some rest. He was clearly going to be incapacitated for some time, but at least his condition seemed to have responded to treatment, however basic that treatment was. And Eduardo showed every sign of being back on his feet soon.

Salah and Fatima joined the others and took part in the conversation, though Salah himself would rather have been in the crew's mess and Fatima would rather have been in the infirmary. John's mind was also much more at rest than it had been almost since the outset. Asha was playing the perfect hostess and clearly enjoying herself so much that her husband just sat back and watched, his pleasure unalloyed even by the thought that it should have been like this for her every night since their wedding.

Next day dawned grey and threatening and the weather reports left them in very little doubt that they would be lucky to get their day's work done before the bad weather arrived. But get their work done they had to and John still had every intention of holding that last lifeboat drill before nightfall. They made an early start, opening the two remaining hatches and spreading out the cargo across the floor of the holds as they had done the previous afternoon.

Cesar and his team finished bracing the bow and Niccolo came limping down the deck on Salah's arm to check that the tarpaulin covers were holding on the containers.

When they broke for lunch, everything was done except the final battening down and making ready. John took pity on them and let them finish their well-earned meal before he sounded 'Abandon Ship'. The lifeboat drill went smoothly in spite of the fact that this time John insisted that the boats actually be lowered into the choppy water and everyone aboard except the occupants of the infirmary, and Fatima who was nursing them, take their place aboard. When that was done, he split the crew into two units: one, under Niccolo, resecured the lifeboats and checked everything was safely stowed in them again; the other battened down everything aboard. Then he and Richard, as they had so often done in the past on so many other ships, completed a tour of inspection which tested every line and strut, every knot, bolt, shackle and fall; everything that might spring loose, blow loose, break free or be washed away. From stem to stern they went, and from keel to truck, and the officer in charge of each section accompanied them. Even El Jefe acquiesced, and conducted them round the engine room – perhaps because only they knew where his beloved telescope had been stowed.

By 18.00 they were finished. There was nothing left for them to do except dismiss the off-watch officers and crew to eat, drink and be merry. For tomorrow the storm was due.

'How are you, my darling?' asked Robin, her voice a distant whisper.

'Fine, darling, how are you?' It was a lie. Richard could not remember when he had felt so lost and lonely.

'We miss you.'

'I miss you two too.' Even though the baby wasn't due for another three months it was already developing emotions and longings, likes and dislikes, according to its mother. Richard played along, indulging her as he always did, because he loved her too much to do anything else.

'What have you been doing today?'

'Nothing much.' A half truth this time. 'We've been battening everything down. We're in for a bit of a blow.'

'I know. I saw the weather forecast.'

'I'm surprised you're not listening to the shipping stations.' He had meant it as a joke. But then her silence told him that that was exactly what she had been doing. 'Oh Robin!'

'Don't, darling! I know it's silly but I promise not to worry too much.'

'I know.' He tried to put into his voice all that deep calm he knew would make her feel safer. But the fact that they were apart for the first time in some years, and at such a point in their life together, was something that both of them were finding very hard to bear. Communication on the satellite phone was a mixed blessing. Without each other, so far apart, they felt less than whole; they needed to communicate. But when they talked on the satellite, the distance between them was only emphasised more painfully. He could hear her becoming more and more depressed on the far end of the faint link and he could do nothing to cheer her because the same thing was happening to him. Had he known it would be as bad as this, he might have hesitated longer before coming aboard.

But he still would have come. There was no real choice in the matter. Robin would not have allowed him to be hesitant even had he weakened himself, for they had both seen the right course of action quite clearly. But their strength was as a team, together. He found it very hard to be so far from her. And she found it harder, he was on a dangerous ship carrying a deadly cargo heading for a destructive storm and she could share none of it with him. Perhaps that was what she found worst of all. That he might die without her. Of course she told him none of this, but he knew her as well as he knew himself and he could read between the lines of their agonising conversations.

'How's the baby?' he asked, after a short, hissing silence. 'Stopped being sick?'

'No! God knows what sort of a sailor he or she will be, but we can't even get in the car without a brown paper bag! It's embarrassing. And, you'll be pleased to know, it's crippling my social life!'

'No! Selfish little brute!'

'The build-up to Christmas just won't be the same. No husband. No wild parties.' She was teasing. They worked too hard during the day to go wild at night, and in his absence Robin was in the office every day. In any case, since becoming pregnant, she had had no alcohol to drink and had been careful to eschew smoke-filled atmospheres; she had avoided parties, in fact. He looked at the clock Jesus kept above the radio. 22.00 local time. It would be eight o'clock in London. Behind the quiet hissing of the air waves, he could hear quiet music. She was at home, curled up in front of the fire, listening to the stereo. How he ached to be there with her.

'What are you listening to?'

'*Don Carlos*.'

'Verdi? Not Mozart?'

'I started to listen to *Cosi Fan Tutte* but gave up. Not in the mood.'

'*Don Carlos* is a bit depressing, though, isn't it?'

'I listened to *Madame Butterfly* last night. All about unfaithful sailors sailing away for ever.'

He caught his breath at that. She *was* getting depressed. Could he hear tears in her husky voice? 'We have a chap called Verdi mixed up in this,' he told her, making his voice light and a little bracing. 'Funny little chap. Works for the owners of the ship, CZP.'

'That's nice . . .' She said more, but the link suddenly started phasing out on them. Her voice drowned under a rising tide of static. She was gone.

He stood, looking down at the instrument, his face set like stone. Then he put it back and stepped out on to the bridge. Marco Farnese was there, lounging in the watchkeeper's chair. 'Good night,' said Richard quietly.

The third officer jumped up and stood to attention. '*Buona notte*, Capitano,' he said.

'I've never seen him look like that,' said John.

'He misses Robin. I hope you're going to look like that whenever we're apart.'

'Yes. It's funny that. I've never known them to be apart for any length of time. I'll tell you what, though.'

'What?'

'I'm glad he's here.'

'Why? You haven't really let him take any responsibility aboard. He hasn't actually done all that much.'

'Well, that's because I'm in charge. I'm the captain. It's my responsibility; my job.'

'I think he feels out on a limb. I think he's come aboard for all sorts of good reasons and now he finds he's all alone with nothing much to do.'

'There'll be enough to do when the storm hits tomorrow.'

'Well, in that case, we should be getting some sleep.'

'We're all tucked up in bed, aren't we?'

'That's not quite the same thing.'

'Annamaria Julietta Corigliano-Calabro,' said Niccolo, rolling it round his tongue.

'That's what it would have been, yes. The same as my grandmother. But when my grandfather arrived at Ellis Island, the immigration people thought Corigliano-Calabro would be too much of a mouthful.'

'So they shortened it to Cable.'

'Yup. A lot of social and racial heritage went that way in the thirties. Nobody argued, they were all too glad to get safely in. Grandpa especially. He'd fallen foul of Mussolini and the Blackshirts.'

'Communist, huh?'

Niccolo meant it as an Italian joke, but he hit a raw nerve. She swung round to look at him full face, her eyes blazing with rage. 'Never!'

'Sorry, *cara*! I was only joking.'

'It's no joking matter. And don't call me *cara*!'

'So, your *nonno* emigrated in the thirties to escape fascist persecution. What did he do?'

'He had trained as an architect in Italy but he couldn't get a job even as a builder in New York. He looked all over. It was bad in the thirties, of course. Grandma took in washing. He did odd jobs. The old thing. Then Dad came along and things got really tough. They drifted west. Ended up in Hollywood and Grandpa got a job with MGM building sets. Solid work. They settled down. Had a big family. Dad grew up in Tinseltown, got some bit parts as a kid. Got married in fifty-nine. I came along in sixty-one, just as he was really establishing himself in the movies.'

'Not *Clark* Cable!'

She had heard that one before. She threw a napkin at him. Some of the other occupants of the officers' saloon looked across at them, then looked away again. Something in her expression settled Niccolo down as well.

'You won't have heard of him, he never made it big. He fell ill in sixty-three. Cancer. He died seven years later, when I was nine. On my birthday. It was my birthday wish that he should stop suffering at last.'

Niccolo looked at her in silence. What was there for him to say?

'You heard of the film star Dick Powell?' she asked after a while.

'Sure.' He couldn't quite see where this was leading, but he was pleased to change the subject.

'In the late fifties he started directing films. The story goes that he made one of them out in the desert in New Mexico. My dad was in it. Bit part, but big break.'

'Yes?'

She had retreated far away from him now. He had the feeling this story was one she rarely told but was important to her.

'The government had just done a test there. A nuclear test. They didn't realise, then, about the way such things worked.

Things like fall-out, radiation. They didn't warn anyone. Certainly not a bunch of actors shooting some movie in the desert nearby. That's how the story goes.' There were huge tears in her eyes. 'They all died of cancer. Dick Powell, my dad . . .'

Niccolo sat silently, looking at her. She had answered the question he had instinctively held back from asking: why she had joined Greenpeace.

Asha and John were interrupted five minutes later by the only person aboard who would have dared thunder on the captain's door like that.

'Look!' said Richard when John answered his imperious summons. 'Salah's just come across this. It's Lazar's. It was hidden in his cabin and it's just come to light.' Richard was holding out an open passport as though it was the Holy Grail.

'Come on, Richard, what's so important about this?'

'You must see, John! Wake up for heaven's sake! It's a dead man's passport with an American Visa in it.'

John's mouth fell open. Automatically he turned towards his office and the safe. 'My God!' he said. 'I've still got Gina Fittipaldi's passport too. That means we have a passport for each of them. If neither of these has been reported missing during the last ten days, we have a fighting chance of getting both Salah and Fatima safely off the ship in Sept Isles.'

'With luck, we could even get them into the United States!'

'I'll check at the earliest opportunity.'

In the short term, however, sleep was a higher priority.

And, as it turned out, there were distractions in the long term too.

CHAPTER TWENTY-TWO

When a great storm crosses a continent, it is the clouds that come first. When it crosses an ocean, it is the waves.

There are other differences. On land there are forecasts; at sea, warnings. If the wind folded fields into hillsides and sent them rolling across the landscape at fifty miles an hour, it would be different; if it tore off their topsoil and hurled it through the air in streaming clouds, if it caused city blocks to rise up and fall upon transports full of people, then there would be warnings. But the wind does none of these things on land. Not so at sea. At sea it can do all of these things.

They knew when the storm left its lair in Hudson Bay because Jesus started getting storm warnings. They knew the look of it, for Niccolo could draw its shark's fin shape, tracing the fronts which met at the low that had spawned it. They heard tell of it, for there were ships to the north and west of them who met it first as it was beginning to flex its muscles, and they radioed to each other and to them, for Jesus had made wide contact as part of the preparations, and to Cape Race radio station in Labrador who broadcast their warnings more generally.

The first they actually saw of it, however, was the rising of a north-easterly chop which cut across the south-westerly set of the Western Ocean groundswell. The new waves seemed to have a different colour, and perhaps they actually were different, for they were reaching over Flemish Cap and Grand Bank before they came to *Napoli*, and there the depth could be as little as twelve scant metres, and the bottom mud came up with each billow.

A dull brown stain was coming south, with the new waves cutting over the green rollers that had kept *Napoli* company since Fastnet. Richard and John saw it when they came on to the bridge the next morning, the new colour and the new set of the sea. Both of them had felt *Napoli*'s new motion even before their feet had touched the deck, but there was nothing yet to make them hurry aloft and they both showered, shaved and dressed in a leisurely manner. It might be a while before they got the chance to do these things again. For the same reason, they both enjoyed an unaccustomed breakfast of sausages, kidneys, eggs, bacon and fried bread. Lots of toast, all of it piping hot, with marmalade and butter dripping. They watched each other going through the familiar ritual with much the same feelings: they had learned to do these things at sea together and may even have learned them from each other. And, when they had finished, together they went up on to the bridge.

It was the last half-hour of Niccolo's watch and he sat in the watchkeeper's chair with his body relaxed but his eyes busy. John went across to the log at once. At 07.00 local time, half an hour ago, the storm centre had been at 60 degrees east of Greenwich, heading westward at thirty miles an hour and just about to be flipped south off its direct track by the monumental high pressure sitting on the Greenland icecap. *Napoli* was coming up to 45 degrees east and more than a thousand miles south of the heart of the thing, but she would soon be under the shark's fin fronts when the whole system came down round Cape Farewell. And, while the storm centre might be moving at a sedate thirty miles per hour, the winds which whirled around it, their direction and intensity varied by the fronts, were moving at least three times as fast.

'What does Cape Race say, Niccolo?'

'Jesus was on to them a couple of minutes ago. Westerly gale force eight, gusting nine. Overcast with thunder and driving rain. They're expecting it to back north and go to storm ten soon with

more squalls and thunder. They've got snow as well, but I don't
think that'll come down here.'

'Don't be too sure.'

John went out to join Richard on the starboard bridge wing.
Together they looked north-west. There was nothing to see yet in
the sky. It was a clear, cold dawn with an unblemished canopy of
blue and a peculiar intensity to the light. It was as if they should
have been able to see over all those sea miles and up through
the crystal air to the towering clouds at the centre of the storm
or at least to the great black battlements sweeping south along
the lines of the fronts. Silently they stood, looking, feeling the
way *Napoli* rode the choppy sea, knowing that the flukes of wind
slapping their cheeks every now and then were parts of a local
microclimate which would soon be overcome, like a rock pool
by a spring tide.

By nine, there were wispy mare's tails of cirrus cloud floating
far on the weather side. By ten Marco came out to report that the
glass was really beginning to fall; and the clouds had thickened
up. The horizon was a hard black line between the greyish sky
and the restless, brownish sea. 'Coming in fast,' said Richard
to John.

'Maybe it'll go over fast as well,' John answered, but he did
not sound convinced. 'I'll just have a word with Jesus. See what's
happening to his friends to the north of us.'

Asha came in to lunch at twelve fifteen having walked through
directly from the infirmary. She had noticed nothing of the gathering clouds outside, nor of the increasingly restless movement
of the ship. She did notice, however, that she was almost alone
in the dining saloon. '*Donde esta el capitan?*' she asked a Spanish
steward.

'*Encima,*' he answered. Upstairs.

'*Il ponte commando,*' supplied Marco Farnese who had arrived
just in time to overhear the exchange.

Asha's eyebrow rose, then her forehead folded into a slight
frown. She got up from her table and went out of the saloon.
She always went up to the bridge by the external companionways

unless it was raining, so as soon as she got outside she registered the change in the weather. The wind had arrived. It was gusting from the south-west, across the main thrust of the storm waves which were still running down from the north-east. As she arrived on the bridge, skipping in from the bridge wing outside, the first spatter of raindrops dashed themselves against the closing door behind her.

John was standing beside the helm which, unusually, had a helmsman steering; the helmsman was Salah Malik. 'Why are you up here, John?' she asked at once. 'It's lunchtime.'

'We're having sandwiches sent up,' answered John quietly. His eyes were on the sky which was now darkening more rapidly. There were no discrete clouds, but a general overcast which was closing down rapidly on the sea to the north-east, on their starboard quarter.

The dark heaving of the waves was abruptly whitened by a gust of wind strong enough to set the foam flying. It buffeted the bridge, and the windows also whitened with foam. 'Gusting force six,' said Richard to Cesar, who was writing in the log. 'It's just building. There shouldn't be any squalls this side of the first front,' he added, addressing John, who nodded.

'Sandwiches?' said Asha. 'Why? Are you not hungry after your big breakfast?'

'No, it's not that. Look, come outside for a moment, would you?'

Outside, the weather seemed to have deteriorated during the few seconds she had been inside. They had to stand well back under the canopy to keep out of the worst of the rain. 'I don't want to leave the bridge,' he told her. 'There's quite a storm coming down that way.' He gestured away to the north-east, where the sky was darkest. 'It's much worse than the one we brushed just after we cleared Fastnet, and this time I'm afraid we'll have to sail right through it. The only way to avoid it is to run for Bermuda and wait it out, and if we do that, the people in Sept Isles may not take the cargo. They're working to a schedule as well. Anyway, it's just a Western Ocean blow. Nothing really to worry about as long as we stay alert.'

'And stay on the bridge.'

'Of course. That's the only way to handle them. You have to be ready to react the instant anything unexpected happens. Can't have the watchkeeper phoning round with a message like "Big sea coming in over the forepeak, permission to wear ship". The captain's got to be here.' The wind buffeted her back, emphasising his words by driving her body hard against his. He slung his arm round her shoulders and guided her back into the bridge. All at once she noticed the concentration on the faces of the others there, the air of quiet tension pervading the place.

'Shall I come round?' asked Salah. 'Put her nose into the waves at least.'

'Not yet,' said John. 'The wind will shift dead west when the first front comes over and they say it was gusting to ten at Cape Race. I don't want that catching us with an unexpected broadside. We're too top-heavy with the deck cargo as it is. Keep an eye on the clinometer, Cesar. If we go beyond fifty degrees, she'll roll right over.'

Asha leaned across and pressed her lips to John's cold cheek. He looked at her as though surprised to find her still beside him.

'Sandwiches,' she said.

The chef was busy putting a series of steel struts across the top of the cooker to keep the pots and pans on it steady. The struts had slots cut into them, which slid into each other like carpentry joints. The whole lot clamped down tight to hold everything still. That just left the problem of their contents duplicating the motion of the waves outside. Everything in the galley was tinkling and jingling restlessly. Unused pans hung from hooks along the deck head, sounding like a carillon of little bells. Cutlery lying on the work surfaces rocked and slithered, clashing quietly like distant sword fights. Glasses and cups were shut away but they rang mysteriously from behind closed doors.

Asha staggered a little coming in through the door and almost collided with a steward. Courteously, he stood back, as though the tray of soup plates he carried was weightless. The deck heaved slowly and he performed a matching movement, keeping the tray steady. The soup stood like six little millponds.

'Madame,' the chef beamed, treating her visit as a high compliment. Her work on his hands had made them fast friends.

'Sandwiches, Marcel, for the captain.'

'*D'accord!* You wish to take them *en haut* yourself?'

He opened the refrigerator, swinging the door right back until it caught on a hook on the bulkhead. The hook was tight but even so, the door rattled against the restraint and the bottles and jars in the racks within it added their merry music to all the other tunes in the galley. The sandwiches were piled ready-made on a platter wrapped in plastic film. She took them and went back across the room.

'Tell them there is soup to come!' called Marcel as she left.

This time she went up the internal companionways to the bridge. If the galley had been noisy, here it was worse. The wind was whistling and buffeting against the walls; the rain was continuous, heavy and noisy. Someone had switched on the bridge lights against the gathering murk and as she entered, John's hand moved on a switch and the ship's running lights came on as well. They were almost all that could be seen through the bridge windows until John also switched on the clearview. The huge, old-fashioned windscreen wipers swished from side to side, hurling the water away, and it was possible to see the afternoon again. It was a pitching, dark, roiling afternoon, like the inside of a great cave floored with unsteady stalagmites of sharp black waves. Asha put the tray on the chart table and pulled the plastic film away. John and Richard came across the bridge, licking their lips. 'The chef says there's soup to come,' she told them, and they paused. Hesitated. Their eyes met.

'Soup,' said John, and Richard smiled.

'Soup,' he agreed.

'I'd *love* some soup;' said John, and took a sandwich.

'What was that all about?' asked Asha later, standing beside John as he watched over Salah's steady shoulder.

'Haven't I told you about the soup?' he asked, amazed at his oversight. He told her about the first *Prometheus* and how her crew had been put out of action in a storm such as this by cups of poisoned soup. He related the story as though by rote, as though his mind was not really engaged in it. It wasn't; he was concentrating on the weather outside and the way in which his ship was reacting to it.

They were under the first front now, the warm front. The cloud was at its lowest, seemingly almost on the water, and the wind was just on the point of swinging to the west. The seas were sharp and the wind still strengthening: force nine gale promising at any minute to topple over into storm ten. There was a weight to it, as though they were a nut being squeezed between the jaws of sky and sea; as if the very pressure of the air could crush them. *Napoli* pitched and tossed like a cockle in the frantic swell. Salah's shoulders rocked independently of the movement of the rest of his body, their movement dictated by the force of the wild water through the rudder and the steering motors to the wheel.

'Come to slow ahead, five knots,' ordered John as he finished his story.

Just as he spoke, and Cesar, who was standing at Salah's left hand, moved to grasp the engine room telegraph, the deck before them seemed to catch fire. Asha gave a gasp of fear, which became in an instant a sigh of pleasure. It was as though the main deck, with its cranes and cargo containers, lines, rails and deck furniture had all been remade out of blue neon. Every item there glowed with that electric brightness. Even the smallest detail was visible in the wavering effulgence. Asha felt that the foredeck should have given off light, that it should have reflected on the waves and brightened the sagging bellies of the clouds. But it did not do so; the glow was of itself and gave out no light.

'I think we should log that, Cesar,' said John, automatically looking up. 'Bang on thirteen hundred local time.'

The wind settled into a westerly gale and they butted into it at five steady knots. Asha stayed with John and Richard on the bridge and Ann joined them when Niccolo came on watch at four. By then the overcast was beginning to thin and there seemed to be the chance that the clouds would clear for the evening. The darkness ahead lightened little by little, a process helped by the gusting out of the last of the rain.

By the time a steward brought tea at five, *Napoli*'s bows were outlined against a dazzling band of pearly brightness lying along the horizon dead ahead. As they moved towards it, the waves became visible again, mile upon mile around them of steep-backed water, white-crested and furious looking. Foam exploded up over the old freighter's flared bows, washing like snow along the deck, foaming up in short-lived drifts, making brief igloos of the McGregor hatches, then thawing instantly into the scuppers and away. The winds whipped the tarpaulins into a frenetic blur of movement so that watching them for any length of time gave a sensation like drunkenness as the eyes tried in vain to focus. The cranes seemed to waver like aspens, their ropes performing the wildest dance of all.

Then the sun came out and it was as though they had come to the end of a long tunnel. A wind tunnel. They blinked like troglodytes resurrected and the mood on the bridge lightened like the afternoon. Asha had the feeling of having come through something monumental. She felt elated, renewed. And stifled. Impulsively, she pulled open the starboard bridge wing and stepped outside. It was miraculous out here. The gale was still blowing hard enough to make her stagger and it was cold enough to cut. Her cheeks felt almost flayed at once. But it was so bracing. And so beautiful. She staggered to the bridge rail and hung on for dear life while she looked around. Never had the sky seemed so high, so blue. And the surface of each great wave hurling past mirrored the blue of the sky exactly. The sun was lowering towards the horizon but its beams were dazzling still. The spindrift was perfect white, the spray like flying diamonds.

One look was all she could take for now, though; she wasn't dressed for this. The sunshine was bright but there was no heat in it. The wind was coming from the west now, but it had been born near the polar icecap. The spray would have been solid ice had it not been so salty.

Within a moment she was back inside. 'It's *beautiful*,' she gasped. 'I have to go out again!'

'Be careful if you do,' said John. 'And wrap up well.'

'Oh, but you must come!'

'Asha, I can't just leave the bridge.'

'Of course you can. Niccolo and I can cope.'

'That's very nice of you, Richard, but there's still a full gale blowing out there.'

'A gale?' Richard's face wore an expression of blank astonishment. 'Niccolo, did *you* know there was a gale?'

Niccolo gave one of his Neapolitan shrugs. English humour was beyond him.

Napoli's head ducked under another crest. John looked forward automatically, but it was only white water. Only foam. He didn't need to worry too much until she started taking solid green water. Then her pumps would really have their work cut out.

But Richard was right. There was no reason he should not take a few minutes outside in the fresh air with Asha. She so obviously wanted to; she was hopping from foot to foot like an excited child. They had ridden out a nasty blow with no problem so far. Half an hour to watch the sunset. What harm could it do?

They went down the internal ladders to their cabin and changed as quickly as possible. In Limassol they had bought only summery kit, suitable for a few days' cruising in the south-east Med, and the last suitcases that Richard had brought contained clothing for a Hawaiian honeymoon, but the lighter from Cork had carried proper winter gear. They donned heavy pullovers and waterproof clothing, then went on down through the bridgehouse, out of the rear doors and on to the afterdeck. Because Salah was keeping *Napoli*'s head dead into the wind, the bridgehouse gave a wind shadow. It also gave a sun shadow, and so even with no wind chill, the air was bitingly cold.

They went quickly under the high gallows and out to their favourite position on the wooden afterdeck. There they stood, admiring the breathtaking evening as it gathered behind the ship. The far east of the sky was dark, and it was difficult to tell towering clouds from thickening shadows. Such was the blueness of the sky above that the sky behind was a shimmering indigo. Across this breathtaking backcloth ran the tall seas, spindrift streaming in bright banners away into the stained-glass night. The wind buffeted them and they cuddled up together, watching the day darken down behind them. Distance began to mean less and less as shadows like a tidal wave washed towards them. The noise of the wind made it almost impossible to speak, but there was little enough to say; they simply stood, crushed together, looking at the view.

And as the eastern sky trembled on the edge of darkness and it seemed that the shadows were piled up against the after rail just beyond their heavily gloved fingertips, the most magic moment of all was born. Stretching back along their wake, sitting like a pale carpet, long and narrow, lifting over the waves, there came a luminescence like the neon brightness of the foredeck. Across the troubled waters, under the cloudy shadows, the bright road ran away towards the east.

'Oh John! I've heard of this but I never thought I'd see it.' Asha supposed it was that strange but beautiful phenomenon caused by the movement of the ship through the water stimulating a phosphorescent display from tiny creatures in their wake.

John did not.

He was in motion at once, tearing away from her to run forward into the full force of the wind.

'John! What is it?'

'It's the cargo!' came his voice, all but lost in the roaring wind. 'It's the bloody cargo leaking.'

She looked back, thunderstruck. Then she was in panicked movement, running after him.

She caught up with him on the foredeck immediately in front of the bridge. She thought he must have stopped to look at the deck cargo. But no, he was looking at the sky.

Right across the golden bowl of the western evening sky from the north to the south horizon there cut a mountain of absolute blackness. Only the very top of the sky showed, with just the promise of a star. Below it stood black battlements of cloud. Like basalt cliffs they fell sheer. Tens of thousands of feet they fell, seemingly from the first pale glimmer of the evening star to the wavetops.

Then a series of flashes came dazzling out of the base of the black monster as bolt after bolt of lightning pounced down out of the seemingly infinite thunderheads. The sudden light defined the actual distance between the cloud base and the ocean; it also revealed the speed at which it was coming towards them.

'*My GOD!*' she screamed at him. 'What is *that*?'

'That's the other half of the storm,' he said. And even he sounded awed. 'That's the cold front, where the big winds live.'

CHAPTER TWENTY-THREE

'I know it's bloody dangerous, but we've got to have a look, at the very least. Richard, what do you think?'

Richard's reply was drowned beneath the screaming of the black wind currently doing its level best to tear the superstructure off, and the group in the bridge along with it. Night had come with the second front as abruptly as if the sun had gone out for ever, like a broken light. The northerly storm lying under the cloudbank had arrived with stunning suddenness, far too quickly to allow John any time to check the deck cargo on his way up here. The storm beneath those tall black thunderheads was so fierce that it had taken nearly an hour just to come to terms with it, to hold *Napoli*'s head at exactly the right angle to the wind and waves, which were at least coming from the same direction now. The thrust of the engine pushing her into the teeth of the storm had to balance exactly the pressure of the weather pushing back. Then there were all the other actions and decisions which made up the handling of a storm-bound ship by a master mariner. Richard could certainly have done it, but only the captain could take responsibility for it.

Now *Napoli* was riding as well as could be expected, and someone had to go out on to the deck to check the cargo. All through the last hour of concentrated ship handling, John had felt the worry of it at the back of his mind. He had visions of the toxic filth pouring overboard from lethally gushing tanks. He had to try and stop whatever was happening as soon as possible. But the only way he could even begin to make a plan was to go out on the deck and find out what was happening. Heaven alone knew what he would do if the chemicals really were pouring out of the containers, but he had to know. So, at the end of that first hour, when his ship was riding as safely as he could make her, he announced that he was going to take a team outside to have a look.

Asha had pointed out the obvious: it was dangerous on the deck.

Richard agreed with John's decision, and not only because of the threat the toxic waste posed to the ocean around and behind them. John was worried about the stuff gushing overboard. Richard was more worried about what might happen if it was *not* gushing overboard. What if it was draining down into the ballast tanks and the bilges below them? He did not know he was confronting a nightmare that visited John every night. Nightmares aside, there was one other factor to be considered. The chemical was leaking. The chemical was corrosive. Quite apart from what it might be doing to the ocean or the hull, what was it doing to the hawsers holding the containers safely in place? If it could eat through a hawser or two, twenty tons of steel box was liable to come in through the clearview and on to the bridge along with the next big sea.

'I agree with John,' he said again. 'Someone has to go out.' But before John could say anything, he added, 'I think it should be me.'

John swung round to face his friend and mentor. 'But . . .'

Richard smiled. He almost let the silence stretch. There was nothing John could say, really, though he had started to say something. Richard was not needed on the bridge. John was. Richard was as competent as John to take a team and look at the cargo. His friend simply did not want him to face the danger. He appreciated that. But they had just agreed that someone had to go. At the moment it made more sense that he should go.

When Richard read reluctant agreement in John's eyes, he nodded once. 'I'll take a team under Cesar, and I'll borrow Marco as lookout,' he decided.

Cesar hurried off the bridge to dig his gang out of their

accommodation below and get them kitted up. Marco Farnese moved with far less alacrity.

Twenty minutes later, they were all assembled by the main deck bulkhead door ready to step out of the bridgehouse into the maelstrom. They each wore bright yellow wet weather gear with extra covering for heads and hands against the biting cold which already seemed to be percolating in through the shaking steel around them. They each held a bright, broad-beamed flashlight. Richard, Cesar and Marco each held a portable two-way radio. Richard had given his orders, Cesar had translated them and the crewmen nodded grimly that they understood.

It took all Richard's massive physical power combined with Cesar's wiry strength to push the door open against the unrelenting pressure of the wind. The huge, counterweighted steel portal trembled like a leaf as they moved it wide enough for their team to squeeze past them. They themselves would have been trapped inside, but the wind hesitated for a second, allowing two of Cesar's men to hold it for them, and they jumped out on to the deck together. No sooner had they done so than the wind slammed it behind them, seemingly deciding to do its best to pitch them overboard.

Had John not switched on the deck lights, they would have been utterly blind. The storm was taking place in absolute darkness. There wasn't even any lightning now, just an overpowering, invisible bedlam of wind, rain, wave and spray. The noise was terrific. The wind buffeted them with breathtaking force and glacial cold, many degrees below zero even without counting the massive chill factor. The water on the deck was moving with such force that it might as well have been ice. Richard was more worried than ever when he noticed that the spray clinging to the deck furniture all around him was in fact turning to ice. Leaning into the incredible power of it, he began to force his way forward, the quick release of his lifeline ready to snap on to the safety ropes along the deck.

There were two teams of crewmen. Richard would take one team down one side, Cesar the second down the other side. Marco was going up on to the forward radio mast to keep a lookout in case the men on the exposed deck needed warning about the state of the seas bearing down on them. All the deck lights were on but the men still needed to use their torches; thin, impenetrable shadows sat under the tarpaulin-covered containers.

Richard caught up with his two men and knelt uneasily beside them, then lay full length on the pitching, running, freezing steel, to shine his torch under the first set of containers. His torch beam married up with those of his men. The underside of the containers lit up, ridged and ribbed with ropes. Little icicles hung down towards the deck until another freezing wash of foam snapped them off. Richard found that he was shaking with the cold; not shivering, shaking. He forced himself to his knees just as *Napoli*'s head swooped. He had a vague impression of distant mountains made of black glass, then a tidal wave of foam swept back towards him. He turned his back to it and let it wash up to his armpits while he held on to a steel hawser for dear life, his safety line wrapped twice round his arm just in case. When it had passed, he simply turned round and crawled forward, dragging his line behind him like a dog's lead. Standing up just seemed too much trouble. There was nothing to see under the second set of containers either. Richard and his two men began to crawl towards the next pile.

On the other side of the deck, Cesar and his men were fractionally ahead. The second officer was a grimly efficient man and, like Richard, had been careful to clip on his lifeline. But, being slighter, and perhaps more energetic, he had relied upon it to hold him safely as the foam swept past and had continued to plod doggedly forward through it. Nor was he pausing to lie flat on the freezing deck. He trusted his men to do that and warn him if they saw anything untoward. He himself was concerned to test the tarpaulin lashings, something he could do while standing up. He did this by taking firm hold of the ropes and pulling them roughly from side to side. When the radio snarled, he put it to his hooded, wool-covered ear and yelled, '*Pronto?*'

'Anything?' It was Richard.

'Nothing.'

'Good. Marco?'

'*Pronto?*' came the distant reply. Cesar turned and glanced up at the forward radio mast. He was surprised Marco had made it up there. But then Cesar was surprised when the stupid boy did anything right. Thoughtlessly, he pulled at the tarpaulin binding. And it came away in his hand. Puzzled that it should have chafed through so quickly, even under these conditions, he brought the frayed rope end up towards his face, allowing the radio to dangle by its wrist strap while he shone his torch fully upon the rope. His puzzlement deepened. It hadn't frayed to the usual wild bunch of fibres at all. Quite the reverse; the hawser end seemed almost to have been sealed. Then he realised. It hadn't chafed at all. It had melted.

It was braided steel, and *it had melted*.

He swung round, looking for Richard, his radio back in his hand, coming up towards his mouth. Whether he looked forward because he thought the big Englishman would have worked faster than he had or because he felt *Napoli*'s head begin to dip, he would never know. But look forward he did, just as the radio came up to his mouth.

And he screamed.

Marco Farnese was fast becoming convinced that life at sea was not for him. Although he never admitted as much to himself, he had come to sea to run away from his father's farm. And now he wished he could run away from the sea. It scared him. It made him feel sick. It did not, as he had hoped it would, guarantee him success with girls because he was a boring person who never noticed anything of interest even in his greatest seagoing adventures. And, even if he had, he could never have made an interesting story out of it. Climbing the thirty feet up to the forward observation post inside the top of the forward radio mast was the most difficult and dangerous thing he had ever done. He knew he was lucky to have got up here without hurting himself and he was not looking forward to getting down again – though he was of course very much looking forward to getting back to the warmth and safety of the bridge.

At least the little eyrie up here above the forward emergency siren was relatively warm and snug. If only it would stop pitching about in quite such a sickening manner. Then again, he told himself, things could be worse. He looked back and down at the unfortunates crawling like vermin on the brightly lit deck. Just as he did so a sea of white foam washed along the length of it, inundating them all. He spluttered quietly, trying not to laugh. The snotty, holier-than-thou Cesar was almost washed away. The huge Englishman had to stay on his knees as it flowed past him. He looked as though he was swimming. How cold it must be! Good! Marco did not like people, captains or not, who volunteered him for unpleasant duties.

The little room pitched again, throwing him around like a child in a fairground ride. His stomach began to heave.

'Marco!'

'*Pronto!*' He hit his lips with the radio and made them bleed. He thought he had chipped a tooth.

'All okay?'

'*Bene*, Capitano,' Marco managed, then his stomach got the better of him and he began to vomit.

The sole reason for his being in the forward lookout post was so that he could warn the men on the deck about any big seas ahead. But he hadn't looked forward once, and he wasn't doing so now.

And so it was Cesar who saw it first, though even as he screamed – an automatic reaction quite beyond his control – his mind refused to accept what he could see. It was a black wall. There was apparently no curve to it at all, neither concave nor convex. It was simply a coal-black cliff, shining slightly with reflected brightness from the deck lights. There were no ends to it. It ran into the wild darkness on either hand. There was no bottom to it that he could see. Its foundations seemed to be far below the surface of the sea, or where the surface once had been, out of sight in the abyssal depth of the ocean. There was a top to it, however. A top, mountainous and snowy white with spume, being thrust forward over the broad, black shoulders of the wall by the unrelenting power of the wind, at least thirty feet above *Napoli*'s falling forecastle head.

When Cesar screamed, Marco looked up. He watched with silent wonder, never thinking to yell a warning into the radio he was holding for that very purpose. The foaming top of the wall of water was exactly level with his eyes. He saw it. He refused to believe it. The spray hurling forward from the crest mercifully blinded him. But only for a moment. When it cleared again an instant later it was as though he was looking through a porthole in a diving bell. There was water breaking gently against the glass in front of him. Glass which was thirty feet above *Napoli*'s forward deck. Oil-black water stretched away as far as he could see and the surface of it was exactly level with his eyes. He looked down. The lower half of the window in front of him showed the absolute darkness of the deeps of the ocean. Tiny streams of water arced in from pinholes along the bottom of the window frame. His brain told him that his mouth was under the surface. His lungs told him they were drowning. He choked. He whimpered. He began to cry in earnest.

It did not break like a roller on a beach. It just slid forward over the rails of the forecastle head and came massively along the deck. It seemed to be hissing, very quietly. All the other sounds of the storm, all the other sights and sounds in the whole world fell away. Cesar stood and looked up at it. In slow motion, it swept up to him and, as though passing through the looking glass, like Alice, the second officer stepped into it. And the force of it, the unimaginable power of it whirled him away from the deck. He felt a slight jerk as his lifeline parted. He did not even hold his breath because this was all so completely unreal. The shock of the icy water going directly into his lungs stopped his heart at once. He was dead before the force in the bowels of that water mountain whirled him in an instant along the length of the deck to smash his rigid body against the front of the bridge with enough force to leave the faintest impression of his face in the steel before it sent him tumbling into the lower depths with the remains of his work team and the tarpaulin torn from the forward container stack.

The sound of Cesar's scream gave Richard warning enough to take one simple action. He wrapped his arms and legs tight round the nearest hawser and hugged it to himself with all his might. There was a prayer in his mind but it could not really be said that he prayed. He was an extremely fit man with an enormous lung capacity and was a trained diver to boot. He could hold his breath for four minutes at a pinch. His eyes closed, his face screwed up, his teeth grinding together, his cheek against the metal – metal so cold it burned his flesh – he hung on. A force took hold of him. It was more than water. It was naked power, an omnipotence like the grasp of a god. It could do anything. It could so easily have torn him free. It could equally easily have ripped the container free, whose hawser he was clinging to. It could have broken the front off the ship altogether – he had seen the sea do that – or it could simply have swallowed the ship whole. He had no idea what it was doing elsewhere while it held him within it. He did not care. He was thirty feet below the surface and he concentrated on trying to protect his eardrums. On trying to move his numb cheek just a millimetre in case it froze to the metal. On little things. On staying alive, and sane.

No one on the bridge said a thing. Possibly they simply did not believe what they were seeing. For them it was black no longer once it had passed the radio mast where Marco was sitting. The lights on the deck lit up the crystal heart of it so that it looked like a mountain of glass – until it shattered against the front of the bridgehouse. Then it was as though they were caught in an earthquake. The pitching and rolling of the storm so far had been sea movements. This was much more elemental. A deep vibration came through every surface. The steel itself seemed to be rippling. The bridge window went absolutely white and Salah later swore that it bulged inwards. The noises from below were indescribable and for a moment John thought the whole bridgehouse was simply being torn off. All five storeys of it.

Everything – motion, time – stopped. And darkness slammed up against the bridge window. It was so sudden, so absolute, so shockingly unexpected that there was almost a sound to it, as though *Napoli*'s face had been slapped by the blackness. As though in answer to the blow, the lights in the bridgehouse died as well. The whole ship shuddered and heeled. And fell off the edge of the world.

The thing that Richard felt most poignantly was amazement that he should feel anything at all. The next thing he felt was cold. It was a cold which had gone far beyond anything of the surface. It existed deep in the very heart of him, like a spike of ice. So numb was he that he didn't even notice the shock of *Napoli* landing in the next trough, though it was great enough to break his grip on the ice-slick hawser and smash him jarringly to the deck. It was also enough of a shock to start his lungs working again, and he breathed in air, which was absolutely miraculous. When *Napoli*'s head came back up, she all but threw him on to his feet but his legs weren't actually working and so he just rolled down the deck in an ungainly bundle until his lifeline brought him up short. He thought, 'If I don't get up and get myself into the bridgehouse, I'll freeze to death in no time.' But when he looked for it, he could see no sign of the bridgehouse at all.

El Jefe had been carrying out an elaborate ritual in the engine room designed to protect the main drive shaft. Every time the ship pitched forward, he gave a signal to cut engine power so that when the propeller came up out of the water it did not begin to race uncontrollably and destructively. There was no way he could be prepared for the water mountain, and when *Napoli* fell off the back of it, having been swept from end to end like a toy boat, he was damn near thrown through the engine control room window. On the other hand, when the power went, he knew exactly what to do. Emergency power was on within minutes and full power not long after. But his responsibilities only began with the restoration of power; he had to start checking all the damage that might have been done when they lost it in the first place. It took power to run the steering motors, power to keep the shaft turning in its long, open bed. Power to keep the seacocks closed and the bilge pumps pumping out.

As soon as the emergency lighting came on, John was in action. The fact that he was trained to act under the most mind-numbing circumstances when lesser mortals stood around and gaped was what made him a master mariner. A Heritage Mariner master mariner. It also nearly killed him. He crossed the bridge while the others were standing gawping and pushed the door to the bridge wing open. 'Niccolo, check in the bridgehouse and below,' he ordered. 'I'm going to see what's left on the deck.' And he stepped out of the door into the night. Only by the greatest good fortune did he keep firm hold of the door handle, and it saved him. He stepped off the bridge with his right leg and leaned forward, expecting his foot to touch the bridge wing. And then he was swinging wildly, holding on for dear life, his left leg twisting agonisingly while the door took his weight until he hauled himself back on to the bridge.

The starboard bridge wing was gone altogether.

When the lights came back on in the bridgehouse, Richard began to crawl towards them. It was an act of superhuman strength and willpower and it was utterly useless. He did not realise that his lifeline was still attached and his frozen hands and knees were simply skidding over the icy deck while he stayed in the same place, exactly halfway between the nearest containers and his bright but battered goal.

And that was where John and the rescue team found him three minutes later when they came rushing out on to the deck.

When he came to, he felt as though he had recently been boiled in oil. His right cheek also seemed to have been branded. As he came spiralling up towards full wakefulness, he became aware of a persistent sobbing and this caused him some deep concern. 'It's all right, darling. Robin, I'm fine,' he said.

But then he realised that the crying was too deep to be

Robin's. And the odours of this place were not the familiar smells of his bedroom either.

Then it all came back in a colossal rush and he sat up straight in his bed. Fatima jerked awake at his bedside and stopped him moving any further. 'Asha says you've got to keep warm!' she whispered.

A shivering fit overcame him. He looked around a little wildly. Fatima watched him, her face worn and lined. Behind her shoulder, a bundle in the next bed shook and sobbed. Dim light on gold curls showed that it was Marco. Beyond him sat Asha herself. Her eyes met his.

'Cesar?' he asked quietly.

'Gone. Everyone on the deck except you and . . .' Asha looked down at the sobbing man.

'My God! So it's just John and Niccolo?'

'He's made up the crewman Eduardo acting third. But he needs you. He *needs* you, Richard. You've got to get better as quickly as possible.'

Richard lay back, shaking again, trying to gather his strength. Well, he thought, every nerve alert, at last she was sitting more firmly in the water. The pitching and rolling had stilled. 'Are we through the storm?' he asked, his voice full of wonder.

Fatima nodded.

'Well, that's a good start!' he said brightly. 'How long have I been out?'

'Four hours.'

'My God! I must get up!'

'No,' said Asha. 'He needs you well and strong. Get some more sleep. Please. We'll wake you.'

He acquiesced, leaning back. They had piled too many pillows up behind his head. He could not get comfortable. He reached back to remove them. And froze. There were none there. It was not the angle of his bed that was so acute. It was the angle of the deck.

The angle of the whole ship.

CHAPTER TWENTY-FOUR

'My God, Richard, you look dreadful!'

'You don't look too good yourself, John.' Richard hesitated on the threshold of the bridge, just a little winded by his rush to dress and get up here. He looked around with narrowed eyes at the shambles in the bridge and the mess outside. 'Still,' he grated, 'you look better than *Napoli* does.'

John was grey with fatigue and had clearly taken no rest since the beginning of the storm. Niccolo looked no better, and was slumped in the watchkeeper's chair. The door of the radio shack was propped open and Jesus sat like a ghost in there with Ann Cable perched on a work surface by one of his radios. Eduardo had replaced Marco as third officer, but he was really only a kind of extra Bosun, his paper qualifications were not sufficient to support his place as a navigating officer. Salah still stood at the wheel. They were all staring through the bridge window down on to the deck.

It was a glorious dawn, still, calm and bright. The sea was a cheerful blue, the long south-westerly groundswell rolling up towards them like billows of peacock silk to caress the length of the ship making her rock gently like a cradle. There was no foam or wrack on them, no sign of present weather or memory of last night's tempest. *Napoli* continued to push through them, doggedly upon her course, as though anyone aboard still thought she and her cargo would make it safely to Sept Isles.

The deck which Richard overlooked sloped down hill. The swell which should have reached the middle lading marks on her hull rose over them near the fo'c'sle and, Richard knew, would be nowhere near them at the poop. The line between her black side and her red-lead bottom was no longer parallel with the water's surface; it plunged below each rising wave which tried to wash the anchor. And, he suspected, that same red bottom would be on view from astern, along with the top of her rudder. But at least the propeller was under water or they would not have had steerage way. That was something.

The angle of the deck was only the start. How the forward radio mast had survived remained a miracle to rank with his own continued existence. The cranes had not been so blessed: all four of them were twisted, hunched. Their arms were broken or gone. This was a serious problem, because now they could not tidy up the deck cargo which lay strewn across the green steel like a child's building blocks thrown down in a tantrum. Richard was surprised the deck had stood up to the impact of their toppling. Surprised that he could see no immediate evidence of the containers themselves having fractured or burst. God alone knew what things were like within those great corrugated boxes, how many barrels were leaking, split or shattered. As for the hold cargo, he didn't like to think what leakage from the deck cargo was doing to it.

'Has anyone been down for a closer look?' he asked. They shook their heads. A captain coming on to a bridge normally consults barometer, compass and heading, log, chronometer. Richard had so far looked at only the deck; none of the other things seemed important beside the state of the cargo. 'What does Cape Race say about this?' he demanded, swinging round to look into the little radio shack.

'Radio's fucked,' said John. Richard, who had hardly ever heard his friend swear, was slightly shocked.

'I get a little incoming. No outgoing,' Jesus explained. 'Is random, yes? No pattern. No control. I think is aerial. I don't know. I've looked *inside* radio. Now I must look outside bridgehouse. See if outside aerial is still there. I don't think she is.'

'God!' Richard paused. But there was more he wanted to

know. 'Well, what does El Jefe say? How are the pumps handling things?'

'Pumps are fucked.' John's voice sounded dead, as though he was beyond caring.

Silence.

Richard looked round at them all; they seemed at the end of their tether. Only Ann Cable appeared to have any energy left. Richard was not particularly strong himself at the moment. He would have to conserve his energy if he was going to be of any long-term use. But they could not continue pounding up towards Canada in this state, dumb, helpless, apparently slowly sinking, with a horrifically dangerous cargo that was damaged and quite likely deteriorating. The deck cargo had been leaking before the wall of water smashed into them. They needed a plan of action and they needed it fast.

His precious energy would be best expended in gathering facts and making that plan while these exhausted zombies continued to sail the ship into the early day. Perhaps they would meet another ship, though the storm might well have cleared even these busy shipping lanes. Perhaps Jesus would manage to fix his set and raise Cape Race. 'Ann,' he said quietly.

'Yeah?'

'Could you find the chef and a couple of stewards. Get some hot coffee and a couple of mattresses up here. Then the captain can catch a nap and the watch officer can keep himself awake. And some food.'

'Galley's probably out of action,' she said. 'But I'll see what I can do.'

'Right. In the meantime, I'll be in the engine room.'

Everyone in the engine control room was asleep and most of them were wearing their life jackets. El Jefe, for all his bull-like strength, was clearly as exhausted as John and it seemed a pity to have to wake him. Information about the weather and the radio and where they were on the face of the Western Ocean could wait; what Richard needed to know most urgently was how long they could expect to remain afloat. The term 'fucked' when applied to pumps was a little vague.

'J'ou understand pumps?'

'Of course.'

'The bilge pumps on *Napoli* are reciprocating displacement pumps. J'ou are familiar with this?'

'Yes.'

'They work with a central piston and four valves. J'ou know?' Richard just nodded. 'The valves must fit exactly or the pump does not work well. If the valves wear out, stop to fit, the pump will cavitate. Will break. All our valves worn out. None fit now. Head pressure dangerously low. I shut down system.'

'All the valves failed at once? At the same time?'

The Spaniard looked at him sideways. Richard had put his finger on the central point. The valves were the most delicate parts in the system, but it was unusual, to put it mildly, for all the valves in a series of pumps to fail at once.

'What do you think it is, Jefe?'

The chief engineer hesitated, thinking. 'The deck cargo. Is in the bilges. Bilge water go through the pumps. Valves suddenly fail. Deck cargo has destroyed the valves. J'ou see this?'

Richard nodded wearily. It was exactly what he had been worried about. 'Can you check?'

'Long job to check. And any case, all valves would need to be re-machined.'

Richard read between the lines here with no trouble at all. It was a question of time. There was probably not enough time to check; definitely not enough time for the re-machining. 'How fast are we taking water?'

'Not fast. Here, at this part of the ship, we have hardly measured any gain in the last two hours. To know more, j'ou will have to check further forward.'

Richard nodded again. He was going to have to go down into the forward hold as soon as possible in any case. Into all three holds, in fact. And he would have to take Professor Faure. If the concentration of deck cargo in the bilge was strong enough to destroy the pump valves, it was certainly strong enough to attack the hull. And, if the hold cargo was under its surface, then the concrete protection round that was at risk as well.

'Can you give me any idea how long she will stay afloat if we can either stop the leaks or fix the pumps?'

El Jefe shrugged, a gesture exaggerated by the bright orange life jacket he was wearing. 'Afloat? Perhaps days. Moving? Not very long. We go down at the head by another metre, I have to shut the engine off. The propeller, j'ou see, is almost out of the water now. Water pressure of the sea on the propeller blades is falling quickly. Soon the revs go up too high and the engine stop or the main shaft break. J'ou look, j'ou see bad vibration already.'

Faure looked just as exhausted as everyone else. Clearly, the fact that he had spent all night in his bunk did not mean that he had actually got any rest. No one aboard had slept, or even relaxed. The state of the main deck did nothing to cheer the distinguished scientist. Like all the rest, he had glanced outside when calm dawn had descended. And, again like all the rest, a glance out of the side windows had sufficed for him. He had collapsed into relief and stayed put. Now, in the company of Richard and Ann Cable, he was kitted up in a white protective suit, carefully picking his way through the lethal litter on the main deck. He was not enjoying the experience at all. Every time he stooped or knelt to take a sample from a pool, the action only served to emphasise the angle of the deck. His samples were in any case a little academic. The bottoms of so many of the pools he paused at were pale enough to make it obvious that some corrosive agent was at work. And there was only one source of that agent.

The forward hatch was smashed open along half its length, though no sign remained of what had done the damage. Richard's torch probed the shadows beyond the sunlight streaming down into the gaping, snaggle-toothed hole, but the morning brightness was enough to establish at once that the hold's ladder was still firmly in place. Their ears were all they needed to tell them about the hold's liquid contents, though the sun also obligingly revealed a restless, filthy lake of sea water below, sluggishly washing over the tops of the concrete containers. At the forward end of the hold, they were deeply submerged; at the rear it was possible to see the grey shapes below the filthy, oily, surface. *Napoli* pitched exhaustedly. A wave of scum and debris slopped back to explode against the after wall of the hold. Richard watched it wash up over the outline of the huge door there, the one that Captain Fittipaldi had had welded shut. His face folded into a frown.

'Wait here a minute,' he said to the other two, though neither of them had yet shown the slightest inclination to clamber down into the forbidding little cavern.

The cover to the next hatch was undamaged and Richard had no trouble opening it. The motor whirred and the sections folded back one by one. Richard looked down into the darkness, at the square of light expanding on the floor of the hold, over the concrete boxes. Over the dry concrete boxes. The ship pitched gently again and a thunder came from against the dividing wall. Richard suddenly found that he was short of breath. It was hope and it winded him as effectively as a punch below the belt. He pulled his headgear into place and switched on the air. Then he swung one leg over the raised lip of the hatch cover and stepped down on to the first rung of the ladder. He descended rapidly, pausing only when the thunder of water against the dividing wall just before his nose made the ladder he was climbing shiver along its length.

At the foot of the ladder he knelt, looking at the flat grey metal. It *was* dry. He touched it almost unbelievingly. He looked up to his right at the massive dividing door welded shut by the dead captain's fear. Not a drop. Dry as a bone. He rose to his feet again and walked over towards the nearest concrete boxes. It was not far, they were spread out and fitted snugly across the floor of the hold. All the pitching and heaving last night didn't seem to have moved them all. Thank God for small mercies.

On closer examination he saw that things were not actually as dry down here as they had seemed at first. The blocks were splashed with darkness; whole areas of them were black and shiny. But it did not seem particularly important at that moment.

What was of overpowering importance was the dryness of the deck. It looked as though *Napoli* was down by the head because of the weight of the water that had poured through the smashed hatch into the forward hold. If the pumps had been working, they could either have pumped it over the side, or at least balanced the weight. As it was, the only way they had of bringing up her head would be to cut open the welded doors between the three holds and let the water flow back and settle at the bottom so that *Napoli* would sit on an even keel. Then they could look at getting the pumps fixed. Or sail in search of help. Maybe even think about getting to Sept Isles after all. As long as that stuff slopping in the forward hold was not so corrosive it ate away their bottom or their hold cargo first. And as long as there was no more water coming in through the hull at the bow.

Back on the bridge it seemed that only Richard and Ann were fully awake. Faure looked around and then hurried below to test his samples. Richard explained his plan to the others and they stood and looked at him as though they didn't understand. Ann listened to his short speech, then hurried below in the wake of the professor. It was clear to Richard that if he was going to get the oxyacetylene equipment out and undo Captain Fittipaldi's work, he would need engineers to help. They at least should have had a little sleep. But he did not want to rush into action quite yet. He had to be sure that John agreed; *Napoli* was John's command, after all. 'John,' he persisted. 'What do you want to do first?'

'Sleep!' John's voice caught on an exhausted half-laugh. 'But we can't. I think we'd better wait just a moment until we get reports back from our experts. We may need to save our energy to abandon ship. At the very least, I want to hang fire until we check up on the crew and get some competent deckhands up here. It's ridiculous to have Salah still at the wheel. I know we have several perfectly capable helmsmen below.'

Richard nodded. John might be at the end of his strength, but he was thinking clearly enough. He caught up a cup of cooling coffee from the work surface near the watchkeeper's chair and gulped it down. He waited, as though expecting either the caffeine or the sugar it contained in such abundance to give

him some extra energy. When it failed to do so, he stretched
and crossed to the helm. Pausing for a moment beside Salah, he
looked out at the morning. Then he crossed to the chart table
and at last tapped the barometer as he passed it. In spite of all
they had been through – and in spite of the exhaustion – they had
kept up the log and movement book. Their current position was
marked as of the 08.00 change of watch – which was, of course,
only a theoretical change because all the watch officers were
here and looked like staying here for the foreseeable future.
Their current position was 41.45N; 49.50W, nearly a thousand
miles out on their current course; four days' sailing at their
current speed.

While Richard was checking their course and position, Ann
Cable was rushing back down the length of the deck. She had
convinced Faure to accompany her because she wanted someone
to check her readings. Side by side they hurried through the
debris of the deck cargo, skidding in the pale-bottomed puddles,
sending them trickling down the slope towards the fo'c'sle. They
were completely unaware of what their feet were doing because
of the depth of their concern. Their protective headgear was
pushed back on their shoulders so that they could talk.
    'There is no doubt that your chemical, whatever it may actually
be, is strong enough in its current concentration to attack almost
everything it touches.' Ann gave Faure a breakdown of what
Richard had told her about the state of the pumps. 'He says he
wouldn't be at all surprised,' she concluded, 'if the stuff hadn't
been leaking right from the start. It could well be the reason the
hold lights stopped working. It would be logical for them to go
first; the circuitry that powers them is all in the space between
the deck and the top of the hold.'
    They were at the top of the forward hold now, beside the
broken hatch. They climbed down, Ann first. As she stepped
off the bottom of the ladder, it moved and she paused for an
instant, shining her torch on it. The bolts securing it to the
forward hold wall had sheered. All the bolts under the water
had failed; all those above it held true. She turned away and

started wading aft towards the shallow end. It was like moving through a tiny, filthy swimming pool. The surface of the restless liquid – she could hardly call it just water any more – heaved gently around her hips and the chill of it struck through into her most vital areas. She had to force her mind to trust what she was wearing; the thought of what might happen should the suit spring a leak made her blood run cold.

A few minutes of determined movement brought her to her goal: the shallow end. Here one or two concrete boxes stood partly above the surface. She knelt and shone her torch down on them. Nothing looked wrong. She glanced up as Faure came sloshing over to crouch beside her. He had his bag of tools as well as his torch. He unzipped it and handed her a knife. She scraped the surface of the concrete just at the water line. Under the stainless steel blade, the concrete turned to powder and for more than a centimetre of its depth it simply crumbled away. The two scientists exchanged glances. Ann tried again on another block. Same result. She gave the knife back, then got out her Geiger counter. As soon as she swiched it on, it started to click so rapidly that Faure jumped. He grabbed it and studied its read-out closely. Then he handed it back very slowly.

They went into the next hold. Movement was easier here as there was almost no water on the floor. Ann had been hoping that the drier conditions would mean that the concrete of these boxes would be much more robust, but this was not quite the case. The dark areas which had been wet by water dripping in from above were pitted and as crumbly as the concrete in the flooded hold. And her Geiger counter sounded just as angry.

Ten minutes later the two of them were back on the bridge. Ann had brought the folder in which she kept her records. She threw it down on to the chart table with a loud *slap*. John and Niccolo, both of whom had been dozing, jumped awake. Richard swung round, a frown creasing his strong face. 'It's bad, then,' he said quietly.

Ann took a juddering breath. 'How long have we got at best speed?' she asked.

'To get to Sept Isles? Four days. Say one hundred hours. At best speed, weather permitting.'

'Then we're dead.'

John cleared his throat. 'When you say "dead", what do you mean, precisely?'

Ann took another deep breath. She looked at Faure as though his gentle, academic, professorial style could rub off on her and allow her to present their findings in a cool, calm, scientific way. 'Your deck cargo is leaking so badly that it is not only eating into your ship, it is also dissolving the protection round your nuclear cargo.' She looked at them, met each pair of eyes. 'It's like a kind of time bomb,' she said more quietly. She opened her record folder and showed them the graph she had drawn based on her readings in the hold. 'I haven't got the kind of time frame I would like and I can't be absolutely accurate, therefore. But the simple fact is that all that nuclear waste down there is heating up faster and faster as the concrete gets eaten away. Unless you can stop the process soon, you'll be sitting on another Chernobyl.'

'How soon?'

'Before it's too late to stop the process? Eight hours. Before the whole lot melts down and blows us all to hell and gone? Less than twenty-four.'

The very instant she delivered herself of this speech, Jesus recieved his first – and his last – clear radio message: '. . . *Napoli*. This is Cape Race. Receiving you strength five. Intermittent. Confirm your position 41.45N; 49.5W. Understand you have sustained damage. Nearest ship to your current position is *Rainbow Warrior*. Say again, *Rainbow Warrior*. Make contact on the following wavelen—'

CHAPTER TWENTY-FIVE

'What did you think?' asked Ann. 'Did you think I was on holiday or something? That Greenpeace employs me to sit around on container ships and wander all over the world doing the odd test on a suspect cargo and flirting with the officers? I mean, it would be a great life if you didn't weaken. But *really*!'

The others looked at each other in silence. Niccolo in particular frowned thoughtfully.

'Maybe when I talked my way aboard at Naples I was content just to look around and keep tabs. I didn't know what was involved then and the fact that Verdi and Nero had been happy enough to let me come and even to bring me out with them on the *Parthenope* didn't look very promising, frankly. You know the way we operate: *Rainbow Warrior* on the Southern Ocean, inflatables in front of whalers and sealers, rallies, books and posters, films and videos, news reports – *publicity*. That's what I was looking for: something to make a story out of. Something to hold up as a warning. Things really started shaping up in Liverpool. I mean, that was publicity of another kind. And suddenly the owners and the charterers wanted me off. Of course I had to stay. Of course I had to keep checking. Of course I had to keep reporting in. Yes, I guess I was setting you up. Did you really think we would be happy for you to go sailing up the St Lawrence ready to drop off in the North American subcontinent a cargo so dangerous that it had already been thrown out of Europe not once but *twice*!'

She took a deep breath. 'I'm surprised I need to telling you this. Where do you guys keep your brains, for Heaven's sake? But the fact is that if I set you up, it's nothing to the way CZP and Disposoco have set you up before me. Captain Fittipaldi must have been really out of touch. The rest of you are all pretty desperate, I know, officers and crew alike. Professor Faure, you and your men were just trapped aboard by bad luck, like Salah and Fatima. John, Asha, for you it was a mistake; good intentions and more bad luck. Richard, you were just helping and God knows we may need more help yet. But I mean to say! Look at the mess you've gotten yourselves into. You're just coming over the most fertile fishing grounds in the whole of the northern hemisphere, heading towards one of the most populous and widely used seaboards in the entire world and you are bringing a high-yield, extremely dirty, nuclear time bomb with you that is going to go off like a huge Roman candle somewhere in the top ten feet of water where it can infect the air as well. You're right where the prevailing weather systems can spread the fall-out from here to Russia, and where the Gulf Stream can pick it up and spread it all the way back to Europe next time it swings north.'

'In these conditions, that will be sometime soon unless we get another northerly storm anyway. And if we do, that would just take the airborne fall-out,' observed John.

'We can't unload the deck cargo which is the root cause of the trouble because the cranes are . . .' Ann looked for the correct technical word.

'Fucked,' supplied Niccolo helpfully.

'We can't unload the hold cargo for the same reason. We can't even pump clean water over the hold cargo and give it a decent wash, because the pumps aren't working either. So we can't stop the process or even slow it down. We can't get this clapped-out old scow to any port or docking facility, or to anyone who could help us. And we can't even warn anyone what is happening because of the radio.'

'But,' said Richard, returning to the revelation which had

begun this impassioned speech, 'you say that *Rainbow Warrior* is on her way out to meet us even as we speak.'

'Right. But aside from filming this mess as it all goes up, I can't think what good she will actually do.'

'Filming us?' he asked, sidetracked for a moment.

'Sure. That's what it's all about. Like I said: publicity. They've got the cameras, the news guys, the inflatables. They've even got a submersible aboard, for God's sake, so they can get underwater shots of you if they need. But they won't have any heavy lifting equipment and they won't have anything to neutralise that stuff on the concrete boxes.'

'The most efficient agent seems to be salt water in any case,' observed Faure. 'Witness Dr Higgins's work on Bernadotte's hands. But we cannot get enough of it to dilute the concentration of chemical already in the hold or dripping through from the deck.'

'But that's insane,' whispered Asha. 'We're surrounded with the stuff. We're surrounded by salt water. There's nothing else as far as the eye can see!'

'Yes, but our problem is letting enough in to stop the process and then *letting it out again*. Otherwise we just sink, *hein*?' Faure's wry observation seemed to have ended the conversation.

Except that Richard added: 'That, of course, might solve everything.'

The others stared at him and he paused, gathering his thoughts. What he was about to propose was so deeply against everything he had been trained to believe as a master and a shipowner that only these circumstances would have made him entertain the thought, and even then, the thought had to be handled carefully, as though it too was unimaginably destructive.

'Our first problem is that the deck cargo is now leaking with dangerous results and it cannot be moved. If *Napoli* sank, the ocean would move it for us. Our second problem is that the chemical cannot be washed off the hold cargo because the pumps have failed and although we can get sea water in, we can't get it out. If *Napoli* sank, the hold cargo would be suspended in the one element which will bring its deterioration to a stop. Our third problem is that if we continue on our present course, we will come over the Newfoundland Banks where the water is shallow, restless and the breeding ground of an incredible range of fish; further, it might also be swept by the Gulf Stream flowing east, back to Europe. But if she goes down here, where she is now, then none of these things apply.'

'Here?' Ann looked out at the early morning ocean as though it would betray some individuality, something special for her to see.

'Our current position, 41.45N;49.50W. John; you started it! Captain Smith!'

'My God!' breathed John and his eyes seemed to light up. '*My God!*'

'*What?*' cried Ann.

'We haven't reached the Grand Banks yet. We're still out in deep water. There's two and a half *miles* of water under our keel. Two and a half miles straight down to an abyss where almost nothing lives. Where the water is still, lightless, below freezing, all but dead. There may be some primitive corals down there, some extremely basic tube worms. Nothing much else. And it's so chemically inert that it can take years just for rust to form.'

'How do you know that?' Ann demanded. 'How do you know what it's like down there?'

'Because *she*'s down there. Two and a half miles straight down. Right under our keel.

'*Who?* Who's down there?'

'*Titanic*,' answered Richard. 'We're exactly over the *Titanic*.'

At that moment the radio sprang back to life and everybody on the bridge looked towards the radio shack. '*Napoli*, this is *Rainbow Warrior*. We hear you strength five. Intermittent. Please respond *Napoli*. Please re—'

In his youth, Jesus had seriously considered *la corrida* as a profession, but Heaven had dictated otherwise. He had kept himself fit, however, and his trim body and quick reactions would have given any bull a run for its money even now. Certainly, he was having no trouble at the moment, on this clear and beautiful morning, in shinning up to the wreck of the radio mast. He was coming up to seventy feet above the deck, well over one hundred feet above the rolling surface of the sea. He was too wise to look down and concentrated on looking up towards the twisted metal above his head. There should have been a set of steps climbing up here, but the storm had ripped them away at the same time as doing the damage he had come to repair.

He was a conscientious man and he had found his inability to communicate from the moment the wave struck extremely frustrating. At the same time, he was sensible and very careful. He had thought of coming up here while the wind was still high, but there had been no real point in risking his life, then. The odds had been too high. Now the risk was well worth taking. He had in mind only to check what might be wrong, to see if there was anything obvious that he could fix. He was a trained electrician in his own sphere, not capable of fixing all of the machines aboard, but well able to take care of the electrical equipment, its fittings and fixings.

The top of the stubby main mast was perhaps four feet square and the thin whip-mast rose from the middle of it. He immediately spotted a badly broken connection. Hanging on with his left hand, hugging the mast itself to his narrow chest, he pulled out a pair of long-nosed electrical pliers. Taking hold of the disconnected wire, he pushed it back into the socket from which it had sprung free.

A flash of electricity jolted through his body. It was not strong enough to kill him, but it was enough to cause his grip to fail. Feeling himself falling, he caught at the mast again and the whole thing tilted over. Still fighting to retain his grip on the slippery, salt-caked, white-painted metal, he felt himself being swung out across the width of the bridgehouse. Automatically, he twisted his body, hoping to catch hold with all four of his limbs, or, failing that, somehow to fall safely and land on his feet like a cat. The movement forced him to look down, and so he saw something which had been invisible from deck level: the top of the bridgehouse was out of line, forced back. The green metal of the top deck was rippled by slight folds. Below, the foot of the bridgehouse was no longer sitting quite correctly on the main deck.

Jesus saw these things in an instant and he had no leisure to consider them. They were simply impressions which burned themselves into his mind during that instant. When the movement of the mast stopped, he jerked free and fell. By now he was far beyond the starboard edge of the bridge. There was no bridge wing there any more to break his fall and he tumbled overboard, falling almost a hundred feet straight down into the ocean. Reacting automatically, he performed one complete action – he pulled the toggle which inflated his life jacket. Landing head first and face down, he felt nothing of the impact his body made with the ocean. An impact so great that it burst the life jacket and killed him at once. He sank immediately and without trace. At the top of the radio mast, however, his wild movement had completed the destruction begun by the storm last night.

'Where's Jesus?' asked Ann.

'He must be up there somewhere,' said John, looking upwards to the deck head above him. But when the radio operator did not come back on to the bridge, Richard went to look for him. He saw nothing of the damage to the main bridgehouse that Jesus had noticed, but then he did not try to climb the crazily leaning mast. He understood what must have happened to Jesus at once, and dashed back down to the wheelhouse with the news. Within a very few minutes, *Napoli* was reversing her course and going back over the long lost *Titanic* looking for their man overboard. They had no second radio officer; Niccolo went into the radio shack to try and raise any ships nearby to warn them to keep a sharp lookout. When he could raise no one, he got out Jesus's book of call frequencies and started to try for Cape Race. The radio hissed promisingly enough but there was no reception. Niccolo doggedly continued to transmit, therefore, in the hope that his messages were still being received by Cape Race and *Rainbow Warrior* at least.

John remained on the bridge and Richard took charge of swinging out the only lifeboat they still had left. Everyone else aboard – scientists, engineers and deckhands, stewards and even the chef's helpers all gathered on high points of the ship, looking for Jesus. Bernadotte came up from the infirmary, leaving the third officer and Fatima as the only people aboard not involved in the search. But there was nothing to see in the water.

They gave up at the end of the morning watch, and all of them gathered below. Niccolo still had had no luck with the system Jesus had died trying to fix. There was one other option: the short-range radio kept ready to go in the lifeboat. But as it became more likely that they would have to use the lifeboat and its radio for real, John decided to keep working with the main set for the time being. Meanwhile, the hold cargo was no doubt hotter than it had been when Ann last checked it, and they were still right over the *Titanic*, no further forward on their voyage to nowhere.

Richard looked round at the expectant faces. Eduardo had replaced Niccolo as third translator, but otherwise it was very much as at John's first such meeting. The circumstances could hardly be more different, however. Then it had been a case of a disunited inefficient group of people being asked to get their act together and keep their ship safely afloat. Now, Richard was explaining to a unified, very much more efficient group of men and women how they might all get safely off the ship before her imminent loss at sea. An abandonment under the current weather conditions would be quite simple. Getting them all into one lifeboat would be a bit of a crush, but short-term it should be possible. He made sure they understood that the abandonment would be completed carefully and with lots of warning, should the captain decide to proceed with it. They would all get into the remaining lifeboat with only their most valued possessions. Then they would withdraw to a safe distance, hopefully towards or even on board whatever ship might come to their rescue. No one but volunteers would remain on board to scuttle the ship, under the direction of the captain, and they would not proceed until the rest of the crew were safely in the lifeboat.

But one way or another, the decision to abandon ship could not wait. They had spent precious hours looking for Jesus. If they did not get *Napoli*'s hold cargo – and *Napoli* herself – down beside *Titanic* soon, there would no longer be any point in putting her down at all. It would be too late to stop the nuclear waste from going critical.

CHAPTER TWENTY-SIX

Richard and John looked at each other across the chart table. Neither man could really believe that it had come to this. They had spent their lives keeping ships afloat no matter what the power of nature or the perfidy of man could do. Ten years ago they had stood side by side, captain and acting first officer on the bridge of a tanker which had broken in half, and they had still brought her to safe haven. Richard had only ever lost one ship, and the price he had paid for that was so high it had nearly destroyed him. John had never lost a ship.

But things were different now. This was far beyond anything even the most outstanding seamanship could control. There was no miracle that could get them across a thousand miles of ocean to port in less than four hours; even if there was, Ann said the filth in the hold would still go critical, and they believed her.

There was only one course of action left and both of them knew it. Everyone aboard knew it. And while these two stood like shadows of their former selves staring in silence across the table, the rest of the men and women aboard were packing their kit ready for the abandonment – except Salah, who was still at the helm, and Niccolo who was still trying to raise an answer on the radio. And Asha who was pounding up the stairway towards the bridge.

She burst into the silent room and ran across to embrace John. It had seemed so unreal before, but now the quiet, hopeless preparations below had really brought home to her the loss he must be feeling; the risk he must be preparing to face. After all

he had been through trying to bring this ship and her foul cargo
safely to port, he had been defeated. And the price of his defeat
– the *immediate* price, for she knew it could not end with the
scuttling – would be to remain aboard until the last, no matter
what the danger – though at this stage she had no idea what the
scuttling of *Napoli* would actually entail.

The greatest of all the things she loved about him was the
self-deprecating way he went about doing the most impossible
things. He seemed so uncertain of himself. He had about him
that old-fashioned air of boyish, amateurish enthusiasm which
she remembered from films about fighter pilots in the Battle
of Britain. And yet, like them, he came through, shrugging
modestly at what it cost. It was a typically English strength,
it seemed to her, and it amused her to remember that he
was a part-Irish Manxman. He seemed out of touch with
the hard professionalism and corporate fanaticism she saw
all around her these days. His integrity was so deep and
inbred it took itself for granted and never made a show of
being out of the ordinary at all. So easy to overlook or
undervalue. So easy to mock. So utterly defenceless. So easy
to love.

'I say, darling, what's the matter?' he asked as she hugged
him with all her might.

She made no answer and at last he was forced, gently, to break
her grip.

'You mustn't hang about, you know. Get all the kit together
you want to take with you. Don't bother with my stuff – there
won't be much room. Better get some emergency supplies from
the infirmary too. And you haven't got very much time. I'll be
sounding "Abandon Ship" soon. And for once it won't be one of
my damned drills.'

She would have liked to have stayed with him a little longer,
but she could see that he was right. She had better get some
warm clothing for them both in case they were in the lifeboat
for any length of time. And he was right about getting emergency
supplies from the infirmary. She would ask a couple of seamen
to look after Marco Farnese who was still in the infirmary,

almost comatose with shock. And someone else to look after Bernadotte, who still could not use his hands. Could she rely on Ann Cable to help Niccolo? His leg would prove a severe handicap on the sloping deck, and on the way into the lifeboat, she suspected.

These thoughts were enough to take her out of the bridge and away from John's agonised gaze.

'So, Richard,' he said, after she had gone, 'how do we go about putting this mess down on the ocean floor?'

'I've been thinking. We'll need to talk through the details with El Jefe for a start. He's shut down the pumps in case of cavitation because the valves don't work. I don't know whether that's just the pumps or whether it's the seacocks as well. I mean, if the seacocks are working, we can just open them and climb aboard the lifeboat. She's down by the head already and so she should just slide under like a lady. We'd have to be careful, though; work it out in detail if we can. We don't really want her breaking up. Professor Faure or Ann can advise us, but I'd have supposed it would be better to try and keep the hold cargo all together in a controlled ride down rather than risk *Napoli* coming to pieces and scattering it all over the place.'

They caught up with Ann on the way down to the engine room and took the opportunity of checking with her. 'Well,' she said, 'it depends. If it does go critical, then if it's all in one place it'll just make a bigger bang. But if it's spread all over the bottom of the ocean, it'll be much messier. If it doesn't go critical . . .' She thought for a moment. 'They've reached the *Titanic*, so I guess they could reach *Napoli* too, if push comes to shove. In which case it'd make much more sense to be able to get it all up together. Yeah, that's what I'd do. Keep it all in one place if you can.'

'Right,' said John. 'We'd better pray the seacocks are working.'

'Seacocks are fucked,' said El Jefe. 'They won't open now. I can't make any of the systems under the holds work at all. Or in the holds either. Is deck cargo who leaks, j'ou understand?'

'Any idea how we make this tub go down in one piece, then?'

'*No*. I make her move until j'ou say stop but I cannot make her sink.'

'That only leaves one alternative,' said John thoughtfully. 'We'd better find Faure.'

'Yes, of course I can set the charges for you,' said the professor. 'I know how to use explosives. I was in charge of the excavation in the desert. The rest of them are just scientists, you understand, but I served in the army, in Algeria. I was trained.'

They took him to John's day room and pored over the drawings of *Napoli* which accompanied her papers.

In the rooms next door, Asha was packing a case for the lifeboat, her movements quiet but plainly audible. For once, her proximity did not distract John.

'Look,' he said, 'it's obvious. We want a small hole punched in the bow just below the water line. We want a hole in the stern too. That way she'll go down quickly and with a minimum of damage to the hull. It's the pressure of trapped air that actually destroys ships when they sink – that and shifting cargo, I suppose. And exploding boilers.'

'That's right,' Richard agreed. 'We'll have to time things carefully and trust to luck. But if we open a hole at each end of the hull, she'll go down very fast with the least possible disturbance from air trapped in the hull because the water coming in at the bow will simply push all the air out of the stern. If we want to be very tricky, I suppose we could open the front and wait for a while before blowing open the stern. That way the holds will flood more slowly, and then they should stay secure. You see the way they're designed? Three huge boxes simply bolted into the hull. The Gdansk shipyards made simple U-shaped hulls and added box holds or oil tanks or whatever later on. But once they're flooded, the holds should sit quite happily through the changes in pressure as she goes down. And the cargo is heavy, laid flat on the bottoms of the holds and as secure as we can make it. The only things we should lose are the

containers off the deck, and we don't want those sitting too near
the hold cargo anyway, even at two and a half miles down. And
if the engine does explode, it shouldn't do too much damage.
Look here: the aft section is self-contained. If *Napoli* is well
down by the head, all the force will simply come up out of the
hole that's already there!' He looked at the two other men, his
expression one almost of elation that he should have solved so
many complex problems so simply and so elegantly. But then
he remembered what it was he was talking about and what the
risks really were. And how great the incalculable elements all
their best-laid plans could never hope to encompass.

'So,' said Faure slowly, 'you want a charge at the bow and
another at the stern. You would like the bow charge to be timed
so that it goes off some time before the stern charge in the hope
that this will allow the holds to flood in a controlled manner
before she goes down fast. That way even the explosion of the
engine should help the process to be more effective, should such
a thing occur. It is asking a lot but I will see what I can do. In
the meantime, do you have anyone else aboard who can handle
explosives? What you ask will take a long time for one man to
prepare.'

The next stage of the discussion started between John and Salah
in the captain's office. 'Yes,' said the Palestinian at once, 'I might
be a bit rusty but if the explosives and the timers are standard
then I can set them.' He laughed drily. 'Though it is Fatima you
should be asking. Her training is much more up-to-date than
mine.' John buzzed up to the bridge at once and asked that
Faure be found and sent to his office.

While they were waiting, he suddenly remembered Richard's
suggestion about the passports. He rose abruptly and crossed to
his safe. 'I don't know what you think of this idea, Salah,' he said
as he span the combination, 'but that passport you found wasn't
the only spare one aboard. I was supposed to check whether they
were still valid but haven't had the chance. Still, you might be
able to use them. What do you think?'

Salah looked at the two little booklets with stunned disbelief.

Had John no idea what they were worth? Had he no conception what people like himself and Fatima would do to get a pair of documents like this? He had not looked closely at Lazar's before he gave it in. He looked closely at it now: yes, there was the treasured American Visa. And Gina's. It actually *was* an American passport. The girl obviously had dual nationality. With these, the new life was really possible. When *Napoli* went down, Salah and Fatima would go down with her. Carlo Lazar and Gina Fittipaldi would be picked up with the rest of the crew. The nearest landfall was the eastern seaboard of the United States. When they were rescued, they would be taken there, and the two ex-terrorists would just vanish westwards. He opened Lazar's passport again. The face looking back at him was not so unlike his own. Height two metres it said. Lazar had added a good few centimetres out of vanity – enough to make the height close to Salah's own. And Gina – dark, brown eyed, plump. If she dieted enough she could be Fatima; and who did not diet, these days?

Salah had been on a roller coaster during the last few weeks. Until Ali ibn Sir had come after him, he had never questioned his place in the PLO or his right to argue against political fashion and expediency. He had never questioned his position in the organisation he had served so well. Until the disturbing silence when he radioed in for help. Until Fatima's chilling question. Until the gunboat had opened fire. But then had come that great upsurge of hope when Tewfik had told him to go to Blackwater Hall, and the death of all hope when the trap there had been sprung. Now there was a new hope here. Hope of a kind he had never experienced before. He felt like the first plainsman looking west across the unmapped prairie and he found it very sweet.

A gentle tapping at the door heralded Professor Faure, and a short conference established that Salah could handle the explosives and the timers, which were designed for general commercial use.

A rather more forceful sound warned that Asha and Fatima had discovered exactly how John proposed to put *Napoli* down beside *Titanic* and had come to talk about it. Richard was just behind them.

'You can't be serious!' snapped Asha at once. 'You expect the rest of us to get off and sit in the lifeboat while half a dozen of you stay aboard and blow the ship up?'

'It's the only way,' said John firmly. 'And it is not as dangerous as you make it sound. I'll keep her as steady as possible while Professor Faure places just enough explosive to blow a small hole in the bow. Salah will place just enough to blow open a small hole in the stern. We will set timers. We will come off into the lifeboat with the rest of you. We'll all be well clear before the timers even detonate. There's really no danger.' John looked around the silent room, rapidly coming to the conclusion that he was not a very convincing liar at all.

But then Fatima sprang to his aid. 'It is no big deal, Asha. If the people placing the charges know what they are doing, it should be quite safe.'

Asha looked from one to the other and she knew she was beaten.'What can I do?' she asked.

'Continue with what you are doing. Get the sick off. As ship's doctor, check your stores for anything we might need. But be calm and keep the crew calm. The only things which can hurt us are panic and bad organisation.'

'And bad luck,' Asha observed. 'Still, I'll do what you say. You are my lord and master now. And anyway, with Fatima to help me . . .'

'Oh, but I am staying with Salah . . .'

'Oh, now look here . . .'

Normally, the first officer would have been detailed to oversee the launching of the lifeboat and the safe disposition of everyone within it, but Niccolo's leg would not allow him to stand on the sloping deck and in any case he was still working as stand-in radio operator. The acting third officer, Eduardo, was officially on watch while John and Richard were below. The second officer, Marco, was in the sick bay.

When everything else was sorted out, John went to talk to

him, for there was no one else who had the training or the time
to take charge. He found the boy awake but still stunned by what
had happened to him. Sitting uneasily on his sloping bedside,
too well aware that time was very limited, John explained their
simple plan and the reasons for it, quietly stressing Marco's place
in the scheme. The young man was distressed to learn of the
loss of Cesar and the deck parties, and of the disappearance of
Jesus. The current state of *Napoli* and her cargo shocked him
too. And, slowly, he began to understand the importance of his
own position: that his captain had no one else to rely on, that
his shipmates and all the other men and women aboard had no
one else to rely on.

Privately John thought that his quiet, patient explanation and
gentle, reasonable insistence was probably a stupidly wishy-
washy way to approach the problem. He knew captains who
would have snapped orders and threats of professional disgrace
in the face of hesitation. He knew one or two who would
simply have hauled the blubbering coward out of bed and
kicked him up on deck. But that was not his way; reason
and calm was. He had been brought up to believe that these
were important strengths, and now above all he hoped they
were, for they were the only strengths he had, as a man and
as a commander.

Asha chanced to come in while the conversation between the
two men was taking place and she waited, unobserved, watching.
She had expected to have Marco carried out of here by a couple
of burly seamen. Instead she watched in wonder while her quiet,
gentle husband, coaxed a resolve and determination out of the
young officer that she had never suspected Marco possessed. By
the time John stood up and turned to continue with his next task,
Marco was ready to get on with his duty. It was little short of a
miracle. Emotion swept over her again.

'Darling!' John said in surprise. 'I didn't see you there. All
ready to go? Young Marco here is just about to get the lifeboat
swung out. I say, what is it? There, you mustn't cry. Everything
will be all right, I promise.'

                    *   *   *

John's action proved the making of Marco. As a blundering, easily frightened boy learning his craft and all too often getting it wrong, he had been the subject of scorn and the butt of the crew's cruellest words and actions. As the officer in charge of the only way off the sinking ship, he instantly acquired status among the men who had despised him so recently. The change was facilitated by the fact that Bernadotte, the ringleader of most of the trouble, was now effectively helpless and utterly reliant on Marco's good offices. In truth, the task of swinging out the lifeboat, uncovering it, loading the last necessities, including the emergency radio, and then lowering it on to the gently swelling sea was not particularly difficult. Even the slope of the deck failed to make the unrolling of the Jacob's ladder too much of a problem. Marco knew who the best boatmen were and he sent two of them down first to control the lifeboat while the others lined up quietly in the order he dictated. When he called 'Wait!', not one of them thought of disobeying, even when he walked away to report to John that all was ready, and ask for his next instruction. He suspected it would simply be, 'Go back and wait for the order to abandon ship.'

In essence, the plan was so simple because it had to be. Both Richard and John knew how many things could so easily go badly wrong. John would stay on the bridge. His task would be to coordinate their efforts and keep the ship steady. Richard would go with Faure to place the first set of charges against the already weakened metal of the bow section. Salah would place the second set of charges against the sternmost section available in the engine room, with El Jefe to advise and Fatima to assist. There would be a fifteen-minute interval between the timers. And in any case there would be a further fifteen-minute delay before the first explosion to allow them all to get safely off.

John stood on the bridge while Eduardo took the wheel. The young acting third's bright blue eyes flicked restlessly from the compass card to the sea and back. He did not have to pay much attention to their heading, which was roughly south-west at the moment; his major, extremely important, task was to keep her head into the swell, holding her as steady as possible while the charges were placed.

John felt the way she was riding, using his acutely honed senses and years of experience to judge whether her movement could be bettered, and decided it could not. So, after glancing at Eduardo, he paid no more attention to the way the helm was and crossed to the port bridge wing where he could look down at the preparations for the abandonment and also watch Richard and Professor Faure hurrying towards the forecastle. They were both wearing environmental protection suits because there was more than a chance that they would get splashed as they placed the charges and neither wanted to run the risk of any of the deck cargo getting on their skin. John tapped the earpiece of the hand-held radio against his strong, white teeth, watching and waiting.

The main shaft lay in an open bed for most of its length. It came out of the direct drive at the aft of the engine where the pistons turned it one hundred revolutions a minute. It went straight along in that bed on top of the sludge tank to the housing which was effectively the aft wall of the ship. Between the bed and the housing, the shaft spanned a triangular depression about three feet deep, down to the keel of the ship. This was called the bilge well and it gave access to the after housing where the explosives would best be placed.

El Jefe brought Salah and Fatima and helped them both into the triangular hollow of the well where they could work side by side. The shaft revolved between them, grey and slick with grease, humming a deep note as it drove the propeller at its unvarying speed, guaranteeing *Napoli*'s headway into the south-westerly swell. It was deafeningly noisy, dirty and dangerous down here, quite apart from the work they were doing with the explosives. El Jefe put the hand-held radio into a capacious overall pocket. It was too noisy to use it down here and anyway there was nothing much to say. He crouched above them, watching them work while keeping a worried eye on the nearest rev. counter and the engine beyond it. He still did not trust that engine.

The chain locker was at a strange angle, the forward wall at such a slope that the ladder was difficult to negotiate. Faure went first with the explosives slung over his shoulder. Richard followed him at once, pausing only to flash the torch he was carrying round the locker. He put the radio to his mouth. 'In, John,' he said, and pulled his headpiece down over his face.

At the locker floor, surrounded by the sprawling coils of chain disturbed by the storm last night, Faure waited until Richard joined him and flashed the flashlight beam round the eerie little room again. They were lucky: the chains had not blocked the trap door that opened down to the inside of the bow itself. Richard lifted it for Faure and shone his torch down. The ladders plunged down the metal walls, past the balks of wood Cesar had wedged there, and into the sluggish yellow water immediately below them.

Faure sat, swung his legs into the opening and stepped down on to the first steel rung. After a moment, Richard followed. The little steel-sided valley was even more claustrophobic now than when he had been down here last. The angle didn't help, making everything lean forward. The water, too, sloshing back and forth just below their feet added its own sinister air to the atmosphere.

When they reached the agreed position, they stopped and Richard shone the torch where Faure pointed so that the Frenchman, science professor and army-trained demolition expert, could complete his task. Faure placed his explosive charges in the angles made by black timbers and the steel of *Napoli*'s cutwater. And all the time they worked, even through the white hoods they were wearing, they were deafened by the thunder of the surf which beat, a foot or so from their faces, on the far side of the steel.

'Keep her head to the swell, Eduardo,' said John automatically. His voice carried in from the bridge wing easily enough, and the young officer nodded, concentrating on doing just that. John's eyes narrowed. He was watching the swells now as they came in that long aquamarine series, automatically counting them. The seventh was always larger than the rest. He had learned that on the narrow beaches of Donegal, with the tall cliffs standing at his back and the huge seas beating at his feet. 'Big one coming, Eduardo, watch her.' He felt the ship give a little extra swoop and looked down to see how Marco was handling things. Everyone seemed to be in place, but the third officer had gone. They should have given him a radio too, thought John, but they had lost one with Cesar last night and the last one Richard had mislaid in the black heart of the water mountain.

Marco came panting up on to the bridge a moment later. '*Pronto, Capitano*,' he announced.

John nodded and crossed to the radio shack. 'Anything, Niccolo?'

Niccolo simply shook his head. His face was bitter. '*Niente*,' he spat. '*Morta!* It's gone dead now, Captain.'

'Maybe you'll have more luck with the radio in the lifeboat,' John said. 'Go on down, Marco. Make doubly sure everyone is ready. When Niccolo comes down, you can cast off and prepare to get clear.'

Niccolo translated, just to make sure the message was understood, and Marco was off at once. John went back to the front of the bridge, narrow eyes scanning the rollers, looking for the seventh one, the whole attitude of his body attuned to the movement of his ship, reading each gentle pitch and roll with every nerve, every muscle. Never, even under the most extreme of circumstances, had he concentrated this keenly before. Two men he respected deeply were relying on him to keep *Napoli* as still as possible while they took their lives in their hands, preparing to send her down.

Behind him, in the shack, Niccolo automatically switched the dead radios to OFF. Even concentrating as he was, John knew the sound. 'Eduardo, take the first officer down to the lifeboat now. Get into it yourself. I'll take over the helm.' He put the walkie-talkie on the console in front of him and took the helm as the other two went down.

The spokes were hot in his hands. Either Eduardo was warm with worry or he himself was cold with strain. That was very likely: his hands always went cool when the stakes got high.

He put the thought out of his mind and looked away over the distant sea, mentally counting, looking for that seventh wave, the big one he knew was out there somewhere.

Marco checked that Asha had everything she required from the infirmary and kept an eye on her stuff when she went back up to the bridge. He made sure that Ann Cable was aware of where she would be sitting in the boat and that she, too, had everything with her that she needed. He also checked the disposition of the scientists waiting there.

First aboard with Ann and Asha would be Bernadotte because of his injuries, then the first officer, also injured, who would assume command of the little boat. After him would come the other supernumeraries, the stewards and the chef, followed by the crew in whatever order they presented themselves. Last aboard at that stage would be Marco himself, and then the boat, fully loaded and ready to move off quickly should anything go wrong, would wait for the arrival of the last people left aboard: John and his scuttling team: Salah Malik, Fatima, El Jefe, Professor Faure and Richard.

The wait was not long and the weather remained so clement that the crew did not become restless as they waited, in spite of the fact that it was early afternoon now and no one had had anything to eat or drink since last night. Asha returned, her face pale, Niccolo came hobbling down supported by Eduardo, and Ann Cable crossed to his other side. As soon as he arrived at the head of the patient line, he nodded and the abandonment began. It went exactly to plan.

Soon all of them were aboard. Niccolo gave a quiet order and the seamen seated along the gunwales took out their oars and settled them into the rowlocks, ready. Marco looked across the quiet ship. There was no one to be seen and nothing for the moment to be heard. He took the lifeboat fall and held it, posing unconsciously like an heroic statue as he looked around. The bright afternoon seemed frozen under the high, unblemished bowl of the sky. The sea coming towards them in long, unhurried waves was all that distinguished the ocean from the heavens. Marco looked at the green sloping deck, littered, rocking gently, the battered bridgehouse leaning forward, dented and torn but agleam with salt crystals. He breathed in the sharp tang of salt and ozone deeply into his lungs. He was trying to fix this moment forever in his memory; it was the climax of a story he would dine out on for years to come.

But then the soles of his feet tingled abruptly. The fall trembled in his hand. The deck rippled. Far down by the fo'c'sle, the deck seemed to buckle. A noise came from down there as though the sinking ship had groaned. And the tilt on the deck sharpened as though the bow had been snatched downwards. A thundering sound overwhelmed the groaning and the ship began to slide under. A figure wearing an environmental protection suit erupted from the forward chain locker and pounded up the deck. Seeing Marco standing there, frozen with horror, the figure pulled back its helmet. 'Get away,' it yelled, in the voice of Captain Mariner. 'Get the boat away! She's going down.'

Marco swung round, looking down into the lifeboat, riven with horror. He registered only the face of the woman who had a husband and a sister still aboard. His eyes stayed riveted to hers but it was to Niccolo that he screamed in Italian: 'Sheer off! Sheer off! She's going down.' Then he swung out and slid down the fall like a circus acrobat. By the time his feet hit wood, the lifeboat was already pulling away. He staggered back and fell to his knees, straining to look back, his horrified face reflecting exactly the sobbing scream that Asha was giving.

The lifeboat slid forward with increasing momentum as the crew rowed wildly for safety. Even Bernadotte took an oar, closing his bandaged hands upon it without protest. Behind it, *Napoli* tilted until her propeller jumped out of the water, screaming into a frenzy of unresisted spin. No sooner had it done so than a puff of smoke belched out of the engine room vents and the sound of a muffled explosion chased them across the heaving Atlantic. '*Row!*' yelled Niccolo, as if the fearful men at the oars needed urging.

Asha was on her feet now, staring in utter horror. She had no idea that Ann Cable was holding one hand while Niccolo held another, keeping her safely upright as the lifeboat surged away from the terrible sight.

After the explosion in the engine room, *Napoli* did not hesitate. The angle of her hull remained the same, she went no further down by the head. But she went down, all right. Down and down and down. She slid under the surface with incredible rapidity, the long deck stabbing into the water like a stiletto. Only the bridgehouse made a fuss, slapping into the surface with an explosion of foam, throwing up great waves which pursued the lifeboat over the otherwise quiet ocean and overtook it relentlessly to leave it rocking and heaving long after the ship had actually disappeared on her two and a half mile dive down to join the *Titanic*.

Asha slowly collapsed back on to her seat. Ann slid her arm round her shaking shoulders. Niccolo at last took action, switching the radio beside him to the open emergency channel. But before he had the chance to say anything, the radio burst into life and a voice announced, '. . . *Warrior*. Say again, this is *Rainbow Warrior*. *Napoli*, we will be at your last reported position in one half-hour. Say again, one half-hour . . .'

CHAPTER TWENTY-SEVEN

John almost didn't see it coming, for it hid among the other waves and the brightness of the early afternoon disguised it too. There was only a slightly deeper shadow, betraying a larger wave; the merest interruption to the geometric pattern of the swell. It was something a landsman would never have seen at all, and, indeed, even the experienced seaman was fooled. It was the keen eye of that little boy who had counted waves so long ago on the wild west coast of Donegal that warned the man the boy had become.

John's head jerked to one side, as though the peripheral retina would see more clearly, like it did at night. His jaw squared. He rose onto his toes, straining every nerve to read the movement of his oddly-angled ship. It came and went, the rogue wave, seeming to vanish and then reappear out of sequence, leaping forward magically with each reappearance, so that its arrival could not be anticipated. John's nostrils flared. He licked his lips and tasted sharp salt. He picked up the walkie-talkie and pressed SEND: 'Big one coming,' he said. But there was no reply. He put the little radio down again and went back to being the helmsman.

His fists trembled on the spokes of the helm. The wave rose up before the bows and washed silently over the forecastle head. *Napoli*'s forepeak swooped, dropped, slammed down. The forward section of the deck seemed to catch something from the water washing over it and the metal itself began to ripple. A sensation rushed through John's body unlike any he had ever felt before. As though he were linked to *Napoli* by nerves that reached into her very steel, he felt his ship cry out. And he felt the deck tilt more steeply and more steeply yet and he knew she was going down. His hand flashed to the engine room telegraph and rang up ALL STOP. But he felt no answer from the throbbing deck beneath his feet; the chief was in his engine room; he must have switched the engine commands off automatic and onto manual. Only El Jefe could stop the engine now.

John stood, panting like a man in shock, holding his ship's head where it was, willing it to remain afloat a minute or two more, trying to keep control a little longer yet: until his people below contacted him as arranged to say they were safe.

All Richard ever knew about the arrival of the wave was the sudden sinister quiet it brought with it. He felt the ship's head go down and he clung to the ladder. Then the most incredible sound he had ever heard swept over him. It was a kind of grinding, tearing shriek. It came from all around: above, below, behind.

Behind! He swung round to look over his shoulder and cried out in sudden shock. The back wall of the space he was in, the front wall of the forward hold, was closing down towards him. Even as he looked, refusing to believe what his eyes were telling him, it ground forward another inch as though it would crush him there and then. Its movement pushed the timbers through the weak steel of her hull and the front of the ship ripped open.

Richard was in motion at once, tearing his lower body out of the maelstrom of water foamimg greedily in through that ragged mouth. Faure moved just as fast and they ran up the ladders side by side as though indulging in some strange race. With each step that he took, Richard felt the angle of the ship increase and the terrible sensation of claustrophobia gripped him as his mind screamed that he was trapped in a rapidly shrinking space at the front of a ship going down very fast a thousand miles from land. He burst up into the chain locker and leaped for the rungs which would take him up to the brightness of the deck. At the top he paused, looking down. Faure was just coming through the trap door and into the locker. He was safe. Behind him foamed the ocean as it tore into the ship.

That one glance back was enough. Richard was out and hurrying up the deck. He peered down through the broken gape of the forward hatch. Water was pouring into the hold already. He paused for a second, surveying the ribbed decking around the hatch. There was no doubt: the whole of the huge metal box which made up the forward hold had somehow come loose from the anchorage points securing it to the hull itself and had slid forward almost a foot. Thank God the movement had stopped for the moment, he thought, and was in motion again himself.

Halfway along the deck, he caught sight of Marco Farnese standing frozen by the lifeboat falls. Richard tore back his headpiece and yelled at the top of his voice. He did not pause to see if his order had been obeyed, but rushed into the bridge at once. As he went in through the door off the main deck, he pressed the walkie-talkie to his mouth. 'Richard, going down,' he said. In more ways than one, he thought.

In the trap door up into the chain locker, Etienne Faure hesitated. His bag of explosives had caught on something and he paused to shrug it off. In the instant that it took him to do so, the angle of the deck canted a degree or two more. The wild pile of anchor chain fell forward and slithered across the floor. The sound it made drowned out the noise of foaming water at his heels, and caused him to glance up. It seemed like some unimaginable serpent to him, slithering down the deck to wrap him in its green steel and seaweedy coils. Then the first loop of it reached him. He actually reached up to push the rounded steel away, but the weight of it was overwhelming and he never stood a chance. It thundered down through the open trap on top of him. Metre after metre of it crushed him out of existence. Then it ripped through the gap-tooth holes the wood had made, tearing and widening, until *Napoli*'s strange new mouth began to scream in earnest.

Richard was never to know the manner of Faure's death. He did not know at this moment that the brave Frenchman *was* dead.

All he knew was that the ship was going down and several of his friends were still aboard. His first thought had been to run up to John on the bridge, but then he remembered that Salah and Fatima were in the engine room and, unless they were paying close attention to the disposition of the ship in the water, her sudden plunge might well take them by surprise.

After his brief message on the radio, he ran on down. The stairways were all at crazy angles now, and he stumbled and toppled down them trying to get to the engine room. He was running unsteadily along the angle made by a floor and a wall when he heard the first explosion. He was halfway along the corridor leading to the engine control room at the time; it was against his nature to turn back, so he rushed on forward instead.

The first the three in the engine room really knew about it was when El Jefe fell over. He had been squatting facing dead aft, concentrating as fiercely as the other two on the placing of the charges – they had not quite reached the stage of priming them yet. But then the Spaniard suddenly found himself flat on his back on the engine room floor. It came as such a surprise that he did not at first register the reason for his sudden upset. But then he went absolutely cold. He did not think to say anything to the other two or to report in on the radio. He simply began to roll over and over, trying with limited success to pull himself erect. He knew in his bones what was happening and the more certain he became of it, the quicker he tried to move. His one overwhelming duty was to switch off the main propeller shaft before it was too late. He fell up the steps beside the engine which were now tilting at an almost unclimbable angle. He pulled himself up, climbing with his arms as much as his legs. His mouth was wide as he gulped in the hot, oil-tainted air. He was a strong man, but not a particularly fit man, and he knew it. With each straining step, he regretted the extra servings of paella, the cervezas, the vino tinto. Whether his undoing was due more to food than to alcohol, he was never to know.

In the final second or two, as the angle of the ship became

increasingly acute, Salah grew more worried. He looked up to mention his fears to El Jefe, but the Spaniard was off doing something to the engine. It was obvious that they had very little time left, but then he had almost finished. He paused in his work and signed for Fatima to climb out of the bilge well first, and she smiled a tight smile, glad enough to go. With sinuous grace she pulled herself up and out onto the tilting deck. Salah paused in his work to watch her, thinking how good it would be to spend the rest of his life with! Fatima looked up to see the figure of the chief spread out like a monkey in a white overall on the steps above the engine. He was trying to reach something. She came to her knees, looking up at him in wonder. And the ship began to scream.

The downward lurch which the anchor chain had caused as it crushed the life out of Faure tore the propeller up out of the water. The massive system, so carefully balanced to support that great brass rotor as it thrust aside ton after ton of heavy sea water, screamed into overdrive as the three broad blades bit only air. The revolutions, so carefully kept at a hundred, leaped towards a thousand. The shaft, designed to meet the torque of keeping the screw rotating in the water, was incapable of meeting the new forces its freedom unleashed. It began to twist out of true at once, bending like dough. It gathered up the man in the bilge well and obliterated him. Then it pulled itself out of the retaining clips which guided it when straight and slammed into the deck. It tore through the thin steel of the deck like a knife blade through eggshell. The engine, trying to come to terms with what the suddenly supple steel was doing, failed utterly and, as El Jefe had warned it might do, it exploded.

Fatima was hurled backwards across the slippery engine room deck. She had no idea at all that she was screaming. Such was the noise around her that she could not hear herself. The man she admired and trusted, loved and relied on, more than any other in the world had disappeared. It was hard to say even that he had been killed, so total had been the fate that overtook him. He had simply vanished, as though passing to another plane of existence in the blink of an eye. The shaft that had done this to him twisted like the neck of a dragon and slammed down onto the deck on the far side of the well. Water exploded up in a wall through the deck-plates it had destroyed. The sound was as though she were trapped in a wildly ringing bell. The pain in her ears was excruciating.

On her back in the debris on the engine room floor, she looked up. At the highest point of the stern, the housing into which the shaft had run scant seconds ago tore away as though it were a door being opened by a giant hand outside. The propeller, no longer secured to the ship by anything strong enough to hold it in place, tore itself free and took the housing, and a good deal of *Napoli*'s stern plates with it.

Fatima dragged herself away from the horrific sight and scrabbled round onto her knees, looking for a way to escape. She looked up just in time to see the engine immediately beneath El Jefe burst into flame. Like Salah, he must never have known what happened to him. He was gone in an instant. The second shock on top of the first seemed to galvanise her. One last wild glance round revealed that the wall of water which had sprung out of the hole the shaft had made was faltering. It had filled the bilge well and then it had stopped. Through the long, ragged gash she could see the bright surface of the ocean sliding by.

She tumbled into motion down the slippery slope of the deck just as El Jefe had, but she ran on past the ladder he had climbed – too slowly – up to the engine controls. She made instead for the main companionway which would take her up the forward wall of the engine room, well clear of the blazing engine and out into the passage leading to the main deck. She was lighter, fitter, far more agile than the middle-aged chief engineer had been.

The slope of the steps was almost impossible to negotiate. She gashed her shins and bruised her hands, running up three flights of steps whose angle was now so great they were like an optical illusion or a drawing by Escher. The engine room companionway steps had no fronts to them – fronts which would by now have become the tops to the steps – and so she found herself running up the last set on the forward edges of the steel slabs, and by this time she was uncertain whether she was running up or down. She was powerfully aware, however, that the temperature of the air she was passing through was spiralling upwards increasingly fast. The engine was belching fire now and screeching like some enraged monster. It was difficult to see how it could stay in one piece for very much longer. And what it would do when the cold Atlantic hit it was something she didn't want to think about.

She concentrated on getting out of here and that was all. She had been in tight spots before. She knew that thought could be the enemy of action and that if she thought about Salah, then she would give up and die here. Salah, who had come so near to killing her three short months ago, would not want her to die now.

She came through the main door into the engine control room at a dead run and smashed straight into the unsteady, white-clothed figure of Richard Mariner. They tumbled backwards together down the slope of the shuddering floor until they ended up in a tangle of limbs in the angle it formed with the wall. 'They're dead,' she yelled before he could even ask. His face went blank. He simply did not believe what she was saying. He stayed, unmoving, looking over her shoulder, expecting to see Salah there. She took him by the shoulders, desperate. 'Salah's dead,' she screamed. 'Let's get out of here!'

They crawled to the door and pushed through it into the corridor beyond. Here they picked themselves up and staggered forward in the same manner that Richard traversed it going the other way – one foot on the floor and one on the wall, with the angle between their ankles seeming to point straight down to the seabed two and a half miles below.

John stood at the wheel, looking dumbstruck down the diminishing length of his deck. *Napoli*'s destruction had been so cataclysmic, so unexpected, he still could not bring himself to come to terms with it. The explosives had not even been placed and yet the ship seemed to be tearing herself apart all on her own. The wheel had ripped itself out of his hands. The deck beneath his feet throbbed and thundered. There was water rushing up the inside of the hull, tumbling in waterfalls from hold to hold, setting the steel he stood on to throbbing like drumskin. And as the water entered, so it drove the air out. In the places that had once been flotation chambers, living and working areas, the still air was being pushed into winds, into gales, by the movement of the water. The movement of the air added its insistent vibration to the steel structures around it and these transmitted it to John.

But what was happening as a result of the hull's increasingly rapid descent into the water was nothing compared to the self-destruction of the engine. Of all the sensations transmitted to the highly sensitive captain, that one was the most urgent, the most insistent, the most worrying. He could hardly bear think what must be happening in the engine room. The noise he received on the open engine room telephone simply told him more vividly what the soles of his feet already knew. But neither sensation told him what he really needed to know: who was alive down there and still relying on him to remain up here? Remaining on the bridge had gone beyond dangerous towards foolish now. The foaming wall of water sweeping up the deck, sportively hurling containers this way and that, would arrive at the bridge front in moments. There was nothing he could do up here – really there had been little for him to do once the helm had torn itself out of his hands as the rudder fell over to one side. But they might be relying on him still and so he had waited. But he would wait no longer. He would not abandon yet; he would check on the engine room first. Salah and Fatima and El Jefe were almost certainly still there or they would have warned him as arranged. And Richard's cryptic 'Going down' told him that his oldest friend was down below too. It was time to go and see if he could help.

He turned and walked up the hill to the stairwell at the back of the bridge. He felt absolutely in control. Calm, quick-witted, in charge. His concentration on the situation and how he was going to help his friends escape from it was absolute.

He never noticed that he had left his walkie-talkie on the console by the useless helm.

The doorway was at an odd angle, of course, and the stairs beyond it were leaning to one side so that the only way to negotiate them was to put his shoulder on the forward – downhill – wall and slide along it while his feet went down the stairs. At the first landing, he had to lower himself down a five-foot drop before he could start again.

It was four decks down from the bridge to the main deck; he would have to repeat this laborious process at least seven more times, he thought. He didn't think to consider that he had no *time* for such a slow method of locomotion. Or, at any rate, he didn't think about it until he heard the unmistakable roaring of the sea coming in at the front of the bridgehouse, and the whole environment around him began to shudder as it had done last night in the grip of that unbelievable mountain of water.

'She's going under!' yelled Richard at the top of his voice. 'She's going to take us down!' He had Fatima by the hand, pulling her up across the landing which would take them up to main-deck level at the aft of the bridgehouse. He had to yell because of the noise. At the bottom – more like a side now – of the stairwell they had just negotiated, the engine was still shrieking frenziedly. After experiencing the movement of the forward hold, Richard was surprised that the engine was still in place; he was half expecting it to sheer its retaining bolts and plunge down through the length of the ship. That would take care of their worries about keeping the cargo together! God! How foolish they had been to try and plan for eventualities like this. What chance had seven people with their piddling explosive charges against the might of the Western Ocean? How had they found the presumption to suppose they could control events? And what a price they were paying for that presumption! The only thing that stopped him slipping into an agony of guilt over the death of his friend was the certainty that he was going to die here too.

There was a stiff gale blowing past them as they continued to battle upwards, and the motion of the air and the shuddering of the decks and walls they were climbing over – and the rolling thunder coming closer – all told him that the ocean would be foaming up towards them any moment now. All they could do was to keep climbing, no matter what, looking for a way out. And if they found one, to take it and pray *Napoli* didn't suck them down after her.

He was being particularly careful not to think about Robin or their baby now. He was thinking of nothing except Fatima and how they were going to get out of this. With a wrenching effort, he pulled Fatima up after him and turned to face another geometrical puzzle which they would have to negotiate fast.

The main after companionways in the bridge house of the *Napoli* all ran port to starboard. Had their slopes run fore and aft, the forward angle of the decks would have made them impossible to negotiate. As John had discovered with his leaps down and as Richard and Fatima were finding with their long reaches up, the landings on these, where the steps turned through one hundred and eighty degrees, were five feet wide and now formed walls instead of floors. They were the only serious obstacles to their dogged progress, however, until they all reached the main deck corridor at the same time. This two-way coincidence immediately became three-way. No sooner had Richard and Fatima slid down across the corridor and John tumbled out of the stairwell behind them, than the Western Ocean arrived.

The corridor stretched from side to side of the bridgehouse. When the decks were level, the stairwells ran up and down immediately aft of it. Four decks up, another, identical corridor ran from side to side immediately behind the bridge. At each end of the main-deck corridor were huge metal bulkhead doors. These had been left secured wide open by the crew as they abandoned ship. No sooner had the three survivors met in that main deck corridor, than the open doors slid down beneath the surface.

John's cry of relief at having found the other two was still echoing in the pandemonium around them when his amazed gaze saw the green water come foaming in through the door he was looking towards. He jerked round. At the other end it was exactly the same: waves of water foamed in through the lower angle of the doorway.

Until now, John had really had no sensation of *Napoli*'s movement down through the water. Certainly he had no idea of how fast she was settling. This changed things at once. The surface of the ocean flashed up the length of the door incredibly quickly. One moment the doors were open to the air. The next they were waterfalls of deep green water, foaming in with incredible force. The ocean had closed off all hope of getting out onto the main deck. They could never fight the force of those walls of water. John felt the air being pushed away as the water snatched at his ankles. 'Back up!' he screamed. It was the only way to go.

Whether or not the others heard him over the numbing cacophony of sound there was no mistaking his gestures and there was nothing else to do. They fought through the foaming rapids that the sea water had cast round their knees already. Three together could move up much faster than two. Richard slung John up first. He handed up Fatima and John hauled her the rest of the way, then they both reached back down for the big white gauntleted hands below them. So they raced the foamed water as it came thundering up the stairwell behind them, with terrifying rapidity.

They were short of breath, the sea was pushing out the last of the air from the place but they could still gasp a conversation.

'The others?' – John to Fatima.

'Dead!'

'*Salah?*' He could not believe it.

'She killed him. She stamped him out. This bitch of a ship. What did they call her? The dockers.'

'A leper ship,' gasped Richard. That was all they could say. They climbed on up.

They were stunned and all but overcome by the situation and by the cost in friends' lives which had been paid to get them here. John could not get out of his mind that his beloved wife was up there somewhere watching him die. Hell of a honeymoon, he thought. Richard and Fatima were both thinking of Salah, insofar as they were thinking of anything other than staying alive. There was no doubt in their minds that they were under the water now and yet they would not stop fighting to get free. What was the alternative? To sit in genteel acquiescence as the passengers of *Titanic* had? No! Never! These were people who fought every inch of the way. Who never gave in. Who would fight the Western Ocean until it snuffed out every last spark of life from them.

They came out into the corridor behind the bridge and fell forward again. The differences between this corridor and the other one four decks down were twofold. To begin with, its forward wall was made of glass and overlooked the main bridge and wheelhouse itself. And the huge bulkhead doors at either end of it were closed. There was air here, trapped like them because there was nowhere else for it to go. The doors were watertight. The windows were holding against the water pressure. The metal of the bridgehouse, lovingly welded in the shipyards of Gdansk all those years ago, remained airtight.

As there was nowhere else for them to go, the three of them had an instant's leisure to look around. To look downwards, at least. John gazed across his empty wheelhouse and through the straining bridge windows down the length of the main deck almost as though his ship were sailing normally into a dark night. All the light was coming from the surface far above them, like a sunset astern. Ahead, the sea they were sailing for this one last time gathered through a dazzling array of hues, passing from the palest blue, still given a green tint by the distant sunlight, to the deepest indigo. Dead ahead it was night-black, starless and icy, giving off its own aura of utter annihilation. The lightless abyss waited patiently, just beyond *Napoli*'s bows.

'God, Richard, she's done for us too,' he whispered.

And the whisper carried, because all the other noise had stopped. An absolute silence seemed to claim them. Even the water coming out of the stairwell behind them was welling up silently.

John looked at Fatima and she looked enough like his beloved

Asha almost to break his heart. 'We're dead,' he whispered. 'There's no way out. No way.'

The engine exploded then. It had built to such a pitch of heat spinning the broken shaft with no resistance whatsoever, that the cold water of the ocean depths simply made it shatter like glass. Glass which had contained many thousands of pounds of pressure. Richard's assessment of what this inevitable moment would bring proved, for once, inaccurate. The force released by the explosion did not just go upwards towards the surface. It went out in a sphere of destruction as well, tearing the whole keel off the ship from the coffer dam behind the last hold to the hole where the propeller had been. It bent out the sides of the ship even against the gathering forces of ocean pressure. And because its joints had been weakened by the mountain of water last night and were now under added strain because of the air trapped within it, it blew the bridge house off.

For the three on the bridge itself, the sensation was what dice must experience during an energetic game. When the wild movement stopped, John found himself flattened against the glass of the forward corridor wall, looking dazedly down. The deck was falling away from him and he simply could not credit what was happening. The water was so clear. The colours were so beautiful. With his face pressed against the glass while the shallowest skim of water flowed across it, he watched the main deck of his lost command fall slowly downwards. It wasn't really green any more, he noticed its colour redefined by the thickening water. The twisted cranes down the middle of it waved at him. Behind them opened a gape in the deck, a crater as though there had been a tooth there, recently drawn. And behind that horrendous hole, he saw the gantry of the after gallows and the poop where Asha and he had loved to stand.

Then so near as to make him shout aloud, *Napoli*'s great funnel fell past and tumbled after the rest of the ship with a kind of balletic grace.

His ears popped.

With his shout, the magic of the moment broke. The three of them were no longer in the grip of that timeless time which

had held them, like flies in amber, eternal. Dead. Instead they
returned to the panicked, untidy, agonising, desperate scramble
for life. The water continued to thunder into the bridgehouse
as the air billowed out. But the physics which had begun with
the explosion of the engine still held them relentlessly in their
grip. The air could not escape fast enough to stop the wreck of
the bridgehouse from following its new course. The air that had
been trapped in the rooms and passageways, pressurised by the
force of the deep water seemed extra-buoyant. The outside walls
of the square construct were of metal, but most of the internal
ones were of wood. Quite apart from the three people trapped
within it, there was much in the bridgehouse that wanted to
float. And float it did, for a while at least. As the hull of *Napoli*
slid down into the dark, her entire deckhouse leaped back up
towards the light.

The three on the bridge held onto each other like children
fighting a nightmare. They screamed as their eardrums flexed
in the explosive lessening of the pressure.

The screaming allowed the high-pressure air to escape from
their lungs. The water tried to overcome them but the friendly
air remained. The coldness of the ocean tried to take them but
their vital warmth survived. Moment after moment after moment
it went on, until with a great, overpowering roar, as though of joy
and understandable pride, the bridgehouse burst out of the water
altogether and seemed to leap up into the air halfway between
the lifeboat and *Rainbow Warrior*'s helicopter.